The Rippe

Nabil Shaban was born in 1953 in Amman… was three for treatment for his osteogenesis impe… and Richard Tomlinson founded **Graeae** (pronou… …professional theatre company of disabled performers. A writer and performer with many film and television credits, he is probably best known to television viewers for his role as ruthless intergalactic businessman Sil in the *Doctor Who* stories **'Vengeance on Varos'** and **'Trial of a Timelord'** (BBC, 1985 + 1986).

On stage he has played **Volpone**, **Hamlet**, and Jesus in **Godspell**, Haille Sellassie in **'The Emperor** and Ayatollah Khomeini in **Iranian Nights**, Mack the Knife in Theatre Workshop's production of Brecht's **"Threepenny Opera"**, for which he was nominated Critics' *Best Actor in Scottish Theatre* (2004-2005). He has also played Hamm in Beckett's **"Endgame"** (Theatre Workshop 2007-2008)

He also played the storyteller Rashid in the Royal National Theatre's production of Salman Rushdie's **"Haroun and the Sea of Stories"**.

He has performed in such movies as **City of Joy** (d. Roland Joffe, 1991), **Wittgenstein** (d. Derek Jarman, 1992) and **Born of Fire** (d. Jamil Dehlavi, 1988), and on television in **Walter** (d. Stephen Frears 1982))and **Deptford Graffiti** (d. Phil Davis 1991) he also made cameo appearances in **Children of Men** (2006) and **Trouble Sleeping** (d. Robert Rae 2007).

Nabil Shaban is a political actor and has worked in plays about Palestine (**The Little Lamp**, 1999 **Jasmine Road**, 2003 and **One Hour Before Sun Rise**, 2006), about the State murder of Northern Ireland lawyer, Rosemary Nelson (**Portadown Blues**, 2000). Also "**D.A.R.E."** (disabled terrorists opposed to genetic cleansing of disabled people) (1997-2004). These were all Theatre Workshop (Edinburgh) productions, directed by Robert Rae.

Shaban has written and presented several documentaries on themes of disability, including the Emmy award winning **Skin Horse** (Channel 4, 1983), about disability and sexuality, the **Fifth Gospel** (BBC, 1990), exploring the relationship between the Christian gospels and disability. He also instigated and presented the Without Walls: **'Supercrips and Rejects'** (Channel 4, 1996), about Hollywood's representation of disabled people. Also in a Secret History documentary "**The Strangest Viking**" (Channel 4, 2003), he argued the case that Ivarr the Boneless, Viking leader, was born disabled.

Shaban's radio work includes writing and presenting a six part series on the life of **Gandhi** (BBC World Service 1984). Playing Benn Gunn in BBC Radio 4 "**Treasure Island**" (1994) and Jaturi the vulture in BBC Radio 2 "**The Ramayan**" (1994).

In 1995, he founded *Sirius Pictures* to make video arts documentary **Another World**. This was followed in 1997 by the award-winning **'The Alien Who Lived in Sheds'** (BBC, 1997) which he wrote, directed and starred in.. He also completed a music film, **Crip Triptych** (2006), which he produced, wrote and directed. In 2007, he wrote, produced and directed short drama film, **Morticia**, about a lonely little girl who yearns to be a vampire.

Nabil Shaban, who has a degree in Psychology and Philosophy, was awarded an honorary doctorate from the University of Surrey for the achievements of his career and his work to change public perceptions of disabled people.

In 2005 Nabil Shaban published his first book, "**Dreams My Father Sold Me**", an anthology of thirty years of his artwork and poetry, with a foreword by Lord Richard Attenborough. Shaban's written plays include "**I am the Walrus"** (about a schizophrenic who believes he made Mark Chapman assassinate John Lennon), and "**The First To Go**" (about disabled people in Germany's Third Reich) published in 2007, premiered in 2008, as a Benchtours Theatre production.

Also by Nabil Shaban

DREAMS MY FATHER SOLD ME

THE FIRST TO GO

D.A.R.E.
a play about the Disabled Anarchist Revolutionary Enclave
(written with Daryl Beeton, John Hollywood, Jim McSharry, Robert Rae)

NABIL SHABAN

The Ripper Code

Sirius Book Works publishing

The Ripper Code

First published in United Kingdom in 2008
by Sirius Book Works publishing

Copyright © Nabil Shaban 2008
All rights reserved

The right of Nabil Shaban to be identified as the author of this work has been asserted by him in accordance with the Copyright, Designs and Patents Act, 1988

This book is sold subject to the condition that it shall not by way of trade or otherwise, be lent, resold, hired out, or otherwise circulated without the publisher's prior consent in any form of binding or cover other than that in which it is published and without a similar condition including this condition being imposed on the subsequent purchaser.

ISBN 9780954829421

Printed and bound in Scotland by
Scotprint, Haddington, East Lothian

Sirius Book Works publishing

6 Vaucluse Place
Jackson Street
Penicuik, EH26 9BF
SCOTLAND

http://uk.geocities.com/sirius_book_works

Front cover design and artwork by Nabil Shaban © Nabil Shaban 2008

To Jamil Dehlavi, who gave me the original motivation to write "The Ripper Code"

The Ripper Code

"Could be the most notorious book of the 21st Century" - George

The Ripper Code

PROLOGUE
The Essex Serpent
23rd July. Monday

Wherever he walks, nothing should grow. His blackness should cast a shadow where all within should wither and die. Or so he wished. Or could imagine. But life was not a Stephen King fantasy or a tawdry John Carpenter movie. No. It's a simple but happy fact that none of the punters in the pub cringed or quaked as he swiftly entered The Apple Tree Inn, a sordid little dive, where rumour has it... Freemasons occasionally meet, lurking uneasily down a forgotten back street in Covent Garden. In fact, not one of the revellers, drunken sots, "Happy Hour" yuppies, Alky Journos, copper's narks, Poofs, Crim de la crim Manor bosses, deadbeat detectives or working whores even noticed his quiet serpentine arrival. Except the Landlord, of course. Nothing escapes his beady eyes or beaky snout. But then, he was forewarned. A terse phone call the night before. Or was it early this morning? Yes, dammit...at an ungodly hour. And here before me is the culprit. The disturber of sweet dreams.

The Landlord quickly glanced at the man with the instantly forgettable thousand and one faces... and yet, still knew those crystal blue piercing eyes that had the capacity to rip your soul apart and plunge your being into everlasting torture and despair. Thankfully, the tall grey-suited, menacingly handsome stranger was an irregular visitor. He only came on business. But what business? Something dodgy, for sure. Drugs? Guns? Stolen goods? Flesh trade? No. Wrong smell. "If I were to imagine what a contract killer should look like, then I'd paint this man's portrait." The Landlord mused but saying nothing, he merely gave the customery nod and indicated the backroom.

To look at, no one would think there was anything particularly interesting about the backroom. And yet...what mysteries have been performed...what initiations...the clandestine deals...the candidates transfigured upward to the Nth degree...if walls had tongues as well as ears, what dark and dismal tales would this backroom with its furniture half-shrouded in dust-sheets and threadbare carpet ground down to a thin veneer of grime through the countless shuffling of secret feet?

On entering the backroom, Mister Mystery inwardly smiled a derisive smirk. The Fat Man, in his garishly loud Hawaiian shirt and his semen stained Bermuda shorts, sometimes known as The Hirer, was impatiently pacing up and down. Mister Mystery gave a short polite ironic cough to announce his unannounced presence.

"You're late, Seekay, or whatever your goddam name is. Half an hour," growled the Fat Man, angrily in his Texan drawl.

"Shut the fuck up, Yank," Seekay snapped back. "I was half an hour before you got here. You arrived 1.43pm precisely, in a black cab, licence number 2748931. I don't take chances and I like to be sure my contracts aren't being followed. Keep it brief. CIA Joe...What's the hit...and how much?"

"The Agency said you were rude and arrogant but I..."

"Listen, Yank," interrupted Seekay. "I don't like Yanks but you pay well... So, just give me what I need to know and fuck off."

The Fat Man, otherwise known as CIA Joe, sat down heavily at a card table that had seen better days...and handed over a large brown thin envelope to Seekay, who pulled out a black and white photograph, and dispassionately studied it.

"The new leader of the Labour Party?" Seekay sighed, pushing the unsuspecting smiley face portrait back in the envelope.

"A million dollars up front and a million on completion," CIA Joe replied. "Mustn't look like assassination, of course. Heart attack or something. Injected adrenalin, hormones, air bubble. Whatever - ". Seekay looked up sharply as if to say, "You telling me how to do my job?"

"You did it before, I heard," the American continued hastily. "They were impressed."

The Ripper Code

"Sterling, not dollars, I'm not a Yank...and I want two million up front... and two million on completion. Sterling."

Seekay turned around and walked brusquely to the door.

"Stop right there, you Limey cunt!" CIA Joe bellowed, standing up so suddenly, he knocked his chair over. "Just who the hell do you think you are? You're good but you're not THAT good."

Seekay swung round and pushed his face right into CIA Joe's, forcing the Fat Man to take a step back, nearly tripping over the fallen chair.

"I'll tell you who I am," replied Seekay, affecting a mock Cockney accent – 'Michael Caine' style. "I'm the Limey cunt who you interfering arseholes need, to kill the next bloody Prime Minister because he is a genuine bloody socialist, which, of course, is scaring you bloody shitless... on top of which, he might just bloody well take Britain out of the fucking United States, which is also bloody well making you brown sauce your piss-yellow pants...And yes, I am THAT good!"

Seekay picked up the chair and helped the Fat Yank to sit back down on it.

"And because I have taken extreme offense to your stinking Texan gob," Seekay continued. "I've upped the demand. Five million in total. Sterling. Two and half now, on the nail and two and half in a week's time when your problem's solved."

With a knowing grimace, CIA Joe tossed another bulging envelope on to the table, which Seekay nonchalantly picked up and counted two and half million pounds in five thousand pound notes.

"Good boy. Now piss off." barked Seekay, stuffing the money into his jacket's inside pocket.

Begrudgingly, CIA Joe got up to leave. "Jesus, I'd love, just one time, to whack that son-of-a-bitch smartass," he silently railed. Instead he put on his dark glasses and attempted to give the contract envelope to Seekay, who shook his head. Shrugging his shoulders, CIA Joe ambled to the door but he couldn't just let the session end like that. Violently turning around, his hand nearly pulling off the door handle, the not-so Quiet American asked, "Seekay? That ain't your real name?"

"Seekay? CK? Contract Killer? Don't be a fucking wanker!"

The door slammed as the Fat Yank stormed out, wishing he was more than just a messenger boy.

CHAPTER 1
A Hot Little Number
30th July. Monday

He wasn't really in a hurry. He just loved speed. To be frank, he didn't even care if he was half an hour late for work at Camden's Job Centre in the High Street. Everybody loved Max. The saucy lovable cheeky Crip. "You're not like other disabled people", they would say to him. "You don't carry a chip on your shoulder." What do they know? Saying that to him is a bit like someone saying to a Jew, "Yeah, but I don't think of you as being Jewish". Or to a black man... "You're different, you're not like all the other Niggers". Yeah, Right. Oh well, what the hell, I suppose they are trying to be nice to him, the small disabled man in a wheelchair, thought to himself for the umpteenth time. At least, they're not trying to stuff me in the gas ovens. Max picked up speed and recklessly hurtled his way through the automatic doors of the Job Centre Plus office, whizzing past Claire, a pretty girl, also in a wheelchair, sitting at the Reception desk. She smiled sweetly at him.

"Hello, Max," she said.

"Morning, Claire," he replied, giving her a wink.

Max wheeled past a row of desks humming with computers and various female office workers sitting in attendance, some with anxious looking clients uncomfortably perched on hard plastic chairs, suffering the soft-gloved interrogation Job Centres throughout Britain were famous for.

Who's a lucky boy, Max? The only man working with all these women. Short, fat, tall, thin, bouncy bosoms or flat-chested. To him, they're all gorgeous. He loved it.

All the women looked up and smiled at Max as he positioned himself into his own desk in amongst them.

"Good Morning Max," Sandra giggled, a bleach-blond twig of a girl.

"Hello Max," cooed matronly plump Jacky.

"How was your weekend, Mr. Maxwell Abberline?" Tracy asked, in her most severe office supervisor voice...which she immediately undermined by giving a sly wink at Sandra.

"Oh, the usual," Max replied. "Gambling, drugs, drunken orgies, wife-swapping parties..."

"Max, you're not married," Tracy admonished.

"Drat. I can't fool you girls, can I?"

"Oooh, I wish someone would swap me," Jacky moaned. "I could do with a change. Simon has become so predictable in bed. Max, bring me along to your next wife-swapping party. I'll happily pretend to be your wife and you can swap me for some nice young dolly bird."

"Maybe I won't want to swap you," Max teased as he slowly slides his personal activation card into the slot of his desk top computer. The screen lit up and an image of TONY BLAIR appeared, which slowly morphed into a Satanic version, then dissolving into the words BLAIR NEW LABOUR. Beneath each letter spelling the words a number appeared which then the computer quickly automatically adds up, summing and reducing each word into a single digit of "6"...so that BLAIR = "6", NEW = "6", LABOUR = "6".

Jacky got up from her desk and sauntered over to Max, and stood behind him, leaning over his shoulder to look at his computer screen, which unconsciously allowed her heavy pendulous breasts to lightly brush the back of his head. Oh Jacky, don't do this to me, Max thinks to himself, as his brains drop to his loins. Yes, please, more, more.

"You and your screensavers," Jacky said. "Blair New Labour - 666. How do you work that out?"

"I didn't," Max answered. "It was my numerology program. As I was explaining to you when I did the numerology on your name, every letter of the alphabet has a number - 1 to 9...A = 1, B is 2, C is 3 and so on until you get to I which is 9. Then you go back to 1 which is J until you get to R which is 9...and S is 1, with Z ending at 8. We don't get a third 9 because there are only 26 letters in our alphabet."

With rapid finger movements, Max tapped the keys and moved the mouse to illustrate on the computer screen, the ALPHA-NUMERIC Numerology Matrix -

1	2	3	4	5	6	7	8	9
A	B	C	D	E	F	G	H	I
J	K	L	M	N	O	P	Q	R
S	T	U	V	W	X	Y	Z	

Max continued to explain, a favourite occupation of his. "You remember when I typed in your name "JACKY", the computer added up all the numbers assigned to the letters in your name..."

With a Magician's flourish, preparing for the climax of his next trick, Max typed in the name JACKY...the computer screen quickly showed the numbers for each letter - J...1, A...1, C...3, K...2, Y...7 and then showed the summation of the numbers - 14

"As you can see, this gives us 14. But in numerology, we are ultimately interested in a single digit result, to give us your final magic number...so the number 14 becomes 1 and 4, and we add up 1 and 4, giving us..."

The computer screen showed the process of addition and, in garish pink, presented the text "JACKY, your MAGIC NUMBER is 5", which the computer also spoke, using a female voice simulator that had an uncanny resemblance to Marilyn Monroe.

"Jacky," Cyber-Marilyn huskily breathed. *"Your Magic Number is Five, which means you are multifaceted, have a quick wit and inquiring mind. Jacky, you are always on the move..."*

"Oh yeah," Jacky whinged. "Then how come I'm still stuck in this dead end Job Centre job!"

"And Jacky, you easily make friends wherever you go." Cyber-Marilyn mechanically intoned, oblivious to all interruptions.

"Jacky, you have a genuine need to keep busy, and you move from one activity to another at break neck speed until you drop. No matter what you do or where you go, you maintain a sense of

humour and excitement which attracts everyone you meet. As a Lover, Jacky..."

"Ah, yes," Jacky interjects excitedly. "This is the bit I like best."

Hmmm. Me too, Max thought as he felt more of her bosom pushing down onto his head.

"...you are provocative and very sensual," Cyber-Marilyn continued. *"You are adventurous to the core. You like to sink your teeth into new and unusual experiences and-"*

Feeling the rising pressure between his legs beginning to swamp his senses, Max reluctantly pressed the "Escape" key and the computer abruptly halted her sexy interpretation and returned to the screen display of "BLAIR NEW LABOUR – 666". Mustn't dilly-dally, Max thought. Let's get back to your question.

"Oh Max, what you do that for?" Jacky cried. "I love it when Marilyn tells me how sexy I am.". So do I, sweetheart, that's why I programmed the computer to say such things. Tsk tsk. Such a naughty boy that I am. Oooh Jacky, put me over your nice fat thighs and give my bare bottom a good spanking....

"You were asking about this screensaver," Max said, trying to steady his thoughts. "Well, out of curiosity I typed in BLAIR NEW LABOUR... and surprise, surprise, it came up with three sixes....the Number of the Beast...666."

"You still haven't forgiven him, have you? He's long gone. Things must change for the better."

"Ahem." They are interrupted by a small shy voice behind them. At the same time Max felt something gently nudge his wheelchair. It's another wheelchair...belonging to the frail looking Receptionist, Claire.

"Max, there's a traffic warden out front," Claire warned. "About to put a parking ticket on your car."

"Oh, Jesus Christ," Max shouted "Why won't they leave me alone. How many times must this go on?"

Frantically, Max charged round his desk and shot off to the front doors, threatening to smash the glass because they seemed so slow in opening.

The Ripper Code

"Claire, how long have I been working here? Don't the idiots realise...."

Like an angry wasp riding a torpedo, Max propelled himself outside, screaming to a dangerously close halt at the kneecaps of a slightly nervous traffic warden, who was never sure how to confront Max's pit-bull terrier like aggressive yelling.

"You stupid morons," Max growled and howled. "How many times do I have to tell you. I work here. I have a disabled blue badge. As you can see, I'm a genuine crip, not like all those other fake crip drivers who nick their aged granny's disabled badge so they can park outside Tescos...can you see my wheelchair? I have no choice but to park here. You know I have to write in and complain and.... always the penalty charge gets cancelled...but why do imbeciles like you keep insisting on wasting my time and money constantly having to appeal...why? I have been working at this Job Centre for over a year and still you wankers...god, I wish I had a gun, I'd blow your fucking kneecaps off, then you fascists will see what it's like to be a cripple trying to get anywhere in this shitty life. I promise you, next time you give me a parking ticket, I'll get a gun and put you in a wheelchair...." And with that, Max pushed his chair into the shell-shocked traffic warden, knocked him off his feet, and sent his hat flying into a puddle of water.

Hearty rousing cheers exploded behind Max, who turned and saw all his colleagues lined up behind the office glass front, applauding him. He reciprocated with an exaggerated bow and a dirty big grin splashed across his face

The traffic warden picked up his sodden hat and shook his fist at the gloating Max.

"I'll have you for this," the Traffic Warden grumbled. "I'm just doing my job. Got a right to do it without fear of violence from the likes of you. Assault, that's what it is. Assault. GBH. You'll be inside for this."

"Who cares?" Max snapped back. "I'm already in prison. What you think this body is? And fascists like you, are the bloody jailers. So go on, report me, I don't give a shit. Wanker."

The traffic warden continued to shake his fist as he skulked off, disappearing around the corner. Max re-entered the Job Centre to even more applause from both clients and staff alike. At her Receptionist Station, Claire's eyes glowed with hero-worship as Max jauntily wheeled past her to his desk.

Later that evening, after the day's work was done and a light dinner consumed, the little disabled man in the wheelchair, took a shower to prepare for his usual night's entertainment. By 10.30 pm Max was driving round the streets of Kings Cross in his metallic gold coloured Motability leased car, a Vauxhall Corsa for the next three years. He seemed to be going round in a circle, covering the same two or three streets, peering through the darkened streets, searching, driving slowly. The night was haunted by lots of women in various states of undress, alluring, tight fitting skirts, fish net stockings, standing at street corners, under street lamps, lurking in shop doorways. Max at his favourite pastime, was curb-crawling and enjoying the sights of feminine flesh for sale. The girls saw his car, smiled, beckoned, gesturing with their heads, thrusting their bosoms, wiggling their hips, rubbing their crotches. One hooker slyly lifted her skirt to reveal she wasn't wearing underwear. Max chuckled, stopped the car and wound down his window. The girl walked over to him, grinning.

"Looking for business, darling?" she said in the usual "working girl" matter of fact way.

"Naturally. I like your technique. You certainly know how to get a man's attention."

"Of course, darling, showing some gash guarantees the cash, as my grandma would say."

"Really, was she on the game too?" Max smiled.

"Probably," the girl airily replied, although her eyes were opened wide as she could not hide her surprise at seeing such a tiny man driving such a big car. "...Because me Gran would also say 'a man is so sex obsessed, he would fuck a snake if he could keep it still' ".

"Well, lucky for you, we are. You certainly screw enough money out of our rampant sex drives."

"Are you feeling rampant, then?" she said, her eyes lighting up.

"Indeedy deed. What do you call yourself?"

"Emma."

"Okay, Emma, get in the car and let's fuck. I've just got paid and I want to blow it on you."

"Darling," Emma whooped with joy. "You're just my kinda guy."

"How much?"

"The going rate for doing it in the car. Twenty pounds. Pay me after we've done and dusted. I trust you."

A few streets down the road, the gold car, parked down a dark and dingy cul de sac, was bouncing up and down on its suspension to the hungry rhythm of Max screwing Emma on the cramped back seat. Finally, accompanied by a brief moan, which he tried to conceal, he comes inside and knowing the rules of the game, he immediately withdrew his spent penis. Emma kissed him sweetly, while swiftly removing the full condom from his 'Jack the Lad'. Max was both intrigued and impressed by the diligence with which she put it in a plastic bag, sealed and then stuffed into the side pocket of her handbag..

"That's interesting," he said "Most of the girls just sling the used condom out of the window."

"Ugh, I know. It's disgusting. They don't care if kids find them. And these rubbers could be containing all manner of horrible diseases...littering the backstreets. So unhygienic. I really hate the attitudes of some of the girls. Me, I take a professional pride in this job." She then looked coyly at Max. "I gave you a good time, didn't I? You got your hour's worth?"

"Oh yes, you were gorgeous," Max replied, his hand cupping and stroking her petite breasts. "I loved having sex with you."

"Me, too." Emma gently removed his hand and placed it onto his cock and giving it a squeeze. "You're quite a nice little fucker. And well-endowed, if I may say so. You got a girlfriend?"

"Nah, of course not. I wouldn't be having to pay for it, if I had. You got a boyfriend?"

"Yes, but he doesn't know what I do on the side. I only do it a couple of nights a week."

Emma wriggled into her skimpy knickers and buttoned up her blouse, while checking her face in the car mirror.

"Oh, what do you do normally?" Max asked, looking at her, wishing she could be his.

"I'm a medical student. I just do this to try to pay off the students loans and fees. It's really hard being a student today. I guess I'm lucky really, I'm able to exploit my body to make easy money."

"But isn't it dangerous sometimes...and what does it do for your normal sex life? I mean, doesn't it have an impact on your relationship with your boyfriend?"

"You ask a lot of questions, don't you?" she queried, looking at him sharply. "Yeah, it could be dangerous but I've not had any trouble yet...touch wood...but then I've only been doing it a few months. True, I think it would do my head in, if it was all I had. And I think I might start to despise men....or sex with men. And I'd hate that. I wouldn't want to become a man-hater like a lot of the girls."

"A few of the women have told me they didn't like men before they became prostitutes," Max pointed out, "...not surprising as they had been abused as children... and that they use the profession to get revenge on men. They enjoy taking money off gullible men who pay for an hour, but the girls get them in and out in less than ten minutes."

"Yes, as my old grandma would often say... 'women were the first slot machines'." Emma held out her hand and Max diligently counted out four five-pound notes, which she slipped into her handbag, and then gave him a quick peck on the cheek. Max sighed wistfully as she ran down the alley onto the main drag.

"Jesus, I'm always falling in love with them," he moaned, mentally beating himself.

CHAPTER 2
The Wrong Side of the Bed
1st August. Wednesday

Who said "I don't like Mondays", Max thought to himself as he drove to work that dismal Wednesday morning. I don't like Wednesdays. Woden's Day, Woe-be-gone day. Bloody middle of the week. Last weekend a distant memory. The next, too far in the distant future. No wonder I'm feeling depressed. But be of good cheer. It's the first of August... Lammas Day in the wiccan or witches calendar... or as the Celts originally called it, "Lughnasadh". The festival of harvests, marriages (and divorce) and sacrifice....In the old days, the Celtic King would volunteer to sacrifice his life if things were going too badly for his kingdom....floods, famine, poor harvests, pestilence...whatever the reason. The King would take all the blame upon himself and allow for him to be killed and his blood would first be drunk by his successor and then shared out between his people. As was his flesh. Cooked upon the communal pyre and eaten by one and all. The energy and power of the King, thus consumed, passes from the dead to the living. The King is Dead. Long live the King. The Once and Future King. So this is where the Early Christians plagiarised the idea for the Holy Sacrament from. The heathen Celts. What about that other Celtic festival of the first of May. The Bealtane fertility ritual where the pagan King first fucks a white mare horse, then kills and cuts her into pieces which are thrown into a cooking pot, whereupon he and everyone partakes of her... and all that was in her, including the King's semen. Funny how the Christians weren't so quick to nick that idea.

Suddenly, Max's thoughts were brought to a sudden standstill, on seeing newspaper hoardings outside newsagents, announcing in big screaming headlines "LABOUR LEADER DIES"

"Jesus fucking Christ!", he cursed and slammed on his brakes, bringing his car to screeching halt. Vehicles behind him blared their horns at him in protest. But he didn't pay any heed as he stopped to read the headlines - "LABOUR'S JACK KIMBLE DEAD FROM HEART ATTACK" and "SUDDEN DEATH OF SOCIALIST REVIVAL"

"Oh no," Max groaned. "Not again". Ignoring for several minutes the mounting anger at his rear, Max simply sat rigid, and blankly stared into a haze of nothingness that quickly succumbed to a swirling black fog which stank of the fetid breath of the Devil himself.

He was snapped out of his doom-laden reverie by the sharp rapping on his windscreen by a traffic cop, warning him to keep his car moving.

" Just like with John Smith," Max explained, back at his desk, talking to his colleague, Claire, who was all ears, her eyes wide with excited admiration. Max always had something fascinating to say. Even if a lot of it seemed a little looney, she could listen to him for hours. Okay so what if she was only twenty-six and he was old enough to be her father. Anyway, I'm only bringing him a cup of coffee...his favourite first cup of coffee of the day, he always said. It's not like we are engaged or anything. He hasn't even asked me for a date. And I've been working here for nearly two months.

"Must be murder" Max continued. "You know, whenever we get a good guy. The bastards make 'em disappear."

"The papers say it was heart-attack. Kimble had been under a lot of stress. Dealing with the mess the last one left behind."

"Huh, that's what they always say," Max retorted. "Heart attack is easy to simulate when they want to kill someone and make it look like death from natural causes. For example.... All you have to do is inject some adrenalin and it makes it seem exactly like a heart attack. And the beauty is..it's nigh on impossible to detect. Unlike poison. We know the Mafia and the old KGB were very good at that sort of thing. Why wouldn't CIA assassins be?"

"Oh gawd, you and your conspiracy theories! The CIA again." she said.

"Just study the public history of the CIA. It's out there in black and white."

"Why would the CIA, I mean the Americans want to kill Jack Kimble?"

"Same reason they had John Smith bumped off back in the mid-Nineties. To make way for their favourite Prime Minister. John Smith was good old fashioned Labour, a proper, genuine socialist...and a decent humane human being...unlike that fraud, Tony Blair. Smith would never have allowed Britain to be run by the US President, would never have made us fight America's imperialist wars. Blair was paid and nurtured by the Yanks. He was their mole, sent to infiltrate the Labour Party and destroy it from within and hand it over to the Neo-Cons. And now, its' happening all over again. Kimble's dead. Let's see who suddenly appears out of nowhere to take over the Labour leadership. Whoever, it is, you can be damn sure, he or she will turn out to be America's new lieutenant....You mark my words."

"You're probably right," Claire conceded. "You do seem to predict some of these things rather well. You said the Americans were going to invade Pakistan, because of their nuclear weapons and six months later, they did. You're a clever bunny."

Max, not expecting this, blushed and quickly turned to his computer to see whose next for interview.

"Peter Davies?" he called out as he surveyed the line of waiting claimants.

MARTHA

Later that evening, flashing gold in the King's Cross "Red Light" district, Max's car was a signal to all the hookers that he was out on the prowl, "curb-crawling", again. He spotted a slim young girl with long blond hair, wearing a red tight pvc mini skirt. As he slowly drove towards her, she was forcefully pushed aside by a 40 plus, who ran to his car side window, thrusting her whiskey smelling face into Max's.

"Hello sweetheart," she exclaimed. "Haven't seen you around here for ages. Where have you been?"

"Do I know you?" Max asked, peeved at this unwanted interloper.

"Course yer do. It's Martha. I always give you a good time, don't I."

"Eh, yes," he said, still uncertain. "Yes, I remember you. You look different."

"None of us are getting any younger, are we," she laughed and ran round to the other side and threw the car door open and gleefully leaped in, and stretched herself out on the front passenger seat.

"The usual, then?" she asked hopefully.

"Eh yeah, sure," he said with barely concealed resignation.

"You got twenty quid?" she demanded, holding out her hand.

Max gave her a twenty pound note, which she carefully examined as if he had handed her a dud. Satisfied she stuffed it into a bulging purse and turned to him with the most fake sweet smile he had seen for a long time.

"Thanks, sweetheart," she purred. "Just go down the road and turn right at the second set of lights...then 3rd turning at the mini roundabout. Then immediately left behind the Barratt's Haulage yard."

Max dutifully followed her directions and they ended up in a darkened backyard, with a faulty street lamp flickering at the end of the block. Max jumped at the sound of a cat shrieking. Martha told him not to worry and began to unzip his flies and pushed her hand into his pants.

"Glad to feel you're still a big boy," she said with a lascivious grin. "Remember the first time? I was worried I wouldn't be able to get it in. You got a johnny, dear?"

"Awfully sorry, I haven't."

"Not to worry," she said. "I always carry plenty. Well, you've got to, haven't you."

She quickly opened her purse and took out a prophylactic, and began to put it on Max's eager member.

"What a beauty," she exclaimed. "Shit. I don't think the johnny is big enough. Don't want it to burst, do we, dearie?"

"Certainly not."

"That's it. Nice and snug," she said, managing to roll all of the rubber over his swollen erect penis. "God, I still can't get over it. When I first saw it. You scared the life out of me. Thought you were going to split me in half. I couldn't believe such a little chap like you could be so well blessed."

"Yes, I remember now. I thought you were just flattering me. You know... like... you say it to all the punters."

"Oh no. I tells the truth, I do. You are big. Jesus," she said, lovingly stroking it.

Five minutes later, they didn't seem to have progressed very far. Martha straddled over Max, who was on his back, lying uncomfortably across the two front seats of the car. Which he didn't enjoy but she said she preferred it this way. Back seat screwing always gave her the creeps.

"I keep wondering if it's just an optical illusion," he said, shifting his back slightly because it felt like it was going to snap in two at any moment. "You know, it looks big in comparison to my small hips and body."

"Nope, it's definitely huge," she insisted. "I always have difficulties getting it all the way in. I don't with other blokes. Jesus, what do you feed it on?"

Or was it that Max's patience was about to snap because she was really annoying him with her farcical rocking up and down as if he was fully inside her when he knew damn well that only the end of his nob was actually penetrating her vagina. And while this charade was being played, her hands were busy searching his coat pocket for loose money. Bingo. She found another twenty, a ten and two fivers, which she surreptitiously pushed into her purse. Max knew exactly what she was up to but he hadn't the nerve to challenge her. He felt a sort of existential acceptance of the situation. Perhaps he deserved to be robbed, he wondered.

Having satisfied herself there was no more money to be pinched from the poor sap's pockets, Martha abruptly stopped her exaggerated struggle to receive proper penetration.

"Oh baby, this isn't working is it?" she said with feigned remorse. "I'm feeling a bit sore today. Better call it a day, what yer say?"

"Eh, yeah, okay...if it's hurting you." came Max's meek reply.

"Yeah, I think we'd better. No hard feelings, eh? Just take me back, where you picked me up, will yer, there's a sweetie."

Feeling like a complete www, weak-willed wally, Max drove her back to where he had picked her up from, and stopped the car. Martha skipped out and blew him a kiss. "Remember, darling," she said. "I'm always available for you."

"Yeah, right," he said, driving away from her as fast as he could. "No way," he continued, muttering under his breath, "Bloody tea-leaf."

After ten minutes of crazy manic driving – he thought it would get the anger out of his system – Max got out a pocket dictaphone from the glove compartment and spoke into it.

"MARTHA. M equals Four; A equals One; R equals Nine; T equals Two; H equals Eight and A equals One. Which comes to Twenty-five. Two and Five is Seven. Thus, Martha's number is Seven." With nothing more to add, he stopped the recording and was about to return the dictaphone to the glove compartment but instead placed it in the side pocket on his right.

Seven. What does that mean? 'More than Freeman'. 'Bad Spliff'. 'Kevin Space-head'. But apart from that. Can't exactly remember. Off-hand. Something like... "A Seven who desires material accumulation is liable to go off the track. Sevens are mystical, spiritual, occultic people. Going against their nature by going for money brings out the worse in them." That's true. Bloody Martha.

Jesus. I'm tired. He looked at the dashboard clock. Eleven Eleven. I don't want to go home yet. I need some satisfaction.

POLLY

On the predatory prowl, Max, still stressed and angry from just having been robbed, cruised down a different street. A flash of white caught his eye. Was it his imagination? No, there it was again, in the darkened doorway. He espied the girl, smoking a cigarette. Short brown hair. Full breasts trying to escape a skimpy tee-shirt and a very curvaceous plump bottom. She saw his eye roving all over her body, smiled and beckoned him over. He slowed down as he drove alongside her, checking in his mirror for possible undercover cop cars lurking around corners. The girl quickly stubbed out her fag, tossed it to the ground and ran up to his car.

"Drive to the end of the street," she said, getting in the car beside him. "Turn right and keep going 'til I tell you to stop."

As they approached the rail goods yard, she lightly tapped him on the shoulder.

"Stop here," she commanded. "This will do."

As instructed, Max stopped the car, switched off the ignition and headlights. Plunged into a darkness that deepened the silence as Max stared ahead. The girl surveyed him with a detached appraisal, giving him time to pluck up the courage. Poor boy, she thought, this is probably his first time. To reassure him, she put her hand out and touched his face, gently caressing his cheek.

"I'm Polly," she said. "What's your name?"

"Max."

"Ah yes," she smiled. I'm wrong. This isn't his first time. "I've heard of you. Some of the girls say you're really nice."

Max remained silent, still staring ahead angrily. She took his hand and put it on her breast. Slowly, he started to fondle her breasts. They felt good. Warm. Comforting.

"You haven't said what you want, Max."

Max turned and looked at her.

"Lie on your tummy, Polly," he said in matter of fact way. "I want to look at your bum." To help her into a reclining position, he wound the back of the passenger seat down

Polly turned over onto her stomach, and Max began to stroke and squeeze her ample buttocks which erotically filled the tight fitting jeans.

"What do you think? Isn't it just the best shaped bum in the world?"

"Oh yes, gorgeous," he replied dreamily. "Hmmm so exquisite to the touch. Divine. I love it." Polly wriggled with pleasure as Max intensified his massaging of her full spongy bottom.

"God, Polly," he exclaimed. "What a difference you are, compared to the last girl."

"When was that?"

"Half an hour ago."

"You randy little beast, Max. Can't get enough of it, huh?"

"Didn't get any, Polly. She took me money, made a feeble attempt to fuck me, made some excuse that it wasn't working and did a runner. A real prick-teaser."

"Really?" Polly queried, looking at him with a shocked expression. "That's terrible. What a bitch! Slags like that give decent working girls like us a bad name. Don't worry, Max, I'll make up for what she didn't give you."

"I hope so," Max said as he squeezed and pinched her rump, giving it a few hard slaps which made her giggle and moan with pleasure. I wonder if she's faking it, Max thought.

"You do anal?" he asked.

Taken aback, Polly pushed his hand away and swivelled round to give him a hard look.

"You want to fuck me up the arse?"

"That's what I asked."

Polly sighed, and then smiled, putting his hand back on her bottom.

"You're in luck, I do anal. Not many girls do. But it will cost you."

"How much?"

"Sixty quid." Polly smiled hopefully, beginning to undo her jeans.

"Sixty," he replied. "Damn. I've only got a fiver."

The Ripper Code

At this, Polly sat bolt upright, rigid as a rock, eyes wide with disbelief.

"You what?" she said in a dangerously low voice. "What you say? Did you say a fiver? You actually said a fiver? You're fucking mad." Now her face was boiling red as she spat out – "I wouldn't even let you breath on me for a fucking fiver. You fucking arsehole, how dare you ask to fuck me in the fucking arse for a fucking fiver." She quickly did up her jeans, screaming furiously at him, "YOU CUNT. YOU FUCKING CUNT. HOW FUCKING DARE YOU. YOU MISERABLE LITTLE TURD."

Max suddenly felt out of his depth. Also her rising rage was making him feel physically vulnerable. There was only three and a half feet of him, and less than thirty three kilos in weight.

"No. No," he said placatingly. "It's not like that. I...the point is...one of you girls robbed me...whilst pretending to screw me, she was rifling through my pockets... took about forty quid...and I...well...I told you.. you know.. about how..."

His words were cut off when her hand slapped his face, the force of which knocked him sideways.

"So fucking what?" she screamed. "That's got nothing to do with me. That doesn't give you the right to treat me like I'm a fucking idiot.. You want to punish me because you were stupid enough to get robbed. And you're such a fucking drip of man, you can't fuck properly to even keep a whore interested. You want to blame me, you bastard. I can't believe you had the nerve to string me along, asking if you can fuck me in the arse, when you had no fucking cash to back it up, you fucking Mong...And I let you have a free fucking feel of my arse...and my tits...I've got a good mind to break your fucking fingers...you Spazzy twat."

Her fury was truly frightening. Polly screamed and wept tears, as she punched at Max, her fingers grabbing and scratching at his face, trying to rip his eyes out. Max, pale and petrified, pulled further away, pleading with her, "Look, I'm really sorry. I was just angry", but she just grabbed his hair and started to yank him towards her.

"Yeah," she snarled. "And you thought you could take it out on me...I never done you any harm. It wasn't me who robbed you.

The Ripper Code

You really imagined you could fuck me in the arse for a fiver! Do you know how painful anal fucking is, you little shit...have you any idea...I wish I had a nice fat dildo on me, I'd turn you over and fuck you up your stinking shitter till I have you shitting blood all week." Then she slapped him again around the face, and again and again... slapping him until his head was ringing, while pulling him towards her by his hair.

"You're lucky I forgot to bring my knife with me tonight.." she said hoarsely. "I'd cut your fucking throat...or least, cut your prick off. You wait, I'll tell my Man, he'll find you and slit your throat..."

By now Polly's anger was lessening and she began to get out the car. Then she stopped and swung back on Max.

"Where's that fiver?" she demanded, her eye glaring at him like daggers. "Give it me. Give me it now before I smash your face in. Give it me." She grabbed him by the hair again and yanked him towards her. His face so close to her raging jaws, he was afraid she might try to bite his nose off.

Max hurriedly looked and found the five pound note, which he nervously held out to her. Polly snatched it from him, and again, as she went to leave, she had another thought, turned back and looked at the Disabled Badge on the windscreen.

"And I'm taking this, you little rat," she snarled, ripping the Blue Badge off the window and waved it, taunting him. She then stuffed it in her bag, leapt out of the car and ran down the road.

Max collapsed, his head sank into his arms on the steering wheel and sobbed. Utterly defeated. Suddenly very ashamed. And utterly humiliated. He hated the feeling of fear and vulnerability. And how could he be such a prick. No longer could he regard himself the hero in his own comic strip.

CHAPTER 3
The Eyes and Ears
2nd August. Thursday

It wasn't exactly sheltered accommodation where Max lived. There were no on-site wardens, but he did live in a ground floor flat that was part of a housing complex for people with special needs. It was early in the morning, around six-thirty. Max, after returning from his disastrous attempts to get laid, just couldn't sleep. His mind turning over and over the scenes of being battered, being screamed at, and being frightened – very frightened. Still, his heart was racing. What if she found out where he lived? What if she sent her pimp round...to slit his throat? Max shivered as he thought about her, Polly and the hate in her eyes. If looks could kill, he would be burnt to a crisp by the intensity of her glare. "Okay", he thought to himself. "Let's hope that's a lesson learnt. I must get back to being Robin Hood." Oh god, that's even more pathetic. Forget it. Forget everything. Go back to being a worm, fit only for turning the soil and then to be cheerfully eaten by a chirpy-cheap-cheep blackbird singing "Oh blood-deee, oh blood, ahhh". That last thought made Max smile. Okay, life must go on.

Max turned on his computer and summoned the Name-Oracle programme. He then typed "POLLY". After playing a little jingle, which Max had composed as one of the gimmicks for his software invention, the computer displayed the text "POLLY, your number is 8". "Eight...Fate, Mate, Gate, Hate", Max thought grimly. "Yes, hate. Polly surely hates me now, and then she ate me."

Max opened the file labelled "Prostitutes", and added "Polly = 8" to the list.

"So, Name-Oracle. Speak. Tell me what is Eight?" Max clicked on the Number Interpretation icon. Of course, I know what eight is, but I like playing this game, thought Max.

"*Number Eight*", began the voice-simulation of Christopher Lee, the actor, Max would have cast in the role of Gandalf in the movie, "Lord of the Rings". He shouldn't have played Saruman. That part should have gone to an American. If Orson Welles had still been alive, I would have given him the role of the evil wizard. Of course, Max would have cast himself as Frodo. "Well, I am a genuine hobbit, am I not?" Unlike that fake, Elijah Wood, that pathetic "Winona Ryder-lookalike". Throughout all three Ring movies, Max griped endlessly in his head, Mr. Wood just had the one pasty-faced pained expression.

"*Number Eight*", the deep resonating voice repeated (Max had a variety of voice simulations programmed into his computer, which he would select, depending on the mood he was in – usually it was "Christopher Lee" when he was at home, especially after a night with prostitutes. The creatures of the night...and Dracula. But why this cliché association? And do I have a thirst for prostitutes that is really vampiric?). "*You know exactly how to handle money and very much, at home in the business world. You are able to take charge in any situation. You are frank and do not hesitate to give orders. Number Eight, you are admired for your executive ability and appreciate your efficiency at any task, from the simple to the most complex.*" She certainly bloody well took charge of me last night. Max squirmed.

"*Number Eight, as a Lover, position is everything. You like to be on top. You are acrobatic and well-exercised. You know which muscles to stretch and which to tighten. You are deliberate in your moves and you make every one count. You love to wrestle with your partner, whether you are man or woman, and you have mastered some good holds.*" Jesus, now you tell me, Max mused, rubbing his still throbbing jaw.

"*Do you want more information, Number Eight?*" the computer asked.

Max clicked "Yes" with his mouse.

"The Number Eight represents two worlds, the material and the spiritual. It is in fact like two circles just touching each other. The sphere of Heaven and the sphere of Hell...and where they meet at the interface are the learning curves that is Earth."

"One side of the nature of Eight," the cyber-Christopher Lee continued to intone, while Max made himself a cup of coffee.

"...represents upheaval, revolution, anarchy, waywardness and eccentricities of all kinds. The other side represents philosophic thought, a strong leaning towards the occult studies, religious devotion tending towards fanaticism, a concentrated zeal for any cause espoused. People with the number Eight in their lives feel that they are distinct and different from the rest. Number Eight people are invariably much misunderstood in their lives, and therefore for this reason they feel intensely lonely at heart. You have a deep and very intense nature, great strength of individuality. You will generally play some important role on life's stage, but one which is fatalistic, or as the instrument of Fate for others." That's also me. I'm a number Eight. Maxwell James Abberline. The full name adds up to Eighty, reducible to the single digit of Eight. Though, not many people know my middle name, James. I try to keep it quiet. Makes me sound like a bloody chauffeur, driving around some posh git. "Home, James, home". Still, there's one "James" I can look up to. "My name is Bond. James Bond".

Max looked down at his cup of coffee. Empty. Bollocks. The first cup of the day always goes too damn quickly. As he went to the kitchen to make another, there was a knock on the door. A sharp knock. A commanding knock. A knock that proclaimed, "Open the door at once or else!". Max chose to ignore it. "Seven o'clock! Too damn early for visitors." He continued making his coffee. The knocking was even more insistent. Max took the cup to the sitting room and nervously placed it on the coffee table, spilling some of it on a recent issue of the cult magazine *"The Ripperologist"*.

"Shit," Max cursed, as he used the ruined magazine to mop up the wasted drink, then on his way to the front door, threw the sodden sticky mess into the bin, which in his haste, he nearly knocked over with the front wheels of his wheelchair. The relentless knocking on the door was really pissing him off.

"Alright!" he yelled. "Keep your bloody hair on, I'm coming."

Hope it's not blasted bailiffs come to do me for unpaid parking fines, worried Max as he opened the door.

"Maxwell Abberline?"

"Yes?" Max blinked at the portly middle-aged man, smiling benignly in his black suit, white shirt and glaringly orange tie.

"Maxwell James Abberline?" His smile vanished and his slate-blue eyes sharpened and hardened into the piercing hooded stare of an encircling raptor.

"Yeah?" Max winced. Jesus, this fat balding fucker knows my middle name. Must be a cop.

"Can we come in?"

"We?" Max queried. There was no one else out there. Was there? Then, from around the corner appeared another man in a black suit, ten or more years younger than the first. Also, much slimmer and slightly taller. He wasn't wearing a tie and his shirt was a pale green, open at the neck.

"Yes, there's two of us," the younger man grinned. "I was admiring your roses. Hope you don't mind."

"I'm Detective Inspector Edmunds," the older man said. "And this is Detective Sergeant Walters. Camden CID. Can we take up some of your time?"

"Yeah, sure," Max wheeled back into the sitting room, quickly checking there were no incriminating porn videos lying around.

"Come in. Cup of tea?" Max offered cheerily.

"That'll do nicely, thank you," Det.Sgt. Walters said as he wandered around the room, browsing the bookshelves. He paused and exclaimed, "Fascinating,", when he saw the highly controversial books, "*The Murder of Robin Cook*" by Mick Cullin, and "*9/11: The Pentagon-Mossad Conspiracy*" by Connie Lisa Ryse.

Bloody typical copper, nosey as shit, Max thought, keeping a strict eye on him.

The Ripper Code

"Mine's a coffee, if it's not too much trouble," requested the older detective inspector, Edmunds, as he sat on the sofa, noting the still damp coffee stain on the small low table in front of him.

While Max made the beverages, he peered into the sitting room and saw Walters pull out a book from the bookcase, on forensic science, examined the title and smiled at Edmunds, showing it him and then returned it to the shelf. He then pulled out another book, on serial killers, glanced at it, with raised eyebrows, and put it back. Max quickly brought in the tea and coffee as Walters found a book on Jack the Ripper.

"Interesting set of books you got here?" the detective sergeant said, gratefully taking his cup of tea. "Read them all, have you?"

"Most of them", Max replied, trying to sound casual.

"What about this one?" Det. Sgt. Walters asked, picking out the copy of *Crime Shadows*. "Any good?"

"Yeah, it's really good," Max replied, taking the book from him and returning it to its rightful place on the shelf. "David Canter, Britain's top profiler. He uses computers to generate algorithms to identify the killers."

"Yes, we know," said Det. Insp. Edmunds. "He's worked with us on a few cases. But he's a bit of a boffin. Number cruncher. Charts. Statistics. Numbers. All too esoteric for my liking."

"But he does get results, doesn't he, Gov?" Walters affectionately wagged his finger at his boss.

"Ah, young people today," sighed Edmunds, shifting his position on the sofa, allowing Walters to sit beside him. "So easily impressed. Give me good old fashioned police work any day."

The two detectives smiled indulgently as Max placed a plate of assorted biscuits on the coffee table in front of them. Why am I being so damn hospitable, the little wheelchair man silently moaned. I should really be trying to get rid of them as quickly as possible. I've got to go to work.

"You're probably wondering why we've come to visit," Edmunds said, helping himself to an Angus shortbread biscuit.

"Don't worry, we're not vice squad," assured Walters jovially, snatching up two milk chocolate Hob Nobs. "We don't give a damn about you curb-crawling. A person in your position got to find his pleasures where he can. Even if he has to pay for it. Can't be easy for you."

Edmunds, not to be outdone by his junior, quickly takes another shortbread AND a Golden Crunch. "No," he noisily munched. "We have better things to do with our time than harass girls trying to make a living whatever way they can. They're not hurting anyone. Drug pushers, that's a different matter. They ruin lives but whores, in my opinion, they provide a useful service. They've saved many a marriage, I'm sure."

"They certainly saved mine," Walters grinned. "Jesus, when my bollocks are aching for it and me missus is on the rag... you know what I mean.... her time of the month and she fucking hates the mess- so I just have go out and shag a tart . Afterwards, I come home feeling relieved, give me missus a box of chocolates, she clouts me 'round the ear'ole and everything is sweetness and light. And our marriage goes on to see the dawn of another day. Yep", he continued, stuffing a chocolate chip cookie into his mouth. "Whores are society's safety valve. I'd give 'em all the MBE. Where would we be without 'em? God bless 'em."

Max was not impressed by this supposedly frank and open confession. He didn't believe a word of it. "What's their bloody game?" Max wondered, as the senior detective picked up the plate of biscuits and handed them to him, much to the chagrin of Walters, who was hoping to nab one more Hob Nob.

"Okay, so we're agreed," Edmunds said impatiently. "We're not here to smack your bum for being a dirty old cripple...we've got a problem....and we're wondering if you can help us out."

"Coz we've been reliably informed that you are the eyes and ears of this here neck of the woods," Walters added.

Max began to laugh with incredulity. Looking miffed at this response, Edmunds held up his hand, indicating to Max that he should wait and hear him out.

"Me the eyes and ears?" snickered Max. "You must be joking."

"We're deadly serious," the detective inspector replied sombrely. "We've been told you're a bright lad, well-educated."

Walters stretched back comfortably on the sofa, evincing a nonchalant air. "It's not your fault with all your qualifications you can't get a better job than junior clerk in the local Job Centre. What's your degree? Psychology and sociology? I mean the Chief Constable's got less qualifications than you....I mean, if you weren't stuck in wheelchair, you could have been my boss."

"He's got more," Edmunds snapped. "Don't talk bollocks."

"What?"

"The Chief Constable. He's got more qualifications. But that's not the point and stop being patronising to Mr. Abberline here. He doesn't want to hear any more of your flannel."

"Yeah but...you know what I mean, Gov." Walters sounded genuinely hurt.

Edmunds ignoring his subordinate, continued, "Just looking at all your many books tells us you're a very knowledgeable chap....and John Jordan...you know John Jordan?"

"John Jordan?" cried Max startled. "He was the Chief of Security at university."

"That's the man...know what he's doing now?"

"Yeah, I bumped into him not long ago. He runs a private detective agency."

"That's right. He's a good bloke. Very good at his job. Excellent Private Dick. Helped us out many a time."

Walters smiled and winked at Max confidentially. "Of course, his Military Intelligence and SAS background has been useful preparation for his work as a private eye."

"I think that's information Mr. Abberline didn't need to know," snorted Edmunds.

"I already knew that," Max said airily. "In fact, I wrote an article in the student newspaper about him, exposing his clandestine background, querying as to why someone so highly qualified in State Security and Intelligence, and been awarded the MBE, was working in a job that was little more than head janitor, and supervisor of campus traffic wardens at the university."

Walters laughed. "Phew, yes, John wouldn't have liked that...being described as nothing more than a janitor and traffic warden."

"I believe my expose got him the sack. He was gone within a week of my article being published."

"Well, you had rumbled him, hadn't you, Mr. Abberline," Walters said, with a hint of admiration. "The Powers that Be couldn't use him anymore."

Inspector Edmunds got up and patted Max on the shoulder. "Anyway, you'd be pleased to know John bears you no grudge and in fact, admires your skills at detection...thinks you got the makings of a great amateur sleuth-" He wandered over to the bookcase to get a closer look at a book that had caught his eye. *The Brotherhood*, a notorious expose by Stephen Knight, on Freemasons.

"Which brings us round to why we need your help," Walters continued. "Do you remember a double murder case about fifteen months ago? Regents Park."

Max thought for a moment. "Erm...two women was it? Taking their dogs for a walk?"

"That's it," nodded Walters. "That's the one. Very nasty case. In broad daylight, around midday. Middle of the week. Two middle aged ladies."

"Middle class, weren't they. Both had husbands in banking or finance."

"Very good," Edmunds said, sitting back down on the sofa, still clutching Stephen Knight's book on Freemasons. "You have got a good memory. John Jordan was not wrong."

Walters brought out from his pocket a notepad and pen. "You took quite an interest in the case, then?"

"Not really," Max shrugged. "I use to go to Regent's Park to eat my sandwiches. I had a desk job in the Zoo. I like sitting near the wolf enclosure, having my lunch. So, not being far from the scene of the murders, of course, it would make an impression on me. Okay, so I took a little interest. That's all."

"Were you there on the day of the murder?" Edmunds asked, also taking out his notepad.

"When was it?" Max asked, trying not to feel they could be interrogating him.

"20th April", Walters answered. "It was a Wednesday."

"Probably. I don't know. It was a long time ago. But more than likely. If it wasn't raining, I'd be sitting there with the wolves, feeding them bits of my ham and egg mayonnaise sandwiches."

Detective inspector Edmunds raised his eyebrows. Ham and egg mayonnaise sandwiches? Wolves? Next he'll be telling me he fed deep-fried Mars bars to perishing penguins! "Did you notice anyone suspicious?"

"I doubt it."

Taking Walters' pen from him, Edmunds made a note. "You say you took an interest in the double murders...what were your thoughts at the time?

"Well, it did strike me that the attacker must have been known to the women...especially to the dogs. I mean, the fact that he or she was able to get close enough to kill them both within minutes of each other and the dogs not doing anything to keep the killer off. I mean, they were pretty big dogs weren't they?"

"Certainly bigger than Yorkies. Ought to have made any would-be-attacker think twice...unless he was using a gun."

"So, what do you want from me? How can I be of any help?"

"This case has got us completely flummuxed. Eighteen months and we've got absolutely nothing. No suspects. No motive. Nothing. We're up a gum tree. We don't want to close the case as unsolved. One of the victim's was wife to a golfing partner of our very own Chief Constable."

"We close the case and he will take it very personal," added Walters

"But we can't afford the man-hours any more. The murder inquiry has gone past its sell-by-date."

"John Jordan says you're a chap with imagination...lots of bright ideas swirling around in that box of yours. If anything strikes you...if you hear anything....you like to swan it with the low life...the girls, the pimps."

Edmunds stood up, and again gave Max a friendly pat on the shoulder. "We know you're on friendly terms with some of the petty crooks on the estate. You know a thing or two.. who's who...what's what...where's where."

Max felt his face go hot. there was a sour taste in his mouth. "You want me to be a grass?"

"We're talking murder here," Walters stood up and leaned into Max's face. "Two very nasty murders."

"We don't want you to be a sneak," Edmunds soothed reassuringly, gently patting Max on the head. "We just want a fresh mind on the case. Someone who thinks laterally, divergently...someone who fancies himself as a Sherlock Holmes in wheelchair."

"Someone like you." Walters picked up *The Brotherhood* book and as he returned it to the bookcase, he asked "Didn't this book get Stephen Knight into a lot of trouble with the Freemasons?"

"Yeah, they put a ju-ju spell on him," Max said "Dead six months later. From a brain haemorrhage."

"Did you read that in one of your books?"

"Nah, I just made it up."

Walter laughed, picked up the dirty cups and carried them to the kitchen. But he quickly came back out and grabbed his notepad from the coffee table. "You didn't think I was going to wash them, did you? I'm not your bloody Home Help."

"You're a bit behind the times. Us, poor cripples, don't get them anymore."

"Did you ever watch Ironsides?", Edmunds enquired as he walked to the front door.

"Yes, it was one of my favourite TV shows as a kid."

"Exactly. Here's my card. Give me a ring if you think of anything. Anything. Doesn't matter how wacky." Edmunds shook Max's hand, as if they were sealing an agreement.

"Yeah, okay, I'll do some background research on the case....try a bit of brainstorming...See what I come up with. Can't promise anything though."

"Nah, of course not," Walters also took his hand and gave it a good bone-crushing shake. "But give it your best shot, eh!"

As Walters opened the front door for Edmunds, Max asked, "What about the dogs? What became of them?"

"The dogs?" Edmunds said. "No idea. What happened to the dogs, Jim?"

"Can't remember, Gov.", Walters shrugged. "Probably got put down."

"Pity," Max replied. "They could have been a key to solving the crime."

"Yes, well, I think they were put down," Edmunds brusquely said, stepping outside. Walters quickly followed and then paused to have one more look at the roses.

"Don't forget," Edmunds said to Max, while giving Walters an impatient but friendly shove. "Give me a call when you come up with something."

ANNIE

You'd think Max would have learnt his lesson from the Polly incident. You'd think he would give up his nocturnal pastime of Curb-Crawling. You'd think he would avoid prostitutes like the plague. Not a bit of it. He was experienced enough to know that most liaisons with these working women were positive and pleasurable. Besides, you know how difficult is it for a junky to kick his heroin habit, well, it is equally difficult for Max to be rid of his addiction to having whores. So, on the day the detectives sought his assistance, Max just had to celebrate by going out that night to find a hooker to fuck.

And within minutes of crawling the streets he saw her. She was a plump black girl, chatting to Phil, a young white rent-boy. Max gave her "the eye" as he drove close by, which she immediately spotted. She smiled at him, and with a sexy wiggle, sauntered over to his purring car... lurking... waiting in the shadows.

"Hi Baby. Do you need a girl?" she asked, her brown eyes smiling cheekily and her sensual tongue slowly caressing a succulent lipped mouth, full of attractive gleaming white teeth.

"Yes. How much?"

"What do you want? Straight sex £40. Anything kinky £30 upwards extra."

"Most of the girls do straight for £20," Max protested.

"That's for doing it in the car, down some grubby street," she said. "I don't do that. I've got a lovely apartment. Very snug and comfortable. We can relax, have a chat, a cup of tea and I promise I won't rush you. I'm not one of those girls who wants you in and out in ten minutes. If you're paying £40 for an hour, I like to give you an hour's worth of pleasure. I'll even tell you my real name, Annie."

Max smiled. "Sounds good to me, Annie. I love getting to know the girl I'm gonna be making love to." Already he was doing the Numerology in his head...*ANNIE. A=1, N=5, N=5, I=9, E=5. That's 1+5+5+9+5 which is 25. 2+5 is 7. Seven, same as Martha, bloody thief. Is Annie going to try to rip me off? Well, not all "Sevens" are the same. Thankfully. Anyway, Annie might not be her real name, even if she says it is.*

"Who said anything about making love?" Annie leaned forward through his window, pushing her bosom closer to his face. "It's a straight fuck, pure and simple. I don't want you getting all emotionally involved. It's just about having lovely sex and that's it."

"You like sex then?"

"Of course, I do. I wouldn't be doing this if I didn't. I love sex big time and what's even better, is getting paid for it."

"Yeah, I love sex," Max enthused. "Wish I could earn money doing it...but you're never going to get a girl paying for it...not from a man. They don't need to. Women are in a sellers' market, they've got something between their legs which most men want and are going to pay for, or even kill for... Men are in a buyers' market. Even if there were a few lonely rich women out there desperate enough to pay for it, they certainly would never be desperate enough to pay me for it."

"Yeah, it's a hard world for you men, me heart bleeds for you. Now can we get to my place, 'cause me arse is freezing out here."

"Oh yeah, sure, sorry," he opened the passenger door for her. "Where to?"

Annie slumped onto the seat beside him and kissed him on the cheek. "You know Royal Yard Road?"

"Yeah. Only five minutes from here."

"That's where I live. Number 33. Put your foot down"

The Ripper Code

"I can't," he smiled teasingly, pointing to his little legs not being able to reach the foot pedals.

"O shit, I'm really sorry. I didn't think," she groaned, horrified, staring down at the empty space where his feet should be. However, she quickly recovered as her natural curiosity got the better of her. "So how do you drive?"

"It's all done with this hand-control, which is attached to both the accelerator and brake pedals," Max handled a lever on the right side of steering column, behind the steering wheel. "If I pull the lever, the car accelerates and if I push, the car brakes. Simple."

"I see you got automatic transmission, so you don't have to worry about changing gears," Annie put her hand between his legs and cupped his bulging crotch. "But you have a lovely gear stick here, I hope it doesn't brake, when we're going at full speed."

"No, it's just my bones that are brittle," Max smiled at his secret little in-joke.

"Your bones are brittle?" Her eyes widened anxiously.

"Yeah, I got brittle bones – technically known as *Osteogenesis Imperfecta*, meaning born with imperfect bones."

"Oh my god! Is it safe for you to be screwing? I mean your bones won't snap, with you humping up and down? I won't be able to straddle you, will I? My weight will crush your hips and ribs. Honey, is this a good idea? Why don't I just give you a handjob or blowjob?"

"No, no," he quickly exclaimed. "It's alright. I'm doing it every night with a different woman, all shapes and sizes. My bones aren't that brittle. Anyway, they've steadily toughened since childhood. Luckily I couldn't have gone screwing when I was a kid."

"I bloody well hope not, you dirty little tike," She grinned, patting his crutch.

Six minutes later they arrived at Annie's apartment. She helped Max get the wheelchair out of the car, and he made a show of a "Tarzan-like" leap into it, yodelling "Arrrgh-ar-arrrghhh!". Annie laughed and then looked up at her block of flats.

"Oh shit," she groaned. "I forgot about the steps. How are we going to get you in?"

"Well, you could lift me...."

"Nah, I don't think so. I'll see if Spud's around. He's usually lurking somewhere."

"SPUD!!!! SPUD!!!!," Annie shouted, at full volume down the street. "Where's your black arse?" Suddenly a muscle-bound giant of a black man popped up behind her from shadows. "What you want, Annie?" he growled heavily.

Annie jumped. "Oh Jesus, Spud, don't do that, you scared the life outta me."

"Who's he?" Spud pointed at Max.

"Punter," Annie replied dismissively. "Can you carry him up the stairs?"

"Me carry him up the stairs?" Spud gawped at her in amazement. "You must be joking, Annie. He's your trick. You carry him."

"Aw come on, Spud, I'll make it worth your while. You know I will. I always do, don't I?"

"No, you do it."

"I can't," Annie whined. "I did my knee in. You know that."

"Yeah but you know I got a bad back. My trainer said no lifting heavy weights for a month."

"But Spudder baby, I need the money and he's loaded. He's willing to pay for all kinds of weird shit.

"Hey, hold on a minute..." Max interjected.

"Shhhh," Annie hissed, then switching on her pearly white smile at her pimp, she cooed, "Spud, please carry him up for me. He's not that heavy and look at his strong arms. He'll hold onto you like a chimpanzee."

Spud looked down at Max, hands on hips. "How much will you pay me for carrying you?"

"Well, I don't think I should have to pay extra just because I can't fucking walk," barked Max bitterly. "Annie, lets just do it in the car and have done with it."

"Spud! See what you've done," Annie yelled accusingly. "You've upset the gentleman. How would you like it if you were a cripple like him. You could be easily. Dutchie is always threatening to kneecap you. Especially after you didn't go down in the second round like you promised."

Spud looked away, shamefacedly, then turned to Max, beefily grasping his hand, and said, "Sorry mate. Yeah, you're right. It aint right. I should carry you. It's not your fault you can't walk." The great lump of a man hunkered down and picked Max up, thinking he was carrying a tiny baby, but immediately gasped in pain. "Fuck, man. You gonna break my back."

"Stop complaining, you woose," Annie slapped his haunches as if he was her mule and not her domineering pimp. "Get up those steps and I'll give your back a lovely massage later."

CHAPTER 4
Jail-bait
3rd August. Friday

Last night with Annie, restored Max's faith in prostitutes. He had a fantastic time. She was fun to be with, as well as very sexy and attentive to his wishes. On top of which, instead of the hour, she gave him two for the price of one. Perhaps that was because she enjoyed me as much as I enjoyed her, Max conjectured as he parked his car outside the offices of the North London Gazette. He had phoned into work that morning to say he had a hospital appointment, which wasn't true, of course, but he wanted to do some research at his local newspaper.

The officer at the front desk was all smiles and bonhomie, said his name was Larry and assured Max he would give him all the assistance he needed. I'm obviously something of a novelty, Max inwardly laughed. Larry can't have met too many private detectives in a wheelchair.

"Fifteen months ago, you remember the double-murder?" Max asked. "Two women with dogs? Regents Park?"

"What date?"

"20th April."

"Go down to archives," he pointed to a corridor to his right. "There's a lift. Say Larry at the front desk says you can use the computer. All our stories from ten years back are on the database. You should find what you're looking for."

The archive room in the basement was exactly as Max imagined. Cobweb encrusted, ceiling high, racks of boxes, stuffed full of old editions that your great grandmother might have read. Thankfully, Max didn't have to search through all these to find what he was looking for. All he had to do, was sit in front of the archive's computer and type into the news database, the relevant keywords, to summon the various articles on the Double Murder. As he read off the computer screen, Max wrote down notes. *"Regents Park. Midday. Two well to do, middle aged women, in smart but leisure clothes. They were close friends and they had in common that both their husbands were bank managers...and Rotarians."*

Probably also Freemasons, Max thought, because nearly all bank managers are either Rotarians or Freemasons or both. Unless of course, they are women, which is a diabolical shame - for women bank managers. Their business will always be at a disadvantage. I'm amazed that the Masonic movement can still get away with it. Women should sue them under the Sex Discrimination Act.

Taking out his dictaphone, Max closed his eyes, sat still for ten seconds, then pressed the Record button. In a monotone voice, he spoke, playing the part of a psychic detective. "The two ladies walking amongst the Spring green foliage, happily chatting to each other. They each have a dog on a lead. A black labrador and a golden retriever. And now, imagine a Stalker following the doomed pair, dodging in and out bushes and from behind trees. The golden retriever keeps looking back at the Stalker, straining at the lead, whining and wagging its tail. The dog is seeing a friend. One of the women turns to see what her dog is fussing about and about to smile but then, there's horror on her face as the hand appears, wielding a knife, which slashes down at her repeatedly. She collapses as the other woman turns to look, screams and starts to run, dragging her labrador behind, which keeps trying to get at the Assailant. The woman trips as her dog pulls her towards the assailant, who stabs her in the back....Screams. Frantic barking from both dogs...." Shaking his head, he stopped the tape recording. "Where did all that come from?" Max asked himself. "Was it real? Or just the product of a fertile imagination sustained by watching too many movies and reading too many books?"

"Onc dog went mad," Max had come to do some afternoon's work at the Job Centre, and was talking to Claire as she sat, all agog, at her reception desk "Had to be put down. The labrador. But the other dog, Goldie the retriever, went to an animal rescue. Battersea Dogs Home, in fact. If I could get to the dog, I'm convinced she will identify her mistress's killer for us. Lets face it, the police are wrong when they say there were not witnesses. There were witnesses. The dogs. Those dogs saw, smelt the murderer and if they could speak our language they would have been questioned."

"But the dogs don't... and one is dead anyway," Claire reminded him.

"There has to be a way we can get the information from the remaining dog, Goldie. If a Bizzy Lizzy can identify her neighbour's destroyer, then a dog must be able to. After all a dog is far more of a sentient and intelligent being than a potted plant.

"I beg your pardon? What do you mean 'Bizzy Lizzy'?"

"Its a plant," Max answered. "I read about it in this brilliant book called *Supernature*. It was an experiment back in the 60s. They got two of these plants - Bizzy Lizzies."

"Why are they called Bizzy Lizzies?" she interrupted him.

"I don't know. Coz they're busy growing to fantastic heights, coz they're busy attracting busy buzzing bees. Who knows...but it doesn't matter."

"And why Lizzie?" Claire persisted.

"What?" Max stared at her. "Because it rhymes with Bizzy probably...but anyway... the thing is they attached a polygraph to one of them-"

"A polly graph?" Claire again interrupted. Is she playing dumb on purpose just to wind him up? "Its the posh word for Lie detector. They attached this device to one plant and then cleared the room of all humans. The computer randomly selected someone to go into the room when no one was looking and that person was told by the computer to massacre the other plant...you know, the Bizzy Lizzy NOT attached to the polygraph-"

"The Lie Detector."

"Yes," Max affirmed excitedly. "The thing is no other human knew who the killer of the poor Bizzy Lizzy was. The next day, the experimenter lined up about 10 suspects including the killer, and had each one go by the plant which had witnessed the murder. The polygraph remained static for all suspects except for the one who had actually killed the plant. The machine went bonkers, indicating that the surviving Bizzy Lizzy was extremely distessed by the presence of her neighbour's killer. This showed that plants had feelings and that they were capable of recognition."

"Wow, that's amazing," exclaimed Claire. "Is that really true? Did that really happen?"

"Yeah, of course. I read about this sort of thing in loads of books. The most famous is *The Secret life of Plants*. But the point is...if you can get physiological and stress responses from a plant, then with the same apparatus you should be able to read the feelings of a dog."

Claire nodded enthusiastically. "Yes, of course, attach the Lie detector to Goldie, show her things to do with the murder and see how the machine reacts...But what could you show the dog?"

"Well, for a start...the police may have photos of possible suspects," Max replied as he glanced at his watch, and realised he had been away from his desk much too long. "Catch you later, kid," he drawled in his best Humphrey Bogart voice and blew her a kiss as he returned to his mountain of paper work.

ROSIE

The curtain of night was a favourite velvet cloak Max loved to wrap around himself, when shopping in the street flesh markets of Kings Cross. To enhance the mood, he would repeatedly play on his in-car sound system, Velvet Underground's *Walk On The Wild Side*. He was listening to this very classic as he brought his vehicle to a sudden halt, to survey a petite willowy feminine silhouette bathed beneath the sickly yellow penumbra of an irritatingly flickering street lamp. There was something uncertain about her. He sat for a few minutes to see if she was simply out having a smoke or waiting for a bus, or whether she was a genuine hooker plying her trade. Eventually, the young looking girl approached Max's car. She looked drugged up.

"Do you want some?" she asked in a little girl voice, which didn't seem an affectation.

"Yes. What do you charge?" Max replied, but he was feeling very concerned as she was swaying about, having to hold on to the side of the car to steady herself.

"Um.....What.....What you want?" she slurred. Her eyes had difficulty focusing on him.

"Are you okay?"

"Yeah. You want...you know...do it all?"

"Yes. Sure."

"Okay...what? Sorry. What did I say?" she giggled as she nearly fell over.

"Nothing. Do you want to get in the car?"

"Yes. Okay. Sorry." The young girl slowly, dreamily staggered to the passenger side, paused as if forgetting why she was there. She then turned and looked at Max, giving him a demure smile and opened the door, and flopped into the front seat, closed her eyes and seemed to have fallen asleep. After a couple of minutes of quietly observing her apparent somnambulant state, Max gave her a gentle nudge of the shoulder. "Where do you want us to go?"

"Eh? What?" She jerked awake. "Oh god, sorry, was I asleep? Didn't mean to. Don't tell anyone."

"Are you sure want to go through with this? Shall I take you home?" Max asked.

"No. No. Please. Don't do that," she pleaded. "Let's go round the corner."

Arriving at the spot where she had indicated, Max stopped the car and wound the girl's seat back. She looked at him through half closed glazed eyes and smiled sweetly while he kissed her on the lips and caressed her small young breasts.

"Do you have any condoms?" Max asked, unzipping his flies.

"Yes," she replied sleepily, "In my bag."

Max opened her bag and after much rummaging around the squalid detritus of her life, he found the all-essential bare necessities of life on the game - several packs of 'rubber Johnnies'. Triumphantly, he turned to her, waving a 'packet of three', but saw that the girl seemed to have fallen asleep again.

"Hey, wake up," he said, softly stroking her face until she opened her eyes.. "What's your name?"

"Rosie," she replied, struggling to show more life. "What's yours?"

"Max."

"Hello Max. I'm Rosie. Did you ever see 'Rosie and Jim'? My mum named me after that kids' TV show." She giggled and started to sing the theme tune to 'Rosie and Jim'.
Meanwhile Max was struggling to undo her jeans and pull them off her hips.

"Here, can you help get your knickers down?"

"Certainly...eh...what you say your name was? Oh yes, Max. Maxwell's silver hammer."

Rosie tried to lift her bottom up so Max could slide her knickers down but she flopped back down again.

"Rosie...Rosie..." Max sighed, exasperated and annoyed with himself, for having so little physical strength.

"Yes, Max?"

"Lift up again," he panted.

"Oh, sorry. You haven't got me knix down yet. Sorry". She lifted up her hips, and this time Max succeeded in pulling her knickers down to her knees. She may have been the smallest whore he had ever tried climb on top of, but he was still only about two thirds her size. "Ahhh," she said, holding him close, like he was her little doll.

"Open your legs, Rosie, so I can get it in."

"Yes sir. Certainly, sir. I like a man who knows how to command a lady. Maxwell's silver hammer..." In mid flow of the upbeat Beatles' song about a serial killer, Rosie fell asleep once more as Max struggled to penetrate her but he was at an awkward angle on top of her and her knickers halfway down her legs didn't allow her to open her thighs wide enough.

"Oh Jesus, this isn't working," Max moaned, rolling off her. "Rosie, wake up. I can't do it. You'd better go home."

"Oh? What? No, Max. Please. You're really lovely. Such a gentleman." She immediately sat up and yanked her knickers off. "There! Is that better? I can open nice and wide for you now." she spread her legs wide and picked little Max up and put him back on top of her. "Get it in me. I want to feel you...all of you...inside me. Push it in. Yes....Just push...that's lovely...hmmmm."

Rosie closed her eyes and began to snore. Despite her seeming to be asleep again, Max tried to have sex but gave up. Withdrawing his insubordinately limp penis, he rolled to the side of her and began to gently stroke her innocent looking face.

"Rosie, how old are you?"

"Why? What you mean?"

"How old are you?"

"Eighteen," she said too quickly.

"Are you really?"

"Yes, of course I am."

"I don't think you are, Rosie," Max began putting his cock away.

"I am. Honest." She put her hand out to stop him.

"I think you are much younger. I can't do it if you are less than 18."

"Oh please, Max. I need it. I am 18. You got to believe me. Don't you like me?" She began to weep a little.

"Yes, I like you," Max put his arm around her. "You are the sweetest girl I've seen in a long while. But I don't do it with children. You must be about 14..13 even. I don't know but you look too young to be doing this. I can't. I'm sorry. Don't worry. I'll give you the money. I'll give you double the money if you let me take home." He looked at her full in the face. She turned away, avoiding his eyes, then looked up into the distance.

"I haven't got a home," she murmured quietly. "I'm staying in a squat with my pimp and two more of his girls. So, you can't take me back there, he'll kill me...and you," she added ominously. "Lets just do the job and I'll go," she urged.

"No. Rosie," he pushed five banknotes into her tiny hand. "Look, here's fifty quid. Get a bus back to your parents."

"My parents?" her voice on the verge of hysteria. "You must be joking. Why do you think I'm doing this? My Dad's dead and my Mum's boyfriend has been fucking me since I was nine...and my Mum refuses to do anything about it. She won't believe me. I told her and she called me a liar and kicked me out. I got nowhere to go. All I know is fucking. Steve taught me all I know, the filthy bastard. So, I can teach you, if you want, Max. Steve liked to fuck me in the arse. So I wouldn't get pregnant, he said. So my mum need never know, he said. I got a great arsehole for fucking, Max. Its been stretched nice and-"

"Stop it, Rosie," hushed Max. "Don't. You don't have to tell me...listen, if I give you an extra hundred quid. Promise you'll go to a women's refuge."

She stared at him, open mouthed. "Another hundred?"

"Yes. Here." Max took from his wallet and counted out ten ten-pound notes. Rosie snatched the bundle and leaped out of the car, shouting, "Thanks Max. I promise. I'll be a good girl from now on. Ta-ra." As she ran gaily down the street, Max wondered if he had been over-generous with his dosh. Reaching the end of the street, Rosie turned and smiled sweetly back at Max and gave an affectionate little wave. No, he thought, in horror situations like this, you can never be over-generous. Before starting his car engine, Max took out his dictaphone and pressed record.

"Friday night. August the Third. A close shave with jail-bait. She called herself Rosie, I'm not going to calculate her number. She's not to be entered into my file of Prostitutes."

CHAPTER 5
Barking Mad
5th August. Sunday

Is there really any difference between visiting Battersea Dogs Home and Wandsworth Prison? Max thought. Both places made him feel sad and depressed. Not that he had had too many opportunities to visit either. The one and only time he was inside Wandsworth H.M. Prison was nearly two years ago, when he visiting an anti-war protester friend of his, who was doing six months for repeatedly demonstrating "without authorization" outside Parliament. What a fucking arsehole of a country, Britain has become, Max thought bitterly. My friend ain't a criminal. The damned Government is. First, for illegally invading and occupying sovereign states. And secondly, for demanding you must first obtain permission before exercising your inalienable democratic right to tell them they are a no-good bunch of international war criminals. Given the blatant hypocrisy of the British justice system, Max had no qualms, at his friend's request, about smuggling some marijuana under the table. They had to meet in the prison hospital unit because, typically, the visitors' room was not wheelchair accessible. It was easy getting the tiny bit of contraband in. Of course, the screws weren't going to search an innocuous-looking little man in a wheelchair. Max, for a brief moment, wondered if he should take this up full time and call himself "Deals on Wheels".

Now, he was visiting Battersea Dogs Home in south London on a Sunday afternoon. As soon as he entered the famous canine rescue centre, a cloud of despair descended upon him. And the noise was incredible. Dogs barking, howling, whining, crying. Max slowly wheeled pass the cages, pausing every now and again to pet and stroke the abandoned, the lost, the frightened.

Bouncing up to the bars, sorry-looking mutts, of all shapes, sizes, breeds, and 'Heinz 57s' tried to get his attention, their manic tails wagging hopefully, all demanding, insisting, often with big sad appealing brown eyes, that he take them to his home. Max looked wistfully at them. "Oh dear, I'd take you all, I really would."

"Is there a particular breed you're after?" asked the young hippy-looking Dog Care Attendant, who was accompanying Max in his search for a dog he hoped he might recognize.

"A Golden Retriever."

"Ah, they go very quickly. Popular breed."

"Actually, the one I want, I'm sure was given a good home ages ago." Max glanced up at the long-haired young man. Perhaps he looked more like an afghan hound than a hippy. Maybe that's what happens if you work here long enough, speculated Max.

"Was it here?" asked "the afghan hound".

"Yes. Apparently. Her name was Goldie."

"Huh. That doesn't tell me anything. Very common name for Golden Retrievers. How long ago was she here?"

"Eighteen months ago," Max said, following the man down another seemingly endless corridor of cages, exploding with the same cacophonous maelstrom of dog noise.

"Phhhhh," the attendant sucked air through his teeth, shaking his head. "No. She'd be well gone by now. Come to the office. I'll see if we got anything on record that far back."

Max had difficulties getting his wheelchair into the cramped untidy office. As he would expect, the walls were festooned with notices of animal protection and welfare charities, slips of paper from heartbroken dog owners, whose family pet had gone missing, clippings of newspaper stories of recent cases of cruelty and barbarism to dogs and cats. Max was particularly shocked to read about a cat found in a dustbin, barely alive, with over a hundred nails hammered into it. Humans can be such cowardly sadistic monsters.

"Here we are." The dog attendant pulled out a folder from a filing cabinet, containing several pages of biographical and health details and a photo of a golden retriever. "Ah. Right. Hmmm.

Well, I'm afraid I can't give details as where Goldie went. But you will be pleased to know she went to a very good home."

"I see. Well, that's good. Do you think she would still be there?"

"Probably. We've had no complaints from her new owners. They never asked us to take her back. Of course, she may have died by now. Or they may have moved her on to another home. But who knows, she's probably still with these people. They're a good couple, very caring. They've adopted quite a few of ours. Real dog lovers. Apart from that, there's not a lot more I can tell you."

"Okay, thanks," Max lingered at the door. "So you won't tell me where Goldie is?" he asked, trying not to appear too pushy.

"Sorry," the dog attendant shook his head regrettably, "Against the rules. We have to protect the dogs and their new owners. Sometimes people change their minds, after dumping their dogs on us...and go chasing after the new owners, demanding their dog's return."

"Yes, of course, I see your point. Okay, well, thanks anyway for your help." Max took one last quick glance at the stomach-churning photograph of the wretched cat resembling a nightmarish pin-cushion. With the distressing bedlam of a thousand cooped-up dogs' anguished yapping howling noise hounding pounding his head, Max was relieved to get away.

CHAPTER 6
The Contract
6th August. Monday

The room was a cliché. A large ornate office, over-ostentatious with too much gleaming glass, golds and reds. On the walls, hung antique guns and samurai swords. Why do British gangster bosses, especially those that run London manors feel the need to mimic their stereotypical counterparts caricatured in the so-called gritty British gangster movie? And as you would expect, there was the ubiquitous gigantic wall-to-wall aquarium, complete with Japanese fighting fish in one tank and piranhas...yes...piranhas in the other. Peering affectionately through the glass at his swimming treasures, loomed the heavily jowelled face of the archetypal tough guy, who couldn't decide if he should look like Bob Hoskins or Ray Winstone, but could quite happily settle for James Cagney. He was short and stocky but then so was Napolean, and it never did him any harm. All muscle and no flab. He was in his prime. Confident and relaxed and this room was his castle, his inner sanctum. The lair of Sinclare, crime boss for north and west London.

Behind him, entered one of his many skinhead henchmen, Mr. Brown, dressed in standard issue black, polo-necked jumper and slacks. "He's here, Boss"

"Good. Send him in." Sinclare dropped a small piece of prime steak into the piranhas' tank and watched with fascinated relish, the short work they made of it. The door silently opened behind him, Sinclare turned and studied the tall man as he entered, wearing a long black coat and carrying an old-fashioned doctor's bag. Seekay or CK, returned an equally cool appraisal. For several minutes, they just stared at each other without a word.

Finally, Sinclare wandered over to his aubergine-coloured leather armchair and sat down.

"You come highly recommended," Sinclare smiled.

CK, saying nothing, turned and looked at the ceremonial swords on the wall. He recognised one sword in particular, that of the Alumbrados, an Illuminatus secret society in Spain. The sword was used in their rituals. He looked closer at it and saw that it was a replica. CK inwardly smiled. He didn't expect it to be genuine.

"SAS wasn't it?" Sinclare attempted a confidential tone. "Northern Ireland, Iraq. Afghanistan. Pakistan. Iran. Venezuela. Death Squads. Nice one. Sweet. My friend couldn't stop singing your praises. Said you were worth every penny."

"Your friend talks too much," softly growled CK.

"No he doesn't," Sinclare said, shaking his head. "He never told me your name."

CK said nothing, continuing to fix Sinclare with a quietly mocking baleful stare.

"I get a little nervous if I don't know the name of the killer I'm hiring."

"Just call me CK."

"OK, CK," began the gang boss. "I pay well for a job well done. I hate fuck-ups. No one ever fucks up twice with me."

"Just tell me the job, will you."

"Listen here, you fucking snot-nose," Sinclare snarled. "I'll tell you all in good time."

"Oh dear, I didn't realise I was working with amateurs," sighed CK, turning for the door. "I haven't time for this. I'm going."

"Just you wait a minute," demanded Sinclare. CK stopped and waited patiently.

"Two million, professional enough? A million down payment and a million when its all done and dusted. That suit you?"

"The Hit?" CK impassively asked, his hand still poised over the door handle.

"Multiple. Anything from five to ten", replied Sinclare, relieved they were talking business at last. He handed CK a photograph of a young woman. "She's number one. The rest are red herrings. You are free to choose the others from my stable. I want total camouflage of real motive. You up to it? Got the bottle for this little number?"

CK studied the photograph and handed it back. "You got the million, in cash?"

Sinclare shouted for his henchman, "Mr. Brown!", who immediately entered, carrying an attaché case.

"Yes Boss?" Mr. Brown asked.

"The Lucky Dip."

"Yes, Boss." The henchman passed the attaché case over to Sinclare, who, placing it flat down on the desk, unlocked it by applying the correct combination of numbers and opened the lid. He then gestured to CK to come over and count the contents, which he did, diligently. Satisfied, he put the million pounds in used notes into the black leather doctor's case he brought in with him. He also picked up the photograph of his contracted hit and put it in with the money. As he turned to leave, Sinclare stopped him with a hand on the shoulder.

"CK, I've got another photograph," Sinclare said. "It's your choice but I'd appreciate if you'd include this little brat in your barrel of red herrings. She's really giving me arse-ache. She's under-age. Gonna get me into trouble with the law. I told the Fishers to steer clear of sprats but do they listen? Problem is, she's a favourite with a bent cop I got on the payroll...which makes him vulnerable to blackmail and he's too valuable to lose to the paedophile squad."

"Look, if you want her dead, just tell me. I'm not interested in any sob sob stories."

"Fuck you," Sinclare snapped and threw a second photograph, which landed on the floor. CK briefly glanced at it, nodded, looked at his wristwatch, saw the time was 15.06 and six seconds, nodded again at Sinclare, and walked sharply out the room, leaving the picture where it lay.

CHAPTER 7
Irish Queen on Cnoc na Rea
6th August. Monday

Max was quite pleased with himself. Proud almost. He had managed to avoid tasting the delights of Kings Cross "Red Light" district for a whole weekend. Of course, it was hard. But, in truth, giving a hundred and fifty quid to Rosie had blown him out. Saturday and Sunday, he just didn't have any ready cash to pay for prostitutes. He couldn't withdraw any money from the "hole in the walls" because they're always at awkward heights for people in wheelchairs. So, he was going to have to satisfy himself, jerking off while watching internet movie porn, which was never a real substitute. Max absolutely loved the feel of warm womanly flesh, the intimate physical contact and the luxuriant scent of feminine smells. He also missed the brief companionship and chat, hiring the real McCoy, offered.

So, at last, on Monday night, after a heavy day at the office, Max with a full wallet, was back on the streets of Kings Cross, ravenously trawling the salacious sidewalks for his nocturnal hit of tasty bit of crumpet. The first two streets he drove down, he didn't see any of the regular girls. Then as he turned into Cheney Road, he saw Rosie standing at the corner with Martha. The young girl, on spotting Max's car, her face flushing with guilt, tried to hide behind Martha's back. She was hoping not to see Max sadly shaking his head as he drove past them. But, of course, she had. Suddenly bursting into tears, little Rosie ran from the astonished uncomprehending Martha, and disappeared into the shadows for the remainder of the night.

SOPHIE

"At last, my port came in view, now that I've discovered you..." Lines from the romantic ballad "To My Lady" by the Moody Blues, one of Max's all time favourite rock bands, were being played on a CD of their greatest hits, just as he swung the car around the bend and saw her. Perfect timing or synchronicity? She was tall, wearing a tight green dress that stopped just above her knees, green high heel shoes, dangerously teetering as she tried to maintain her balance, caught like a moth in a curtain of light, radiating out from a seemingly mesmeric street lamp. Max, slowly motoring pass her, was immediately smitten by her as she quickly and shyly glanced in his direction. Being cognizant of his breathing suddenly becoming rapid and the emergence of a dull ache in his loins, Max knew he had to have her this night, whatever the cost. He turned the car round and pulled up beside her, his electric window purred as it whirred all the way down. She effortlessly swung her voluptuous hips as she valiantly attempted to glide towards him, determined to deny the awkwardness of her impossible shoes.

"Would sir be looking for business?" the Green Goddess tempted.

"Oh indeed, I am," Max grinned. She ran around the car, laughing joyfully and quickly got in beside him.

"You from Ireland?" he asked, looking at her admiringly.

"That's right. My accent too much of a giveaway? Or is it the emerald green dress?"

"The accent... the burning red hair and the Celtic fire in your eyes. What part are you from?"

"Dublin's fair city," her eyes sparkled. "And where are you from? You don't look English, if you don't mind me saying."

"I was born in London but my Mum was Sicilian. She's dead now. Both parents are, actually."

"Oh dear, I am sorry," she said, touching his hand. "You're all alone. One should never be alone. You have a sweetheart? No, I suppose not. You wouldn't be wanting to pay for the likes of me if you had. Oh dear, I am sorry. I'm talking too much. I'm not very good at this. Poking my nose. Terry is always telling me I ask the Tricks too many questions. Tell me if I'm being too nosey."

"It's okay. I like chatting to the girls. I'm nosey myself. Anyway, if you get too beaky I'll just have to spank that shapely bottom of yours."

"Ooooh, I'd like that," she purred, wriggling teasingly in the seat.

Max slipped the car into forward gear. "So...where do you want to take me?"

"You say," her eyes shone like cut glass. "But not around here. These are not nice streets. To be honest, I don't like doing it in the car. I prefer somewhere more comfortable."

"We could go back to my place," Max suggested hopefully.

"No, I don't know you well enough for that. Later maybe." She winked and gave his hand a light touch.

"Well, where do you suggest?"

"My apartment but how would you get up there? Its three flights up."

"You look like a big strong lass to me. You could carry me up the stairs."

"Really?" Her face lit up. "How much do you weigh?"

"Nothing," Max said, leaning forward, trying to hide his tubby tummy. "I'm just a baby. You could swivel me on your little finger."

"That sounds a bit kinky to me, we'll have none of that." The vivacious redhead pretended to be shocked. "Bad boy."

"So...where are we going?"

"My place. Head down Euston Place and then, turn left at The Doctor's Scalpel."

"I know the place. Weird name for a pub", Max laughed. "Popular with medical students, I'm told."

"And members of the S and M fraternity. And barbers", she giggled.

"What name do you give yourself?" Max took a short cut onto the Euston Place.

"Sophie," she said, while indicating with a nod that the pub, The Doctor's Scalpel was coming up on their left.

"Ah. Sophie," said Max as he turned the car into her street. "Sofia. Sophia. The Goddess of Wisdom. Philosophy. Lover of Wisdom."

"Pardon?" Sophie raised her eyebrows quizzically.

"Philosophy. That's what the word means. "Philo" - "Love of"...."Sophy" - "Wisdom"

"Well now, Mister Philosopher, here we are. Now the fun begins."

Sophie got out of the car, and under instruction from Max, took out his wheelchair, unfolded it and placed the chair cushion. Max did his "Tarzan leap" from the car and landed in the chair. Door slammed shut and they raced down the street like a pair of lunatics to the tower block where Sophie stayed. Max whooped and yelled as Sophie, laughing, pushed his wheelchair like a maniac racing driver, swerving him from side to side, terrifying oncoming pedestrians who quickly leaped out of the way. When they reached the inside of the building, she instantly sobered and put her finger to her lips, gesturing to him to keep silent.

"I don't want people here to know my profession," she whispered.

Arriving at the formidable looking staircase, Sophie turned and looked anxiously down at Max. "How shall we do this?"

"Might as well leave the chair downstairs," Max suggested. "No point in lugging it up as well. Can we hide it somewhere?"

"There's a cupboard under the stairs. Here, I'll pick you up and sit you on this table for a minute."

Sophie bent down and lifted Max up.

"Bloody Nora! You little fibber. You're heavier than you said," she complained.

Max wrapped his arms around her neck. "If I hold you like this, I can take most of the weight."

"Don't kid yourself. Jeezus," Sophie panted as she struggled to hold him aloft and steady herself on her high heels. "And all them stairs. You'll be the death of me."

Sophie plonked Max on a very wobbly hall table, and then folded the wheelchair, She opened a cupboard door beneath the stairs and pushed it in. She turned back to Max, made a show of flexing her arm muscles.

"Right, you little darling. Let's climb the mountain."

"Stairway to Heaven, I hope," he said, as she briskly grabbed him and tried to run up the stairs, carrying him, not the easiest of things, wearing a tight dress and high heel shoes.

"Bloody Hell, I'm not dressed for this mullarkey," she giggled.

Suddenly, there's a sound of a door opening above them and footsteps of someone coming out of a room. Sophie froze.

"Jeezus. Someone's going to come down and catch us. I don't want them seeing me carrying you to my room. What would they think?"

She swung round and ran back down the stairs in near panic. On reaching the bottom, she unceremoniously dumped Max into the cupboard under the stairs, closed the door on him, plunging him in darkness. Suddenly, the door opened again. She quickly popped her head in. "Sorry," she smiled. "I'll be back. I promise."

She quietly closed the door, and ran up the stairs to chat with the neighbour coming down. As soon as he'd left the building, Sophie charged back down, opened the cupboard and swooped up Max, and began to run back up the stairs with him....when, again, she suddenly stopped halfway as she heard another door opening.

"Oh bloody Nora," she yelped.

"Not again!" Max groaned.

"Jeezus," Sophie cursed. "I can't believe it. Am I never going to get you into my bed?"

Sophie swivelled round and again ran back down the stairs, panting and giggling with Max. It was all getting highly surreal and slapstick. Again at the bottom, she dumped him in the stairs cupboard, slammed the door on him, and tried to walk nonchalantly and calmly back up the stairs.

"Well, hello Mrs. Ferguson, what grand weather we had today," she said as she passed her neighbour coming down. For the next couple of minutes they continued to exchange pleasantries, much to the impatient annoyance of Max, who was beginning to feel claustrophobic in the stiflingly heavy darkness.. At last, the gossip was over and the second neighbour bade

Sophie goodnight and was gone. "Now, third time lucky, please," Sophie exclaimed, as she ran, pell mell, back down, threw the cupboard open and hoisted Max up into her arms, gave him a quick peck on the cheek and ran like a half-crazed Olympic champion back up the stairs. Max, at this point, was looking very anxious as he was bounced about in her iron hug. He prayed that there would be no more interruptions. "I don't think my brittle bones can take much more of this. Much as I love being pressed against her bosom." He pushed his face further into the softly mounded twin peaks of her chest, feeling the hardening of a nipple against his cheek.

They arrived at a door which was appropriately painted bright Leprachaun green.

"My God, we made it," Sophie wheezed. "Here, hold tight while I get the key. Oh Jeez. I can't open the door. Take the key, you try."

Holding on for dear life with one hand, Max took the key with the other and managed to unlock the door, which Sophie shouldered open with a loud bang.

"Shhhhh" Sophie whispered at the door, and ran to the bed and collapsed, still holding Max on top of her. They frantically kissed and cuddled, rolling about, trying to laugh quietly. Suddenly Sophie threw Max off her and leaped across the room to the open door. "At last," she breathed, closing the door and locking it.

Max, lying on his back, head propped up on her fluffy pillows, looked admiringly at her. "Hooray," he said, feeling happy. "At last."

She came over and sat on the bed beside him and held his hand. They looked into each other's eyes. For a moment, Max allowed himself the luxury of imagining they were normal lovers, but with a small sigh, he knew it was time to burst the bubble.

"We didn't talk about the price," he said, trying to sound business like.

"After all I've had to go through to get you here, I should charge you a hundred."

"You what?" Max was genuinely shocked.

"But we'll call it fifty," Sophie grinned. "But if you want to stay the night, it'll be seventy."

"I think I better stay the night to give you a chance to get your breath back, build your strength." Max took seven tens from his pocket.

"You're not wrong there, darling." Sophie took the cash and went over to a dressing table and took out from the drawer, a little music box. On opening the lid, it chimed a tinny rendition of "It's a long way to Tippery." She placed the seventy pounds in the little wooden box and shut the lid, halting the tinkling tune but she continued to softly sing "That's the wrong way to tickle Mary. That's the wrong way, you know."

"Is there a right way to tickle you, Max?" Sophie smiled, taking her clothes off. Max nodded as he undressed, just leaving his underpants for her to remove, which she slowly did with her teeth while he lovingly caressed her bottom.

"I could eat your bottom," he said, wolfishly licking his teeth. "It looks as juicy as a peach."

"Be my guest," she purred, turning onto her tummy.

CHAPTER 8
Tiw, the God of War
7th August. Tuesday

There was a big smile on his face as he drove, that Tuesday morning, to work. Sophie, what a woman! The best hooker in town. how many different girls had he had in the past year alone? Must be in the hundreds. Yet, Sophie tops the lot. There's no sophistry in her. Sophisticated? Maybe not. But sexy as hell. And kind. and fun to be with. And loving. As far as a professional lover can allow themselves to be loving. Sophie. Sophie. Her real name? What's her number?   **S** -1, **O** -6, **P** -7, **H** -8, **I** -9, **E** -5. 1+6+7+8+9+5 = 36 = 9.

Sophie is Nine. Nine, the number that always comes back to itself. 2 x 9 = 18, 1+8 = 9... 3 x 9 = 27, 2+7 = 9.....4 x 9 = 36, 3+6 = 9..... 5 x 9 = 45, 4+5 = 9.....and so on. What is it about the number Nine? "999" our emergency call. "911", the Yank emergency call. "9 / 11", the day the Americans declared war on the world. Number Nine symbolises the Planet Mars and is the number of force, destruction and war. Today is Tuesday, named after Tiw, the Anglo-Saxon god of war. The French call this day of the week, Mardi...named after Mars, the Roman god of war. Max wondered how many wars began on a Tuesday? "9/11" was a Tuesday...

In the esoteric traditions, we have the Secret Chiefs, those Hidden Masters known as the Nine Unknown Men. These semi-divine Supermen, also known as the Great White Brotherhood, ancient Aryan adepts lurking in a subterranean city, somewhere beneath the Himalayas or Gobi desert or beneath the ice sheets of the Antarctic, worshipped by Bulwer-Lytton, Blavatsky, W.B. Yeats, Crowley, Hitler and other Rosicrucians, Occultists and black magicians. And in Freemasonry there is an Order of the

Nine Elected Knights, with a ritual where 9 roses, 9 lights and 9 knocks have to be used.

But back to Sophie and her Nine. Max pulled into the side of the road and stopped the engine. Taking from the glove compartment the book of numbers, he quickly found the section about the number "nine", and from it, read out loud some notes into his dictaphone. "Number Nine is a free spirit, believing in live and let live. Nine is charming and has a zest for life... a dramatic flair and love of art and music...a one-person show, capturing the social spotlight...generous to a fault...selfless sees the best in everyone...a broad-minded soul who loves everyone....the key word for number Nine is Humanitarian...Number Nine is all things to all people." Max wondered how all this squared with Nine also being the number of war and destruction. As he was about to speak some more, there was a sharp tap on the window. A traffic cop. "Sir, you can't stop here. Move along now." Max nodded his obeyance and continued on his way to work.

Mid-morning coffee at the Job Centre always has Claire sitting next to Max. Today, she was full of great excitement and admiration, as she watched him speaking on the phone.

"Detective Inspector Edmunds? Maxwell Abberline here. You know, the Sherlock Holmes in a wheelchair. I've got an idea for finding the murderer, I want to run by you. Can I pop in to the station later this afternoon? When I finish work? About half-five? Good. See you then."

Must be newly built, this police station, Max thought as he arrived at the fortress-looking steel and glass building. It's wheelchair friendly, if nothing else. They actually have a ramp to the front entrance. They must be anticipating an increase in disabled criminals...or disabled protesters, now that the Government plans to abolish all our benefits and allowances, and repeal the Disabled Discrimination Act, which they made preparations for by getting rid of the Disability Rights Commission.

The detective inspector was already waiting for Max in the reception. "Max, good of you to take the time," Edmunds greeted enthusiastically. "Come into my office."

Edmunds opened the door to his office, where a man and a woman were already seated

"Det. Sgt. Walters you know. And this is D.C. Eloise Warren", Edmunds introduced the woman, who sharply stood up, beaming and shook Max's hand.

"Call me Ellie," she said. Max stared at her, thinking he had seen her face before.

The three police detectives settled down, notebooks at the ready. Surveying the expectant eager faces looking at him, Max momentarily felt shy.

"So, what do you have for us, Max?" Edmunds asked business-like.

Max opened his briefcase and spread a chaos of documents, notes, newspaper clippings, charts on the table

"I found Goldie," he said triumphantly.

"Goldie?" Edmunds looked dumbfoundedly at his subordinates. They shrugged.

"She didn't die," Max explained. "You were wrong. Only one dog was put down. The golden retriever was retrieved or should I say repreived."

"What are you talking about?"

"Goldie. She is your key witness. She knows what the killer looks like. She saw it all. She saw her mistress getting knifed to death."

Edmunds turned to his sergeant. "Who is this Goldie? Jim, I thought we interviewed everyone. Did we miss someone out?"

"Goldie is the dog, Guv," exclaimed Walters, the penny dropping.

"I know she's the bloody dog," Edmunds snapped. "But why are we talking about a bloody dog?"

Max pointed to some of his material on the table. "Look, did you read about the Bizzy Lizzy experiments? If you can detect emotional responses in plants using a polygraph, you know, Lie detector, then surely you can do the same thing with dogs. What I propose is... we hypnotise the dog."

"Hypnotise the dog?" growled the inspector.

"Yes, Goldie, hypnotise her. I mean, I read somewhere that police often use a hypnotist when dealing with witnesses who are so traumatised that their consciousness blocks all information and the only way to unlock it, is to get them hypnotised. It's amazing what little details people remember when hypnotised. 'What colour was the car that knocked the kid over?' 'Can't remember.' Look into my eyes, follow the swinging watch - and *boof* - 'The colour of the car was RED, Master'. It's incredible. The police have solved thousands of cases using hypnotism."

"Not in this station, they haven't," Edmunds caustically retorted.

"What crank books have you been reading, sunshine?" Walters smirked.

The woman detective constable, Warren, tried to be less bellicose. "Max, even if hypnotism had some validity in police work, how do you know it could work with a dog? I mean, can a dog be hypnotised? And even if they could be, so what? How do we get the dog to tell us anything useful?" Max looked appreciatively at Warren. He sensed a possible ally in..... Ellie? Was that the name she told him to call her? Nah. He preferred her proper name, Eloise. Suited her looks more, he thought, as he continued to discuss his idea. "You wire up the dog to all sorts of physiological detection devices, measure galvanic skin response, heart rate, brain waves...basically a polygraph...then you show the dog specific stimuli relating to the event of the crime-"

"What kind of things?" Edmunds laughed bitterly. "We haven't got anything. We don't have the murder weapon. We don't have any clothing. We've got zilch."

"But have you photographs of possible suspects? Do you have a computer programme for building up an identifit picture. Show the dog various combinations, permutations of facial and head features. I'm convinced one of the permutations will trigger off some memory of that traumatic event and the lie detector will pick up the dog's physiological response."

The Ripper Code

The detective inspector stood up impatiently. "I think your idea is totally crackpot...and I think we've wasted enough valuable police time listening to your mad ideas."

Walters shook his head in disbelief. "John Jordan must have been winding us up when he said you could help us. You're a bloody nutcase."

They can call him what they liked. Max was used to it. But he was determined to make them hear each of his proposals for solving the murders.

"Look. Yes, of course, its possible it could never work... you know, perhaps dogs can't be hypnotised...or they can't detect images in two-dimensions, you know, like they can't see things in photographs...but...but-"

Edmunds and Walters grabbed the handle bars of Max's wheelchair and politely but firmly pushed him towards the door. Max wasn't having any of this. He slammed his wheelchair brakes on. The two cops couldn't budge him. Thinking he can't have much more to say, they sat back down to hear him out.

"But...the murderer doesn't necessarily have to know that," Max continued. "What if we say all this in a newspaper article...that the key witness to the murder, Goldie the Wonder Dog, who is going to be hypnotised, etc, etc, blah blah and that she is going to be kept one night at a certain kennel, awaiting tests and... of course, if I was the killer and thought a dog was going to give me away, well, I'd go to where it was and try to knock it off. That's what you do, tell this story, set a trap, using the dog as bait. It doesn't matter if my theory is a load of bollocks so long as the killer falls for it."

Edmunds leapt up and bellowed. "GET OUT! Get out before I nick you for taking the piss."

Five hours later, attempting to recover from the ignominious eviction from the police station and the unreasonable rejection of his ideas for ensnaring the Regents Park killer, Max was out cruising his favourite streets, where he knew the working girls hung out. Of course, he was hoping he might see Sophie again. She would surely know how to heal his wounded self-esteem. It was a busy night. the girls were out in full. But no sign of Sophie. There were also many other punters like him, slowly driving around, stopping every now and then, and a girl approaches. And just like him, the drivers open their side windows and deals are struck, and the cars seem to swallow up the girls, carrying them off, like beasts of prey, into the anonymous shadows of the dark city's concrete undergrowth.

As Max turned into Cedar Way, he sees little Rosie get in a car. She seemed to notice him but looked quickly away, laughing with the punter. Max was sure she was exaggerating her gaiety for his benefit as she climbed inside the car. He sighed sadly as he watched it speed off down the street. He wondered if his paternalistic feelings were not rather hypocritical. After all, if it were not for men like him who were willing to spend money to have sex, desperate people like Rosie wouldn't be tempted to go on the game. Even having arrived at this conclusion, Max decided to continue looking for a hooker. He moved on round the corner into Camley Street, and groaned. Martha. She turned on hearing the car and recognised him, and began to rush towards him.

"Oh-oh. No way," Max muttered, as he drove away quickly. But not quick enough. Coming towards him was a police patrol car. All the girls scattered in every direction.

"Oh shit," Max muttered as the patrol car pulled up alongside him. The police driver glared at Max and aggressively gestured at him to wind down his window, which Max reluctantly did.

The policeman leaned at of his side window. "You're getting to be quite a regular," he said menacingly. "We've spotted your car too many times. Curb crawling is illegal. Clear out. I don't want to see you around here again."

The second police officer who sat next to the driver, said something in his ear.

"Bollocks," the first cop replied. "I don't give a shit if he's a cripple. He's still breaking the law and being a fucking menace on the streets." He turned back to give Max another filthy look, viciously jabbed his finger at him and spat out, "Do as I say, Cripple. Piss off or I'll book you." Max drove away pretty sharpish, but not so fast that they would have had reason to do him for speeding.

KATE

Max, to get as far away from the patrolling police as possible, headed down Pancras Road, across the Euston Road and right into Cartwright Gardens where he knew there was the occasional hooker looking for business. He wasn't going to let that nasty cop deter him from getting laid. Nonetheless, he drove slowly down the road, keeping an eye out for those orange and white "wasps on wheels" that love to lurk behind corners, waiting to pounce. As he hurtled passed the British Museum he saw her, a girl in the shadows. He slowed down and flashed his headlamps. On seeing him, the girl in a red dress stepped into the light and gave him the nod. Max halted beside her and wound down his window. She smiled and leaned into his car window. Then, when she saw him properly, her face changed to a look of deep concern.

"Is it a blow job or a handjob you're wanting?" she hesitantly asked. "Handjob is £10 and Blowjob £15."

"How much do you charge for the full works?"

"You want normal sex? I mean, proper sex," she enquired taken aback.

"Of course," Max grinned.

"Oh. Um. I don't want to seem rude or offend you but...can you...I mean...do it?"

"Yes, of course I can. You think because I look like this, I can't fuck?"

"Oh! I'm sorry. Really, I didn't mean to offend you. Its just... I've never met anyone like you before. I mean, I've never done it with...you know..."

"Well, I can," Max gave her a gentle smile. "I can assure you. Ask some of the girls. I'm a regular punter."

"Aw, right, I see. I'm so sorry. Didn't want to upset you. I offered blowjob and handjob coz I was worried if I said the other, you'd feel hurt coz you couldn't.... yer know what I mean," she tried to explain.

"I take it, you're new round here."

"Yeah, my usual patch is Brixton and Streatham," she said, relieved he wasn't angry at her apparent ignorance.

"Right," said Max. "So how much is straight sex?"

"Normally I charge 30 quid in the car, but coz I'm sorry I was rude... Special price tonight...Twenny."

"No, I'll pay your usual, if you don't mind," Max insisted. "You want me to drive you where you normally do it?"

"Yeah, I'll get in the car. There's a place not far from here, called Weir's Passage. You know it?"

"Oh yes, that's a very popular bonking spot. What's your name, by the way?"

"Kate," she replied.

"Hmmm. Kate. 'K' 'A' 'T' 'E'. You're a Number One."

"That's nice of you to say but you haven't tried me yet." Kate said as she opened the car. At that moment Martha appeared around the corner, and saw Max.

"Fuck off, slag! He's mine!" she yelled, starting to run towards him.

"Oh, shit, it's Martha," Max pulled Kate in. "Quick, lets go."

As Max sped off, another car pulled up alongside Martha. It looked very posh. The electric tinted window whirred down. Martha peered into the darkened interior. Her face lit up with big triumphant smile.

"Are you looking for business, sir?" Martha politely enquired.

"Yes. Get in," commanded a suave voice.

Thirty-six minutes later, Martha was lying on the back seat of the posh car, with a man dressed in black, on top of her. She was up to her old tricks, faking an orgasm with lots of exaggerated and badly acted moans of ecstasy...while surreptitiously searching his pockets for loose cash.

"Oh sir, yes, yes, that's good, yummmm, ahhhhh, YES, ride me, fuck me, you feel so good, YES..."

Suddenly, a knife-like bayonet appeared above her...and slashed down. Briefly Martha saw the glinting blade plummet. she barely had time to scream as it struck her throat, slicing the windpipe. The scream became a gurgle as she drowned in her blood. The blade continued to jerk up and down, stabbing again and again in the throat, her neck....all over her body including her private parts. The killing of Martha was ferocious, relentless, with the assailant counting each plunge of his deadly bayonet –

"....30, 31, 32, 33, 34, 35 , 36, 37, 38." At "39" he stopped his stabbing and opened the car door. He grabbed her bleeding, mutilated body and threw it out into the darkened derelict yard. He slid into the driver's seat and drove the car away.

Later, the police and the fire brigade arrived down a side street, not far away. There had been a report of a car on fire.

Then, someone was heard shouting "MURDER!"

A policeman, holding a torch, came to investigate the shouts.
"Jesus Christ!" he cried out after nearly tripping over Martha's ripped body.

CHAPTER 9
Not Bad...for a Man.
8th August. Wednesday

Max was in too much of a daydream to notice, as he was driving to work the next morning. He was luxuriating in erotic memories of Kate. Even the Radio One DJ was talking about it, but Max wasn't listening. He was on auto-pilot. Which is not a good idea in London traffic. But his mind was still gripped between the heavenly thighs of Kate. So he didn't see the newspaper hoardings, with their screaming headlines - "WOMAN FOUND MURDERED" - "VICIOUS STABBING OF WOMAN" - "WHITECHAPEL MURDER". And he nearly didn't see the recklessly impatient Mercedes trying to overtake him as he was attempting to overtake an oil tanker. Max suddenly realised what was about to happen and swerved back behind the tanker lorry just in time. It was a close shave but it did remind him of a certain song of his childhood – "Keep your mind on your driving, keep your hands on the wheel and keep your filthy eyes on the road..." or some such lyrics.

Claire was beginning to really like her lunch-breaks. Now that Max was having them with her. In fact, she would often volunteer and get his sandwiches order from the deli round the corner. "I've got it right, haven't I?" Claire asked as she handed him his lunch. "Ham and egg mayonnaise?"

"Perfect, sweetheart. You're an angel. Thanks."

"Horrible, isn't it?" she commiserated, tucking into her tuna and sweetcorn pannini.

"What?" Max looked at his sandwiches with suspicion.

"You read the morning papers? Woman murdered. Found in Whitechapel. Prostitute, apparently. Stabbed many times."

"Prostitute?" Max looked up. Mention the word "prostitute" to him, and he has this Pavlovian guilt feeling.

"Yes. But the article says she isn't local to where her body was found. The police are still trying to identify her."

"Then how do they know she's a prostitute?" Max could feel his face reddening.

"I don't know. The papers don't say."

"Maybe they're deliberately keeping back information," Max said, tapping his nose significantly.

"Is this going to be another of your murder investigations, my Sherlock Holmes in a Wheelchair?" Her eyes shone excitedly.

"Uh-uh no way," Max said with his mouth stuffed full of sandwich. "Once bitten twice shy. I'm not going to be humiliated again by those bloody PC Clods. Why should I waste my brilliant brain power on them idiots? They couldn't investigate their way out of a paper bag."

"Oh dear, you are in a grouchy mood," Claire hastily ate her pannini. Lunch break was just about over.

"No, not really," Max gave her a cheerless smile. "But this murder has depressed me. Killing women. What a waste."

L ISA

Ten fifty-three. Max was at it again. A different girl. Hadn't ever seen her before. Hard, tough-looking. Surprisingly, it was her masculinity that attracted him....Such women don't normally...but there was something Amazon about her...in a Nordic kind of way...as if she has stepped out of a Conan the Barbarian movie. They were in his car down a darkened alley. He half expected at any moment, Arnold Schwartznegger to step out of the shadows and claim her for his own.

"Have you come yet?" She asked lying on her side, getting very bored with Max's physical exertions.

"No, not yet. Nearly," he gasped, frantically pounding her from behind, sweat pouring from his forehead..

"I'm sorry, love but you're taking ages," she complained, taking another surreptitious glance at her watch.

The Ripper Code

"I thought women didn't like men coming too quickly."

"When its business, darling, we do. You've been at it ten minutes."

"It's coming, coming, nearly there...nearly," Max panted.

The Blond Titan sighed, prepared to endure his exertions just a little longer.

"Come on. You must have come by now." She looked at her watch again, her irritation increasing. Max worked harder and faster, desperate to make the most out of his money. Suddenly the Blond Bombshell lost patience. "I've had enough," she shouted. "You're giving me a sore fanny." She disentangled herself, pulling herself free of Max's appendage and roughly groped the end of the condom and found that it was full of his spent semen. She gave him an accusing look.

"You little bugger, you have come. You were trying to keep it inside me as long as possible. You cheeky bugger. The rules are - when you come, you take it out."

"Yeah, but I paid for an hour," Max tried to argue.

She glared at him as she unceremoniously yanked the damp condom off his glistening slimey nob, and threw it out of the car window. "Listen, baby, if you think I'm going to let you go on working like a piston inside me for a whole bleeding hour, you got another think coming. You don't think I could put up with a man inside me for an hour. No way, darling. The very thought. I'm sore just after ten minutes of you."

"You don't like men?"

"They're all right in small doses. So long as you keep them in their place. On a leash. Preferably chained to a kennel in the back garden. Never let them control you." She handed him a tissue to clean his penis.

"God, you're harsh," he complained.

There was silence for a few minutes as he performed the personal hygiene with the flimsy tissue and she pulled her knickers and jeans back on.

"So you don't actually enjoy sex with us men?" he said as he offered to give her back the soiled tissue.

"Jesus fucking Christ, you must be joking", she cried, pushing his hand away. "Yuck, horrible smelly cocks."

"Thanks." Max muttered, struggling into his underpants. He still had an erection. Why, he couldn't understand- all this kind of talk should have been a real turn-off.

"Nothing personal but men just aren't my scene." She opened her bag and counted the night's takings. Satisfied she snapped the bag shut.

"But you're a prostitute and you make money from them", Max zipped up his flies.

"Exactly, that's all men are good for, to screw money out of them."

Max looked at her. Yes, her face was hard. Sharp featured and tense. Yet, her eyes told a different story.

"Do you like sex at all?"

"Oh, yes, I love it," she replied with a smile. "But with women."

"You're a lesbian."

"That's right darling," she said with an even bigger smile. "They don't call me 'Lezzie Lisa' for nothing. I love girls so much, I'll even pay for it. Would you believe it?"

"Why do you hate men so much?"

"I don't hate them, I just don't enjoy sex with them. I fucked you because you're stupid enough to part with loads of cash to stick your thing in my hole. Period."

"Well, don't worry. Next time I see you, I'll avoid you like the plague." Max slid back into the driving seat. "Do you talk like this with all your customers? Coz you're going to end up losing money. You'll alienate so many men, you'll lose business."

"No, I don't talk like this with every one." Lisa paused for a moment. Shook her head and glanced back at him, with suspicion. "I'm surprised at myself being so up front with you. It's you. You've got this knack of getting people to talk. You're not an undercover cop by any chance?"

"No," laughed Max and pointed to his body, as if to say, *do I look like a bloody cop?* "I'm just nosey," he continued. "I like people. I'm dead curious about all aspects of life. I want to experience everything."

"Everything?" Lisa asked slyly. "Ever tried S+M? Fancy a couple of lezzies torturing the bollocks off you, fisting you in the arse. We would tie you up and turn your pleasure into a hell on earth."

"Um...maybe not everything." Max backed further into his seat.

"I'm joking, kid. Anyway, gotta go. And please don't avoid me like the plague. For a man, you're quite sweet, really. Bye." Lisa kissed him on the forehead and was gone.

By midnight, Max was back in his flat, his face illuminated by the glare of the computer monitor. He typed on the keyboard "LISA". The screen displayed the result. "Lisa, your number is 5." Should it be Lisa? Max wondered. Or should I type 'Lezzie Lisa'? After all, that is the name she uses. He typed "Lezzie Lisa" into the computer, which instantly returned with the text message, "LEZZIE LISA, your number is 7".

"Hmmm. Another seven." Max thought. "I think that's three in eight days" He opened the "PROSTITUTES" file and double-clicked on the list of names. The computer screen flashed with a drum roll and crash of cymbals and the record of the last eight days' whoring was revealed;

        Martha = 7
        Polly = 8
        Annie = 7
        Sophie = 9
        Kate = 1

Max typed "Lezzie Lisa = 7", adding it to the list.

CHAPTER 10
A Nasty Kettle
13th August. Monday

The Dead of Night. The poor hapless Polly. The girl who had been so insulted by Max. A decent working girl like her. She didn't deserve it. The fucking little creep. Wanting to fuck her in the arse for a fiver. A miserly bloody fiver! The fucking nerve of the nerd. And now she felt jinxed. Nothing had gone right for her ever since. Not a single punter in eight days.

It was a dark street. Unusually dark. None of the street lamps seemed to be working. Really she shouldn't be walking down there. But Polly was a tough old girl. She knew how to fend for herself. Even though the sudden squalling of a cat frightened the life out of her. But still, she kept walking down that empty eerie street.

Then it happened. An arm from the shadows grabbed her from behind. Hand clamped across her face. Another hand holding a long knife, which slashed twice across her throat, from ear to ear. A deep long sigh escaped from her severed windpipe. Yes, she really was jinxed. Were these her last dying thoughts?

* * * * *

Lying on the autopsy table in the morgue at the London Hospital in Whitechapel, poor Polly certainly had no more thoughts. Whatever consciousness that belonged to the personality formerly known as "Polly" was now far far away, possibly, traversing the stars to a better place. Meanwhile, her physical body, now a lifeless corpse, was fated to continue to suffer indignities, at the hands of the police doctor, Llewellyn

Hawkey, dissecting her for forensic investigation. Also in attendance were Inspector Edmunds and Sergeant Walters.

"The subject has been dead for at least an hour," announced the doctor as he read the thermometer he had taken from Polly's rectum. "Her neck has been slashed twice, cutting through the windpipe and the oesophagus. Was she killed where she was found?"

"No," replied Walters, still staring at the corpse in shocked disbelief. "She was found lying in Buck's Row, on a plastic bag, which was obviously used to carry her body to the location. I would say she had already been killed somewhere else and transported, probably by car to Whitechapel."

His boss, Edmunds, looked at him. "Jim, I don't know how you manage to assume so much from so little....Where the bloody hell is she?" He exclaimed, looking at his watch.

At that moment, WDC Warren entered, all in a fluster, still in her "street-walking Emma" disguise of purple fishnet stockings, pink leather ultra mini-skirt and scarlet red low cut blouse.

"Sorry, I'm late, Gov," she panted.

Edmunds raised his eyebrows. "Llewellyn, this is Detective Constable Warren. The most punctual woman on the force."

The coroner took a rubber glove off and stepped forward to shake her hand.

"Hello. Dr. Llewellyn Hawkey, police surgeon," he said enthusiastically, eyeing her up and down in her prostitute outfit.

"Yes, I think she got that," Edmunds tutted. He turned to Warren. "Well?"

The policewoman stepped nervously up to the barely human remains on the dissection table. "Oh Jesus!" she cried out in anguished recognition, her face drained of colour.

"You know her?" Edmunds asked. Warren wanted to break down but managed, with extreme difficulty, to control herself.

"It's Polly," she said, choking back the tears. "That's two from King's Cross. Martha and now Polly."

"Murdered and then dumped here in Whitechapel," Walters shook his head.

"Or were they murdered here?" countered Edmunds.

"I don't see it," Warren shook her head. "Why would two working girls from King's Cross suddenly start operating out of their patch?"

"Well, maybe that's why they were killed," posed Walters. "Didn't you say King's Cross was getting over-grazed? So Martha and Polly went poaching on rival territory and paid the price."

Edmunds walked over to Dr. Hawkey who was slicing a section from the victim's liver. "What else do you have for us?" he asked, wrinkling his nose at the smell. The doctor put the piece of liver into a sample dish and pointed at Polly's chin. "There's a bruise on the lower left jaw, which suggests a hand had grabbed her from behind from the right. Since the knife wound across the throat starts from right to left, this would all indicate the killer is left handed." Dr. Hawkey moved round the table and pushed his hand into an opening in the victim's stomach. "As you can see, her abdomen has a long deep jagged wound, done with the same instrument that cut her throat. There are several other mutilating cuts to the abdomen running downward, again with the same long-bladed knife. Her uterus has been removed. And her left kidney. The blood from the abdominal wounds have largely collected in the loose tissues. Such a pattern proves that the subject's injuries were inflicted when she was lying on her back. This suggests to me that she was already dead."

"This long-bladed knife? A bayonet?" surmised the detective inspector.

"Possibly," nodded Dr. Hawkey.

"Her womb was taken out? With a bayonet?" Warren asked aghast.

"Yes," Dr. Hawkey said. "And her left kidney. Looks like it was done by someone who knows their anatomy. And highly skilled. To do it with a bayonet and not a surgical knife."

Edmunds looked at Hawkey in surprise. "An army doctor? Military surgeon? Someone with experience of performing emergency surgery in the field?"

"That's what it suggests to me," concluded Dr. Hawkey.

"What about a medical student?" Warren asked.

"Um, possibly," admitted Dr. Hawkey. "But he'd have to be top of the class."

"Could the murder instrument have been the same as that which killed Martha?" inquired Edmunds.

"In Martha's case, I think the killer used two weapons. Martha's multiple stab wounds indicate both the bayonet and a pen-knife."

"Thirty-nine stabs wounds I think we counted," said Edmunds

"Why thirty-nine?" Walters wondered.

"Why not," Edmunds shrugged. "He just happened to stop at 39. He has to stop somewhere. I can't imagine the killer counting the stabs so as to arrive at a certain special number."

The woman detective constable Warren put her hand up excitedly. "Excuse me, sir it could be a coincidence but...well, I think Martha was, in fact, 39 years old."

CHAPTER 11
Snookered
13th August. Monday

Like most things in his life, Max took his job seriously. He didn't find working in the job centre either boring or a waste of time. This was probably because he genuinely liked people. He finds everyone he meets interesting. He's fascinated by the myriad of life stories that lay hidden in all those he met. He was not a particularly political animal. By no stretch of the imagination could he be considered a rabid left wing radical...but he did believe his job of helping people to find work, of vital importance. As a disabled person, he knew the hardships and desperation that poverty brings, and all because society, which thrives on inequality, refuses or is ill-equipped, to give you gainful employment. Eighty-seven percent of all disabled adults are unemployed and its not through want of trying. Max knew he was lucky and was grateful that not only had he a job that enhanced his self-esteem...he was a civil servant, after all...he was performing a civic duty...but he was also helping those less fortunate than himself. He enjoyed the irony of being a "poor unfortunate", a disabled person being a beacon of hope to those non-disabled who before entering his office, considered themselves superior to people like him. But Max was a nice guy. It wouldn't cross his mind to rub their noses in the unpalatable truth of tables being reversed. He wasn't one of those civil servants who took sadistic pleasure in making claimants grovel.

The man in front of him, for example, was nervous as hell, unable to look Max in the eye. His jeans were ripped, revealing underneath a Death's Head tattoo on his right inner thigh. His puke yellow T-shirt was stained and grubby and his chin unshaven. The bags under his eyes and the enlarged red nose spoke volumes of a man with a drink problem. Max felt genuine pity and was determined to be a friend in the short time he had this man trapped within his orbit.

"So, lets see what you've written in your diary, eh," Max said as he examined the claimant's documents.

"Good. On the 2nd you searched the job sections of the Camden Herald. Didn't find anything for car mechanics. On the 7th had an interview for warehouse supervisor...how did that go?" Max asked the unlikely looking would-be supervisor.

"Promising," replied the claimant, shifting his position in the uncomfortable bucket of a plastic chair. "It's a warehouse for body parts, so they thought I had the right background and that."

"Body parts?"

"Cars...trucks...you know, vehicles...body parts."

"Ah...of course. You had me worried for a moment," grinned Max. All of a sudden, Max noticed some of his colleagues were gesticulating at him, trying to get his attention. Now what? Out of the corner of his eye, Max saw Claire hurriedly approaching his desk. She looked anxious and was frantically beckoning him over.

"Excuse me for a second," Max apologised to the job seeker, who was desperate to go outside for a cigarette.

"Max, there's a traffic warden," whispered Claire in an urgent tone.

"Oh, no. Why won't they leave me alone?" moaned Max. He hurriedly returned to the waiting claimant, took his "job search diary" and signing it, said "Very good, Mr. Reid. Just sign here. See you in two weeks." With that, Max spun round and rushed out of the building, onto the street, in time to catch the Traffic Warden placing a penalty ticket on Max's car windscreen.

"What is the matter with you people?" Max yelled furiously. "There's a disabled badge, I use a wheelchair, I work here. How many times..."

"No there isn't," replied the Traffic Warden emphatically.

"'No there isn't' what?"

"There isn't a disabled badge," the Traffic Warden retorted with a smug grin. "You don't have a blue badge."

"Yes, there is," Max bellowed.

"Not on display, there isn't," came back the contrasting quietly confident tone of a self-satisfied Traffic Warden, knowing that a longed-for victory was at hand.

"Yes, there is," screamed Max, astounded that the Traffic Warden could be so stubbornly cretinous.

"Where?" mischievously asked his old adversary. "I can't see it."

Max leaned forward to point it out, and to his dismay, saw the Blue Badge was missing. For a moment he thought he was going mad, then slapped his forehead.

"Oh shit, I forgot. It was stolen," he said, beseechingly.

"Oh shit, you forgot. It was stolen," parroted the Traffic Warden sarcastically.

"It's true. Anyway, you know I normally have the blue badge. And dammit, you can see my bloody wheelchair."

"That's irrelevant. Without the blue badge, your wheelchair is invisible. So the ticket stays. Gotcha this time," said the Traffic Warden, triumphantly swaggering away

"BASTARD!" Max yelled at his victorious enemy's retreating back

Back inside the job centre, Max sat despondently, his face in his hands resting on the desk, surrounded by his colleagues, all shaking their heads sympathetically.

"What are you going to do?" asked Claire, her arm around his shoulders.

Max sighed and then sat up straight, and putting on a resolute mien, said, "I'm going to have to report it missing, get a Crime Number and then apply to the Council for a new one. Damn, I should have done this immediately."

Max did not want to be at the police station, giving details to the desk sergeant, but he had no choice. The Blue Badge was an essential and valuable item in the disabled driver's life.

"And you say it was stolen, Mr. Abberline?" the Desk Sergeant looked with scepticism at Max.

"Yes. Yes. It was snatched from the car," Max reiterated.

"When was this?"

"Eh..yesterday.. yesterday evening."

"You don't seem very sure, Mr. Abberline." the Desk Sergeant who was standing, had to lean forward to see Max, half concealed by the tall reception desk.

"No, no, I am sure. It happened last night."

"Did the thief break into the car? Or did you leave the car unlocked?"

"Eh, well, I was in the car, actually..."

"When the blue badge was stolen?"

"Yes," Max replied for the thousandth time. Jesus, this Desk Sergeant is so infuriating, Max thought. Why must I say everything three times?

"You were in the car when your disabled badge was stolen?" asked the Desk Sergeant with disbelief.

"Yes."

"I see. So, I take it, you saw the thief?"

"I did. Yes."

"Was the thief acquainted to you?" asked the Desk Sergeant hopefully.

"Eh. Sort of."

"Sort of. I see."

At that moment, the policeman, Max called the "nasty cop" entered, and on seeing Max, gave an unkind smile.

"Well, well, well, if it isn't the Dirty Pervy Cripple," jeered the Nasty Cop. "No more curb-crawling, I hope. Keep away from the slags. They're bad for your health. Old bags full of nasty diseases." The Desk Sergeant whispered to the Nasty Cop.

"Indeed," exclaimed the Nasty Cop, turning on Max with mock sympathy. "Lost your cripple badge, have you?"

"Stolen," Max grumpily replied.

"Ah yes, stolen. Sarge here says you 'sort of' know the thief." The Nasty Cop placed a heavy sarcastic emphasis on "sort of".

"Yes. I know her," Max did not want to be dealing with this jerk.

"Her? Was it one of the whores?"

"Yes," mumbled Max.

The Ripper Code

"Sorry," shouted the Nasty Cop. "Speak up a bit. I didn't quite hear you."

"Look, can I have the crime number?" Max said, losing his patience.

The Nasty Cop snapped the report book shut with a loud thud. "Would you mind coming into the interview room?" Max acquiesced. He knew this was not a gentle invitation.

Max was shoved into the Interview Room. The door behind him was slammed shut and he was left alone to stew. Max didn't like any of this. This Nasty Cop was bad news. He looked at his watch. Ten minutes must have gone by. What game was this bastard playing? Maybe he shouldn't have come in person to the police station. Perhaps he could have phoned for a crime number. Damn, he should have thought of that.

The Nasty Cop re-entered and puts a blank audio cassette into the **interviews** recording machine. Max looked round and saw behind him, standing in the doorway the silhouettes of Edmunds and Walters. The Nasty Cop pressed the record button.

"Which Crime Number would you like? The one for a stolen cripple badge..." asked Nasty throwing Max's Blue Badge onto the table, "...or the one for *murder*?"

"Murder?" Max asked bewildered. Edmunds stepped forward and sat on a chair in front of Max at the table. "Thanks, Reece, we'll take over from here," he ordered. Peeved, Reece left the room but very reluctantly. He was enjoying seeing Max squirm.

Walters came into the room and stood behind Max. "Hello Max," he said. "You just saved us a journey to your place of work. Bet you're relieved you came to us first."

"Well, Mr. Maxwell Abberline," said the detective inspector. "I hope you don't mind helping us with our enquiries?"

"What's this about murder?" inquired Max. "And what's it got to do with me."

"Good question, Max. Very good question." said Walters, giving Max's shoulders a gentle massage.

"Do you have a name for the person who nicked your badge?" questioned Edmunds.

"I knew her as Polly."

"And when do you say she committed this heinous crime?"

"She snatched the badge.. um.. yesterday," lied Max.

"Any idea what time?"

"I don't know. Eleven. Twelve."

"That the usual time you go sniffing fanny for hire?" Walter sneeringly asked.

Max tried to turn round and look at Walter. "I thought you were supposed to be Good Cop and he the Bad Cop."

"We like to take it in turns," Walters replied impassively. "Keeps us from getting bored."

Edmunds stood up and leaned over Max, "So, you was with Polly some time between eleven and midnight. Which means you were one of the last people to see her alive."

"So that's the murder," said Max. "Polly? Polly's been murdered?"

"Oh very much so," Walters moved around to the right of Max. "You can't get more murdered than poor Polly. Very nasty. Not so Pretty Polly. A very sick sadistic bastard did her in."

"Know anything about it, Max?" demanded Edmunds, moving in close to the left of Max, who sat frozen, feeling caught between a rock and a hard place. He looked first at Walters, then at Edmunds. He decided it wasn't particularly nice being interrogated by coppers who are looking for a murderer. And he's crap at telling lies.

"Okay, I'll come clean," Max confessed. "It wasn't last night she stole my badge. It was nearly two weeks ago."

"Really?" Edmunds exclaimed in mock surprise, looking quickly at Walters.

"Why did you say it was yesterday?" the junior partner asked grimly.

Max tried to explain. "Well, I had to get a crime number today and I thought it would get too complicated asking for one for something that happened two weeks ago. And I dreaded trying to explain that it was a prostitute who nicked it."

"Oh dear but it has got very complicated for you, hasn't it Max?" Walters commiserated.

"Well, Max, don't worry, you were never a serious suspect," said Edmunds, walking to the door and opening it. "For now. But be a good boy, don't go leaving town without telling us first."

"Can I have my Blue Badge back?"

"Fraid not," Edmunds shook his head. "It was found on her. Vital piece of evidence."

Max sighed and wheeled towards the door.

"But don't worry, little laddie. I'll tell the Sarge to give you your crime number," reassured Walters, picking up the disabled badge and placing it in a thick folder.

CHAPTER 12
In the Eye of Gemini
14th August. Tuesday

There's always a first time for everything. Max was in Claire's flat. Ground floor, of course. Wheelchair accessible. And, glory be, he was actually spending the evening with her. The two of them were sitting together on the sofa, watching the television, with about twelve inches distance between them. Out of the corner of her eye, Claire, every now and then, looked at the gap between them and sighed wistfully. Max tried to focus intently on the movie they are watching, but could feel her restlessness beside him. However, he was determined to keep his body rigid and unyielding. So, he continued to resolutely lean away from her demure vulnerable body. You'd think he was a priest, he was so fanatically avoiding any possibility of the slightest physical contact. It wasn't that Max didn't like Claire. He probably liked her more than he was prepared to admit, but it was just that he was unable to relax in any relationship with a woman... unless he was paying for it. Or so he endlessly tried to tell himself. He looked at Claire. Her eyes met his. They nervously smiled at each other and still... their tongues were tied. How to break the ice? Pretend you are someone else? That usually works.

"Yeah, it's funny, the detectives are coming to me more or more often nowadays, you know, to help them solve various murders," said Max grandly.

"But I thought they rejected your last brainwave for solving the case," said Claire, "Didn't you say they thought your idea was completely mad and you were off your trolley?"

"Did I say that?" laughed Max. "Well, no, it wasn't quite as bad as that. No, Detective Inspector Edmunds thought it was an interesting idea but he didn't think he could get my proposal past the Chief Constable. He reckoned the experiment would be too expensive and the 'money boys' higher up would have his guts for garters if the dog didn't deliver."

"So, the police want you help them solve the two prostitute murders?" Claire inched a bit closer. Max pretended not to notice.

"Yeah. Amazing, I went into the station to report my missing crip badge and Edmunds asked me into his office and said they were desperate for my Sherlockian sleuthing mind," boasted Max.

"Gosh, how exciting!", her eyes shining. "I'm so proud of you, Max. Were you able to give them any ideas?"

"Oh no, its too early. I have to do some private investigation, go to places the police can't get to before I can begin making deductions. I need to get some background info on the two girls killed. The murderer could well have been someone they both knew, not necessarily a homicidal customer. So, I better be off. Thanks for the movie."

"Oh!" a look of panic on Claire's face. "Do you have to go right now? Wouldn't you like to stay for a coffee?"

"Nah, thanks anyway, but I've got to go," Max slid off of the sofa into his wheelchair. "Now's the time they start to come out...the creatures of the night...I got to catch up on some street research." He grabbed his car keys and wheeled towards the hall.

"Oh, okay," Claire said, disappointed and quickly got into her wheelchair and followed after him." Well, be careful. The maniac might not just be killing prostitutes."

"I'll be careful, don't worry," Max smiled and blew her a kiss. "See you tomorrow morning. I'll give you an update at lunch break." Claire closed the door behind him, feeling, once again, the unbearable weight of loneliness descend upon her.

CHAPTER 13
The Run Around
14th August. Tuesday

Unsurprisingly, given the nocturnal horror now stalking the streets, the night hung like a heavy oppressive curtain, panic-stricken fear woven into every fibre. Max drove down Wharfdale Road which, at that hour, would normally be full of working girls, chatting, laughing, smoking, showing off their wares, salaciously distilling a balmy atmosphere of delicious heady hedonism. And yet, despite an unusually warm night, there seemed to be fewer women patrolling the pavements. Several cars slowly crawled furtively past, inviting but the girls didn't seem too eager to jump in. The uneasiness was palpable.

As Max was wondering if he should give up and go home, he swung the car round into Killick Street and saw Jail-Bait Rosie, touting for business. Max sighed. How depressing. This is no good. He thought perhaps he should give up this sordid life. On seeing him, Rosie gave a friendly little wave. He waved back and was about to do a U-turn and head for home, when emerging out of the shadows, from All Saints Close, a car appeared and stopped beside the little girl. Initially, Rosie enthusiastically leaned forward into the driver's window. Max tried to see the man at the wheel. He got a shock. It was the Nasty Cop, clearly driving an unmarked car. Reece waved money at Rosie, who, all of a sudden, seemed reluctant to get in the car and began to walk away. Reece clearly was not a man to take no for an answer, spun his car round and drove it on to the pavement and blocking her with the opened passenger door. Rosie shrugged resignedly and got in. The door slammed shut, swallowing up the helpless child. As the Nasty Cop's car sped past Max in his parked vehicle, he quickly ducked down and crouched low in his seat, keeping out of view, hoping to avoid the car head-lamp's sweeping beam.

FRAN

Suddenly there's a rat-a-tat on his window which made Max jump. He turned and saw the smiling face of a skinny weasel looking woman peering at him. He opened the window. "Looking for business?" she asked, her face withdrawn and pinched, eyes hungry for custom.

Max looked her up and down. She's a new one in this area. There was something dodgy about her. She looked like a crack addict. Max had doubts but after an evening with Claire, in such close proximity, and his groin aching for her, yet too nervous and shy to try to seduce her, he was still feeling steamed up, wanting relief. But with a "crack slut"? Could end up another bad experience.

"I would do but I don't have much cash on me," Max lied.

"How much you got?" she asked.

"Only a tenner, I'm afraid."

"That'll do." She smiled desperately.

"You what? Really?" Max was unsure. "What's your name?"

"Fran," she said hurriedly, looking over her shoulder. "Serious like, I'll do you for ten quid!"

"But I'm not interested in just a handjob," insisted Max.

"Yeah, of course. I'll give you a good fuck for ten."

"Honest?"

"It's a favour," Fran said conspiratorially. "I'm feeling really flush. There's hardly any competition tonight and I've made loads. I mean, I'd offer you a freebie, especially with you being...you know.. but a working girl's got to keep some dignity... and I know people like you are proud and don't like charity...so, coz I'm feeling good, the night is balmy, I'll give you a damn good screw for a token price of ten pounds. How's that sound?"

"Sounds great," Max couldn't believe his luck. "Where shall we go?"

"There's a flat on the ground floor," Fran pointed behind her. "I got to get a key for it first, from some bloke. He's a friend of a friend, you know what I mean. You stay here. I'll be back with the key. And then I'll take you to the place and we'll have a fucking good fuck. You stay there. I won't be long. It's just round the corner."

"Okay."

"You got the tenner?" asked Fran quickly. She turned and looked at him directly for the first time.

"Yeah."

"Give us it, then." She held out her hand.

"Oh, well, I'd prefer to give it you when we get to the place."

"Oh come on, don't you trust me?" Fran said, squinting her eyes at him. "Oh that really hurts. I'm offering you a lovely juicy fuck for ten quid and you're casting asparagus on my intentions!"

"Aspersions," Max said helpfully.

"Exactly," she grinned. "Look, I just need the ten quid to give the guy for the key. See. In reality, I'm actually giving you the fuck for free...coz I'm not going to really see the tenner...and I don't need to...I'm happy. Tonight was rich pickings. Whoopee. Listen. If you don't trust me, doesn't matter coz I still like you and I think I want to fuck you anyway coz I've never fucked a cripple before and I think it would be very interesting. In fact, maybe I should be paying you...ha ha ha...so forget the tenner...I'll go and see if I can find the man with the key and I'll be back."

"But don't you need the tenner to hire the key?"

"Probably," she said, knitting her eyebrows. "Probably. That usually is the case but...you know, maybe tonight he won't be such a stickler for the rules."

"Okay," shrugged Max.

"On the other hand, he is a total bastard and without the money up front, he'll probably shove my face in dog shit..."

"Why don't you get in the car, we go somewhere quiet, I give you the ten and we just do it in the car?"

"I've been doing it in cars all night," Fran shook her head. "My back's giving me jip. I need a bit of comfort. There's a nice soft bed back in the flat. Give me the ten quid and I'll be straight back." She put her hand out again. Max was still unsure but he felt guilty about not trusting her, so he handed her a ten pound note.

"Just wait there, I'll be back in no time," she smiled. Max watched her as she ran down the street. He shook his head and started the car to follow her. She swivelled round and ran back towards him.

"No no. It's all right," she panted. "Don't move. Be patient. I'll return. Don't worry."

"Why can't I follow you to the flat? It'll save you having to come all the way back."

"No. You don't understand," Fran said, standing in front of the car. "Doesn't work like that. He doesn't like to be seen by the punters. You have to keep back. Otherwise he won't give me the key." Fran quickly turned and saw a thick set man, crossing the road, coming towards her. She walked up to him, and pointed at Max. "Excuse me, mister, can you do me a favour," she whispered. "That car keeps following me. I'm really scared."

"Shall I sort him out?" the man asked, glaring menacingly in Max's direction

"Oh no," she said placatingly touching his muscular shoulder. "No need for that but if you could just walk with me part of the way, he'll give up."

"Yeah, alright," he growled, giving Max another filthy look. "You sure you don't want me to smack him one?" Fran slipped her arm through his and pulled him towards her.

"Nah, just act like you're my boyfriend, just til we get to that building," she cooed.

Max, undaunted, continued to follow the couple but keeping his distance. Fran looked back at him tauntingly and laughed out loud, as they passed under an arch, which led into a pedestrianised street where Max couldn't take his car.

"Bollocks," Max thumped the steering wheel angrily. "Oh well, its my own bloody fault. Can't blame her. She took advantage of my fucking greed. Jesus, I'm such a wanker at times."

"First sign of madness, talking to yourself, you know that?" came a woman's voice.

Max turned and saw a cigarette-smoking Sophie, grinning at his side window.

"Jesus, Sophie, you made me jump."

"Been having trouble with Fran?"

"Nah, not really. I could see she was as high as a kite."

"Keep away from the Crack Girls. They'll razor you for a few quid," Sophie warned, taking a long drag on her cigarette.

"Yeah, yeah, I know. I told her I wasn't looking for business tonight," lied Max, blushing pink.

"Well, you don't have much choice. It's like a ghost town tonight. Mind if I hop in for a minute?" Sophie turned her face from him and blew out a series of dancing, twirling smoke rings.

"Of course not," said Max, suddenly feeling very happy. Sophie got in the passenger side.

"Fancy a mad drive around the city, listening to Techno music?" Max asked, feeling wild and impetuous.

"Yeah, let's go bonkers," laughed Sophie, sweeping Max's face with her burning red hair. With a maestro's flourish, he started the ignition and revved the engine. Sophie let out a whoop of joy.

"Lets give it some Welly, it's too damn quiet", he shouted, pumping up the volume of a techno CD. "I've only seen a couple girls. Fran and the kid, Rosie. Actually, I'm sure I recognised a cop picking her up. I think his name is Reece." Sophie face went ashen.

"Oh yes. That'll be Greasy Reecy. He's in the Vice Squad and he's pure vice. Dirty bastard. On the make. Takes bribes from the Bosses and demands 'freebies' from us girls. When the 'Crims' call the police 'Filth', with Reecy, you can understand why."

"He warned me to stop curb-crawling. Said he'd do me, next time he catches me."

"Did he indeed! Such a hypocrite. I mean, I don't have problems with coppers being bent. We wouldn't be able to ply our trade if all cops were straight. But it's when the bent cops try 'the holier than thou' routine and give paying customers like you a hard time when they have us for nothing. Cops like Greasy Reecy are the lowest of the low because they have a taste for child prostitutes. And poor Rosie has got caught in his headlights. He's constantly abusing her."

"How old is Rosie?" Max asked.

"Twelve."

"Twelve?" Max was horrified. "You're joking. I thought she was perhaps fourteen."

Sophie swung round and glared accusingly at him. "You didn't have her, did you?" She clenched her fist like she was about to punch his lights out.

"No I didn't," he stammered. "I told her to go away, gave her a hundred quid and made her promise me she'd go to a women's refuge."

"Oh you mug. You're such an innocent fool."

"Yeah, I know." For a moment an awkward silence descended upon them both. Then, Sophie gave Max's hand a little squeeze. Max turned and looked at her, and saw tiny tears in her eyes.

CHAPTER 14
Rose Tinted Bi-focals
14th August. Tuesday

The night hides many things. No one saw the Watcher as he inched towards the car parked in the murky shadows of a back alley. No one, except the Watcher, witnessed Sergeant Reece of the Vice Squad, also known as "the Nasty Cop", having illegal sexual intercourse with a minor, a twelve year old girl...the child prostitute called Rosie. The Watcher felt a burning fury brewing within. Yet, to act as he must, he knew he had to remain calm, dispassionate. Slowly he moved forward with the deadly stealth and silence of the professional assassin that he undoubtedly was. Creeping towards them, keeping in view their bobbing heads and shoulders, the Watcher noted the depraved policeman's thrusting, violent inhuman movements. To stop Rosie from crying out in pain, Reece had a hand clamped tight around her mouth. His other hand around her throat seemed to be throttling her. Deciding enough was enough, the Watcher deliberately scraped his shoe along the ground as he dodged behind another parked vehicle. Reece startled by the sudden noise, stopped, and looked in the direction of the sound. Spooked, the crooked copper shoved the wretched Rosie to the ground and threw a hundred pounds in notes at her.

"Keep your trap shut, and there's more where that came from," Reece snarled, as he got into his car and drove away. Still crying from the pain and humiliation, Rosie bent over to pick up the notes, and from behind her back, the Watcher...the hired killer...CK... rushed towards her. He grabbed her and before she had time to cry out, placed a cloth on her mouth and nose. The chloroform worked instantly and she passed out. CK lifted her into his arms and carried her to his waiting vehicle. The night hides many things.

***

Careering down the Marlebone Road, dodging in and out of the traffic, dangerously overtaking on the inside, the loud Techno music providing the adrenalin booster, Max joyously showed off his driving skills to Sophie.

"Jesus, Max, you drive this car like you've stolen it," shrieked Sophie as if she was riding a roller-coaster. Max laughed. He liked that and to show his appreciation, executed a crazy double swerve around and between a minicab and a bus.

"We should do something about Reece," Max said in a more sombre tone.

"We?" asked Sophie, raising an eyebrow.

"He shouldn't be allowed to go around fucking kids. If cops behave like monsters then there's no protection for anyone."

"Max, there have always been corrupt cops. And some of the biggest child porn, and child prostitution rackets, and drug rings have been aided, abetted and even run by bent cops."

"Well, for Rosie's sake, shouldn't we do something about Reece?"

"Be honest, Max, it isn't just for Rosie, is it? Wouldn't you like to get him off your back?"

"Maybe," conceded Max. "I'm still going to get hassled for curb-crawling but I would rather it was an honest cop giving me a hard time than some pervy hypocritical creep like Reece."

"What do you suggest?" asked Sophie

"I don't know. Get an incriminating photo of him with one of you girls."

"Not me. And don't even think about a pik of him with Rosie."

"What you take me for? Max sharply retorted. "I'm not into child porn."

Sophie touched his hand in an apologetic gesture. "Anne will do it," she said after some thought. "She'll set him up. He quite fancies her, so it should be easy."

Max smiled grimly and took the car left into Baker Street.

"How do we get the pictures?" Max asked.

"Have you a camera?"

Max nodded, "Several. Stills. Camcorder. Night vision."

"Okay", replied Sophie. "You get the gear together. And I'll put you in position so you can take great pictures."

* * *

It could have seemed like an empty warehouse but for the eerie echoes. And at the far end of the cavernous building, crouched the darkened office, like a forgotten giant she-spider. And inside this womb-like structure, the solitary naked light bulb swept its gloomy pool of timid light around the piteous, though mercifully, still clothed Rosie, tied to a wooden chair in the dead centre of the bleak Spartan room. As the child emerged from unconsciousness, she saw something that made her wish she could slip back into oblivion. Standing in front of her was the tall imposing figure of a man, cloaked in a red cape and on his head, he wore a wolf mask. She screamed in unqualified terror. This was worse than any nightmare and when he spoke to her, she screamed even louder.

"Maybe I should let you wear the red cape," offered Wolf Man. "See, it has a riding hood." He laughed softly, which made the prisoner scream some more. The Wolf Man got down on his knees and stared into Rosie's petrified eyes.

"Don't worry, Rosie," he soothed. "I'm not going to eat you. For you...and you alone, I'm not the Big Bad Wolf. You are lucky. Tonight is not a full moon."

Rosie stopped screaming. "You're not a real werewolf," she said defiantly between the gasps for breath and tears. "That's a stupid Halloween mask."

"Yes, of course, you're right," he smiled. "It is a stupid mask...but it's a mask that keeps me from killing you. So long as you don't see my face, you can continue to live."

"Why have you taken me?" she answered back, still snivelling. "Why have you tied me up here? Where am I? I don't want to see your stupid face, anyway."

"Rosie, do you know someone has paid me a lot of money to kill you. But I don't want to kill you. Personally, I don't like the idea of trying to save a bent policeman's bacon."

"Greasy Reecy? He's paying you to kill me?" Rosie gulped.

"No," he stood up and began to circle her. "He would never be able to afford my services. Even with all the kickbacks he's making."

"So who?" she asked as her eyes followed the Wolf Man pacing up and down.

"If I told you, I would have to kill you. But I don't want to kill you. So, forgive me if I don't tell you."

"Why don't you want to kill me? Is it because I'm a kid? Because I'm only twelve?"

"I've killed younger children than you," he coldly replied. "No more questions please. Just listen. And then, I will free you, unharmed." The Wolf Man pulled up a chair and sat opposite the scared little girl.

"The man who wants me to kill you, is paying me for a much bigger job. You are just an extra he wanted me to throw in. But, your death upsets the grand scheme of things, disrupts the symmetry. There is a pattern that cannot be interfered with, what is Above, so it is Below. Laws of a Cosmic Numerical Significance must be obeyed. The Apocalyptic Precipitation requires...."

"I don't know what you are talking about," interrupted Rosie.

"Of course, you don't," said the man smiling behind the wolf mask. "I wouldn't expect you to...and I shall not bore you any more. Suffice it to say, I cannot spill your blood. It has no value and will put things out of sync."

"So you are going to put me back on the streets and let someone else murder me," she yelled at him accusingly. "That psycho who killed Martha and Polly? Or Reece? He'll kill me one day. One way or another. I can't take him any more. What he does to me. Why do people do things like that to me? I'm only a little girl. Really. He's killing me inside. Maybe you should kill me. I don't really want to live anymore anyway." Rosie started to cry, which infuriated the Wolf Man who immediately sprang up and shouted in her face, "STOP CRYING, YOU SNIVELLING LITTLE BRAT. I HATE CHILDREN CRYING."

The Ripper Code

Shocked by this terrifying outburst, Rosie instantly stopped her wailing. She knew he would strangle her if she continued. The Wolf Man waited. When he was satisfied she had definitely ceased her weeping, he spoke very gently and quietly to her.

"I have no intentions of putting you back on the streets. I am going to take you to a very nice place, a long way away from here. You will live with some nice people who will look after you, see that you have a proper education. This couple, who have no children of their own, live in the country with dogs and cats and other animals..."

"Will they have horses?" Rosie asked.

"They have horses," assured the Wolf Man. "And I will pay them lots of money to take good care of you. I will also put money in trust for you, so that when you come of age, you will never be poor again and you won't have to do what you have been doing."

"Can you really do this?" demanded the child sceptically.

"I can."

"But why?" Rosie was astounded. "You don't look a Fairy God Mother to me." The Wolf Man laughed.

"There is evil in you," she added fearfully.

"There is ", he agreed simply.

"Why are you doing this for me?"

"Because I can."

"But why?" persisted Rosie

"I like....to be unexpected," answered the Wolf Man, softly stroking her hair. "I like....to surprise myself." He picked up the bayonet. Her eyes widened in terror. She knew she couldn't trust him. He knelt down beside her and carefully cut the ropes that bound her.

* * *

"Thanks, darling. Just drop me off here," Sophie said, unbuckling her seat belt. Max slowed down and brought the car to a stop. He turned and looked hopefully at her.

"Oh Sophie, must we part so soon? I don't suppose you're available..."

"Oh, god no. No offence but you weigh a ton. You nearly knackered my back last time. Three times up and down those bloody stairs," she groaned, stepping out of the car with a grossly exaggerated stagger.

"Sorry...but does that mean... we.. well.. I mean, won't ever be able to again? Because you don't like doing it in the car, do you?" asked Max, creasing his elfish face in alarm.

"That's right but... never say never, darling. I'm sure we can find a way. Where there's a willy there's a way, as my grandma would say."

"Huh, these grandmas, always quick with the easy quip," laughed Max. "Do you do home visits?"

"Of course, sweetie," Sophie squeezed his hand. "Costs more but if you can afford the extra, just phone me and I'll be in your bed in two shakes of a lamb's tail."

"Oh great," Max's face cheered up. "Fancy coming back to my place now?"

Sophie looked at her watch and sadly shook her head. "No, sorry, darling, got another assignation booked but here's my card. Just phone me and if I'm available, I'll pop over and brighten up your evening."

Max stared at the business card like a hungry man. "Thanks, I'll definitely ring you," he said, feasting his eyes on her sumptuously rounded posterior, which she flirtatiously flaunted at him, as she skitted away down the street.

CHAPTER 15
Candid Camera
15th August. Wednesday

Max was seriously worried about his eyes. He was spending far too much time staring at a computer screen or watching television. The constant bombardment of radiation was bleaching the retina and thickening the cornea. All day and all night, except, of course, when he was out whoring. He was paranoid he would be blind by the time he was sixty. Even during his lunch breaks, he was unable to drag himself away from the computer. Right now, as he ate his sandwiches, he had opened Cyber-Road Atlas and was studying a street map of London on his work computer.

"What you looking at?" asked Claire as she came alongside his desk, with a burger in a bun and a carton of banana-flavoured milkshake. He looked to see if the "junk-burger" was a Macdonalds, and was relieved to see it was not. His harangues were beginning to have an effect.

"Street map of Whitechapel," he said, tapping the computer screen.

"The murders?"

"Yes," he nodded. "I'm trying to locate the streets where the bodies were dumped."

"You agree with the papers, you don't think that's where they were murdered?" Claire bit into her Brit-Burger. She proudly showed him the label on the wrapping. Max briefly smiled, at least she's no longer eating Yankie-burgers.

"These two prostitutes didn't work in Whitechapel. I found out last night, their normal patch was Kings Cross," Max told her.

"Wow," Claire shook her in admiration. "You really are a detective. Did you have to question other prostitutes for the info?"

"Yeah. I found out their names - Martha and Polly. Martha's body was found just off Wentworth Street...and Polly's near Durward Street, about 150 yards north of the Royal London Hospital. Hmmm. Interesting." Max paused for thought. Claire waited patiently for him to continue, and then she couldn't bear it any longer.

"What?" she eagerly asked.

"I don't know," Max replied cautiously. "Its just...well, me mentioning London Hospital, is like stirring up a feeling...a memory. London Hospital seems to mean something here. I don't know why. Can't quite put my finger on it." Max screwed his face up, wracking his brains.

"What about the numbers of their names?" suggested Claire.

"Good idea. Let's type Martha and Polly in my numerology program..." Max typed on the computer, calling up the Name-Oracle program. The screen asked him to type in the name. Max knew the answers. He had already done this but he decided to go through the routine just so as to entertain Claire. Also she may see something he hadn't. So he typed in "MARTHA". The computer quickly showed "25", and then "7".

"DO YOU WANT ANALYSIS?" The Computer asked in the sim-voice of Dana Scully from the "X-files" TV series. Max clicked "NO".

"ANOTHER NAME?"

Max tapped "YES", and quickly typed "POLLY". The computer responded with "26", then "8".

"Martha equals 7...and Polly equals 8," Max summed up.

"Does that mean anything?" asked Claire.

"I don't know. Except of course, this 7, 8 could be the beginning of a number sequence."

"If there's another murder, could that victim's name add up to 9?"

"Well, lets hope there's not another murder," Max replied grimly. "But it would be just too weird if we've discovered a numerological sequence in the killings. No. Seven - eight. It's just a coincidence. And anyway, what happened to one to six?" Max closed the Name-Oracle. "I don't think numerology is going to help us solve the murders?"

"You said 'us'. Does that mean I'm now your assistant?" Claire asked, half in jest.

"Er. Well, possibly," Max replied, feeling slightly sheepish. "Looks like it."

A big smile lit up Claire's face.

"Fancy coming round to watch another video this evening?" she asked hopefully. "I'll cook you a meal."

"Um. No. I need to be at home this evening. I wanted to carry working on the computer." Max lied, and felt bad doing so. Claire dropped her head down, unable to hide her disappointment and was turning to go back to her reception post, when he piped up.

"But.. if you want... Another evening this week, come over to my place. Another brain on this case. You'd be welcome."

"Really? Cool," beamed Claire.

Max smiled back and then looked behind him, saw a long queue of Job Seekers waiting.

"Okay, who's first?" shouted Max.

Sitting alone, parked in his car, waiting in Yorkway, just off Kings Cross, Max looked at his watch. *9. 15*. She was late. Oh well, Max sighed, the prerogative of women. He again picked up the book he was struggling to read in the dismal light; *Hitler, Demon Sorcerer : Occult Roots of the Nazis* by J. B. Yeagher. He had a terrible feeling the book wasn't going to tell him anything he didn't know already. Just another regurgitation of previous treatises on the Satanic origins of the Third Reich.

'In the last days, Hitler, suffering from horrible nightmares, would wake in the middle of the night, screaming, "He is here. Angry with me. I have failed him. Can you see him?" ...'.

The car door suddenly opened, making Max jump out of his skin.

"Got your camera gear with you?" Sophie asked as she quickly got in beside him.

"Jesus, Sophie," Max croaked, putting his hand on his pounding chest, "Yep" he added, giving her a warm smile.

"Good," she said, giving him a quick peck on the cheek, "You know Bagleys Studios Night Club? I fixed us a room on the second floor, overlooking Goodsway Yard, where Anne will try to get him to take her...in more ways than one."

"Is there a lift to the second floor?" asked Max, as he started the car and began moving.

"No, but it's all sorted. Don't worry, I won't be carrying you."

"I don't mind you carrying me. It's lovely snuggling close to your bosom."

"Saucy sausage," she winked, putting her hand between his legs, giving his groin a light squeeze. She pointed ahead, and continued with directions, "Go up and then take the first left....and then first right."

They arrived outside Bagleys Studios Night Club, where three hefty-looking bouncers greeted Sophie with cheeky grins and hugs. They then took it in turns to shake Max's hand, each with a vice-like grip, making him fear for the survival of his delicate fingers, and slapped him on the back as if he was a long-lost friend, though this was the first time he had ever seen any of them. It must be because he had been vouched for by Sophie. The three bouncers then picked Max up in his wheelchair and carried him into the building. Sophie took the camera gear, but a fourth bouncer eagerly relieved her of the burden and rushed up the steps, carrying the stuff, squeezing pass and overtaking his colleagues who were huffing and puffing, as they struggled with the arduous task of hauling Max up the tight narrow winding stairs to the second floor.

"Watch where yer going, you fucking Mong," yelled one of them as the eager one reached the top of the stairs ahead of them.

"I gotta open the fucking door for you, ain't I?" shouted back the fourth bouncer, turning the key in the lock, "and don't be calling me a Mong in front of the cripple. It ain't PC."

"Fat lot you know, arse-wipe. He ain't a cripple, he's a 'person wiv a disability'," came back the reply.

Max, miraculously still in one piece, breathed a sigh of relief when the three bouncers finally set him and his chair down on the ground in the room on the second floor. Now he understood why they were called bouncers, having been shaken and bounced all the way up. Sophie kissed each of the tough guys a 'thank you' kiss as they made their exits back downstairs.

The last one as he was leaving and closing the door, popped his head back in. "You sure you don't want me in this 'ere porno?"

"Another time, Harry. This one's for a specialist market," Sophie hurriedly said, while helping Max set up the camera equipment.

"Oh, yeah. Yeah. I get ya," replied Harry slowly. "Give her one for me, Titch." He grinned lasciviously at Max as he finally left the room.

"Sophie, what did you tell him we were doing?" inquired Max.

"Making a porn movie, of course," she replied po-faced. "Don't worry. This room is used lots. Part of the deal is the bouncers get a piece of the action."

"That's handy," Max said as he wheeled over to the window. Sophie having put the camera on the tripod brought the assemblege over to him. Max looked down towards the Goodsway Yard. Suddenly he stiffened. "There's a car coming into the yard," he quietly announced.

"That should be Anne and Reece. Jesus, we only just made it," Sophie said, switching the light out. Max pressed the record button on the camcorder and followed the car as it halted, and zoomed in on Reece as he climbed out. The plain-clothes police sergeant swiftly surveyed the area, checking that the coast was clear. Satisfied that his suspicions were unfounded, he beckoned to his passenger to quickly get out the car. The available light in the yard wasn't sufficient for proper recording, so Max switched on the 'night vision' infra-red mode, which immediately enabled him to see the beautiful black mama, Annie cautiously emerge from the copper's vehicle. She walked to the bonnet of the car and bent across it, offering her rump to Reece, who positioned behind her, forcefully pulled her trousers and knickers down.

Max began to feel uneasy as he filmed Reece's brutal use of Annie, alternating between close-ups and wide shots of the policeman's tight, hard, bestial face, and of Annie, biting her lips, stifling cries of pain. Keeping the camcorder on record, Max turned and looked at Sophie at his side, who was busy taking stills pictures with the digital camera, wondering what she thought of what she was photographing. Wasn't she finding this prurient voyeurism distasteful? Max looked back at the sex scene down in the yard, in time to see Reece take from his trouser pocket, a policeman's truncheon.

"Oh Jesus, Sophie," whispered the horrified Max, "He's just got out a truncheon. He's going to beat her. Call the bouncers. Quick. Stop him."

"No, he's not," she replied. "He likes to use it for double penetration."

"Oh Jesus, he just shoved it up her -"

"Exactly," Sophie said, snapping a dozen shots in quick succession.

"And he's still rogering her with his cock," exclaimed Max in disbelief. "Oh, Jesus, poor Anne."

"Poor Anne, my arse," Sophie grunted. "She loves a bit of Double-P. The harder it is, the better." Max turned and stared in astonishment at the woman next to him. She must have seen everything. Nothing could shock her, he thought. Sophie gave him a nudge as his camera began to tip down, "Focus on the task in hand, Max. Your camera's drooping," she admonished. Max quickly swung back and, with reluctance, continued to video the nasty sex scene in the Goodsway Yard below. Or was it really so nasty? Anyone would think he was a damn Puritan. Which, of course, wasn't true, because an hour later when he and Sophie were packing the camera equipment away, he found he had been completely turned on by what they had just been witnessing.

"Want to come back to my place?" he asked.

"It'll cost you," she replied. "And you'll have to bring me back to the street. I've lost custom tonight, spending time doing this."

"It's for a good cause, though isn't it?" said Max, slightly annoyed at this constant harsh mercenary quality of hers.

"Maybe. Could make things worse. For Annie especially".

"Oh shit. Should we forget it?"

"No. What the hell. Annie was up for it. So if she wasn't worried, why should I be?" Sophie shrugged, snapping shut the camera cases.

"My place, then? We can choose stills from the video and the pix you shot."

Sophie took his face in her hands and kissed him, full on the lips, "To your pad, Max," she said, licking his nose. "I can't wait to see your den of inequity," she added, offering him her bottom for a little slap.

CHAPTER 16
Click-er-ty-click
15th August. Wednesday

Max liked his flat. It was an extension of himself. And he wanted Sophie to like it. As she wandered around, exploring his domain, he busied himself, first, plugging the video camera into back of a computer, and then pressed "LOAD TAPE", so that the computer would begin downloading the evening's footage. At a second computer he downloaded the pictures taken with the digital camera. A third computer had his Numerology Program - "NAME ORACLE" on display. Sophie shook her head in amazement.

"You got enough computers, haven't you? You could start your own Internet Caff," she suggested as she sauntered over to a wall of books.

"And look at all these books!" she exclaimed. "I've never seen so many. Have you read them all? You're not moonlighting as Camden Public Library by any chance? Anyway, how do you find the time when you're out all night screwing us girls. And how can you afford all this shit, when you seem to blow all your dosh on us tarts?"

"Jesus, Sophie, so many questions," laughed Max. "You're worse than the law."

Sophie swung round and stared fixedly at him, pretending to be outraged at the insult.

"Hark who's talking," she sniffed. "You never stop asking questions. And look at these books. Most of them are true crime, East End Gangland, Forensics, serial killers, Jack the Ripper, the Maybrick diaries...that's Jack the Ripper, isn't it?" she asked, pulling out the said volume, waving it at him.

"That's the belief. But it's bollocks. The diaries are bullshit," replied Max with disdain.

She pulled out another book, "*The Final Solution*...that about the Jewish Holocaust?"

"No, its referring to the final solution of the Ripper case. Stephen Knight claims Jack the Ripper was a Freemason and thinks he can identify him. Actually, he's wrong. Not about the Ripper being a Freemason, I've got evidence he was but Knight was wrong about who Jack was." Max went to the kitchen and came back with a tea caddy in one hand and a jar of coffee in the other and waved them at Sophie. The kettle was boiling.

"So you think you know who he was, then?" she asked, pointing to the coffee jar.

"I don't *think*. I *know*," he snootily replied as he returned to the kitchen to make them both hot drinks.

"Who was he then, smarty pants?" she shouted.

"A Freemason of the Occult school," he shouted back. "He was an initiate of the Hermetic Lodge of Alexandria. He was also a member of the English Rosicrucian Society....you want milk and sugar in your coffee?" he yelled from the kitchen.

"No milk, and three spoons of sugar."

Max rushed back into the sitting room and stared at her in astonishment, "Three spoons of sugar?"

"Yes. We got a lot of fucking to do," whispered Sophie, smiling sweetly. With a big grin across his face, Max hurried back to finish the coffee.

"I also believe the Ripper joined the Hermetic Order of the Golden Dawn when it was founded by two Freemasons, William Woodman and William Westcott on the first of March in 1888, at the Temple of Isis in London," continued Max.

"The what Dawn?" shouted Sophie.

"The Hermetic Order of the Golden Dawn," shouted back Max. "They believed in an ancient race of Supermen, possibly living in a subterranean city beneath the Himalayas, and that after an Apocalypse, they will come to the surface and rule over us...or those of us who have not yet transformed into Supermen. The aim of the Golden Dawn was to discover and employ the magic rituals that will transmute their members into Super beings, and summon the Adept Masters from the Underworld, and thus hasten the Age of the Super Race. You'd be amazed at who were members. Two of your countrymen, poet W. B. Yeats, and Bram Stoker, writer of *Dracula*... Another of their more infamous members was, of course, Aleister Crowley, who tried to claim he was the Great Beast 666. Crowley was the father of today's Black Magic movement. Actually, another of Crowley's claims was that he knew the identity of Jack the Ripper, which shouldn't surprise us, since they had both been members of the Golden Dawn."

"You've lost me," groaned Sophie, completely confused with this sudden information overload.

"What I'm saying is, the man I believe to be Jack the Ripper, was a Black magician," explained Max, returning with their drinks, "...who also used his Masonic knowledge to perform blood sacrifice rituals. The unfortunate prostitutes he killed were his human sacrifices for some perversion of an ancient Masonic cabalistic ceremony."

"Oh gawd, I wish I hadn't asked. Can't you just tell me his name?"

"Roslyn D'Onston. His real name was Robert D'Onston Stephenson."

"Did he call himself Rosslyn because of the Rosslyn Chapel?"

"How do you know about Rosslyn Chapel?" Max asked her, surprised.

"Coz I read the novel *The Da Vinci Code* and saw the movie. Oooh, Tom Hanks, he's so sexy," she winked, licking her lips.

"Da Vinci Code," winced Max. "I thought that book was superficial, dumb and designer-written to be Hollywood garbage."

"Well, I enjoyed them, you elitist little shit," huffed Sophie. There followed for several minutes, an awkward silence, until finally Sophie poked her tongue out at him, making Max laugh. He reached out to take her hand. At which point, there was an electronic beep-beep from one of the computers. Sophie took the sonic interruption as an excuse to leap up and investigate the rack of computers.

"I think the video is downloaded," she shouted, beckoning him over.

"Great. Lets run it and capture stills for prints." said Max excitedly, going over to the computer and clicking the curser on the PLAY button on the screen.

"How much are you going to blackmail him for?" asked Sophie, looking at the computer screen showing the video footage of Reece and Annie.

"I'm not going to blackmail him," replied Max as he froze a suitable frame and clicked CAPTURE. "I don't want his dirty money," he continued. "I just want to tell him to stop hassling me, and that I know, and he should try to treat the girls with a bit more respect."

"Oh yeah, and pigs may fly." replied Sophie, at the same time pointing out a particular freeze frame for Max to capture, of the cop undoing his flies.

"They do. In helicopters," he responded, cringing at his own cliché joke.

"Ha-funny-ha ha," Sophie laughed derisively. Max didn't mind. He was enjoying her bending over his shoulder, breathing in her smell, as she helped choose the images. "Yes," he nodded when she picked out an extreme close-up of Reece's sweating face as he sodomizes Annie. Max then selected a medium wide-shot, depicting both Reece and Annie and truncheon.

After half an hour or so, the two had built up a file of ten porno stills, which Max then worked on individually, cropping and enhancing them, employing PhotoArtClass software. Finally, he printed out the incriminating images, in three different sizes on glossy paper. They looked very professional.

Max and Sophie then went to work on the digital photos Sophie had snapped. This took nearly an hour. But eventually, Sophie was able to flop down on the sofa and take out well-deserved cigarette. She thought of asking Max if it was alright to smoke but as he was already bringing over an ashtray, she didn't bother. Instead, she asked, "Are we going to fuck now? Coz I got to get back soon."

Max smiled and from behind his back, brought out a phallic-looking loofah.

"Fancy giving me a bath?" he asked.

Max relaxed back in the bath tub, luxuriating in the steaming hot sudsy water, wallowing in the womb-like warmth as the naked Sophie, kneeling on the floor beside him, scrubbed him all over, laughing and pretending to be a randy lunatic nurse, who is unable to resist man-handling his erect member and grope his testicles.

"How about getting in with me?" invited Max, splashing her like a demented sea-lion.

"Thought you'd never ask," she said in her best Mae West, and climbed in, creating a deluge of lavender smelling lather all over his hair. In retaliation, he grabbed both her breasts and, like a hungry goldfish, nibbled and kissed the hard pointing nipples, while she lovingly caressed and squeezed his small soft bottom. For several minutes, they played, feverishly kissing and cuddling and biting each other. Then, suddenly, she pushed him from her, looking rather thoughtful.

"So, your Jack the Ripper suspect, did he call himself Rosslyn after Rosslyn Chapel?"

"I think so." replied Max. "Although D'Onston spelt Roslyn with just one "S", whereas the Chapel is spelt 'R', 'O', 'double-S', 'L', 'Y', 'N'."

"Why did he spell it differently?"

"Numerological reasons."

"Oh gawd, here we go again," groaned Sophie, flicking water at him. "Another complicated answer to a simple question."

"Numerology isn't complicated," he protested, flicking water back. "I'll show you on the computer."

"Another day, darling. I've got to go soon. You have to take me back."

"Actually, do you mind if I give you money for a cab?" asked Max.

"Okay, 10 quid should do. That'll be on top of the 50 quid 'Home Visit' you owe me."

"We haven't done it yet," Max wagged his finger at her.

"I know," she said, taking his finger in her mouth and gently bit it.

"Have you ever done it in the bath?"

"Yes, lots but its not a favourite."

"Why?" inquired Max, slowly tracing the curves of her breasts with his finger, repeating a figure of eight.

"I don't like soap getting in my fanny. But if the client insists," she lay back in the foam, offering up her glistening vulva to him.

"Oh no, if you rather not. Don't want to make your fanny sore. We'll do it in the bedroom."

Max's bedroom was also full of books, from floor to ceiling. The man is book mad, Sophie thought. There was a small portable television, on a chest of drawers beside his bed and a notebook computer on a desk at the foot. He doesn't have a wardrobe. Or a mirror. The bed was kingsize, which was funny when you saw how tiny Max actually was. No more than three and a half feet tall. You could mistake him for a dwarf, but he'll be quick to inform you, brittle bones has nothing to do with dwarfism. Though, none of that mattered to Sophie who was rubbing Max's naked body down with a towel, as he sat on the bed, because he was the sexiest client she'd had until now. One of the things she loved about him being small was that when he lay on top of her, his feet just reached her groin, so his toes would play with her clitoris and probe her vagina while his hands caressed her breasts, and they snogged. There aren't too many men who can do that. And he had the cutest most gorgeous tiny bottom she could cup with one hand. It is true what they say; 'small IS beautiful", though thankfully, he isn't small where it counts, she thought with a smile, as she dried him between his legs.

"What was this numerological reason your Roslyn spelt his name differently?" asked Sophie, giving Max the towel and turning onto her stomach, so he could dry her back and bottom.

"The way he spelt it, allowed his whole name to add up to 6, which was a number that had demonic meaning for him." explained Max, his strong hands gently kneading her buttocks.

The Ripper Code

"Like 666?" Sophie closed her eyes, enjoying the sensual massage.

"Exactly. In fact, he used sixes in most of his aliases."

"How many ali-arses did he have?" she asked dreamily, thinking what naughty fingers he has. Max laughed, then continued, "I don't know but certainly at least three, each of which came to six. He was obsessed with six six six. I'll show on the computer...after we've had sex sex sex."

"Hmmmm, sounds good to me," she said, suddenly turning round and throwing Max on his back and taking his cock in her mouth.

"There you are, a crash course in Numerology" said Max sitting at his computer six minutes later, with Sophie looking over his shoulder. The two of them, in the darkened sitting room, were eerily-lit by the neon colours of the "Numero-Alpha Matrix" displayed on the screen.

"I wonder if you can make three letter words from the chart to help you remember a number belonging to a letter?" asked Sophie.

"Well, there's 'C', 'L', 'U'. These are the letters that have the value of '3'."

"C,L,U? Oh, CLUE!" twigged Sophie.

"Yep," affirmed Max. "And then there's 'E', 'N', 'W'. They are the three FIVEs, which spells NEW."

"That's great! You can always remember the FIVEs and the THREEs by thinking NEW CLU."

"Exactly, my dear Watson," intoned Max. "And there's one more."

"No, no! Don't tell me. Let me find it." Sophie ran her finger along the matrix of letters and numbers, until she stopped at the column headed '6'.

"Yes," she shouted. "The SIXES. 'F', 'O', 'X'. The three sixes spell FOX."

"X-actly, my dear girl. FOX is 666. 20th Century Fox...owned by Rupert Murdoch who I'm certain is a servant of the Antichrist."

"What about Fox Mulder in 'The X-Files'? Is he part of the Antichrist, too?"

"Could be," hinted Max. "Look at the title, 'The X Files'. 'The' is 6. 'X' is 6. 'Files' equals 6. Three sixes - 666. AND Fox Studios produced the series. Personally, I've never trusted the 'X-Files', especially when it keeps telling you 'The Truth Is Out There', and you know its owned by Murdoch, the "Lord of Lies". I watched all nine series and concluded that the producers were just playing with us, deliberately creating confusion, making a mockery of the paranormal and UFO phenomenon, stuffing our heads with an incoherent mish-mash ragbag of conspiracy theories, telling us nothing and leaving us frustrated and thinking its all a load of bollocks and will never take the subject matter seriously again..." Max stopped, suddenly embarrassed that he was on a rant.

"Anyway, lets get back to Roslyn D'Onston," he said, and inputed names and words into the Name-Oracle on the computer, which rapidly performed some calculations and then unfolded the following results:

Roslyn D'Onston Stephenson MD
```
   31      29      45      9 = 114 = 6
    4       2       9      9 =  24 = 6
```

aka Dr. Morgan Davies
```
       13      32      24       = 69 = 6
        4       5       6       = 15 = 6
```

aka   "Sudden Death"
```
           22     20    = 42 = 6
            4      2         = 6
```

The computer startled Sophie when it suddenly said in a Dalek voice, "Six-Six-Six. Xterminate- Xterminate- Xterminate." Max burst out laughing and drew Sophie's attention to what was now displayed on the screen.

"You see, all three of his pseudonyms come to 6. Clearly, he knows about numerology, he is obsessed with 666 and by giving himself these names, designating himself as 666, he either thinks he's the Antichrist or he's the servant of the Antichrist."

"Did he really call himself 'Sudden Death'?" Sophie asked disbelievingly.

"Yes, he did."

"God, that's creepy. I think you're right. He must have been Jack the Ripper."

"I'm not the first person to claim Robert D'Onston Stephenson was the Ripper," Max confessed, "but its my numerological analysis which proves it. I've got more examples to show you...." He was interrupted by the doorbell..

"That will be the taxi," Sophie jumped up, and grabbed her coat and purse.,

"Thanks for a fascinating evening, darling," she said and gave Max a quick kiss on the cheek. "Let's hope we have more sex sex sex."

As she ran out the front door, Max shouted "SOPHIE! WAIT."

"What?" She yelled back, leaping into the cab. Max charged down the garden path and quickly pushed something into her hand.

"You forgot your money," he whispered. "Sixty quid, wasn't it?"

CHAPTER 17
Taking Charge
16th August. Thursday

There was a lull in business at the Job Centre that Thursday afternoon. Not many people were coming in, claiming their Job Seeker's allowance or needing interviews, so Max took the opportunity to make an illicit phone-call. On the computer screen was a detailed street map of Whitechapel. He beckoned Claire over to him. She was at his side like a shot, all smiles.

"Is that the Whitechapel Gazette?" Max spoke into the phone. "Hello, I'm a researcher for a Channel Four documentary..." Max winked at Claire, who responded with a stifled giggle. The other Job Centre staff opened their mouths in horror, as Max continued, "Do you have any more information on the exact locations of where the bodies of the two murdered prostitutes were found?" Jacky stormed over to him.

"Max, the Supervisor will go ape-shit, if she catches you," she interrupted, wagging her finger at him. Max covered the phone mouthpiece, and whispered back, "She's at a conference, isn't she?", and quickly resumed talking to the Whitechapel Gazette.

"...George Yard?" Max queried. "That's where the first woman, Martha, was found? George Yard.... And the second? Yeah, her name was Polly.... How did I know that? It's my job to know... as researcher for Channel Four....the police wouldn't tell you? Well, aren't you glad I rang. Yep, thanks. Cheers. Thanks a million." Max hung up, and proceeded to type, '*Polly found at Bucks Row, Whitechapel*'. He followed this by placing a "skull and cross-bones" icon on the map at Bucks Row. He then typed: '*Martha found at George, Yard, Whitechapel*' and placed another "skull and cross-bones" icon over George Yard on the map. He clicked "SAVE" and returned the screen to normal Job Centre business.

The Ripper Code

"George Yard...Bucks Row?" pondered Max. "Why do these names mean something to me?"

"And London Hospital," Claire reminded him. "You said that stirred some feeling in you."

"That's right," he exclaimed, patting her arm. "London Hospital also. Yes. I'll have to sleep on this." Or better still, take a trip to Whitechapel tonight, Max thought, and then, afterwards, try and see Sophie.

The night came quick enough. From Camden Town it is just under five miles to Whitechapel but even at this time of night the drive can take at least half-an-hour. Sometimes, it has even taken Max an hour and half to cover as little as three miles. Bloody London, the city that never sleeps, and the traffic always hell, Twenty-four Seven. So, Max wondered, how is it possible for anyone to get away with murder in such a restless bustling insomniac environment?

Max in his car, tried to drive close to Bucks Row but found a criss-cross of crime scene tapes blocking his access. Not wanting to draw attention to himself, and feeling vulnerable, he decided not to get out of the car and explore the murder scene in his wheelchair. Maybe the access will be better at George Yard.

It wasn't. In fact, it was worse. There was a vigilant policeman on guard duty at the taped off scene of crime. When Max arrived, he was immediately accosted by the police constable and ordered to clear-off. It was only as Max drove away, the policeman suddenly realised he should have asked for some identity. Snatching at his notebook, the dozy copper quickly wrote down the car's registration number just before Max disappeared into Wentworth Street.

Back at Kings Cross, Max felt at home, cruising the 'red light' district. He loved watching the working girls strutting their stuff. A few of the regulars gave him a wave as he drove past, but he wasn't interested because he had just seen Emma. He needed to talk to her, so he pulled up beside her. Quickly looking over her shoulder, she walked up to his window warily.

"Emma, you seen Sophie?" asked Max.

"Sophie?" she queried. "I don't know any Sophie. She may be giving you a special name."

"Irish, redhead, green eyes."

A look of recognition crossed Emma's face, "Sounds like Maeve to me. No, haven't seen her for several nights."

Max looked hard at Emma. Where else had he seen her, apart from that time, over two weeks ago, when he paid for her services? And then it hit him. "And Emma, that's your special name?" he grinned. "I never thought I would get to do it with a real cop." He thought her tarty undercover outfit very convincing.

"Shhh. Not so loud, idiot," hissed Emma, also known as Detective Constable Eloise Warren. "We let you in on the secret because we thought you could be trusted. Thought you were going to be working for us. You're not going to compromise me, are you?"

"I didn't think your chief wanted anything more to do with me, the way he threw me out."

"His bark is worse than his bite. He just thinks you're a crank. Its John Jordan he's annoyed with, making him think you were some genius."

"Thanks a million," Max tried to sound hurt. "You do wonders for a poor guy's self-esteem." Warren smiled, and as she turned to walk away, Max whispered, "So...um...are you on duty, so to speak? What do you charge if you wear your uniform? I fancy a policewoman tonight."

"Another time," replied Warren, sadly shaking her head. "Tonight, I've got bigger fish to fry. Anyway, you better not hang around here. Reece is on patrol."

"Okay. Another time. And don't forget your handcuffs," Max said to her as she briskly strode away. Oh dear, Max thought, now she's walking like a policewoman – dead giveaway. Why didn't I notice that before? Because, Maxwell, you are not as smart as you like to think, he said to himself as he drove off down another back street. And then, he drove down another street. It was empty. He did the usual big circuit covering Kings Cross, Caledonian Road, Pentonville, Gray's Inn, Tottenham Court, Euston and back to Kings Cross. And still nothing. All the girls had disappeared.

*A*LICE

Suddenly, the larder was bare. Max decided to try Berners Street, near Middlesex Hospital. There's a student nurses home nearby. He knows poorly paid nurses are sometimes found, hanging around in adjacent streets, doing a spot of moonlighting. When he reached the street parallel to the hospital, he thought he was in luck. He saw a woman standing in a shop doorway, half in shadow. He slowed down, wound down his window and made a point of obviously looking at her. She saw him and nodded. Max nodded back and she quickly ran over to his car and got in.

"Hi, I'm Alice," she said. collapsing into the seat beside him. "Thank God you came along. No one's interested. Been standing around for hours." Max smiled at her until he noticed the 'tracks' on her bare arms. Looks like she's jacking up with heroin. Oh Jesus, a bloody junky. Some of the tracks looked fresh. Her face was puffy and her nose red and dribbling. She looked half dead. Max wondered if this was going to be a good idea.

"Go down the street and...turn left," slurred Alice. "No, I mean, turn right."

Max drove as directed, but was feeling uneasy. Alice squeezed his shoulder excitedly.

"That's it," she smiled with a crooked leer. "Now go left in this street."

Max stopped the car at the entrance of the street she indicated, and saw that there were no street lamps, and that it was a dead end. He thought he could see a shadow hiding behind a dustbin. Was it a trap? Spooked, Max suddenly drove on past the cul de sac.

"No," Alice yelled angrily. "You were suppose to turn left. Go back."

"I'd rather not. I know a better place."

"No. It's okay there. Nice and quiet. Very cosy. Won't get disturbed. You can have me all night. Do anything you like to me. All my holes are yours. Lets do it there please," she begged, pointing behind her. Max kept driving, "No. Looks too dodgy."

Max took the car right into a side road with some lighting and parked between two skips. He turned to Alice and was astonished to see that she had already pulled her jeans and knickers down, "Jesus. Alice, you're keen," he exclaimed, as she wound back the seat to reclined position, and lay back, with her legs spread open, offering the goods.

"Yeah, well, you know. You want it. I want it. So let's do it. Quick open your flies. Get it out and fuck me. I've been desperate all night and I need the money. What you going to pay me?" she said, her eyes half- closed as she played with her clitoris.

"Its normally £20 for a straight fuck, isn't?" Max pointed out.

"I'll let you have all my holes for fifty."

"Okay," agreed Max.

"Got the money?" Alice held out her hand.

"Yeah, but I don't have a condom. Do you?"

"Yeah, of course. A working girl must always carry condoms because men are pricks and they are too fucking lazy and too fucking inconsiderate to supply their own." She searched in her bag for a packet...but after much looking and failing to find any, she groaned, "Oh, where are they? I had some. Oh Jesus, where the fuck are they? I didn't use them already, did I? No. Can't have. Haven't done any fucking tonight." She emptied the contents of her bag all over the floor in front of her seat and examined every item, half expecting, half hoping, it would metamorphose into a packet of condoms.

"Oh, no. Did I forget them? I can't believe I forget the fuckers. Shit," she cursed, and turned to Max, with a pleading expression.

"Oh well, it doesn't matter, does it? We can fuck without a condom. I hate the bloody things. They always burst. I can't stand rubber anyway. I like the real feel of hot throbbing flesh inside me. Come on, baby, just stick it in me, now. Its all yours," she urged.

"No," replied Max.

"No?" Alice was stunned.

"No way. I'm not doing it without a condom. Uh uh. No way," reiterated Max.

"Oh come on. I'm clean."

"I don't know that. I'm not taking any chances. No way."

"Oh please," begged Alice. "I need the money. I haven't eaten for days."

"No. Absolutely not. Not without a condom. Never," said Max shaking his head.

"But you got to. I really thought I had condoms. I don't how I forgot. Once won't do any harm."

"Out of the fucking question," shouted Max. "I mean look at your arms. You're a heroine addict. Its too risky."

"No I'm not," she wailed. "I don't do 'H'. Them varicose veins. My Mum had them in her arms. Its genetic." Frantically, Alice bent down again, searching for the non-existent condoms.

"I'm sorry. You're going to have to go," said Max, leaning across her and opening the passenger door.

"No no, look, they're here," she shouted triumphantly, showing Max a packet.

"That's a packet of chewing gum," Max contemptuously retorted.

"Is it?" Alice peered myopically at the packet. "Oh yes. Oh but please, you got to help me out. Okay, if we don't do it, will you give me some money, anyway."

"You must be joking," he spluttered.

"Please. Just give me something. I'm really broke. Anything." Alice began to weep.

"No way," replied Max but in a less harsh tone. He wondered if her tears were crocodile or genuine.

"Just a little something," she entreated. "Something for my time. I gave up valuable time to be with you."

"Get out of here. Go on out the car."

"Give me tenner and I'll go." The tears had stopped and her eyes were full of hate.

"No. Get out the car," demanded Max, beginning to feel a little frightened.

"A fiver. I'm not going unless you give me a fiver," snarled Alice.

"Fuck off out, will you," Max yelled, pressing the car horn angrily, hoping the noise would scare her away.

Suddenly, the inside of the car filled with reflected blue and red flashing lights. Startled, Alice looked behind her and quickly got out the car. There was a shout, "You stop." but she didn't and kept running, rapidly disappearing in the shadows at the far end of the street. Max cursed. He knew what was coming. As expected, the police patrol car pulled up alongside on his right. Reece stepped out and approached Max.

"Did I just see Alice Aids?" asked Reece. "Hope you had appropriate protection, Cripple?"

"I don't know what you're talking about. I stopped to ask her directions," Max replied innocently.

"Don't give me that. How much did you pay her?"

"I didn't pay her anything. I wanted directions to the Bagleys Studio Night Club. You don't know, do you? You know what street it's on?" inquired Max.

Reece did a double take, stared intently at Max and then quickly glanced over his shoulder at the policewoman in the driver's seat, who was busy speaking on the radio. He turned back to Max, eyeing him suspiciously.

"Never heard of it," Reece muttered. "And stop pissing me off. I told you before I don't want to see your ugly Quasimodo face on my patrol. And here you are, flagrantly disregarding my gentle warning. This is not good. Looks like I'm going to have to book you for curb-crawling. Let me see your driver's licence."

As requested, Max took the licence from his wallet but he also placed a small photograph of Reece with Annie over the top and handed both over.

"What the fuck is this?" yelped Reece, who nearly dropped the photo in shock.

"I suppose you'd like to see my MOT certificate?" suggested Max, taking another document and covering it with another incriminating picture.

"Hey, Sergeant, any problems?" asked the policewoman who was bored, and started to get out of the car. Reece quickly turned, and waved her away with one hand, while the other hand went white, so tight was he clutching the documents and photos.

"You probably want to see my insurance certificate as well," Max quietly said, handing a third photo to a seething Reece, who stared in total disbelief at the images.

Max continued, "Of course, I always keep duplicates, triplicates even, of all important documents in a nice safe place like bank deposit box."

Reece looked up from the photographs at Max with eyes that would kill if they could. He threw the motor documents back at Max but managed to pocket the photos without the policewoman seeing. With a face that was purple with bottled rage, he stepped menacingly close to the smiling little man.

"What's your game? You trying to fleece me? Blackmail, is it?" he whispered threateningly.

"Me fleece Reece?" Max exclaimed in mock surprise. "No. I'm just wondering if I have freedom of the city, at night, like? If you know what I mean? I suffer terribly from insomnia. I'm a restless nightbird. I like to drive around, enjoy the nocturnal entertainment on offer."

Reece looked at Max in stunned silence. Then he coughed and said, "Yeah, yeah, I get your point. Your documents seem to be in order. Mister Abberline. Now move along."

Max wanted to laugh gloatingly as he drove away but thought the rush of victory would be stronger if he maintained an impassive face. Nonetheless, he had to admit, it was definitely better than an orgasm, getting one over that nasty bent copper.

CHAPTER 18
A Wind-Up Lemon
17th August. Friday

It was Six minutes after Mid-night. Looking at her watch, Annie, standing on the corner of St. Chads in Kings Cross, was thinking of giving up and going home. Turning on her heels, she saw the car slowly move towards her. She smiled and started to walk towards it, when suddenly another car appeared, seemingly from nowhere and cut in front of the first car. The intruder halted beside the startled Annie, in a scream of tyres. It was Reece.

"Annie, get in here. NOW, before I break your fucking neck," he thundered.

Annie's face went a deathly pale and looked like she was going to bolt. Reece immediately leaped out of the car and grabbed her by the hair. He forcefully bent her over the bonnet, violently twisting her arms behind her and snapped a pair of handcuffs on her wrists. The psychotic cop then shoved her onto the back seat of his car, and slammed the door. He turned and looked back at the car behind his and started to advance menacingly towards it. The car immediately reversed and speedily fled. "That's right. Run, rabbit, run." Reece chuckled nastily and got in his own car, picked up his truncheon and hit Annie in the stomach. She yelped but that was all she could do, she was so petrified. Reece sat down in the driving seat, put a CD in his stereo of the music soundtrack from Kubrick's movie 'A Clockwork Orange" He turned and looked back at Annie who lay crumpled and fetal on the back seat.

"You ever see 'A Clockwork Orange'?" he asked her. "It's one of my favourite movies. Made a big impression on me when I was a kid. Inspired me to become a cop, actually. Licensed thuggery, you see." He laughed and put his foot down hard on the accelerator, shooting off in the direction of Whitechapel.

Motoring along Pentonville Road, Reece continued to give Annie a lecture on his favourite film, while periodically battering her with his police baton. "You know why Kubrick banned his own movie? Because the police threatened him. Didn't like the way he portrayed their brutal natures. Warned him that if his film continued to give the police and the government a bad name, they wouldn't guarantee his safety, should his isolated house come under attack one night by a marauding gang of hoodlums with theft, rape and murder in mind. So he very wisely pulled the 'Clockwork Orange'."

As Reece took a right fork on to City Road, a car came racing up behind him but he didn't notice. Neither did he notice the same car still following him as he sped down Great Eastern Street, and on to Commercial Street. In fact, the car doggedly tailed the police sergeant as he hurtled along Old Montague Street and turned right into Regal Close, where he brought the car to a stop in the quiet cul de sac with no street lighting and empty derelict buildings.

Reece dragged the bruised and bleeding Annie out of the car and held her up, still handcuffed, by her hair, "You fucking whore. I'll teach you," he snarled, and began hitting her in the face, chest and stomach like she was a punchbag. "You thought you'd get away with setting me up. Thought it was all a fucking laugh, did you. You stupid fucking cunt. Know where we are? Whitechapel. That's right. Whitechapel...where your other little whore friends snuffed it. And if your body's found here, it'll look like the same sex killer's been at it again." Reece took out his truncheon and was about to ram it down Annie's throat, when someone swiftly stepped up behind him, and delivered a sharp rabbit chop to the back of his neck. Reece instantly dropped to the ground, unconscious. The understandable euphoric sense of relief and overflowing gratitude Annie felt at being rescued, was cut short when her face was smothered by a hand, holding a chloroform-soaked cloth. She, too, immediately passed out.

Three Thirty-Three in the morning. Once again, the empty warehouse and the darkened sparse office with its single bleak light bulb hanging from the ceiling, radiating the same dismal comfortless glimmer. In the middle of the room was the wicked police sergeant Reece, tied to an office swivel chair. His hands were handcuffed behind him. His own handcuffs. The first thing Reece saw, as he regained consciousness, was a tall man advancing purposefully towards him. The man was wearing a Halloween mask of "*Hannibal Lecter*", as portrayed by Anthony Hopkins.

"What the fuck is this bollocks?" jeered Reece. In answer, 'Hannibal' turned Sergeant Reece round to his right, so the cop could see the naked Annie, bound to an "X" cross. Reece groaned and shook uncontrollably when he perceived that her throat had been slashed, right round the neck, so deep, it almost severed the head. She had only just been killed. For the first time in his life, Reece experienced real mind-numbing, heart-stopping fear.

"Oh God," wailed Reece. "Jesus. God." He vomited copiously. 'Hannibal' quickly wrapped silver coloured industrial tape around Reece's mouth. The man behind the mask would countenance no interruptions while delivering his monologue.

"I am very annoyed with you, Sergeant Reece," began 'Hannibal'. "I was having everything beautifully organised. The timing, the locations, the victims who, incidentally, had to be in pristine condition, not a blemish, so that they could be offered up unto the Holy of Holies...but you, being the brute philistine that you are, had to ruin the Hexatron's need for perfection with your bullish testosterone-driven nastiness. I do not like my sacrificial lambs to be sullied and soiled by bruises and cuts and unwarranted swellings that were not within your gift to bestow. When I cut their throat...it must be kosher...halal...pure."

To reinforce the point, 'Hannibal' strode across to Annie's dead body and with a black gloved hand, held up her drooping head for Reece to see.

"The Cosmos will not be appeased by damaged goods," bellowed 'Hannibal'. "Look at these cuts, these bruises, ugly discolourings, such unseemly swellings. You hit her so hard, you nearly knocked her eye out. And her jaw is broken. And she's got teeth missing. Really, Sergeant Reece, this will not do. When the police find Anne, when the good Inspector Edmunds examines my handiwork, it will be thought she was killed by an animal, a drunken thug, they will think she is the victim of some tawdry pathetic domestic squabble. Happily, however, I was able to prevent you from completely ruining my work."

'Hannibal' quickly walked to the back of Reece and pulled out a revolver. "But in all seriousness, Sergeant Reece," the masked man continued. "I will never be able to forgive you." Pointing the gun to the back of the frantically struggling policeman's head, 'Hannibal' pulled the trigger. Reece was promptly killed. 'Hannibal' then picked up a black plastic bag, lying on the floor beside Reece, and swiftly pulled it over the shattered, bleeding head. The killer secured the bag on the expired policeman's head by wrapping sticky-tape around the neck.

Before turning his attention to Annie's body, strapped to the "X" cross, the killer first removed from his head, the 'Hannibal' mask. It was CK, who stepped up to Annie, and rotated the huge cross structure, which was pivoted in the centre of the cross beams, by 180 degrees, so that poor Annie was now upside down. The effect was that of an inverted five-pointed star, i.e. the "Black Arts" pentacle of Lucifer.

CK took a black ceremonial sword, kissed the scabbard before removing it and gently touched Annie, with the sword blade, in the sequence of five points; her two ankles, two wrists and her forehead. He then plunged the blade into her abdomen.

CHAPTER 19
The Black Madonna
17th August. Friday

It was 6 a.m. when he had gone to put out the rubbish. John Davis, the resident of 29 Hanbury Street, Whitechapel, had never seen anything like it in all his sixty-six years. And he devoutly hoped he would never have to see anything like it again as long as he lived. Why him, he kept asking himself? Why did it have to be in his own backyard? What had he done to deserve this? Why him, he kept asking the two police officers who were now questioning him at the crime scene? Would they believe him that he had nothing to do with this terrible business? All he had done was have the misfortune of discovering, early that Friday morning, the body lying on the ground,... in his backyard. Why in *his* backyard? Who had such a grudge against him that they would choose to dump a horribly mutilated murder victim on his property? No, he didn't know her. Never seen her before. A total stranger, he tells them. Then he asks again, why him? Why his property? Who could do such a ghastly thing to such a young lady? And why? And then he broke down and wept.

For the moment, the two 'Scene of Crime' officers had no answers. All they had was the naked body of a black woman, with her internal organs removed and placed on the ground, above her right and left shoulders. A police photographer was quickly taking photos of everything contained within the taped-off rectangle that enclosed the crime scene before the victim's body, her bowels and intestines were packed away in the waiting body bag.

Dr. Llewellyn Hawkey was one of the first to arrive, and was now reading aloud from his notebook to the grim-faced Edmunds. Standing at his side was Walters, looking most decidedly green at the gills. He was regretting the fried egg and bacon roll he had just hurriedly eaten on the way to the murder scene.

"The body of the deceased was found, lying on her back, by John Davis, here in his backyard..." recited the police doctor.

"What address is this?" interrupted Edmunds.

"29 Hanbury Street, Guv," Walters answered. "Do you think this is a Black Madonna Murder?"

"No, this MO isn't in the Yardies' style. Second, there's been a truce in their prostitution wars for the past six months. And third, the Black Madonna slayings have never been outside Brixton."

"There's always a first time, Guv."

Inspector Edmunds shook his head, turned back to the doctor, and told him to carry on.

Dr. Llewellyn Hawkey sniffed before continuing, "...The left arm was across her left breast, and her legs drawn up, feet resting on the ground, knees turned outwards. The face was swollen and turned on the right side... The small intestines and other portions were lying on the right side of the body on the ground above the right shoulder. A part of the stomach was above the left shoulder...There was very little blood, indicating she wouldn't have been killed where she was found. The body was cold, except that there was a certain remaining heat, under the intestines, in the body. Stiffness of the limbs is not marked, but commencing. The throat was dissevered deeply. I noticed that the incision of the skin was jagged, and extends right round the neck. I'll tell you more when I've done the autopsy."

Edmunds made a few notes on a slip of paper, and then told the doctor they will meet him at the London Hospital in an hour. "WPC Warren will be there to identify the corpse. Ten to one it's another prostitute from the Kings Cross area," continued Edmunds.

Dr. Llewellyn Hawkey nodded and left the two detectives.

"What about Reece? He should be able to tell us," said Walters.

"Where the hell is Reece? demanded Edmunds impatiently. "Didn't anyone call him?"

"Yes but he's not answering".

Edmunds walked over to the spot where the corpse had been found. Walters knelt down to examine what looked like a small blood stain on the concrete.

"Jim, this looks very bad," Edmunds said, shaking his head. "And I think its going to get worse. The third found in Whitechapel. In the space of how many days?"

"Ten," replied Walters, checking his notebook

"We have a serial killer," deduced Edmunds. "And a very, very nasty one. Never seen anything quite like it."

"Psychopathic sex killer?" conjectured his sergeant.

"Sex could be the driving force behind the killings but is he actually having sexual intercourse with the victims? The Doc can't tell, what with the victims being prostitutes, who will have had one or more sexual encounters with other clients before they were killed...and what with their genitalia having been mutilated. So far, there has been no traces of semen anywhere on or in their bodies." Edmunds always seemed to have a problem with articulating the word 'semen'. The word somehow left a bitter taste in his mouth. Wondering if there could be something Freudian in this, Edmunds shuddered at the very idea.

"The level of mutilation seems to be getting greater with every victim," observed Walters.

"I know," agreed Edmunds. "That's what's worrying. The killer looks like he is not content with what he has done before. He has become a serial killer because he is seeking something new with each kill. He has developed a need to kill. And he will kill again."

"When?"

"I don't know...but he will kill again... and again... and again... until we catch him... which we will... eventually. Because the more he kills the more he will betray his pattern... and there is a pattern... and with each kill, that pattern will become clearer and clearer. However, I would prefer to catch him before too many more women have to lose their lives just so that we can detect a bloody pattern." Edmunds said with distaste, and then indicating they should get a move on, he and Walters walked briskly to their car.

Police doctor and coroner, Llewellyn Hawkey was intrigued. Throughout his examination and autopsy of the Hanbury Street corpse which had been delivered to the morgue at the London Hospital in Whitechapel, he had a sense that this was no ordinary murder. He looked up at Edmunds and Walters, who were watching him with rapt attention, waiting for him to speak. They were hoping that his findings would confirm that there was a simple motive for the killing. He was going to have to disappoint them.

"The abdomen had been entirely laid open," Llewellyn Hawkey pointed out. "...the intestines, severed from their mesenteric attachments, lifted out of the body, and placed by the shoulder of the corpse... whilst from the pelvis the uterus and its appendages, with the upper portion of the vagina and the posterior two-thirds of the bladder, had been entirely removed."

"Have any of these parts been found?" asked Edmunds, turning to his side-kick.

"No, Guv. answered Walters.

Edmunds frowned, stared at the ceiling as if he was trying to do some mental arithmetic, gave an exasperated sigh and nodded at Dr. Llewellyn Hawkey to continue.

"The incisions were cleanly cut, avoiding the rectum," informed the doctor. "...and dividing the vagina low enough to avoid injury to the cervix uteri. Obviously, again, the work of an expert - someone who had such knowledge of anatomical or pathological examinations as to be able to secure the pelvic organs with one sweep of the knife."

"Is it the inference that the operation was performed by the perpetrator in order to obtain possession of these parts?" Edmunds asked.

"Yes, that's how it seems to me," affirmed Llewellyn Hawkey. "The body has not been dissected, but the injuries have been made by someone who had considerable anatomical skill and knowledge. There are no meaningless cuts. It was done by a person who knew where to find what he wanted, what difficulties he would have to contend against, and how he should use his knife, so as to abstract the organ without injury to it. No unskilled

The Ripper Code

person could have known where to find it, or have recognized it when it was found. I would say it was done by someone accustomed to the post-mortem room."

"A renegade doctor servicing a black market of illegal human organ transplants?" suggested Walters.

At that moment they were interrupted by the door banging open. Without a word of apology, Warren barged in and made straight for the autopsy table. She stared at the body. The mutilation was an abomination, a total negation of womanhood. It was at times like this she could really hate men. Men. Menace. Yes. Any more of this and she could tip into Radical Feminism.

"Well?" Edmunds asked impatiently.

Warren had to stop herself from screaming into his face, "You pig-ignorant male prick..." Instead, she replied, through clenched teeth, "Her name is Annie, sir. She usually does Argyle Square, south of Kings Cross."

"Annie who?"

"Annie Craig, sir," she said.

"Have you kept a log of her known and regular clients?"

"Yes sir."

"Right. As of today your undercover duties stop," decided Edmunds. "I'm not having you exposing yourself in that fashion in Kings Cross. Not with this lunatic killer at large."

"But sir, I'm in an excellent position to entrap him," argued Warren.

"Absolutely not, Eloise, I'm not serving you up as bait."

"I can't see how else we are going to catch him, sir."

"Through good solid police detective work, WDC Warren, that's how. We are not living in some flash TV fantasy cop series. Now, get back to base and start collating details of the regulars of all three prostitutes."

"Yes sir," obeyed Warren reluctantly.

"And Ellie, I mean what I say," Edmunds said in a much softer tone. "I don't want to see your guts and intestines decorating some grubby little back street in Whitechapel."

"No sir," sighed Warren, as she stormed angrily out of the autopsy room.

CHAPTER 20
"Dear Bob....."
17th August. Friday

Even though he didn't manage to get laid that night, Max was still feeling pleased with his blackmailing stunt the next morning, as he drove up Camden High Street, on his way to work. The look on Reece's face when he saw the photographs last night, was absolutely priceless, Max chuckled to himself. "I can go - curb-crawling now - to my heart's content," he sang out loud to the melody of "Rock and Roll is here to stay, it can never die," as the *Sha-Na-Na* hit was being played on the car radio. Max's mood changed suddenly when he heard the smarmy voice of the Radio One Deejay cut in with, "Did you see Big Brother last night?"

"Will you shut the fuck up about Big Brother," shouted Max at the radio. "It's not even on bloody BBC, so why are you talking about it, you moron!"

"...I mean, did you see those underpants he was wearing? I mean, those alone are reason to be voted out the house..." continued the Radio One Deejay, sadly oblivious of Max's vitriolic tirade.

"Will you shut up, you arsehole," harangued Max. "I don't want to hear about boring bollocks like Big Smother. You're supposed to be a pop music station...Play some fucking music. Less of the fucking inane chat. God, you Radio-One wankers are so mindless with your 'Hello' magazine banality..." The disgusted Max was about to switch off the radio, when a jingle announced the half-hourly radio news summary

"It's 8.30 and here are the News Headlines," introduced the radio news presenter. "Another woman has been found murdered in Whitechapel early this morning. This is the third Whitechapel killing in ten days..."

"Oh Jesus...no," Max groaned. "Not another." Utterly distraught at the news, his face blanched white, Max had difficulties breathing, and thought he was going to faint.

At the Job Centre, Max hurriedly wheeled passed Claire at her Reception desk.

"Morning, Max. A woman rang for you about five minutes ago," she shouted out after him.

"Oh?" Max halted in his tracks. "She leave a name or message?"

"Just a number for you to ring back," Claire replied, handing him a piece of paper with the phone number scribbled on.

"Thanks," mumbled Max, squinting at the note, wondering again if his eyesight was failing.

"A 'Good Morning, Claire' would be nice," Claire said, somewhat sniffily.

"Good morning, Claire." Max moved to his desk, with Claire following him, which at this particular moment he found slightly irritating.

"Breakfast News on TV said there was another one," she told him. "Whitechapel again."

"I heard. That's why my head is somewhere else."

"Do you think there's a pattern emerging?"

"Yeah I do. But I don't want to say at the moment. I first need to know where this morning's body was found." Max switched on his desktop computer.

"Whitechapel," Claire reminded him.

"Yeah I know that, but what street? I think I can guess and if I'm right, then I think... I know the pattern... which will suggest there are more murders to come, possibly three, before its all over."

"Oh Max, don't say that," Claire said, looking genuinely concerned. Just then, the telephone rang on Max's desk, making them both jump. He snatched up the phone

"Yeah...hold on a second..." Max put his hand over mouthpiece and turned to Claire.

"If you're not doing anything this evening, come over and we'll go over my theory," he whispered. Claire nodded and wheeled back to her Receptionist Station. Max returned to his telephone call.

"Listen. Let's meet for lunch. I can't talk about it here. Regent's Zoo. Outside the Wolf enclosure. 1pm. Okay. Keep calm. Don't worry. I'll be there." Max wanted to sound confidently comforting but he wasn't convinced he had much to offer the caller.

Edmunds surveyed the hundred or so police officers that had gathered in the Incident Room for debriefing and allocation of investigation duties. He was in a foul mood but he was glad to see that Warren had obeyed his orders and was sitting in the front row in her regular police outfit.

"When I say I want all Vice Squad to be present, I mean all Vice Squad. Where the hell is Sergeant Reece?" thundered Edmunds. He was glaring particularly at Walters, who shrugged, knowing he can't be expected to be in two places at once. Either he is here assisting his Chief with the conference paraphernalia of flip-charts and maps, or he is out shepherding Reece back into the fold.

Walters attention is drawn to a policewoman who had just entered the room. She seemed to be signalling for him to come over.

"This had better be good," he whispered fiercely, sideling up to her.

"Sir, I've just had an urgent message from His Lordship's secretary. An email has just arrived in his inbox... he must see," she hissed back.

"Lets hope for your sake its not spam."

Walters quickly went to his boss, who was seething with impatience, and gave him the message. Edmunds cursed and tutted with annoyance, and then turned to address the room full of officers, still silently sitting in rapt anticipation.

"Don't go away," he commanded. "And don't be using my temporary absence as an excuse for gossip and idle chit-chat. When I get back, I want your constructive thoughts and some worthy proposals." With that, Inspector Robert Edmunds, with Sergeant James Walters in tow, marched out and down the lengthy corridor to his office, where he read the email that had so disturbed his secretary.

"'*Dear Bob....*' How does he know my name?" Edmunds demanded of Walters, who was also reading the email off the computer screen. "And how did he get this email address?" he added, and then continued to read out loud, "'*...I hate whores and I shall not quit ripping them until I get caught. Great work my last handiwork. I didn't give the whore time to squeal. Expect in the post a trophy of my endeavours...perhaps a portion of bladder or vagina. Catch me if you can. I love my work and shall start again soon...very soon. You will soon hear of me and my funny little games... The next job I do I shall slice the whore's ears off and send to you just for merriment sake...Keep this email back till I do a bit more work, then give it out straight. My knife's so nice and sharp. I want to get to work right away if I get a chance. Good luck. Yours truly, Tau Tria Delta*'". Edmunds, severely shaken, turned and stared perplexed at Walters, "Jesus, the sicko is going to send me her bits. As soon as any packages arrive, don't open them, send them straight to forensics. And I mean all packages."

"Tau Tria Delta? What kind of a name is that?" questioned Walters.

"Its Greek or something...but get a language expert on to it. It's probably a red herring. The arsehole just wants us to think he's educated." Edmunds replied dismissively.

Suddenly the air was sliced by the shrill trilling of the telephone. Walters picked it up, listened, and his face immediately seemed to drain of blood.

"Bloody Nora. Where?" exclaimed Walters, clearly shocked at what he was hearing.

He turned to Edmunds and said quietly, "Guv. It's Reece."

"About bloody time. Pass him over. I want a word with him." Edmunds reached for the telephone. Walters shook his head, "He's been found dead, sir. Shot in the back of the head. Looks like an execution, paramilitary style. Apparently got the hallmarks of the Islamic Revolutionary Avengers."

"What?" bellowed Edmunds. "That's absurd? What the bloody hell is Reece doing messing with terrorists. That's not his jurisdiction."

"Could be gangland reprisal hit," suggested Walters. "I don't know what he was up to half the time. Maybe they thought he knew something of our Red Canary Project?

"Well if that's the case, it's a good job we deliberately kept him quarantined from that baby."

"I know, Guv. You were never convinced Reece could be trusted with knowledge of our best yet witness against Sinclair."

"I still think we should put her in protective custody. With two months before the trial and this lunatic serial killer at large and now Reece topped, can we be sure she won't bottle out or disappear?" bemoaned Edmunds. He hated police work that depended on informers for results.

"It's a tricky one, Guv."

"Anyway, right now, lets try and shed some light on this Reece murder. Get hold of Commander Chambers at the anti-terrorist squad and chief inspector Moore in Special Branch. Find out if they know something about Reece we don't," growled the Inspector, suddenly feeling very tired.

CHAPTER 21
Zed and Two Naughts
17th August. Friday

He couldn't remember the last time he had visited the zoo at Regent's Park. It was at least six months ago, he was certain. But, here he was, in his favourite spot, sitting in his wheelchair, opposite the Wolf enclosure, next to a park bench, eating his sandwiches. Max was mad about wolves. Since early childhood, he had wished he could have one for a pet, or rather, a companion. Wolves are far too independent and noble to be anyone's pet. Was it the haunting eerie quality of their moonlight howling? Or was it that these most unjustly maligned creatures, with their amber-gold all-seeing eyes, are such exemplary teachers for humanity in the arts of group cohesion, communal cooperation and loyal domesticity.

There was one wolf in particular who always came to greet Max, whenever he came for a visit. He gave her the name of Luna and as usual, she was sitting there on her haunches, behind the bars, gazing expectantly at him, anticipating a share of his lunch. However, on this occasion, before Max could throw her a small titbit, a sudden sound sent the she-wolf scurrying to the far end of the enclosure. He turned and saw that Sophie had arrived, wearing dark glasses and a long coat. It's a fact that wolves are very nervous of people wearing dark glasses. It is very important for them to be able to see the eyes.

Sophie sat down on the park bench along side him. There was silence as they both stared ahead, not daring to face each other. Finally, Max twisted in his chair and looked at her, and saw tears slowly sliding down her face.

"What is it?" he asked, taking her hand.

"Annie. It was her they found this morning," she said, quickly looking away.

"Oh God," choked Max. "Oh fuck. Oh poor Anne. Oh shit, I killed her."

"What? Don't be stupid," snapped Sophie.

"I did. It's my fault. To get Greasy Reecy off my back, I showed him the photos. Jesus, I never imagined he'd react like that. Oh God, if only I'd known."

"Max, it had nothing to do with you. Yes, Reece is a vicious bastard but he's a cop, he's not going to do something so stupid as murder Anne for that. It wasn't him."

"Why couldn't it be him?" argued Max. "He has the perfect set up. With two murders in Whitechapel already, Annie's death will just be seen as another serial killing of prostitutes. No one would suspect him. He killed Annie out of revenge, for compromising him, jeopardizing his future, dumps her body in Whitechapel and the sex killer gets the blame."

"Max, you're wrong. I know who killed Annie...and Polly ... and Martha."

"You do?" Max was astounded. "Who? Have you gone to the police?"

Sophie shivered and looked around fearfully.

"Well...I...don't exactly know who," she whispered. "I mean, I don't know his identity. I couldn't point him out in an identity parade... but I know why my colleagues have been murdered. At least, I think I do. But I'm pretty sure I know who is behind it. Oh God, I'm so scared. I don't know the monster who is doing the actual killing but I know the monster who's responsible. And I don't know what to do? I can't go to the police because I can't prove anything. But I feel it in my guts. Like a knife ripping me apart. I know I'm going to be next. None of us girls are safe. He won't be satisfied until we are all dead...and the police will never imagine it was all his idea."

Max grabbed Sophie by the shoulders and shook her.

"Sophie, you're not making sense. You say you know who killed your friends..."

"They're not my friends," she strenuously countered and abruptly stood up and walked away. Then, just as suddenly, she returned and sat back down. "OK. Annie was my friend," she conceded. "Oh god, Annie, I'm so sorry. But Polly and Martha? No way....but I wouldn't wish them dead, not like that. How could anyone do things like that. But what am I saying? I know why he did those horrible things. It was all deliberate. He did it not because he's a nutter, a raving lunatic. No. he mutilated...he dismembered...he..." Sophie broke down. At first he didn't know what he should do but finally, Max took her in his arms and she began to sob into his shoulders. Someone walked by, and stared at them both. Sophie pulled away and attempted to calm herself...but she held onto Max's hands.

"Is there a way we can start at the beginning?" he tried to ask calmly. "I don't understand how you can possibly know why the girls are being murdered and in this gruesome fashion."

"I don't really know anything. I don't have the evidence. But I know the story that's going around us Kings Cross girls. I don't know if you realise but we're not freelance. None of us are. Kings Cross, Camden, Holloway...nearly all of north west London... is totally owned by one man. He controls all the rackets, gambling, bouncers, protection, the meat market..."

"Meat market?"

"That's us girls... and rent boys, of course. He runs the drug trafficking, he creams off the top of all crimmy capers..."

"Crimmy capers?" queried Max, somewhat bewildered.

"You know, criminal business, robberies, heists, burglaries, thefts, muggings...nothing happens on his patch without his say so and without his cut. You know, he even runs the beggars."

"But what has your Mister Big got to do with the Whitechapel Murders?"

Sophie stiffened and again glanced nervously about her. She looked back at Max and tried to smile but couldn't. Instead she looked like she was going to vomit.

"Can we move on from here?" she demanded, suddenly standing up and grabbing the push-bars of his wheelchair. "Lets talk somewhere else."

"The Big Cat House," suggested Max. "Its usually so smelly, I don't think anyone will bother us there."

As he expected, they were all alone in the Big Cats house. A black panther in one cage paced restlessly up and down, as did as the two tigers. In the third cage, however, the lions were being typical lions, in that they were lazily lounging about and constantly yawning.

Sophie wrinkled her nose in distaste. "Jesus, you're right. It stinks," she gagged.

Yes, the stench was awesome but Max loved it, because it was intrinsic to the thrill and humility he felt whenever he was in such close proximity to these powerful and beautifully wild untameable beasts.

"So this Mister Big...the Godfather of Camden, the King of Kings Cross..." began Max, in a seemingly jocular manner.

"He's no laughing matter, Max. If he was running a country, Saddam Hussein would seem a pussy cat compared to him. I had no idea what I was getting myself into when I first started this line of work. And now its getting so dangerous, I just want out..." Sophie fell silent and stared at the black panther.

"You know Emma?" Sophie suddenly asked Max.

"Yes."

"You had her?"

"Yes," admitted Max.

"She's an undercover cop," whispered Sophie, looking at Max to see how he would react to this revelation.

"I know."

"You knew?" she exclaimed, sounding slightly disappointed. "What was it like fucking a cop?"

"I didn't know at the time," he replied. "She was better than most...but not as good as you," he quickly added.

"She probably took your semen to add to the national Police DNA database."

"Is that what she was doing, getting sperm prints of all us dodgy sex fiends?"

"Why are we joking at this time?" sadly asked Sophie. She returned to gazing at the now supine big black feline. Max watched fascinated, as she began making stroking motions with her hand as if she was actually in the cage with the panther. Suddenly Sophie caught herself doing it. She stopped and smiled sheepishly at Max, and then said in a serious tone, "No, she was gathering intelligence on Sin-Clare, to put him behind bars for good. She was trying to infiltrate his organisation."

"Sin Clare?" interjected Max.

"His real name is August Sinclare, but he likes to put a hyphen between Sin and Clare...for obvious reasons."

"She can't be a very good undercover cop if you knew." objected Max.

"I didn't know until she told me," Sophie explained. "She needed an accomplice on the inside, who would cover for her, provide alibis, a back story where I was an old friend of hers who had suggested she take up the oldest profession."

"But how did Emma know she could trust you?" questioned Max.

"You'd make a great cop if you weren't disabled," teased Sophie. "She thought she could trust me because I was relatively new to Sin-Clare's set up. I wasn't yet in as deep as the others.

The pair moved on to the Monkey House. They continued talking amidst the screaming chatter of chimpanzees. Sophie wasn't too keen on the apes, they reminded her of too many of her clients. She turned her back on them, especially one particularly annoying chimp, who kept wanting to show off his bottom to her; and looked straight at Max as she presented her theory.

"I don't think these deaths are the work of serial sex killer," she proposed. "I think these horrible killings and mutilations are camouflage. It's a set-up to make the police think its a mad man."

"But it is a mad man," Max responded. "No sane person would do to Polly and Martha and Anne..."

"But it's not a random looney doing it. It's a professional killer hired by the Super Boss, Sin-Clare. I think there's a contract out on a particular prostitute who is due to appear in court... as a police witness, testifying against him."

"How do you know this?"

"Emma told me," she flatly replied.

"She told you there was a contract out on this informer?" probed Max.

"No," said Sophie. "Just that there was a woman grassing on Sin-Clare and prepared to give evidence for the Crown. The contract killer is my theory. I thought of this today when I heard that poor Annie was murdered."

"So, you believe Sin-Clare wants the informer dead but is trying to disguise from the police the real motive behind her killing?"

"Yes, with the deliberate murders of other seemingly unconnected prostitutes...." began Sophie

"...before he carries out the hit of the intended target," interjected Max. "And then, when the trial witness is killed in a similar grotesque fashion, the police won't connect it to their investigation of Super-Boss, Sin-Clare. So all this serial sex killer activity is aimed to make a monkey out of the police." Max had caught Sophie's drift very quickly. Her suggestion made complete sense to a Conspiracy Freak like Max.

"He's killed three women so far. Do you think he's content with that and will now kill the informer?" asked Sophie.

"No. He can't stop at four, if he wants to convince the police it's an unrelated serial killer running amok. The textbooks define a serial killer as someone who has killed a minimum of five people in a time separated sequence."

"Oh dear God, so there's going to be at least another two women murdered," groaned Sophie, very upset and shaking.

"Afraid so, if what you're saying is true," replied Max, taking her hand, wanting desperately to comfort her. "And I think you're right," he continued. "I already suspected there's a pattern in the killings. This business of dumping the Kings Cross women in Whitechapel. Why would he do that unless he wants the police to think along certain lines."

"What does he want them to think?"

Max paused before answering. He knew what he was going to say may seem mad, but he was convinced of it. He beckoned to Sophie to bend towards him, so he could speak quietly into her ear, "The contract killer wants them to think he kills because he has a fanatic obsession with past cases of serial killers...that he admires them...that he wants to emulate them...If my guess is right as to where Annie's body was found, then I think her killer wants the police to think he is a stark raving nut who kills because he is a fan of the Whitechapel Murderer."

"You mean Jack the Ripper?" gasped Sophie, looking at Max in horror. At that moment, the conversation was prevented from continuing by the sudden deafening screams of chimpanzees, as if they were terrified of the very mention of Jack the Ripper. Max gave a grim smile at the weird timing. "Let's go," he said. They left the zoo and headed east down Pentonville Road. Max was driving as fast as he could.

"Where are we going?" Sophie asked.

"Whitechapel," replied Max. "I've still got about forty-five minutes left of my lunch break. Because I think I know where Anne's body was dumped, we're going to drive straight there. If I'm right, we'll find the street cordoned off and "crime scene" banners everywhere."

CHAPTER 22
The Shape of Things to Come
17th August. Friday

Unusually, Max was able to reach Whitechapel in less than 30 minutes. The lunchtime City traffic was unnaturally sparse. And as anticipated, he had to stop the car at the junction leading into Hanbury Street, being prevented from going any further by the "crime scene" taped barriers.

"Hanbury Street," he said bleakly. "As I thought. It's Jack the Ripper all over again." Sophie shuddered at these words. Yet, at the same time, she was impressed with the uncanny accuracy of Max's prediction.

A policeman on guard duty appeared around the corner and seeing them, walked towards their car. He ordered them to clear off. Max was just about to argue with him, when another car arrived, and out stepped Walters and Warren.

"Oh look, there's Emma," exclaimed Sophie

"And Walters," groaned Max. "I think we'd better scarper." But it was too late. The policeman had already pointed Max's car out to Walters, who, on recognising Max, immediately walked quickly over, accompanied by Warren. Max tried to put his car into forward gear and hoping to speedily drive away, but Warren ran to stand in front of his car.

"Abberline! Stay right there," shouted Walters.

"Oh, fuck it!" Max softly cursed.

"What's wrong?" asked Sophie, surprised. "Don't you want to tell the police your theory?"

"They'll just take the piss."

"Max, what the devil are you doing here?" demanded Walters, leaning into Max's window.

"We both knew Annie," Max replied.

"Oh indeed. Oh yeah, of course, you'd know all the street girls, wouldn't you?" the detective smirked.

"Hello Maeve," greeted Warren, leaning into Sophie's side of the car.

"Hello Emma," Sophie smiled back. "Finished moonlighting, have you? Back doing your proper job?"

"As opposed to an improper job, you mean?" quipped Warren.

"I don't have a problem with it," Sophie said resolutely. "A girl's got make a living."

Walters laughed with bitterness, "Doesn't look like Annie and the others were making a living. Seems like they were doing a lot of dying." He turned to Max, "How did you know Annie's body was found here?" questioned Walters "We haven't released that information to the press yet."

"I worked it out," Max calmly responded. "Because I found a pattern in where the murderer is leaving his victims."

"Another of your crackpot theories?" Walters sneered.

"You asked me how I knew and I'm telling you."

"Alright. Tell me."

"The killer is copying Jack the Ripper," Max said with a flourish.

"So he's going to kill two more women to make up the Ripper's five?" asked Walters with deep scepticism.

"No. Jack the Ripper killed six women, not five," corrected Max. "Most Ripperologists have got it wrong. They shouldn't discount Martha as Ripper's first victim."

Sophie who was getting more and more agitated, suddenly lost her temper and screamed at them both.

"Can you have this conversation somewhere else, please," she cried. "You're talking about people I knew." She burst into tears, which made Walters feel awkward. Warren tried to comfort her by softly stroking Sophie's shoulder, but she turned impatiently to Max, "Get me out of here. Now," she ordered, tears streaming down her face.

"Yeah, you're right," agreed Max, feeling abashed. "I should be back at work now, anyway. Where shall I drop you off?"

" Anywhere. I don't care. Just away from here." she hissed.

As Max drove away from the police officers, Walters shouted after him, "Max, find a time this week to continue this conversation back at the station." Max flashed his hazard lights to let Walters know he heard.

He was half an hour late, but he didn't care. Max always thought of himself as his own boss, no matter who was his employer. And they forgive him because he was normally a hard, reliable worker. Right now, however, he was feeling impatient. He really didn't want to be interviewing this woman in front of him, with her three young children mewling and crawling all over her, clinging at her skirts. He was eager to be at his investigations, and wanted the workday to be over.

"That's all in order, Mrs. Tumblety. If you could just sign here," Max said hurriedly, looking sadly at the vastly overweight woman, the latest victim of the American Disease crossing the Atlantic, spending all day watching junk TV, eating junk food, and using her car for everything, never walking anywhere. Mrs Tumblety signed and with a lot of huffing and puffing, waddled out of the Job Centre. One day, because of the highly contagious American Disease and it's virus of rampant consumerism, everyone will be so obese and indolent, their legs will fail to carry them and they will all be needing electric wheelchairs to get around. Then I shall be King of the Crips, Max mockingly thought as he closed her file. Seeing that there were no more Job Seekers immediately seeking his attention, Max opened his "WHITECHAPEL MURDERS - THE SEQUEL" folder, and clicked on the Whitechapel street map file. He typed "*Annie found at Hanbury Street, Whitechapel*" and placed another "skull and cross-bones" icon over Hanbury Street on the map on the screen. He then saved the changes and removed the disk from the floppy drive, putting it into his brief-case, and returned the computer's function to the proper Job Centre business. Well, at least I'm not one of those employees secretly using the computer to look at Internet porn during office hours, thought Max in a feeble attempt at self-righteous justification. He turned and saw that there was now a queue of six claimants. Jesus Christ, just turn your back for five minutes, and bumph! Oh well, no peace for the wicked.

"Who's next?" Max asked wearily.

At last, the day was done and Max shut down his work station, stuffed documents and folders into his brief-case, and hurriedly headed for the exit, waving and winking as he whizzed past the other staff, "Good night, everyone," he shouted, and at the Reception desk, "Goodnight Claire," he whispered, blowing her a kiss.

"Max?" Claire cried out, startled.

"What?" Max said, stopping abruptly in his tracks and turning impatiently towards her.

"Is it off?" she asked, looking slightly panic-stricken.

"What? Oh. Right. Of course. No. No. It's still on," Max reassured her, trying to cover up the fact that he had completely forgotten, "If you're still up for it, seven thirty?" he quickly added. Claire smiled and nodded. "Want me to bring anything?"

"No. Just yourself," Max replied, looking directly into her eyes, with an open-hearted softness that put a blush to her face and sent her pulse racing.

CHAPTER 23
Cacophony of Emotions
17th August. Friday

She thought he had cooked a lovely meal. In fact, she was rather surprised. This was the last thing she had imagined Max to be capable of. But, it was all very cordon bleu...and dare she think it? Romantic. The candle-lit dinner, the soft music. She really didn't think Max had it in him. Mind you, if he was trying to woo her, his patter was hardly Don Juan or Casanova. There, she thought, he was a bit of a disappointment. Throughout the evening, thus far, he seemed reticent and tongue-tied. Which for him, she thought, was rather out of character.

Max looked up at Claire again. Oh God, he thought, she really has "dolled herself up". I hope I haven't gone too far and given her the wrong idea. They were still sitting across each other at the dinner table. Claire, gazing open-faced at him, was trying to convey her deep longing for him. Max tried to match her glances but felt awkward, and kept looking down. He wasn't very good at this game, if indeed it was a game. Was it? Finally he made a decision and pushed himself away from the table.

"Shall we withdraw to the computer room?" he said in a pseudo upper-class accent. He smiled as he pointed in the direction of the sitting room, which in moments of Sci-Fi. surrealism he liked to label 'The Computer Room'.

"Yes, lets," replied Claire. "Did you like the wine I brought you?"

"You're a naughty girl. Yes, I did. It was lovely, thank you."

"I didn't want to come empty-handed, you might think I was common." Claire followed him into the sitting-room but gave a furtive glance in the direction of the bedroom door.

"Oh? I thought you just wanted to get me drunk... so you could have your wicked way with me," Max joked light-heartedly, positioning himself in front of a desk-top computer and switching it on.

"I think you could teach me a thing or two about 'wicked ways'," Claire teased, seeking to match his banter, as she manoeuvred her wheelchair alongside his. Max quickly gave her a sidelong glance. What does the sly little minx know, he wondered?

The computer whirred and bleeped as the screen unrolled an image of an old map of Whitechapel circa 1888, with flashing icons showing the six murder sites of Jack the Ripper, naming the streets, and labelled with each of the victims' names.

"So you can see," Max said, pointing at the screen, "when I realised the names of the recent prostitutes killed and where they had been dumped exactly matched the sequence of names and locations of the original 1888 Ripper murders, I knew we are experiencing a 'work in progress' of a Jack the Ripper copycat serial killer."

"The first Ripper victim was called Martha?" queried Claire.

"Martha Tabram," elaborated Max. "And the prostitute killed ten days ago was called Martha. Both were found in George Yard, Whitechapel."

"And the second was called Polly?"

"Two Pretty Pollys murdered," said Max. "Polly Nichols in 1888 and poor Polly four days ago, found dead in Bucks Row, the same place as the Ripper Polly. Same name, same location. And now, today, the third victim, Annie, whose namesake, Annie Chapman, was also third. I told you, I suspected a pattern and this lunchtime I checked out my theory, based on what seemed like two coincidences. I expected Annie's body to be dumped in the same street as her predecessor. And it was. Hanbury Street."

"Wow. That's weird. So, there will be more murders of prostitutes with names identical to the Ripper victims," Claire exclaimed.

"Only as far as their first names...I think."

"And you think they will also be dumped in identical streets in Whitechapel?" questioned Claire excitedly. She couldn't believe she was getting intimate with a real-life murder mystery. She had always been an avid reader of detective novels by Agatha Christie, Ruth Rendell and P. D. James.

"Or as near as dammit. Its more than 100 years since the Ripper struck. Some street names will have changed."

"But you think today's killer will try to dump the bodies as close to the original as possible?" Claire started to wheel up and down the room, mimicking those television detectives pacing up and down, lost in deductive ponderings.

"I'm sure of it," answered Max. "As you can see from the map, the names of the girls will be Elizabeth; she'll be found in Dutfields Yard in Berner Street; Kate will be found in Mitre Square and the last victim will be Mary; found horribly mutilated in Miller's Court, Dorset Street."

"Are they all going to be King's Cross prostitutes?" Claire went back to the computer to study the map's diagram.

"If my theory is correct."

"But there might not be prostitutes with these names operating in Kings Cross."

Max opened the prostitute's file and displayed the list of names, "Well, I know there's a woman called Kate...and there's a Lisa, which, of course, is short for Elizabeth."

"How do you know these names?" Claire asked, giving Max a severe look.

"Because I'm Sherlock Holmes in a Wheelchair, ain't I?" replied Max, winking at her cheekily. "I've done me investigations, ain't I?"

"What about Mary?"

"I haven't come across a Mary," frowned Max.

"I see the full name of Ripper's sixth victim was Mary Jane Kelly. Maybe the King Cross Ripper will select a prostitute called Jane?" Claire conjectured.

"Or Kelly. Kelly can also be a first name," Max pointed out.

"Have you in your... research...come across a Kelly?"

"No. Or a Jane. I've met a Sophie, an Alice, a Fran, a Rosie but no Kelly or..."

"You've met all these prostitutes?" interrupted Claire, clearly shocked.

"Er. Yes," Max stuttered sheepishly.

"You have been busy," she replied caustically.

Max gave a weak smile, but quickly continued, "There's another coincidence, which I don't think is a coincidence. Our Martha...."

"Our Martha?"

"The Kings Cross Martha was killed on exactly the same date, 7th August, as the 1888 Martha of Whitechapel. In fact, the same day of the week, Tuesday."

"That's creepy," Claire shuddered, staring hard at the dates displayed on the screen.

"If that's not deliberate, I don't what is." Max said with conviction.

"What about Polly and Annie?"

"No. Different dates. Look."

Max pointed to the displayed chronological tables, which showed '*Present; POLLY - 13th August –Monday*' and '*POLLY NICHOLS - 31st August 1888*'

"See. Our Polly, 13th August. 1888 Polly, 31st August." He reads out loud.

Max then pointed again at the screen showing '*Present; ANNIE - 17th August Friday*' and '*ANNIE CHAPMAN - 8th September 1888*'

"Annie Chapman in 1888 was murdered on 8th September and today is 17th August, when Anne..." Max paused to take a deep breath, he needed to suppress a surge of emotion. Poor Annie...he closed his eyes and counted to five. When he had recovered, he continued to speak, and point, with the curser, the pertinent dates of Ripper murders on the screen, "As you can see, the six Ripper murders took place over a two month period. Whereas, we've already had three murders in ten days. I think the killer is in a hurry, so he won't be sticking to the Ripper time-table. Perhaps within the next ten days, he will kill the remaining three."

"You think he's working to a deadline?" Claire asked, surprised.

"Today, I had information that he might be."

"That was your lunch date?" Claire tried desperately to remove the hint of sarcasm from her voice. She was worried she was beginning to sound like a jealous harpy.

"Yes."

"Is she beautiful?"

"Probably," Max said, evasively, trying to sound indifferent.

"Probably?" she replied scornfully. "What kind of an answer is that?"

Max was beginning to get irritated by Claire's scolding tone. She didn't own him, and he didn't owe her anything.

"Let's not get distracted," he said abruptly. "What is vital right now, if my theory is correct, is finding Lisa and Kate, and trying to persuade them to disappear for the next two or more weeks."

"Are you going to throw me out now? I suppose you can't wait to go out and search for your prostitutes," Claire said harshly, and then immediately regretted her tone.

"It could be a matter of life and death." Max quietly insisted.

There followed an awkward silence between them, as they both looked down, avoiding each other's eyes. Finally, Claire moved closer, her arm reached out towards his shoulder.

"Would you hate me if I asked if I could kiss you?" Her finger lightly touched his cheek. Max smiled at her.

"No, I wouldn't hate you," he said reassuringly. "I could never hate you. But I don't think it would be a good idea."

Claire pulled away from him, "Jesus, now I feel humiliated."

"No, please, don't feel humiliated," Max said apologetically. "It's got nothing to do with you. I think you're lovely. But..."

"But what? Are you Gay? Girls just don't turn you on?" attacked Claire bitterly. She knew she was probably behaving unreasonably but her pride was hurt and she felt scorned.

"Gay?" laughed Max "No way. I'm crazy about women."

Another brittle moment of silence, which Claire again broke, "Is it because I'm disabled?" she demanded. "You are only turned by women with perfect bodies? Even though, you're not exactly perfect yourself."

"Claire, now you are demeaning yourself, talking like this," Max snapped back. "It's got nothing to do with you being disabled. I told you, I think you're lovely...and I wish but I can't...because I'm really fucked up. I'm not a nice person. If you knew the truth, you wouldn't want to kiss me. I lead a very double life. When I finish work, I become a dark rat, covered in slime, wallowing in the sewers of London. I'm petrified of a proper relationship. I have never had one.. and I'm incapable of giving genuine love."

"I don't believe you."

"It's true. I'm frightened of feelings. If we had a relationship, it wouldn't take you long to hate me...because I would only want to use your body. I wouldn't give you love. I would just want to fuck you endlessly because I have a pathological addiction to sex. I would just make you my fuck-slave." Max snarled viciously, even though he knew there were no real feelings of enmity towards her. All he knew was that a chilling darkness had somehow entered the room and he had a weird sensation of being possessed by it. Words seemed to be tumbling involuntarily out of him.

"Max, why are you talking like this?" wailed Claire. "Are you trying to scare me away?" She began to sob.

"I am a degenerate," Max tried to explain. "I have been corrupted. I cannot have a relationship with a woman unless I pay for it. I must have control in a relationship because I fear the chaos of emotions...and paying for sex gives me that control. I can avoid feeling."

"Max, please stop," begged Claire in between sobs.

"This is what I do every night. Go to prostitutes. It's the safest sex I know." Max said as he punched the keys on the computer. The screen filled with the names of the prostitutes he had known...including their Magic Numbers.

"I don't want a relationship with a woman who wants to love me," continued Max. "There's a cold-eyed vulture inside me, ripping my heart apart." He moved the cursor and dragged an image of Roslyn D'Onston and puts it in a box labelled 'Jack the

Ripper'. Another box immediately opened and spewed out a flood of sixes, that collected into groups of three...so the screen quickly filled with lots of 666...Then, another box opened and out flowed a river of symbols from Freemasonry, Knights Templars, Rosicrucianism, such as the Eye in the Triangle, pyramids, Skull and Cross-bones, Compass and Set-Square, Rosy Crosses, the Kabbalah Tree of Knowledge, Pentacles, Winged Orbs and Winged Egg-timers. And then, a third box, labelled 'Black Magicians', exploded and released images of Aleister Crowley, Hitler, Himmler and various politicians of the past three decades such as Thatcher, Reagan, the Twin Bushes and Blair. While the computer graphics danced demonically, and out of the speakers came harsh discordant electronic distortions of Wagnerian music, Max finished by saying, "The problem is, with me only ever having sex with prostitutes, well... I'm afraid it's making me cynical about women, and their capacity to give a man genuine love."

"Then I think it's time you stopped because you're getting a gross distortion. Give us women a chance, will you?" said Claire, softly touching Max's hand. He glanced up at her and thought how gorgeous she looked. Now he wanted to kiss her.

"Well. I'd better go," she continued, putting on her coat. "And you'd better go to Kings Cross and try find the girls."

"...Kate...Lisa. And Kelly, whoever she may be," reiterated Max.

"Yes, find them before the killer does," encouraged Claire. And she was gone, out into the night. Max had the feeling of a whirlwind leaving behind a vacuum.

CHAPTER 24
Bad Timing
17th August. Friday

Max was panic-stricken in more ways than one, as he prowled the "Red Light" streets of Kings Cross, driving very slowly, peering into every dark corner, shadowed doorway.

First, he was really frightened for the prostitutes. He felt extremely protective towards them, good and bad, even those who flagrantly tried to rip him off. For years, he couldn't help but regard these wayward girls as the only friends he had.

And second, he felt panicked, in turmoil over what had just transpired between him and Claire. This cute doe-eyed girl in a wheelchair was beginning to dig her claws into him. If he ended up rejecting her or even having a relationship with her, he was worried he will have to give up working at the Job Centre, if she was going to continue being there. It probably isn't a good idea to be romantically involved with someone in the same office. As it is often said, one should never mix business with pleasure...unless, of course, the pleasure is business, like paying for prostitutes.

Anyway, maybe Max was jumping the gun. Perhaps he was mis-reading Claire. Perchance he was blowing her feelings for him out of all proportions. He had a terrible habit of doing this sort of thing. The fact was, he was useless at reading women's minds or their intentions. Likely as not, Claire and his relationship won't change and will continue to maintain its banal platonic level.

Max called a halt to these thoughts and focused on the job in hand. After driving for over half an hour, round and round the same circuit of 'streets of ill-repute', he had to accept that everywhere the erstwhile salacious streets were bare of hookers.

The Ripper Code

The only women standing in the street were either innocently waiting at bus stops or having a cigarette outside a pub or club.

Giving up, Max finally stopped the car and took out his mobile-phone, with a shaking hand, dialled *her* number and waited as the ringing tone seemed to go on forever. Eventually he heard a recording of Sophie's soft Irish lilt, "Hi there. How are you doing? Sorry to disappoint you but I'm not here right now...but please, please... *pretty please* leave me a message after the tone, and I promise to give you *full* satisfaction."

There then followed a long *PEEEEP,* after which Max spoke urgently on the phone to her answer machine, "Sophie, it's Max here. I know who the killer is going to kill next...."

Three miles down the road from Max's parked car, in Sophie's apartment, there was someone listening to Sophie's answering machine as Max spoke, but it wasn't Sophie. The Intruder didn't stop his business of searching the dark empty apartment, as the telephone answer machine continued to relay out loud Max's voice.

"...In fact, I think I know the next two people. If my theory is correct, first, he will kill Lezzie Lisa and then Kate," Max's voice announced. On hearing this, the Intruder stopped rifling through Sophie's kitchen cupboards and he went over to the answer machine.

"I want to warn them to clear out of town," continued Max, "but I don't know where to find them. They're not on the streets. Quite wise, too. You probably know where they live. If you see either of them, please tell them to disappear for the next month. Maybe more. Tell them to go to Glasgow. It's the best meat market in Britain. Maybe you should also do a runner. Give me a ring back when you get this message." The answer machine clicked and beeped and then went silent. With his milky white gloved hand, the Intruder pressed the 'PLAY' button.

"You have six messages. Message One," the Answer Machine voice intoned. Before the machine could continue to play the messages, the Intruder pushed the 'Delete' button...and the Answer Machine voice said "Message Deleted". The Intruder repeatedly pressed 'Delete' until the Answer Machine announced, "All messages deleted. You have no more messages." The Intruder satisfied that the Answer Machine was no longer a threat, he returned his attention to searching Sophie's apartment.

CHAPTER 25
Twilight of the Caribe King
18th August. Saturday

The Sin-Clare Lair was famous throughout London's underworld, and quite possibly the whole of Britain. It is often said that if you enter uninvited, you will never leave alive. And even if you were invited, there were very good odds you still wouldn't. There are rumours that most uninvited guests, end up chopped into tiny tasty morsels, to be served up as fish food for Sinclare's piranhas. One might wonder who this Hood of hoods was currently dropping, little piece by little piece, into the large tropical fish-tank, as Edmunds and Walters entered his office, accompanied by three of Sinclare's meanest minders. The two policemen were most impressed at sight of the boiling bubbling water caused by the wild frenzy of the piranhas ferociously eating bloody pieces of meat.

Sinclare turned to the two cops, offering his most charmless smile.

"Detective Inspector Edmunds and his Boy Robin, Detective Sergeant Walters. To what do we owe this unexpected pleasure?" he asked with sham amiability, gesturing that they be seated, which they ignored.

"Do you have a licence for those piranhas?" asked Walters.

"I didn't think you needed a licence for tropical fish," Sinclare replied.

"But those are dangerous animals and the Dangerous Animals Act specify..."

"They are only dangerous," interrupted Sinclare, "if someone is stupid enough to stick their fingers in my tank. Personally, I don't *quite* see these cute little fishes escaping out on to the High Street and taking huge chunks out from the bottoms of unsuspecting pedestrians."

"What can you tell us about Sergeant Reece?" demanded Edmunds.

Sinclare sat down in a well-upholstered armchair, sat back comfortably, adjusted his crotch and spat into a gold spittoon, which lay near his feet.

"Reece? He's your normal regular pain in the arse...but then all Filth are, aren't they?" Sinclare laughed, looking round at his three stooges to follow suit, which they did, of course, with exaggerated enthusiasm.

"When was the last time you saw him?" Edmunds asked.

"Why would I see him? E's not quite my cup of tea, is he? I'm hardly going to invite him over for morning coffee, am I? I mean, what is it going to do for my "street cred" to have a copper for a bosom pal?"

"Bosom pal, nah. Bum chum, more like," jeered Walters.

The gangland boss shot Walters a nasty look. He didn't like the inference.

"Sinclare, even in the police force, I'd be the first to admit, there are the occasional bad apples," said Edmunds. "They are rare but they crop up from time to time...from recent evidence gathered, it appears Reece was our rotten apple. We now know he was taking payments from you. On a regular basis."

"Don't delude yourself, Edmunds. Every apple in the orchard is rotten. All cops are crooks. As they say, it takes a thief to catch a thief. I bet if I was to visit your home, I'd find loads of gear from burgled houses, which, somehow, you never bothered to return because of all the tedious paperwork that would involve."

Sinclare smiled. From the look on Walters' face, he did not like that. Good, thought Sinclare. If the smarmy git can't take the mud, he shouldn't sling it.

"Anyway, Sinclare said, standing up, "much as I love talking philosophy with you chaps, I really am a busy man, so if there's nothing more..."

"Why did you kill Reece?" barked Edmunds, sharply.

"What?" Sinclare exclaimed, unsure if he heard correctly.

"Was it because you knew we'd rumbled him and we were going to put him on the stand in our forthcoming case against you?"

"Reece? Been killed?" Sinclare was genuinely stunned, as were his three stooges.

"Oh that's very good, Sinclare," gibed Walters. "The look of shock. Most convincing."

"I don't know what the fuck you're talking about," yelled Sinclare, wide-eyed. "What do you mean? Reece is dead? How? When?"

"How? When?" mimicked Walters, moving in to the right of Sinclare.

"You put a contract out on him," insisted Edmunds, moving in to the left.

The three stooges looked at each other, they weren't sure if they should be allowing their Boss to be interrogated in this disrespectful fashion, especially on his own turf.

"It was a professional hit. Bullet in the back of the head. Execution style," stated Walters.

"Though, I wouldn't have thought it was your style," Edmunds scoffed. "Much too clean and precise for the likes of you."

"Mind you, Guv, he does have the dosh to pay for a really classy hit man."

"True. True," agreed the Detective Inspector.

"I don't know what the fuck you're talking about," snarled Sinclare, getting very angry. "This is the first I've heard about Reece getting topped. Why pick on me? I heard the maggot had many enemies. He probably got his fingers caught in one too many cash-tills. I heard rumours he was even doing deals with some of the dodgier East European gangs. He probably fell foul of them or the Russians. Why don't you go after them?"

Walters bent down low, putting his face close to Sinclare's. "Because we're interested in you, Sinclare. Only interested in you. Isn't it nice to be wanted," he said.

"Piss off," growled Sinclare.

Heaving a huge sigh of pity, Edmunds walked to the door and out into the corridor, and then, as if a new thought had occurred to him, turned and beckoned Sinclare over to him. As Sinclare swaggered over, his three minders moved to join him but Walters stepped in their path, blocking them. Unsure what to do, the three heavies, stood looking at each other and at Sinclare, who with a shake of his head, warned them not to make trouble.

Looking very gratified, Edmunds put his hand on Sinclare's shoulder and drew him closer. "The thing to remember, Sinclare," whispered Edmunds, paternally, "is, we're not going to have any problems pinning Reece's murder on you. And no one likes a Cop-Killer - even if that cop is as bent as a ten bob note. I guarantee you'll go down for a very long time. And of course, the kind of free-bird that you are, not being able to cope with the prospect of decades of penal servitude, I anticipate within weeks of starting your stretch, you'll be found hanging in your cell. As I say, the authorities don't like cop-killers."

And on that note, Edmunds and Walters left. When he was sure the two cops were no longer in the building, Sinclare erupted, screamed "FUCK," and rushed back into his office. Raging, he took hold of the aquarium and pulled it over. The glass smashed, with the water cascading all over the carpet and the piranha and Japanese fighting fish bouncing up and down, rows of tiny razor sharp teeth gnashing in a futile martial ballet, drowning in air, while the three stooges stared at the mayhem, in horrified silence.

Sinclare swung violently round at the trio of muscle-heavy flunkeys and pointed accusingly at them.

"Two of you," he roared, "find me that bloke I hired to do the contract. Mister Fucking S.A.S. That fucking Smart Arse Soldier."

"But Boss, we don't know his name or nothing," moaned Stooge Number One, he that was known as Mister Brown.

"Well, find me the fucking Joker who gave me his fucking contact details."

"We don't know his name either," whimpered the second stooge, known as Mister Pink.

Sinclare, who had been tramping up and down the room, manically pacing back and forth, seemingly oblivious to his crunching of the broken glass and stepping on his precious fish, snapping gasping piranhas included, scattered all over the deeply expensive Persian carpet, stopped in his tracks and glowered in utter disbelief at what he was hearing.

"Well, how the hell did I get landed with this bastard in the first place?" he demanded.

"Search us, Boss," shrugged Mister Brown.

"It was all down to you, Boss," Mister Pink said nervously

"You wouldn't let anyone else handle the arrangements, Boss," said Mister Brown in his most apologetic tone.

"It's not our fault you kept us in the dark," bitterly complained the third stooge, known as Mister Yellow.

"You what?" asked Sinclare in a dangerously low voice. Before Mister Yellow had time to answer, the Boss turned to Mister Pink and ordered, "Shoot him."

Without hesitation, Mister Pink pulled a gun from beneath his jacket and shot Mister Yellow in the head.

"Good," Sinclare said with disdain. "Now, clear up this fucking mess." He stepped across Mister Yellow's dead body, and walked out of the room..

Saturday night found Max searching the streets of Kings Cross again, driving around in circles, desperately worried. Empty. Everywhere a courtesan wilderness. Although he should be relieved that the hookers were still keeping away from their regular playgrounds, he nonetheless needed to see someone who could pass his warning message on to both Kate and Lezzie Lisa. After an hour of useless motoring, he stopped the car and used his mobile phone. His face lit up when he heard her voice.

"Sophie!" Max yelled ecstatically, "Sophie, thank god, I got you. Did you get my message? Yesterday. Oh, I dunno. Some time around midnight, probably. No? Anyway, I wanted you to warn Kate and Lezzie Lisa to keep off the streets for a couple of weeks. I think they're next. How do I know? I'll explain later. You don't know where they live? Do you know anyone who can tell you? Are you doing anything tomorrow afternoon? I know it's a Sunday. You don't work on a Sunday do you? Oh, you do dirty vicars and bawdy bishops on a Sunday. Listen, Sophie, you know

I said after Annie, there would be three more girls killed, making it six in total. Well, are there any girls working Kings Cross...called Mary, or Jane? Because it will be a Mary or a Jane that will be the sixth. Hey, I just thought. The final and sixth victim has to be the police informer and her name must be Mary or Jane. And if we can get to her, we can show the police how the serial killings tie in with their prosecution of Mister Big. You don't know any Mary or Jane. What? You are! Great! See you tomorrow afternoon."

All the time Max was talking to Sophie on the phone, his car window was wide open. And because he was so happy to be speaking to her at last, his exuberant voice was perhaps a little too loud. There are shadows that have ears.

CHAPTER 26
Viddy Well
19th August. Sunday

On a wet Sunday afternoon at home, what else is there to do but record a 'video diary'? That was Max's idea. He was in front of the camera, speaking earnestly and quickly, wheeling forward like some roller-coasting David Attenborough, while the naked Sophie, who was operating, retreated backwards, occasionally bumping into the furniture behind her, which, of course, added to the jerky hand-held feel, that is still so fashionable nowadays.

"Jack the Ripper was a Numerologist and he was a Freemason," began Max, staring directly into the camera lens. "But he was a Freemason of a special kind. He was an Occultist Freemason, one who dabbled in the Black Arts. But most importantly, he was a renegade Freemason. I don't believe the six murders he committed were in any way sanctioned or organised by the mainstream Masonic movement. This is where all the other Masonic-Ripper conspiracy theorists have got it wrong. He was not a doctor doing a favour... murdering... for brother mason, Eddie, Prince of Wales, covering up the future sovereign's indiscriminate dalliance with prostitutes. This Jack the Ripper Freemason was acting completely alone. But he was perverting the esoteric and occult knowledge and rituals he had obtained whilst a member of the Masonic Brotherhood....Can you keep the camera still, please," Max pleaded, interrupting himself because Sophie had backed into the sofa, and was now in fits of giggles.

"CUT," shouted Max. "This isn't working. May be we should have done what you said. Keep the camera on a tripod. Perhaps, I'm trying to be too arty."

The Ripper Code

"No, no. I'm beginning to enjoy this," laughed Sophie. "I think the wobbles are good, they could add a sort of sinister quality to it...I've got an idea..."

She gave the camera to Max and began pushing him out of the sitting room, "...why don't we go into the bedroom," she suggested. "I lie on the bed, on my tummy and we put the camera between my shoulder blades, pointing down my back...."

Max thought this was an extremely good idea. So, Sophie flopped on to the bed, and on to her stomach. Max tried to place the camcorder between her shoulder-blades but with the bounciness of the bed and her constant wriggling and fidgeting the best he could hope for, was a very precarious balancing act. He rolled on to his stomach and slid down her back until his diminutive body was between her spread-eagled legs, and then resting his chin between her buttocks, he continued his talk to the camera. Every now and then, he paused to bite and chew her bottom, but with the delicate tenderness and softness of a budgerigar kissing a dolphin.

"I realised Jack the Ripper was a Freemason," continued Max, "because I discovered he used numerology...and numerology is a very important system of coding and creating secret identities within the higher degrees of Freemasonry.... Oh shit. CUT" Max had to stop because Sophie being convulsed in giggles, due to his nibbling tickling her bottom, made the camera wobble off-balance and flop over.

"Bollocks," hooted Max. "I think we had better stick to the tripod."

"Stick in the tripod?" squealed Sophie. "Oooo, you kinky beast." She turned over onto her back and pulled Max on top of her.

Fifteen minutes later Max was back talking to the camera. This time he and Sophie were next to one of his desktop computers. Sophie had the camera on the tripod and would pan across to the computer whenever Max in his lecture indicated graphic illustrations. Having got the sex out of the way, and Sophie was paid her fee of fifty pounds, they were able at last to concentrate on shooting the video.

"Numerology is a clandestine language of numbers," explained Max, assuming a serious tone. "It was the forerunner of cryptography, and had it's origins in both the Hebrew and Greek alphabet–number systems, and the Kabbalah. Freemasons believe, like Pythagoras, that everything is numbers, that the universe is governed by laws of sacred geometry. The Freemasons are secretly a religious cult. Their religion goes beyond Christianity. Its bigger than Christianity. It's a mystical mix of ancient pagan wisdom blending with science and mathematics. Freemasons were the midwives to the Renaissance, midwives to the Enlightenment. Freemasons are agents of change. Freemasons have been behind every revolution for the past 300 years. You may have noticed that these revolutions, American, French, Russian, Latin American, Chinese or Arab, have as one of their emblems, the five pointed star, which is the signature of a conspiracy by Freemasons. And the five-pointed star, or the Pentacle, is the the Morning Star, which for the Masonic secret societies, is...."

"Max, you're beginning to bore me," moaned Sophie, stifling a yawn. "I'm not interested in Men Only Clubs. What's all this got to do with Jack the Ripper and how is it going to help us catch this fucking killer."

"I'm coming to it. I'm coming to it. But I have to put in all this as an intro to the video, so that people fully understand where my theory is coming from."

"Well, just do it quicker."

This slightly annoyed Max. He was damned if he was going to be hurried. He clicked on the word *"Conjuration"* and in response, the computer screen displayed the words *"The Great Architect"*.... Max continued directing his speech to camera.

"The Freemasons worship a supreme deity and they call it "The Great Architect". Numerologically, this name gives us 6 6 6..."

Max clicked *"Numerization"*, resulting in the computer presenting the numerological calculating process of the three words "THE", "GREAT", "ARCHITECT" arriving at "6" "6" "6". ($T=2$, $H=8$, $E=5$...$2+8+5 = 15 = $ **6**. $G=7$, $R=9$, $E=5$, $A=1$, $T=2$...$7+9+5+1+2= 24 = $ **6**. $A=1$, $R=9$, $C=3$, $H=8$, $I=9$, $T=2$, $E=5$, $C=3$, $T=2$...$1+9+3+8+9+2+5+3= 42 = $ **6**)

"666 is the secret code name of the Masons' god," said Max in an exaggerated whisper, "which is why many people in the Church, both in the past and the present, believe Masons are Devil worshippers, Satanists, in league with Lucifer, agents for the Antichrist...because at the top of the Masons cosmic hierarchy is 666."

Max swung round to the computer and moved the mouse and clicked on an icon labelled *"Graffiti"*. A box appeared on the screen and opened, revealing the infamous Jack the Ripper "Juwes" graffiti-

> *"The Juwes are*
> *The men That*
> *Will not*
> *be Blamed*
> *for nothing."*

Tapping the screen with his finger, Max pointed at the graffiti's text and said, "When I was studying Jack the Ripper a few years ago, I found he was trying to tell us, through a numerological code hidden in some graffiti he had written on the wall, that he was killing on behalf of 666, that his intention was to sacrifice six Whores of Babylon to invoke the powers of the Masons' god. He believed that this was the real purpose of Masonry...to bring about the final and ultimate change in the cosmic order. He wanted to bring on the Apocalypse. I think he believed the Millennium would commence with the beginning of the 20th century. His ritual killings took place in 1888, twelve years before the start of the 20th century. Twelve is Twice Six. He probably would have preferred to have performed the human sacrifices six years previous, in 1882, which would have given him Thrice Six before the 20th century began...but then, he did not have the freedom to do as he pleased, he had just got married the year before. He had to get rid of his wife first, which he did in 1887, the year before the Whitechapel murders. So, he had to content himself with Twice Six, which he still believed contained powerful enough magic."

"This is your Roslyn chap?"

"Yes, Roslyn D'Onston. His wife mysteriously disappeared in 1887. A few weeks later, six portions of a woman's body, minus her head, were found in the Thames.

"Six again," said Sophie thoughtfully.

"That's right. Six again," nodded Max. "Now, at the time I discovered the Ripper Code, I didn't have a name for a suspect...but I hoped the code and numerology would confirm his identity if I looked at the list of suspects at the time. Roslyn D'Onston with his army doctor background, his obsession with the occult, masonry and a variety of other reasons I can't go into now... you'll just have to read my book when I eventually get it published... turned out to be the perfect candidate for the Ripper. He gave himself names that would give him the power of six, he geometrically plotted the locations of the murders to give him the power of the six..."

Max paused to move the cursor to drag open a map of 1880s Whitechapel. The computer played out some graphic animations of the geometry of the Whitechapel murder sites. Whilst the animations unfolded, Max continued to speak,

"Roslyn D'Onston wanted the world to know that the Ripper was a freemason, so he embedded numerological clues as to his identity and his Masonic intentions, within graffiti he had written just after he had slaughtered and mutilated his fifth victim, Kate Eddowes. The numerology and summations of the graffiti also tells us that there would be a sixth victim and would confirm the name of the victim and where she would be killed."

"That would be Mary Jane?" interrupted Sophie, suddenly becoming much more interested.

"Mary Jane Kelly."

"Kelly?" exclaimed Sophie.

"Yes," replied Max.

"Jesus. I need a break," Sophie said, switching off the camera. "You bombarded me with too much in too short a space of time. Mind if I go out and have a fag for a minute?"

The man watching the house, parked in his black car on the opposite side of the street, saw Sophie come out of the front door at no. 53 Primrose Hill Park Road. He waited to see what she was going to do next. When he saw she was not leaving but just leaning against the front gate while smoking a cigarette, he slowly drove the car up alongside her. Sophie looked up at him and smiled in recognition.

"Hello there. Fancy seeing you here," she said, leaning in towards him to caress his smooth cheek.

"I could say the same thing to you. Making home visits, are you?" the Man replied.

Sophie laughed, and looked back at Max's front door with affection, and then looked back at the Man.

"I am, actually," she said, with a cheeky twinkle in her eye. "I don't normally but, well, he's disabled...so, you know. He is a lovely lad, though. A real sweetie."

"When do you finish?"

"In five minutes. Are you looking for business?"

"With you, always," he answered, licking his lips. Sophie giggled and gave a little growl as if she was a bitch on heat.

"Okay, darling. I'll just tell him goodbye. Don't go away," she said, running up the garden path to the front door.

Max watched everything from the sitting room front window. He was still looking out, feeling pretty pissed off with her when she ran back indoors.

"Isn't that an incredible coincidence, him just turning up like that?" she said happily, putting on her make-up.

"Who did you say he was?" Max asked.

"Some posh bloke. Used to be an officer in the army or some such," she replied airily, as she tidied her hair. "Really loaded. Trained in Sandhurst. Real gentleman. Very generous. Apart from you, he is my most regular client. Okay, sweetheart, got to dash.

Catch you later." Sophie snatched her coat and rushed up to Max, kissing him on the cheek and rushed out, like a hurricane.

Max was even more annoyed and a little jealous, as he watched her run to the waiting car, and get in beside the driver. Max was hoping to catch a glimpse of his rival but the man was in shadow. As the car drove off, Max was startled to see it's registration number plate - ***MIB 666R***.

"My God," he thought, feeling the blood in his veins freeze, and his heart skip a beat. "That is fucking weird. M.I.B. 666 R. No way. That is one hell of an impossibly weird coincidence."

Around ten o'clock that night, Max was driving around the near empty wet streets. The evening had brought a deluge of rain. Again, he was patrolling the Red Light district, hoping to find Kate and Lezzie Lisa at their posts but apart from a brief glimpse of Alice lurking in the shadows, he saw no other prostitutes.

He widened his circuit to cover Islington, Holloway, St. Pancras, Bloomsbury and Holborn but he searched in vain. After several hours of going around in ever-increasing circles, Max decided to give up for the night and on his way back home, he stopped at a pedestrian crossing because of a woman pushing a pram, crossing in front of him. Suddenly his car gave a big jolt forward. Max only just managed to halt his car in time before the pedestrian and baby were hit. He saw in his mirror that the car behind him, had crashed into his rear. The driver, looking a bit unsteady on his feet, quickly got out and stumbled over to Max's window.

"Ay, sorry mate," slurred the driver, breathing heavy alcoholic fumes into Max's face. "Didn't expect you to stop so suddenly."

"Didn't you see someone was crossing the road?" yelled Max furiously. "I could have killed them, you blithering idiot."

"Sh'not my fault. Couldn't break in time. Must be the wet road. Just skidded forward. Are you alright?" he asked, nearly slipping over.

"May have hurt my neck," complained Max. "Give me your insurance details and your car registration."

"Sure, mate. Hold on a sec. I'll get the documents from the car." And with that, the apparently drunk driver got back into his car and quickly drove off.

"Fucking bastard!" shouted Max as the car disappeared round the corner.

CHAPTER 27
The Year of the Ox
20th August. Monday

Max was lucky to get an eight-thirty appointment at the doctors' surgery that Monday morning. He was even luckier to see his own designated G.P., Dr. James. Nowadays in Britain, you may, in theory, have a personal physician, who should be familiar with your medical history but the reality is that it's a lottery as to who you end up seeing. And the amount of valuable consultancy time wasted having to bring each unacquainted doctor up to speed is frustrating and tedious. Gone are the happy days when you had a family doctor who knew you from cradle to grave, and who never felt the pressure to kick you out after three minutes. In the six visits Max has made to the surgery in the past eighteen months, this was the first time he came face to face with Dr. James.

"He was gone before I could even see his number plate," said Max, wincing at the sharp pain shooting up his neck as Dr. James prodded and squeezed the flesh between the shoulders and base of the skull..

"I'm not surprised," replied the doctor. "He would be in even bigger trouble if it was found he was drinking and driving... Well, young man, apart from a bit of whiplash, I think you're fine. Take the week off. Doctor's orders. I'll write you a sick note."

Back at his flat, taking advantage of not having to go to work, Max brought out his video camera and continued to shoot his home-made documentary on Jack the Ripper. Putting the camera on a tripod and pressing the record button, he placed himself six feet in front of the camera and began to lecture the imaginary viewers who he hoped would one day be seeing this on television.

Holding up a photograph of Roslyn D'Onston, Max spoke earnestly, "Roslyn D'Onston wrote many articles on the Occult and Black Magic. One of his articles was on African Magic and he signed himself as "Tau Tria Delta". This is another name he gives himself which adds up to "6". D'Onston was a self-confessed murderer. He brags that he killed an African sorceress. In his writings, he shows he believes he is a Black Magician and that he knows how important it is to kill harlots and take from them certain organs to be used in rituals for the evocation of demonic spirits. For twenty years before the Whitechapel Murders, D'Onston has been going to prostitutes. In fact, he was fired from his post as customs official for this unquenchable thirst of his, which led to him contracting V.D. Perhaps it was syphilis that made him go mad and turned him into Jack the Ripper."

Several hours later, after having added still shots of text from various D'Onston manuscripts and computer animatic graphical displays of his numerological examples, Max stopped to have a well-earned coffee-break. And as if on cue, the front doorbell rang. "Perfect timing," Max thought, smiling at the synchronicity. "If it's a friend, then it could be a sign I'm doing something right." He opened the door and was overjoyed to see it was Claire.

"Is the invalid receiving visitors?" she asked, handing him a bunch of grapes.

"Of course," laughed Max.. "Come in. I'm surprised you'd want to remain friends with me after revealing to you my dark sordid side."

"You know us women. We can't resist sinners. Its part of our vanity to think we can save their souls."

"Huh. Anyway, why aren't you at work?"

"Today's a training day, remember," she replied as Max took her coat. "And I'm taking the opportunity to skive." Claire added, giving him a sly wink.

"Tut tut tut. Us Job centre staff are supposed to set a good example," said Max as he ushered her into the sitting-room.

"Yeah, right," Claire smirked. "What are you doing?" she continued, looking with interest at the camera set-up.

"These murders which seem to be a copycat of Jack the Ripper have made me think I should put my ideas into some kind of home video documentary."

"What ideas?"

"Well, who Jack the Ripper was and why he killed?" answered Max.

"So who was he?" Claire got out of her wheelchair and made herself comfortable on the sofa.

"Let me show you the video lecture I've shot so far", Max said as he attached a lead from the camera to the television set. He then leapt from his wheelchair on to the sofa and settled beside Claire, who was now absent-mindedly munching the grapes she had brought for Max. She turned to him and offered him a grape, which he gratefully accepted as he pressed play on the camera. A shaky image of Max jumped into life on the television screen and attempting a mock theatrical sinister voice, he began with the words "Numerology is a clandestine language of numbers."

Half an hour later, the pair were still watching Max's talking head on the TV screen, except Max was now resting his head on Claire's lap on sofa, as she softly stroked his hair.

Max on the video was doing a very poor impersonation of Vincent Price, as he said "...Roslyn D'Onston was attempting to perform black magic by killing six prostitutes. By summoning up supreme evil, he wanted to turn the next century, the 20th century, into the Age of the Antichrist." Max looked up at Claire who was watching the screen, mouth open wide, transfixed, enthralled as the "TV Max" continued to argue his case.

"Roslyn D'Onston wanted to be the Cosmic Father of the Coming Antichrist. He believed that the perfect person to be the Antichrist would be someone like him, someone who had the same Zodiac sign as him - Aries, who had the same birthday as him and born in the same Chinese year. D'Onston was born on the 20th April 1841, the year of the Ox. O is 6. X is 6.

"D'Onston began his rituals for conceiving the Antichrist on the 26th of July 1888, when he admitted himself as a patient at the London Hospital, Whitechapel."

"Nine months later, on the 20th of April, 1889, another year of the Ox, Adolf Hitler was born. Roslyn D'Onston otherwise known as Jack the Ripper, ritually sacrificed six prostitutes to plant a demon seed in-"

Suddenly the television screen went blue and the sound cut out.

"Oops. That's when I ran out of tape," Max said, turning to Claire with a big schoolboy grin. "Fancy a cup of tea?"

With their cups of tea and pieces of chocolate cake, Max took Claire over to look at the computer monitor, to continue his lecture.

"Jack the Ripper used the London Hospital as a base from where he went out at night to commit his murders," said Max as he started the computer.

"Why was he in hospital?" Claire asked, only half-interested. She would prefer to be back on the sofa with Max, engaging in a more physical activity. She tried to position her wheelchair as close to his as possible..."Why can't our wheelchairs be made up of our flesh and blood, instead of the sterile cold lifeless metal and plastics?" she inwardly moaned. Her body leant in towards his, her shoulder lightly touching his. Max felt the touch and half-wished he could stop talking and get on with a mad passionate embrace, smothering her with furious kisses...but he couldn't. He had made up his mind that he couldn't emotionally afford to have her as his girlfriend. So he continued the Sherlock Holmes act and set about answering her question.

"D'Onston complained of something which today we would probably call 'ME'. In those days, it was called 'neurasthenia'. a mental disorder caused by emotional stress or anxiety but not by any underlying physical problems, so he would still have been physically fit to carry out the murders. He was a voluntary patient and stayed in a private ward called Davies, which incidentally adds up to '6', and was free to come and go as he pleased. An interesting coincidence is that London Hospital adds up to 66. Double six is important to the Ripper and he employs it when marking out the locations for the six murders, which he does according to an occult geometry. I've got an 1888 map of

The Ripper Code

Whitechapel, where I've drawn the Ripper's geometric pattern. I'll show you on the computer."

As Max talked, he opened the Ripper Files on the computer, and then opened the Whitechapel maps folder. Clicking on the Whitechapel 1888 map, there sprung to life an animated sequence, that drew lines and angles from London Hospital to the six murder sites.

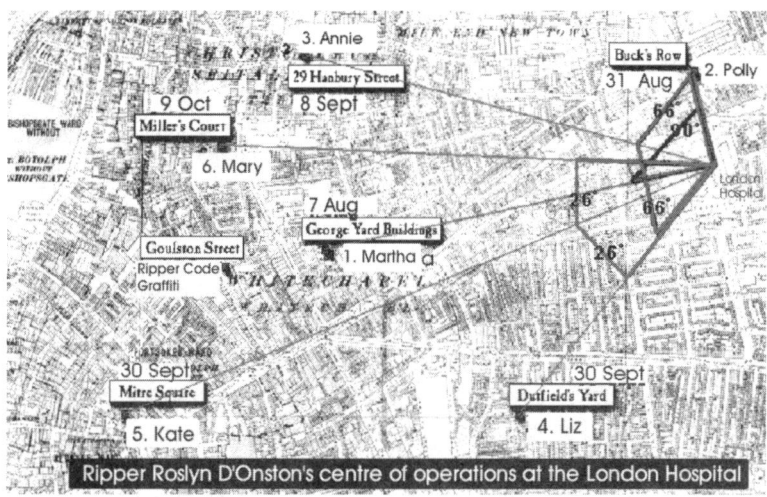

"As you can see from London Hospital, we have three of the murders at a sixty-six degree angle from each other," Max pointed out, tracing the lines on the screen with his index finger. "The six murders are contained within an arc of 132 degree angle. 1 plus 3 plus 2 equals the ubiquitous 6."

"So, you think Jack the Ripper planned all the murders beforehand, using a map of Whitechapel, plotting and drawing all the lines and angles?"

"Absolutely. I'm convinced of it. My studies and analysis shows that everything he did, has a numerological and geometric logic."

"Yes, but looking at your map, not everything fits into the '6' motif," queried Claire, jabbing he finger at the screen. "Murders 4,5,6, you've got 26 degree angles separating those three."

The Ripper Code

"Well, for one thing, don't you think its amazing on either side of murder number five, you have angles of exactly the same value - 26? Secondly, 2 plus 6 is 8. So, we have two eights. The murders are committed in the year 88. The Black Magician Ripper, for his ritual killings to be effective, needs to include the number of the year in his geometric pattern."

"Hmmm. That's one piece of your argument that seems weakest."

"Well, it makes sense to me," rejoined Max sniffily. "Anyway, here's another weird coincidence that points directly to Hitler's birth, which I believe was created by the Ripper's occult murders."

To demonstrate the coincidence, Max moved the curser to an icon on the map and left-clicked the mouse. Instantly, a red line was drawn from Hanbury Street, the site of the third murder, and headed towards London Hospital. As the line graphically travelled across the computer screen, Max explained, "If we continue the line to London Hospital and beyond in its south-east direction... we will find that it goes straight to Hitler's birthplace in Austria - Braunau, which, by now, will be no surprise to you, adds up to six."

Claire watched in amazement as the straight line which had been exactly in the middle of the area of all the murders, bisecting 132 degrees with 66 degrees on either side, passed through London Hospital, and continued on in it's south-east direction...and as it did so, the map of London zoomed out, and then, out of England as the line hurtled on... across the continent of Europe... where it finally stopped in Austria, at the town of Braunau, the birth-place of Hitler. Claire gasped as the word BRAUNAU resolved into its numerological equivalent... '*2913513*' = 24.... the number '6'

"If all this is true," Claire whispered, relishing the tingling shiver shooting up her spine, "then what sort genius mind Jack the Ripper must have had, to have worked it out to such crazy detail. He must have been totally mad... to have dreamed up... AND believed... all this."

"Well, I think Roslyn D'Onston was completely off his rocker. Look at all the facts of his life, at the articles and letters he wrote for the Pall Mall Gazette and for the magazine, 'Lucifer'... and at how he tried to recreate himself numerologically."

At this point Max excused himself to go to the loo, but before he went, he opened a file on the Chronology and Brief Biography of Roslyn D'Onston,

"Take a look at this whilest I have a slash. It's something I put together based on a book by Ivor Edwards *"Jack the Ripper's Black Magic Rituals"*, where he also argues D'Onston is the Ripper. I came across this book after I reached the same conclusion on account of my numerology discoveries. So you can see, I'm not alone in thinking that D'Onston was the original Whitechapel Murderer."

Claire nodded and hurriedly read D'Onston file on the computer screen, while Max was in the bathroom.

Robert Donston Stephenson, *better known to his contemporaries as Dr. Roslyn D'Onston*

Hair: *Light brown, fair, greying, thinning at the sides, full moustache which was mouse or fair-coloured and occasionally waxed, turned up at the ends. Could be manipulated to give various styles.*
Eyes: *Pale blue.*
Complexion: *Pale, sallow, no colour.*
Height: *5ft 11in.*
Build: *Lean and slim, military bearing showing strength and power.*
Voice: *Pleasant and cultured.*
Face: *Full.*
Appearance: *Military; known to observe strangers with an eyeglass; on occasions carried a short military-style cane. Wore a brown wide-brimmed, soft felt hat; wore a long overcoat. Clothes worn through brushing rather than wear; respectable shabby appearance.*
IQ: *Exceptional*
Marital Status: *Married Anne Deary in 1876. By 1887, his wife has disappeared. In 1888, D'Onston is registered as unmarried and in 1889 as single.*
Habits: *Pipe smoker, took drugs, considered a "soaker" (not a drunk) with alcohol use. Bathed every day and was known to be clean and tidy.*

Hobbies: *The Occult, Esoterica. Collector of Biblical texts - 120 of the Greek and Latin fathers from the 2nd to the 10th century, from the 26 old Latin versions of the 2nd century, from 24 Greek uncials and some cursive, from the vulgate, Syriac, the Egyptian and other ancient versions, all the Greek texts from 1550 to 1881.*
A known gambler. Sought the company of prostitutes in Hull, London, Brighton, Paris.
Work experience: *Customs officer, army surgeon, writer, reporter, occultist, magician, soldier, self-confessed murderer, prospector, businessman. Well travelled (France, Italy, USA, Africa, India, Germany)*
Income: *Grey area. Used women as a convenience and was known to have been a kept man. He also wrote articles for cash. The Stephenson family were very wealthy, but D'Onston was an outcast.*
Other: *Contracted VD from a prostitute in Hull. Dismissed from Customs Service because of his association with prostitutes. Known to have fasted for great lengths of time due to his occultist beliefs.*

CHRONOLOGY

1841: *Born - Robert Donston Stephenson, 20 April, Sculcoates, Hull. Lives at Willow House, 60 Church Street. Mother's maiden name, Dauber. Parents wealthy mill owners.* **Known aliases**: *Dr. Roslyn D'Onston. Wrote under the names of Tau Tria Delta", and "One Who Knows"*
1859: *Visits Paris where he meets Lord Bulwer Lytton's son, who then introduces him to Lord Lytton, writer of "Last Days of Pompeii", "The Coming Race" and other works on the occult.*
1860: *D'Onston's initiation into the Lodge of Alexandria is performed by Lord Bulwer Lytton.*
1860: *Lives in Islington with a friend.*
1860-63: *Fights with Garibaldi in Italy. Works as army doctor on the battlefield.*
1863: *Goes to the West Coast of Africa to study witchcraft. He murders a woman witch doctor while there and writes of the deed later.*
March 1863: *Takes a post at the Customs House in Hull*
1867: *His father is a prominent manufacturer and holds the elected post of collector of Hull Corporation Dues. His brother, Richard, is a ship owner, partner in the firm of Rayner, Stephenson and Co., Vice-Consul for Uruguay and a Hull City councillor and Freemason, member of Minerva Lodge (250) Dagger Lane, Hull.*

***July 1868**: Shot in the thigh by Thomas Piles under suspicious circumstances. Sacked from Customs because of his association with prostitutes, which led him to contracting VD.*
***1869**: Living in London.*
***14 January? February? 1876**: Marries 32 year old Anne Deary (born: Thorn, Yorkshire. Father, Charles Deary, profession: farmer), his mother's serving girl, St. James Church, Holloway. Married under the name of Roslyn D'Onston Stephenson.*
***1878**: Goes to India to study magic. Bulwer Lytton's son, Edward, is Viceroy of India.*
***1881**: Living at 10 Hollingsworth Street North with his wife, Annie. He is an MD, not practising but is a scientific writer for the London press. He is 39, his wife, 37.*
***1882**: Joins the Cunning Men witches coven at Canewdon, Essex, where he is initiated by Satan's Magister, George Pickingill (1816-1909).*
***1886**: Vittoria Cremers comes across a copy of Light on the Path by Mabel Collins in a New York bookshop.*
***July 1886**: D'Onston applies for the position of Secretaryship of the Metropolitan and City Police Orphanage Benevolent Fund, part of the Metropolitan Lodge (1507). He hoped that him being a Mason would guarantee his selection, but he is not even short-listed.*
***1886**: Anne Deary is known to be alive at this time.*
***May 11 (+ June) 1887**: Six finds of portions of a woman's body, minus head, in the Thames and the Regent's Canal. Possibly Anne Deary (both in the same age group). Done by someone with surgical knowledge. No death certificate for Anne Deary has ever been found. D'Onston resided at several addresses near the Regents Canal, including Salmon Lane and Burdett Road.*
***August 1887**: Inquest of victim. After which D'Onston refers to himself as "unmarried".*
***1888 :** Vittoria Cremen arrives in the UK going to the HQ of the British Theosophical Society to enlist. She meets Madame Helena Petrova Blavatsky, the head figure. She obtains work as an associate editor of Lucifer, a work printed by the movement. First contact with Mabel Collins.*
***1888 :** D'Onston moves to The Cricketers Inn, Black Lion Square, Brighton, a well-known 18th-century inn frequented by prostitutes. When D'onston is at The Cricketers, Edmund Gurney (founder member of the Society for Psychical Research and English spiritualist, who was investigating psychic fraudsters including Blavatsky, who was known to D'Onston) is found dead in his room at The Royal Albion Hotel, only a*

few minutes' walk from where D'Onston was staying. The day after the inquest (held on 25th July) D'Onston moves from The Cricketers Inn into the London Hospital. It is believed D'Onston had been contracted by Blavatsky to kill Gurney.

1 March 1888: *The Hermetic Order of the Golden Dawn founded on by masons Dr. William Woodman and Dr. William Wynn Westcott with Samuel Liddell "MacGregor" Mathers. The aim of Golden Dawn magic was to become the Superman. As an experienced magician, D'Onston is initiated into the Golden Dawn.*

26 July 1888: *D'Onston admits himself as private patient in London Hospital, Whitechapel, registered as 47 yrs, unmarried, journalist, in Davis ward, Physician - Dr. Sutton, complaint - neurasthenia.*

Tuesday 7 August 1888: *Martha Tabram, 39, prostitute, found murdered in George Yard Buildings, George Yard, Whitechapel*

Friday 31 August 1888: *Mary Ann Nichols (Polly), 45, prostitute, found murdered in Buck's Row, Whitechapel,*

Saturday 8 September 1888: *Annie Chapman (Annie Sivvey), 45, prostitute, found murdered in Rear Yard at 29 Hanbury Street, Spitalfields.*

Sunday 30 September 1888: *Elizabeth Stride (Long Liz), 45, Swedish, prostitute, found murdered in yard at side of 40 Berner Street, St Georges-in-the- East. It should be noted that King Oscar II of Sweden was Grand Master of the Masons in the year 1888. It is suggested that this Swedish factor was another reason Stride was selected to be killed as D'Onston wanted to tell the Masons how angry he was at having been rejected for the Orphanage Secretaryship.*

Sunday 30 September 1888: *Catherine Eddowes (Mary Ann Kelly, Catherine Conway), prostitute, 46, found murdered in Mitre Square, Aldgate, City of London. Jack the Ripper chalks a Masonic message on a wall in Goulston Street. Sir Charles Warren, Metroplitan Police Commissioner, as a top Mason, recognises the message to mean a Brother Mason was the Ripper, and immediately has the graffiti washed off, but not before it is noted down. Sir Charles Warren was a founder of the Quatuor Coronati Lodge of Masonic Research (2076) and a Past Grand Sojourner of the Supreme Grand Chapter, and so knew the Masonic myth (Hiram Abiff) and ritual centres on murder.*

16 October 1888: *D'Onston writes a letter to the City of London Police about the message left by the killer known as the Goulston Street Graffito.*

Friday 9 November 1888: *Mary Jane Kelly (Black Mary, Marie Jeanette Kelly), 25, prostitute, found murdered in 13 Miller's Court, 26 Dorset Street Spitalfields.*

1 December 1888: *D'Onston writes a piece to the Pall Mall Gazette suggesting that Jack the Ripper was a black magician. He tells how to conjure demonic powers by ritual murder of harlots, and that a goat's horn is first used to sodomise the victim.*

Mabel Collins reads this article and writes to D'Onston. Later the two meet and become lovers, then business partners.

Friday 7 December 1888: *Discharged from London Hospital. 134 days in hospital. Condition on discharge - Relieve. Moves to a lodging house, St. Martins Chambers, 29 Castle Street. The landlord, Mr. Cullingford, also owned the property at 66 Leman Street.*

24 December 1888: *Christmas Eve, George Marsh, unemployed who had dreams of being a private detective, goes to Scotland Yard to make a statement to Inspector Roots (D'Onston's friend of 20 years and Brother Mason) to the effect that D'Onston was Jack the Ripper. He is especially disturbed by D'Onston's apparent eagerness to re-enact how the Ripper killed his victims, including the simulation of sodomy. Marsh claimed D'Onston would do this with relish.*

26 December 1888: *Boxing Day, D'Onston goes to Scotland Yard and makes a statement to his friend, Inspector Roots that Jack the Ripper is Dr. Davis. He says he had a deal with George Marsh to share the reward.*

3 January 1889: *D'Onston writes an article for the Pall Mall Gazette dealing with the magical cults of the West Coast of Africa.*

15 February 1889: *D'Onston writes another piece for the Pall Mall Gazette.It contains his own views on devil worship. He admits to the murder of a woman witch doctor in the article.*

March 1889: *Cremers visits Southsea to meet with Mabel Collins. She finds Collins living D'Onston. Collins and D'Onston return to London 14 days later. D'Onston moves to a lodging house run by Cremers's landlady for two weeks. Collins wants to be discreet about the affair.*

13 May 1889: *Moves from HQ London College Mission, 304 Burdett Road, MileEnd and admitted to the London Hospital with an acute case of "Chloralism". Registered as 50 (but really 48) yrs, single, author, in Davis ward, Physician - Dr. Sutton*

Wednesday 17 July 1889: *Alice "Clay pipe" McKenzie, found murdered in Castle Alley, Whitechapel.*

25 July 1889: *Discharged from hospital after 73 days. Condition on discharge - Cured.*

1889: *D'Onston's father dies and leaves him nothing.*
July 1890: *Collins lodges a libel action against Blavatsky.*
1890: *D'Onston starts the Pompadour Cosmetique Company with Cremers and Collins. D'Onston lives in a small room at the back of the first floor. Collins starts to believe that D'Onston is Jack the Ripper, and begins to fear for her life.*
November 1890: *Blavatsky commissions an article from D'Onston entitled "African Magic". The piece appears in Lucifer.*
D'Onston is arrested at least once for the Whitechapel Murders prior to this time.
1891: *Marks the end of the Pompadour Cosmetique Company .*
1891: *D'Onston takes Collins to court over stolen letters; the case is dismissed.*
Friday 13 February 1891 : *Frances Coles, prostitute, found under railway arch, Swallow Gardens, Whitechapel.*
1891 : Census he is listed as a boarder at the following address: The Triangle Hotel, Charterhouse Street, St Sepulchre's, London Charterhouse Street is immediately adjacent to St. Bartholomew's Hospital
In the census return his details are given as follows:
Name: Roslyn D'Ouston - Boarder: - Marital Status: Single - Age: 50 Profession: Journalist ("author" added)
Where born: Elsham (Elsham is in North Lincolnshire, east of Scunthorpe)
1893: *D'Onston is converted to Christianity by the converted prostitute Victoria Woodhull.*
1896: *W.T.Stead, editor of the Pall Mall Gazette, introduces articles by D'Onston in his quarterly magazine Borderland. Stead asserts that D'Onston is Jack the Ripper. D'Onston works on his book The Patristic Gospels.*
1901: *Profession: Dispenser (worker). Residing in St. Mary Islington Parish Institution (workhouse), S. John's Road.*
1904: *The Patristic Gospels is published.*
(1904: *D'Onston disappears. May have gone abroad or stayed in England and changed his name. No record of his death has been discovered) N.B. No longer the case. It is now claimed that....*
9 October 1916 *: Roslyn D'Onston dies at Islington Infirmary, Highgate Hill, Islington. The cause of death is listed as carcinoma of the oesophagus and gastrostomy. His name is spelled as Roslyn D'Ouston, Male 76 years old. His occupation is listed as author. His address is given as 129 St John's Road, Islington. The death was registered on the*

10th October 1916. It has been suggested that the death certificate is a forgery.
D'Onston is buried in an allegedly Masonic private plot in the cemetery at High Road, East Finchley, London.

"Yes, I think you're right about Roslyn D'Onston being Jack the Ripper," Claire said to Max when he returned, which pleased him no end. "But what about today's Whitechapel Murderer?" she went on. "Have you warned his next intended victims?"

Max shook his head. "I haven't been able to find either Lisa or Kate," he said disconsolately. "No one's walking the streets at the moment."

"Can't say I blame them. Must be very terrifying for prostitutes at the moment. What about the final woman? Have you found out who she is yet?"

"My contact says she's never heard of a Mary or Jane."

"You mean your whore?" remarked Claire sarcastically.

Max stiffened and gave Claire a sharp look, who immediately felt ashamed.

"I'm sorry that just came out," she pleaded. "That was completely uncalled for, I know. It was very childish of me. Forgive me."

The awkward silence that followed was unbearable. Max involuntarily glanced in the direction of the front door. Thinking it was a hint, Claire backed away.

"I think I've outstayed my welcome," she said regretfully. "I'd better go."

With a shy look in Max's direction, Claire picked up her bag and coat.

"No, no, stay," urged Max, attempting to block her exit. "If you want. There are still a few things I want to discuss with you about the case."

"Really?" squealed Claire, her eyes lighting up. "Do you mean that?"

Max nodded reassuringly and went back to the computer. Claire with a big smile on her face, sat next to him, again, her right resting lightly on his shoulder. He in turn, while secretly enjoying the renewed intimate proximity, nonetheless, attempted

The Ripper Code

to affect the dry, academic tone of a detached schoolmaster as he said, " If I'm right that our current killer is trying to copy Jack the Ripper, picking victims with the same names and dumping the bodies in the same locations, then, is it possible to predict when he kills based on the original Ripper dates?"

Claire stared intently at the monitor as Max clicked on the Whitechapel murders file, which immediately revealed the following list of dates and victims' names -

Tuesday 7 August 1888 -Martha Tabram
Friday 31 August 1888-Polly Nichols
Saturday 8 September 1888-Annie Chapman
Sunday 30 September 1888 –Elizabeth Stride
Sunday 30 September 1888-Catherine Eddowes
Friday 9 November 1888 -Mary Jane Kelly

"The three dates we've got so far regarding today's Ripper - 7 August, 13 August and 17 August," began Max as he typed *'7 August'*, *'13 August'* and *'17 August'*. "The first date is identical - Now, lets see. Between 7 and 13 is six days interval, between 13 and 17 is four days. Six, four could be a descending sequence of numbers which would predict that the next number in the sequence is two, suggesting that the fourth murder would take place on the 19th, which was yesterday and so far, we've had no news of any more Whitechapel murders. Besides this number sequence would end at '2', which would nullify my theory of six Ripper-type murders, so that can't be the answer."

"Max," Claire exclaimed excitedly. "Have you noticed the two Pollys, the dates are reversed. *'Polly 1'* is 31, *'Polly 2'* is 13. Is that just a coincidence?"

"Probably because with the two Annes, the numbers are not reversed. *'Annie 1'* is 8... and *'Anne 2'* is 17...."

"But Max, look! Could the dating be numerological? We have *'Anne 2'* which is 17... 1 plus 7 is 8. And the date for *'Anne 1'* is 8."

Max stared open-mouthed at the screen. "You could be right, Claire," he said, as a smile slowly crept across his face. "My God, you're a genius," he chuckled. "The bastard could be using numerology. In which case the date for the next murder - Lisa...well, Lisa and Kate," Max corrected himself. "....because the Ripper killed Lisa Stride and Kate Eddowes on the same day, with just an hour between-"

"It says here they were killed on the 30th September.." interrupted Claire.

"Forget September. I think our man is working to a shorter timescale. He is going to kill all six this month. So 30 is 3. What numbers add up to 3?"

"Three, Twelve, Twenty-One..."

"Twenty-One!" shouted Max. "That's it! The Twenty-First. Tomorrow's date! Fuck! He's going to kill Lisa and Kate very early tomorrow morning!"

"Why do you say early morning?" questioned Claire.

"Because if he is really copying the Ripper, both girls will be dead within two hours after midnight tonight."

"Are you going to tell the police?" asked Claire, starting to put on her coat because she knew what he was going to say next.

"Yeah. I'm going there right now." Max replied, rushing to the front door. He opened it and let Claire out.

"You were brilliant, Claire. Thanks," Max said, putting his arms around her. Claire was really happy but nonetheless slightly disappointed that instead of the lips, he kissed her lightly on the cheek.

CHAPTER 28
Dear Boss
20th August. Monday

Max thought he would never get there, the Monday afternoon traffic was so appalling. "God, why do I bother continuing to live in this shit-hole of a city?" Max groaned to himself. "It's such a time-waster. Oh for a dream cottage in the country. Nah, not a hope. Not with my wages...and with me blowing what little I have on professional tarts. Bloody toss-pot that I am."

The bored desk sergeant at the police station immediately went on the defensive as soon as the little man in the wheelchair came through the door.... "Before you start, young lad. Parking tickets are not our business, any more. Put your complaint...in writing... to Camden Council. They're generally sympathetic to people like you," he said wearily.

"Are they bollocks! You condescending pratt," Max thought to himself. "Can I speak to Emma?" he asked out loud.

"Emma who? I don't think we have an Emma working here," the duty officer politely replied as his patronising smile grew.

"She's a policewoman," Max urged.

"No, sorry sir, we have no policewomen here by that name. Do you have a surname?" he asked, picking up his pencil and notebook

"She's a prostitute."

"You what? Excuse me! How dare you!" demanded the duty officer, slamming down his pencil. Glaring fearsomely down at Max, he growled through clenched teeth, "You may not like the police but you don't have to insult our women officers like that."

Max's first impulse was to laugh out loud. Where does this cardboard cut-out think he is? On some crappy peak-viewing TV Cop Opera? Instead, Max tried his most ingratiating wheedling voice..."No. You don't understand. I mean, she's an undercover cop. A detective posing as a prostitute. I met her here once. She told me her real name. What was it? Something similar to Emma."

Down the corridor, in the CID office, Inspector Edmunds looked at the wall map of Whitechapel. Scratching his head and groaning with frustration, he turned to WDC Warren who was writing notes.

"Three murders," he said pessimistically. "Still not enough to go on, which is a pretty grisly thing to have to say."

"I'd prefer we didn't have any more, sir," Warren answered back.

"And so say all of us," chanted Detective Sergeant Walters, breaking off momentarily from the heated whispered conversation he was having on the telephone.

"So do I," Edmunds retorted gruffly. "But if we want to locate his home we need more than three. Did any package arrive? You know the one he threatened to send us?"

"Nothing containing body parts, sir," replied Warren.

"Maybe it was all just bluff. Could have been just a crank," conjectured the Inspector, sounding as if he was mildly disappointed.

"Still doesn't explain how the writer knew that internal organs were taken, sir," said Warren.

Edmunds held out his hand, "Show me the letter again."

At that moment, a loud commotion was heard down the corridor. One voice was particularly angry.

"How many times do I have to tell you," it bellowed. "I can't remember her real name. I just know her as Emma."

The woman detective looked at her boss. "Sir, is that Max?" she said with a hint of a smile.

"Get him in here," ordered Edmunds.

Walters put his phone down, and went out to fetch Max, who on entering the office, was immediately relieved to see WDC Warren, grinning at him.

"Thank God, Emma," Max cried. "What was your real name?"

"Eloise. Or Ellie," she replied.

"W. D. C. Warren, if you don't mind," reminded Edmunds. "Maxwell Abberline, don't you realise it's extremely bad luck to be disturbing the peace in a police station?"

Continuing to ignore the Inspector, Max addressed Warren.

"Kate and Lezzie Lisa, I've been trying to find them for the last three days... but they've disappeared."

The burly Inspector was not going to be so easily affronted, and stepped between his subordinate and Max.

"Who is Kate and who the blazes is *Lezzie Lisa*?" demanded Edmunds menacingly.

"They are the next two prostitutes to be killed," barked back Max, returning the Inspector's basilisk stare with equally grim determination. "And you will find their bodies in Whitechapel early tomorrow morning. 'Lezzie Lisa' will be found in Berner Street, and Kate in Mitre Square."

"What the bloody hell are you talking about? Is this another of your crackpot theories?" Edmunds sneered.

"Guv, Max did know about Anne's body in Hanbury Street," interjected Walters. "I was going to bring him in to question him as to how he knew."

"Are you working with the killer? Aiding and abetting in the murders?" charged Edmunds, thrusting his intimidating face into Max's. "Close the door, Jim, I think we'll make this a formal interview. Warren, set up the recording equipment."

As commanded, Walters pushed Max further in to the room and closed the door. Warren opened new cases of audio-cassettes and inserted them into a recording machine situated under desk. Edmunds sat down in front of Max, while Walters stood behind his boss.

"Maxwell Abberline," began Edmunds. "I'm not going to formally charge you, for the moment....you are not under arrest, for the moment - but if you want to consult with a solicitor, you are free to make a phone call."

"I don't need a solicitor because I have nothing to worry about. I came here of my own free will, to give you information, to try to save lives."

"Fire away. We're all ears."

"It's my contention based on the available facts that the current spate of killings, that is, the murders of prostitutes, who are known to me as Martha, Polly and Anne, are part of a pattern which exactly copies the Jack the Ripper Whitechapel murders of 1888 and in view of this fact we can expect three more murders, the victims names will be Lisa, Kate, Mary or Jane, and the bodies will be found in Berner Street, Mitre Square and Miller's Court in Dorset Street, respectively."

Edmunds guffawed in derision, and leapt up from the desk, to stand behind Max, breathing down his neck.

"Dear-oh dear-oh dear, Max," sang Edmunds sarcastically. "You really have surpassed yourself this time. You seriously expect us to believe this load of cods wallop?"

"The Detective Sergeant already told you I knew the location of the third body... and that was before there was any mention of it in the press. How did I know?"

"That's what we want to know."

Max turned and eyeballing the Inspector, announced triumphantly, "Because I saw a pattern that followed that of Jack the Ripper. I bet I can tell you more stuff that hasn't yet been released to the public. Martha had been stabbed 39 times, probably with a bayonet but there were no mutilations unlike in the cases of Polly and Anne, who had both had their throats slashed through to the windpipe and oesophagus and attacks to the abdomen, with the uterus, parts of bladder and vagina removed from Anne.. I can guess in what postures the bodies were found. There's lots of information I can give you like that."

All three detectives looked at each other, taken aback at Max's accurate familiarity with the case. Edmunds moved slowly back to his chair facing Max, and sat down.

"Perhaps you can name the killer for us?" scoffed Edmunds. "Maybe I should arrest you and charge you with the murders, you seem to know so much. The only problem is you're such a pip squeak, a Tiny Tim, that no court in the land would take the prosecution seriously. But you are in league, obviously, with the killer, so I could make a case stick of you aiding and abetting the murders. We all know it's a regular hobby of yours, fucking prostitutes. Maybe your role in these murders was to chose the victims, point them out to the killer. He did the kidnapping and killing and after he'd done some of the principal cutting up, as a reward he let his evil little dwarf sidekick partake in the more gruesome mutilations."

Utterly furious at her boss, Warren suddenly stood up. Edmunds turned on her.

"You have something to say to me, detective constable?"

"Sir, I really don't think this is necessary," she said which was as much as she could muster.

"Jesus fucking Christ," Max yelled. "No wonder you cops are so useless at solving crime...it's no wonder you're called PC Plod, you're as thick as shit."

"Book him for obscene language," boomed Edmunds.

Max mockingly put out his wrists as if he was expecting handcuffs.

"You cops," he jeered, "only appear to solve crime because... you've either had to rely on informers or you fit some poor sod up...the Guildford Four, Birmingham Six, Tottenham Three, 7/7, the Mohammed Twelve... Oh, the examples are legion... Because, the fact is, you Bobbies... or should I say, Boobies... haven't got the intelligence to do real detective work."

For a few seconds there was a stunned silence at his tirade. Then Edmunds laughed out loud.

"What shall we do with him, Jim?" he said. "He's got bloody balls, I'll give him that."

"Perhaps, we should listen to what he has to say, Guv," suggested Walters. "I have to agree, we could be dealing with a Jack the Ripper copyist. The email we received... could be a similarity there. Didn't Jack the Ripper send letters to taunt the police?"

"Email?", Max exclaimed incredulously. "The killer sent you an email?"

"Show him the letter," Edmunds sighed, pointing at the desktop computer.

Warren printed out a copy and handed it to Max.

The Ripper Code

" '*Dear Bob*'," began Max, reading it out loud, then stopped. "Hummm interesting," he said, looking up at Edmunds. "The Ripper actually wrote *Boss* in the original."

Max continued reading, "...*I hate whores and I shall not quit ripping them until I get caught....* Caught? I think Jack wrote '*buckled*' not '*caught*'... Looks like this next bit is word for word - '*Great work my last handiwork. I didn't give the whore time to squeal*'...I don't suppose you have a copy of Jack's original '*Dear Boss*' letter?" Max looked up hopefully.

"You what?" laughed Edmunds.

"Never mind," Max sighed. "Is this computer connected to the Internet?"

"Yes. I'll get us online," volunteered Warren.

"Go straight to the *Clue-So* search engine," suggested Max, "and type '*Ripper Dear Boss*'. Put quotes around *Dear Boss*."

Warren did as he suggested and within seconds an image of Jack the Ripper's "Dear Boss" letter appeared on the computer's monitor.

"Dear Boss, I keep on hearing the police have caught me but they won't fix me just yet... I am down on whores and I shan't quit ripping them till I do get buckled. Grand work the last job was. I gave the lady no time to squeal. How can they catch me know? I love my work and want to start again. You will soon hear of me and my funny little games... The next job I do I shall clip the lady's ears off and send to the police officers just for jolly... Keep this letter back till I do a bit more work, then give it out straight. My knife is nice and sharp. I want to get to work right away if I get a chance. Good luck. Yours truly, Jack the Ripper"

Max looked at the Jack's letter on the screen and then read out loud the email in his hand, constantly making comparisons between the two.

"Expect in the post a trophy of my endeavours.. See, this is new," Max pointed out. Then, he continued, "...*perhaps a portion of bladder or vagina...* Definitely not in the "*Dear Boss*" letter

The Ripper Code

Catch me if you can... That's certainly a phrase of the Ripper *...I love my work and shall start again soon...very soon. You will soon hear of me and my funny little games... The next job I do I shall slice the whore's ears off and send to you just for merriment sake...* The Ripper says "*Lady*" - our writer says "*whore*"... *Keep this email back till I do a bit more work, then give it out straight. My knife's so nice and sharp. I want to get to work right away if I get a chance. Good luck.*" Yep, there's a very strong resemblance. Most of the words are the same. But he has updated it. However, clearly, the writer of this email is a Ripperologist. He knows his stuff. But this last bit is what interests me most - *Yours truly, Tau Tria Delta.*"

"Why didn't he sign himself as '*Jack the Ripper*' as in the original?" asked Edmunds, completely mystified.

"He wants you to know his game but, obviously, he doesn't want to give it all too quickly. He has a certain vanity. He's trying to be subtle. He wants to say '*Jack the Ripper*' without actually saying it. He's a real expert in Ripper knowledge because he has used the pseudonym, '*Tau Tria Delta*', of one of the known suspects. It appears our killer..."

"Hold on there sunshine," Edmunds quickly interrupted, "we have no evidence that this email was actually written by the killer."

"It was. I'm convinced of it. He wants us to know that he strongly identifies with Roslyn D'Onston. He believes... as I do... that Roslyn D'Onston was Jack the Ripper."

Walters raised a hand. "What does this '*Tau Tria Delta*' mean?"

Max smiled. Now he was in his element, talking like an expert in one of those detective TV dramas. "There are two ways of looking at it. But they both come to the same thing. Numerologically, all the letters add up to six...."

"Numerology? What kind of bunkum is this?" groaned Edmunds.

"Don't worry, I've bought some videos which will explain all that. The other way is more basic. Tau is the 21st letter of the Greek alphabet. Delta is the 4th. Tria means three times. So 21 plus "three times 4" is 33. The writer is suggesting he is a Freemason of the 33rd degree... which is what D'Onston wanted us to think?"

"Your Jack the Ripper," reiterated Walters. He was becoming quite fascinated by these ideas of Max.

"Yes," Max replied. "Also notice, 33 is a 3 and a 3, which adds up to six. Both ways of interpreting the name brings us to six."

"Meaning?" queried Walters.

"Erm, well, now, its going to start getting weird..." Max tried not to sound too apologetic.

"Like it isn't already?" growled Edmunds caustically.

"Let's just say for now, that both Rippers – yesterday's and today's - are obsessed with the number six... that's certainly true of Jack. And the use of '*Tau Tria Delta*' could indicate that today's Ripper has a similar obsession. If I could take a copy of the email home to study. I may find more indications. I mean, just look at how he changed '*Boss*' for '*Bob*'. He's changed the word but he's kept the number meaning. '*Boss*' equals one. '*Bob*' equals one. Also, look, he's substituted '*Lady*' for '*whore*'. Both are words with the same number - 6."

"Jesus, you've lost me," moaned Edmunds, throwing his hands in the air in despair.

"I'll leave you the videos," Max said reassuringly. "You look at them. The reason why I can predict that two women, one called Lezzie Lisa, and the other, Kate will be murdered after midnight tonight, is because my findings conclude our killer is a numerologist... and seeing this email simply confirms it... but it also tells me that this Ripper clone thinks he's Roslyn D'Onston, a black magician who sacrificed six whores for occult purposes... to bring about the Antichrist... another future Hitler... or worse."

Walters and Warren looked at each other in astonishment, not quite believing their ears. Max has really gone too far.

What!" shouted Edmunds. "That's it. I've heard enough of this twaddle." He leapt up and threw the office door open. "Get out!" he screamed at Max. "And take your cranky videos with you. And hand back the email. Go on, clear off."

Max refused to budge. "No," he said resolutely. "I'm not leaving until you assure me you will order a watch tonight in Whitechapel, at both Berner Street and Mitre Square. I promise you, you will have a chance to catch the killer."

"Don't you be telling me what to do, you silly little prick."

"Well, I refuse to leave. I will occupy your office until you agree to stake out Berner Street and Mitre Square tonight."

Everyone was aghast at Max's audacious defiance. The inspector turned to Walters in exasperation. "Jim, am I going mad?" he cried. "Or do we really have a little twerp sitting in my office, threatening to occupy a police station in protest? Listen, if you want to occupy this nick, fine, no problem, I'll arrest you, and leave you to cool off in a cell for a couple of days."

"By which time," snarled Max, "you will have had two more horrible murders on your hands. And when I appear in court for causing an obstruction or an affray or nuisance or whatever charge you dream up for keeping me in a cell, the press will have a field day, when they hear I gave you information forewarning you... and you locked me up to keep me quiet."

"Listen, even if I wanted to do what you ask, I can't. Whitechapel is not within my jurisdiction. When I go there to investigate, I go by invitation. And there's no way, I'm going to make a monkey of myself, trying to persuade Whitechapel CID to organise a watch on the basis of all this nonsensical hocus-pocus you're gibbering about."

"Okay, if you don't want to do it officially, why can't you get a couple of officers, like Jim or Ellie, to volunteer during off-duty. If I was a policeman, I'd volunteer."

Warren looked at Walters but he shook his head. Nonetheless, she stood up, "Chief, maybe we should do that."

Edmunds turned in fury at her, waving his finger...

"Don't even think about it," he shouted. "I'm not having some outside crack-pot amateur start telling me how to catch villains."

"Well, if you're not going to send anyone, then I will have to go myself," challenged Max. "I will sit in my car in Berner Street all night if I have to."

Edmunds gave a nasty laugh. "You can do what the fuck you like in your free time, so long as you're not causing me grief. Now, are you going to vacate these premises or do I have to nick you?"

The atmosphere in the office had boiled to a standstill. No one had anything more to say. Sitting rigid in his wheelchair, Max just stared daggers at Edmunds, who was now preparing a charge-sheet. Finally, Max let out a sigh and sadly shook his head and, to everyone's relief, left the building.

"Chief?" Warren ventured.

"Shut it," warned Edmunds

"Yeah, but Guv..." tried Walters.

"I said shut it," Edmunds snarled as he marched out of the office.

CHAPTER 29
Desperation-ville
20th August. Monday

At the corner of Caledonia Street, Max saw her. All through the evening and then on into the late hours, he had scoured the streets, round and round the Kings Cross manor, with a rising panic-stricken desperation. She was just a white luminous blur when he first caught sight of her...and with her frantic beckoning, he knew, at last, he would be in luck. He drove towards her and saw with an overwhelming sense of relief that it was Sophie.

The car screamed to a halt beside her and, throwing the door open, she leapt in, breathless. It looked like she had been running the three-minute mile.

"Max, I've just seen Kate," Sophie triumphantly announced. "I tried to tell her to go home but she's as pissed as a Kilkenny Bishop and won't listen."

"Where is she?" Max asked excitedly.

"Keystone Crescent just off Caledonia Road."

Like a pair of TV cops, Max and Sophie drove off very fast.

Three streets south of Keystone Crescent, they spotted Kate staggering along, using the walls to stop her from falling over. Max careered up to her. At first, she swung towards them and threw up her fists like a punch drunk pugilist, then she recognised Max and shrieked with joy, "Maxie, darling". Thrusting her head through the open car side-window, she slobbered all over him, then she blearily saw Sophie.

"Oooh, got a lady friend with you," she teased. "I don't mind, lets make it a threesome."

"Kate, it's me," said Sophie.

"Oh you, how are you, my darling? Didn't I see you just now?" Kate said apologetically as she lurched around the car to where Sophie sat.

"Kate, can we take you home?" asked Sophie, getting out of the car to help her in.

"Home?" yelled Kate, pulling away belligerently. "What do I want to go home for? The night is still young. I've only done four blokes tonight. I'll call it a day... or a night... when I've scored a minimum of... ten."

"Don't silly, Kate, you can't do ten men in one night. Go home."

"Four's a respectable number, Kate," reasoned Max. "That must be at least eighty quid in your pocket. Not bad for a night's work."

"Eighty quid bollocks," cackled Kate, falling over onto her behind. "I made one hundred and fifty so far... but... course... been celebrating... and then some cunt robbed me of fifty, pushed me over and took the money right out of my hand. The bastard."

"Kate. It's not safe for you tonight. Please let us take you home," pleaded Sophie.

With an immediate mood swing from jovial bonhomie to hostile posturing, the inebriated woman picked herself up and twisted her face into snarling smirk, breathing intoxicating fumes into Sophie's face. "I know whats bothering you," she belched. "I'm too much competition. You want the streets to yerself."

"It's not that, Kate," protested Sophie. Kate pushed passed her and nearly fell into the car to get at Max.

"Oh Maxie, you wouldn't do me a favour and fuck me for forty would you? I promise you, it'll be the fuck of the century. You know I got robbed, don't you," she begged, beginning to sound maudlin.

"Kate, you're drunk," soothed Max, stroking her hair.

"I know and I'll get a bloody hiding when I get home, specially if I return empty pocket-like."

Max gently held her face and looked directly into her eyes as he spoke, "You know about Anne and the others? The

Whitechapel killer, he's still at large. You gotta get off the streets tonight. Better still, keep away from London for a week."

Kate pulled away and laughed raucously. "Don't be silly, Max," she said. "I'm a working girl. I can't afford to take time out. Don't worry about me. I'll take care of myself. I shan't fall into his hands." The luscious lush stumbled and turned to run away, but as if struck by a momentous thought, swivelled back round on her precipitous heels, and with a cheeky gleam in her eye, bellowed at full volume, "Oh well, Max, if you don't want to fuck me, I'll find someone who will. Bye." Max groaned as Kate lurched out of his reach and ran across the road.

"Max, just say you'll fuck her, so we can get her away from here," urged Sophie.

Max tried to drive towards Kate but was suddenly blocked by a bus. Before Max could negotiate around the obstructing vehicle, another car which seemed to appear from nowhere, pulled up beside Kate and, with a triumphant yell, she quickly got in.

"Shit," Max cursed as Kate was driven away. Max frantically tried to reverse back but another bus pulled up behind him, boxing him in. "SHIT! We fucked it up," he shouted, punching his steering wheel.

Max turned to Sophie and asked without much hope, if she saw the car's registration number?

"No, it was all too quick," she replied disconsolately.

CHAPTER 30
Crip-napping
20th August. Monday

Careering around in a maniac driven car, Max and Sophie continued to patrol the gloom-ridden empty streets of Kings Cross.

"Do you think we'll see Lezzie Lisa?" asked Max, still annoyed that he had allowed Kate to escape.

"Lets go to Holloway Road, there's a club there, where she likes to hang out, called 'The Dirty Dyke'," replied Sophie.

"Seriously?", Max laughed. "It's really called that?"

"Only lesbians are allowed to call it that. To other mere mortals it's 'The Dirk and Pike'."

As the Intrepid Pair drove off towards Holloway, neither of them noticed a car stealthily following behind them.

Max and Sophie arrived at "The Dirk and Pike", with ears assaulted by a thumpingly loud cacophonous mix of disco/techno music, and eyes half-blinded by the stroboscopic coloured lights that swept the dance floor that was enshrouded in a swirling dry ice fog. The club was heaving with the frenetic gyrations of ghostly silhouetted patrons of both sexes, although there were plenty of female couples dancing together. Someone waved at Sophie, who smiled and waved back.

"Doesn't look like it's a strictly Lezzies Night but Lisa still might be here," Sophie said to Max, her body already responding energetically to the music's contagion. "Stay there. I'll have a scout around." Max nodded as she disappeared amongst the jiving bodies on the dance floor.

A camp-looking young man on seeing Max, immediately went over, and squatted down on his haunches to be at the same level as the wheelchair man.

"Oh hello, I haven't seen you here before?" the young man cooed, fluttering long dark eyelashes. Max turned and looked at him, quickly assessing the young man to be gay and was probably about to chat him up.

"It's my first time," replied Max, inwardly groaning. "I thought this was a Lesbian Only club," continued Max, determined to remain polite and friendly, even though the young man was irritatingly very touchy-feely.

"That's Wednesdays and Fridays. Tonight is Bi-Night. So what brought you here?" asked the young man, unable to keep his hands off Max.

"I'm looking for a woman."

"Oh dear... and I thought my luck was in. It's just not my night." He nonetheless kept hold of Max's hand.

"I don't mean to...it's not like that. She's a lesbian."

"Oh, so I'm in with a chance, then?" responded the Gay Guy eagerly, licking his lips perhaps unconsciously.

"Well, ur, sorry but I came with my girlfriend," quickly replied Max in near panic. "She's just gone to look for Lezzie Lisa. Do you know anyone called Lezzie Lisa?"

Shrugging his shoulders, the Gay Guy shook his head sadly. Then, suddenly perking up, he asked "So what's your name, my pretty?"

"George," lied Max.

"Ooooh, Georgie! Well, you can call me Ralphie," he whispered in Max's ear, giving his hand a little squeeze and then began to sing, "Georgie Porgie, Puddening-pie. Kissed the girls and made them cry. When the boys came out to play. He kissed them too. Because he's a little gay. Are you a Little -"

"Oh look," Max interrupted, turning to the sound of very loud laughter. "There she is," he exclaimed relieved, pointing to Lezzie Lisa who was dancing with another woman.

"Lezzie Lisa! Lezzie Lisa!" Max shouted, desperately trying to attract her attention, but the clubbing noise was over-powering.

"Lezzie Lisa! Lezzie Lisa! Lezzie Lisa!" shrieked Ralphie, with exuberance. When she seemed oblivious to their joint shouting, the Gay Guy ran up to her and brought her and her partner over to Max.

"Max!" yelled Lisa above the noise, looking genuinely pleased to see him."What are you doing here?"

"Looking for you," replied Max, with a big grateful smile on his face, as he notices that Ralphie, obviously feeling he didn't belong, had disappeared off into the shadows.

"Really?" Lisa enquired. "You want to take up my offer? A bit of S & M with a couple of She-devil Lezzies?"

"Uh I'll pass on that one." Max said hurriedly. "I've come with Sophie. We need to talk with you."

"Sophie? Don't know a Sophie. She a working girl?"

"Yeah. Maybe you know her as Maeve?"

"Oh Maeve, yes. Lovely Maeve. If anyone lives the life of Riley, it's our Maeve."

"Riley?" queried Max.

"Yes, really," quipped Lisa cheekily. "Ha ha ha. Maeve Riley, that's her name."

"Oh, really?"

"Yes, Riley. Ha ha ha." Lisa couldn't stop laughing at her own joke until her partner playfully jabbed her in the ribs with her elbow.

"Lisa, stop being so corny," admonished the girlfriend. "Nice meeting you, Max. Come on Lisa," she commanded, trying to pull Lisa back to the dance floor.

"No, wait, Lisa!" shouted Max.

Lisa swung round and dragged her friend back to Max.

"Max, you want to dance with us?" she invited with a saucy swing of her hips.

"I can't dance," Max replied in a mock self-pitying tone.

"You don't need to. Does he, Sharon?" prompted Lisa, turning to her partner. "Come on, let's pick him up and dance with him between us."

Before Max could make any more objections, Lisa and Sharon swooped him up from his wheelchair and cradling Max in their arms, they waltzed together, taking it in turns to smother him, and each other in kisses. While Max felt he should be feeling acute embarrassment, and possibly, humiliation at being treated like some kind of Tiny-Tot, he had to admit he was actually enjoying the two women's playful attentions.

With the music getting faster and the Trio waltzing round and round in an ever-increasing spiral, clearing the dance floor of other dancers, who stopped in astonishment, forming a crowded circle, to watch with loud applause and cheers, it was inevitable that Ralphie would want to get in on the act.

"Ooooh!" he squealed out loud. "Let me have him. Give him to me!" He rushed up to Lisa and Sharon, trying to snatch Max from their grasp.

"You can't have him. We've got him!" Lisa shouted, holding tight onto Max, pulling him away from Ralphie's reach.

"But I want him," pleaded Ralphie. "Please let me have him, he's so cute."

There followed a crazy tug of war between Lisa, Sharon and the Gay Guy with poor Max as the piggy in the middle, who was getting more and more anxious by the second.

"No!" snarled Lisa with menace. "He's ours! Let go of him."

"Yes, let go," demanded Sharon, tightening her grip on Max.

"But I saw him first!" protested Ralphie.

Max, finding himself about to be torn in half, cried out plaintively, "Ladies, please. A three-way stretch is not quite my idea of fun. Perhaps... if you let him... for just one –"

Just then, a booming woman's voice rang out, "Put that man down! He's mine!"

Everyone stopped. Even the music. The owner of the commanding voice was none other than Sophie, who marched up to the struggling Quartet and eased Max from their hands. After putting him back in his wheelchair, Sophie turned back to Lisa and gave her a big hug, while caressing her bottom.

"Lisa darling, come outside with me and Max for a moment," whispered Sophie.

Lisa nodded her acquiescence, and signalled to the now slightly peeved Sharon to stay where she was. However, the girlfriend was going to have none of that, and accompanied them to the exit.

"I'm not going to let some man scare me off the streets," Lisa angrily remonstrated with Max and Sophie, as the four of them stood outside the club, trying not to draw too much attention to themselves but without much success.

"But he's a killer and he's got your number," warned Max.

"Literally," Sophie hinted.

"Look, I'm enjoying myself tonight," growled Lisa stubbornly. "Me and Sharon are back together again and we are celebrating and I refuse to be men-aced by men."

"Well, can't you go home and celebrate," asked Sophie. "Max will give you a lift. Won't you, Max?"

"Yes, of course," assured Max.

"He's not going to attack two women together, is he? Not a pair of butch dykes like us.

"He's a vicious animal, Lisa. Worse than a rabid dog," insisted Max.

"Yeah, well, I've got this, haven't I," retorted Lisa menacingly as she took from her back pocket, a nasty-looking flick-knife...she flicked the catch and the sharp blade sprung out.

"Anyway, thanks for your concern. It was sweet. Now, you two go home and enjoy yourselves." Lisa grabbed Sharon and together they marched pulled back to the Club's entrance. At the door, Lisa paused to shout a cheeky parting shot, "And Sophie, imagine it's me when you're screwing Max." Seeing Max's crestfallen face, she continued, "Oh Max, don't look so glum, I'm only joking. Catch you later." With a wave at them both, she and Sharon re-entered "Club Dirty Dyke", leaving Max and Sophie feeling like failures.

***

The huge, dark, cavernous space that was trapped within the old disused aircraft hanger, groaned like a giant whale's empty stomach. Or were the whimpering sounds coming from what, on first impression, looked like a large elongated punch-bag suspended from a chain in the middle of the over-arching ceiling.

The man, who occasionally called himself CK, hidden in a long black cloak and wearing a scary *Tony Blair* Halloween mask, stood silently, watching the hanging bundle wrapped in a blanket, sway gently, relishing the tiny plaintive puppy-like sounds.

Panther-like, he moved up close to the swinging heavy lump of a body, gently took hold of it and gave it a spin round, so he could examine the face shrouded beneath the blanket. It was Kate, alive and unharmed but obviously quite sedated.

"Hello, my Precious," CK spoke soothingly. "Just another little prick. We're going on a trip. It's your big night tonight." He spun her a 180 degrees and lifted the blanket to expose her right buttock. From the old-fashion doctor's medical bag, he took out a syringe and stuck the needle into her rump.

"My Master is waiting to eat your soul," he said as he unhooked the semi-comatose Kate bundle, "Up-si-daisy," he continued, lifting her over his shoulder.

"Are you nice and comfy?" he asked, giving her bottom a light pat and squeeze.

"Then, off we jolly well go." With the helpless Kate over his shoulder, the scary *Tony Blair*-masked man walked swiftly to the hanger's exit.

CHAPTER 31
Baits Hotel
20th August. Monday

They were parked in Berner Street, Whitechapel, Max and Sophie sitting motionless in the car, keeping vigil. The night seemed endless. The street may have been empty but not Max's head. His mind was in turmoil. Finally he broke the accusatory silence.

"I don't know what more I could have done," he said. "The police weren't interested. Bloody morons. Neither of the girls would take me seriously."

"At least, you tried," comforted Sophie, giving him a gentle squeeze of the shoulder.

"Guess we'll just have to sit here all night and wait."

"Are you sure he'll come to this street tonight?"

"If he's rigidly following in Jack the Ripper's footsteps, yes. He'll come here first, around about one o'clock, with Lisa. I hope to God, he doesn't kill her beforehand. If he needs to kill her on the site, then there's a good chance, we could scare him away before he does anything."

"But if he sees your car waiting, he's going to turn round and piss off. He'll kill Lisa somewhere else," warned Sophie, trying very hard to sound calmer than she actually felt.

"I know. That's what I'm afraid of. But I don't know the best way to conceal the car."

"Why don't we park down that side street there?"

"We won't get such a good view of the whole street," Max pointed out. "If only I knew which way he was going to come in."

"What are we going to do when we see him with Lisa?"

"I don't know. Beep my horn, flash my lights, shout 'Murder'. Haven't a clue."

"He might try to kill us, if he sees us. He probably has a gun," Sophie said fearfully.

"Well, I'll try to run him over."

"Yeah, but you'll probably hit Lisa. He's bound to use her as a shield."

"I wish I had a gun. If I was in Yankland, I could easily have had one." There was a moment of silence as Max thought about this notion. Then he gave a little laugh and shook his head.

"No, that's stupid. I don't wish I had a gun. I hate guns...And I'm bloody glad I don't live in Yankland." he said with a slight shiver.

"Only pricks carry guns," proclaimed Sophie.

"Yeah," agreed Max. "Actually it's men without pricks who carry guns." He turned the ignition and nodded at Sophie, "You're right. This isn't a good surveillance spot, it's much too exposed. We'll try that street across the road." He slipped the car into gear and moved slowly forward. On reaching the street opposite, they both felt more secure.

The man, CK, also sat in his car...watching and waiting. His patience was finally rewarded. The two unsuspecting women came into view, walking down the street, arm in arm. They would stop, every now and then, to embrace and kiss passionately. CK felt disgust at Lisa and Sharon's flagrant display of lesbian amorousness. He started the engine and slowly crawled towards them. As he drove alongside them, Lisa suddenly turned on him, waving her flick-knife.

"Hey, creep, what the fuck do you want?" she shouted menacingly.

"I'll give you two thousand pounds for a lesbian show," replied CK, as he held out two thousand pounds in notes. Lisa and Sharon looked in amazement at the proffered wad of money and then at each other. They started to giggle.

"Make it four grand," coaxed Sharon. " and we'll perform for you all night."

"Ladies, you got yourself a deal. Get in the car," CK ordered.

With a whoop of joy, the two women got in the back seat.

"We are we going?" asked Lisa.

"Tower hotel. Good enough for you?" replied CK.

"Ooo-uh! Living it up!" laughed Sharon, excitedly thinking of what she was going to be spending her two grand on.

As CK drove speedily away, his cat-like eyes watched the pair in his rear-view mirror as they cuddled up to each other, singing their version of "Living it up".

Half an hour later, Max and Sophie were still sitting in the car, parked in the side street, off Berner Street. Max was feeling very agitated.

"No, I don't like this," he moaned. "We can only see about a third of Berner Street."

"What about the other end of Berner Street?" suggested Sophie "Aren't there a couple of skips? We could hide the car in between."

Max nodded in agreement and drove the car back into Berner Street, heading towards the very end of the block. Suddenly a car came out from a side street and stopped in front of them. Out of the obstructing vehicle, a man and woman emerge, and began to approach Max and Sophie. The man stopped halfway while the woman continued up to their car window. They were relieved to see it was Detective Constable Warren.

"Hello Max," she said, "switch your headlamps off, you're blinding poor Jim."

"Emma... I mean, Ellie," cried Max overjoyed. "Well, well, well. And the Detective Sergeant! That's a real turn up for the books."

"Hello Maeve," greeted Warren, giving Sophie a friendly smile. "You shouldn't be out. It's not safe for girls like you."

"What about girls like you?" riposted Sophie "Anyway, I'm helping Max, who's now having to do your job, keeping the streets safe for girls like me."

"Well, you don't have to any more. The cavalry have arrived. Jim and I have taken up your suggestion, Max. We've just finished work, so we're now volunteering to go on stake out duty. Jim will watch Mitre Square and I'll watch this street."

"Oooh, are you disobeying Edmunds?" asked Max, making no attempt to hide his delight.

"Not really," replied Warren. "He's choosing to turn a blind eye. Anyway, you can both go home to your beds. So, move along now."

"Yes, officer," said Max as he obediently drove away.

After they had been motoring for several minutes, Sophie turned to Max with a deep look of concern on her face.

"Are we really going home?" she asked.

"Are we fuck!" he replied, as he turned the car into Christian Street and brought it to a halt.

The Bridal Suite at the Tower Hotel was exactly as the receptionist described - regal, decadently enormous and lusciously en suite. CK sat in an armchair, dispassionately observing the lesbian sexual antics of Lisa and Sharon, who were both naked and romping about on the King Jumbo-sized bed.

Lisa was wearing a strap-on 2-inch thick, 11-inch long, chocolate-coloured dildo, and lying on her back on the bed, and was fondling Sharon's breasts, who was in the process of straddling her. As Sharon lowered herself down onto Lisa's up thrusting penis-substitute CK swiftly moved behind her. Lisa followed CK with her eyes and smiled, thinking, "I knew the dirty letch couldn't resist joining in. He wants fuck Sharon in the arse, while she rides me."

"Oh yes, your Lordship," encouraged Lisa. "Sharon loves Double P."

In less than a second, CK brought out a gun, placed the barrel against the back of Sharon's head and fired. Her skull instantly exploded, sending bone, blood and brains all over Lisa's face. Before Lisa had time to scream, Sharon's lifeless body was shoved aside, and with his other hand, CK forced a chloroform-soaked cloth onto Lisa's nose and mouth, smothering her, causing immediate loss of consciousness.

Six minutes later, CK was in the hotel's underground car park, pulling a tarpaulin to cover the two unconscious bodies of Kate and Lisa, who were lying on the backseat of his car. Satisfied that the two supine women were completely concealed, he got into the driver's seat and quickly drove from the premises.

It's amazing how careless people can be sometimes. Fancy dropping a lighted match into a wastepaper bin full of paper! Thankfully the bin was made of tin...and the fire was unlikely to spread. Perhaps it wasn't carelessness, after all. Looked all very premeditated, in fact. The smoke from the burning paper drifted up towards the hotel room's smoke alarm, which was immediately above the carefully placed wastepaper bin.

On the King Jumbo-sized bed, staring with unseeing eyes at the incipient conflagration, lying on her front, was the naked, dead body of Sharon. Other than the headshot wound, there were no other injuries.

Suddenly the deathly silence was interrupted by the harsh strident sound of the smoke alarm, which, sadly, was still not fit enough to wake the dead.

CHAPTER 32
Dutfield Yard Revisited
21st August. Tuesday

12.30am. The woman police detective was snatching a quick doze in her car, when suddenly, her colleague's voice on the police radio snapped her out of her illicit slumber.

"Ellie, come in," crackled Walters voice. "WDC Eloise Warren, speak to me."

"Gotcha, Jim," responded Warren. Speaking sleepily into the mic transmitter. "What's happening? Is it the Bogeyman?"

"No. Zero activity," came back Walters' radio voice. "But we have to abandon the watch. Situation at the Tower Hotel. Homicide. You're needed to identify."

"Oh Jesus. Kate or Lisa?"

"That's for you to tell us."

"I'm on my way," shouted Warren, starting the engine. "Bloody Max. Why did we listen to him?" She slammed a portable flashing blue light on the car roof, put her foot down and screeched away at break-neck speed for the hotel that would now, forever, share the same bloody reputation as it's notorious neighbour, the Tower of London.

12.45 am. Max loved eating doner kebabs, still the best value and highly nutritious takeway meal money can buy. None of this cardboard and plastic tasting Yank junk food shit. He gave a sidelong glance at Sophie to check that she was enjoying hers, and was gratified to see the look of pure bliss in her eyes as she ravenously munched into the pitta bread stuffed with ample portions of thinly sliced mutton and a hefty salad of tomato, cucumber, lettice, chopped raw cabbage and onion, spiced up with a smattering of chilli sauce.

The intrepid pair were still sitting in their stationary car, on self-imposed stake out duty. The street was quiet and the stillness undisturbed.

"Why are we waiting in this particular street?" asked Sophie, her mouth full.

"If I'm right that the killer is a copycat of my Ripper suspect, Roslyn D'Onston," answered Max, "then he will be coming from the direction of his base, the London Hospital. This is Christian Street, the most likely road he'll take to get to Berner Street, where he will attempt to sacrifice Lisa."

"You actually think we will see him drive down this street?"

"If my theory's correct, yes... Hello... here's a car coming now." Max announced, noticing in his rear view mirror, a pair of headlamps approach behind them.

"You said that about fifty times already," said Sophie, dismissively.

They both watched a black car drive past. The dismal street illumination momentarily caught the vehicle's number plate. It read *MIB 666R*

"Jesus!" exclaimed Max. "It can't be a coincidence! MIB 666R. Let's follow it."

Max still with his hands full of doner kebab, clumsily tried to start the car, spilling food everywhere. The car started, then stalled, jolting Sophie, causing her to drop her food all over her. After three more attempts he succeeded in getting the car moving but grease from the kebab made his hand slippery and he lost his grip on the steering wheel, which caused his car to collide into a parked vehicle. Pausing briefly to ascertain that his car only suffered a minor dent, Max swiftly reversed away from the other more severely damaged car, and slammed the gear stick into forward and sped away.

Meanwhile, MIB 666R had disappeared out of view, but Max tore towards Berner Street, confident that that was where the black car was aiming for.

As Max raced along Fairclough Street, heading for the right turn into Berner Street, he looked at the dashboard clock.

"Twelve fifty! Shit!" he cursed. "The bastard could be killing her right now." He pressed the car horn, and didn't remove his thumb, so as to keep up a continuous blaring racket.

"What the fuck are you doing?" shouted Sophie, trying to make herself heard above the din.

"Trying to save a life," Max yelled back. "If that car belongs to the killer, he'll be put off if I wake everyone in the neighbourhood."

"You idiot, he'll just drive somewhere else to kill her. Stop it," she screamed. But Max ignored her, and continued pressing the horn as he drove.

A primary school was now built over what was once Dutfield's Yard, the site of the fourth Jack the Ripper Whitechapel killing, just off Berner Street. With no difficulty at all, employing the usual tools of the skilled burglar, CK had managed to unlock the gate leading to the school playground. Propping up the unconscious Lisa with his left arm, CK held a small bottle containing a strong-smelling antidote for chloroform, under her nose.

"Wakey wakey. Rise and Shine," he softly whispered in her ear.

A few seconds of having the pungent antidote pass back and forth under her nostrils, Lisa regained consciousness, opened her eyes, and as soon as she saw her kidnapper, tried to scream, but before she could, a large bayonet-looking knife slashed her throat twice. Air escaped from her severed windpipe. The knife then plunged down to rip her abdomen but stopped at the sound of approaching car horn blaring

"Damn, Little Lezzie Lisa! Coitus Interruptus! Again," hissed CK sardonically, as he dropped Lisa's body on the ground, and quickly fled off the school premises.

Max's car, horn blaring, was hurtling along Berner Street, towards the old Dutfield Yard, when the black car, MIB 666R, charged out from a side road by the school, and rammed his vehicle out of the way, sending it crashing into a parked truck. Max didn't know what hit him. Neither did he see the black car escaping westwards, heading in the direction of Aldgate.

Dazed and shaken, though relatively unhurt, apart from a bloody nose, Max asked Sophie if she was okay. She nodded reassuringly, although he could see that she was, understandably, on the verge of hysterics. Satisfied that she was more or less coping, Max turned his attention to trying to reverse his car, in an attempt to disentangle it from the truck but the car wouldn't budge. The crashed metal of both vehicles were locked into each other.

"Fuck! The fucking car's fucked," groaned Max. "Come on. We'd better get down Dutfield's Yard."

"Oh Jesus, do we have to?" asked Sophie, looking very frightened.

"We have to see if Lisa's down there," insisted Max, "and if so, if there's anything we can do for her."

"You're right," she replied, getting out of the car, went round to the boot and took out the wheelchair and quickly unfolded it, for Max to get in. They then charged down to the yard and found the school gate was, not surprisingly, unlocked. At the centre of the children's playground, they arrived at the dead body of Lisa, her head was barely hanging on to her neck, the cuts to her throat were so deep. Stuffed in her mouth was a red rose.

Naturally, this was too much for Sophie, her bottled hysteria finally broke. Collapsing to her knees, she started screaming, partly in grief but also in terror. Max hadn't a clue what to do. He was at a loss as to how to help or comfort her. Instead he just stared at Lisa, stupefied. The wailing of Sophie quickly brought other people to the scene. Several vomited on seeing Lisa's bloody corpse. Someone finally suggested calling the police, which immediately brought Max back to his senses.

"Sophie, we have to go," he whispered. "There's Kate,"

"No," she croaked, shaking her head, exhausted, her hysteria spent. "Tell the police."

"They won't believe me."

"Ellie and Jim will."

"Why aren't they here? They were supposed to be here," growled Max angrily. He looked at his watch. "Shit, there's no time," he shouted. "Come on, we have to run to Mitre Square."

Suddenly as if from nowhere, Sophie found new energy and leapt up. "Ok, let's go," she said, grabbing the wheelchair, and pushing it in front of her, ran down the street while Max gave her directions.

It was exactly six minutes after Sophie and Max had left Dutfield Yard that the police arrived at the crime scene, headed by Edmunds who had by now been formally given charge of the Whitechapel Murders Task Force, even though this part of London was not part of his normal jurisdiction.

"Well?" Edmunds asked Warren, who just nodded in reply as she knelt down at Lisa's slaughtered body. Walters, with notebook in hand, came up to them from a knot of bystanders, that had gathered beyond the scene of crime tape. Screens were hastily being assembled around the victim.

"Gov., they say there was a little man in a wheelchair here," reported Walters.

"Max. Bloody Mad Max," snarled Edmunds.

"A woman was with him," added Walters.

"Maeve?" asked Warren.

"Probably, since we know they were here earlier," Walters replied. "Anyway, they ran away. Well, she was pushing him."

"Maeve Riley should not be running around like this," exploded Edmunds. "WDC Warren, why the hell aren't you keeping an eye on her?" He stormed off towards his car, as much angry with himself as he was with her. However, he soon came back with a thermos flask of hot sweetened tea, and proceeded to pour himself a drink.

"So, a prostitute found shot at the Tower Hotel and now this one. Are they connected?" he asked, offering his cup to Warren who gratefully accepted it.

"Sharon and Lisa," confirmed Warren. "They were lovers."

The Chief Inspector took his empty cup back and poured out another cup for Walters. "Great. Nothing is ever simple, is it," he grumbled. "Are the killings connected? One was shot. The other, throat cut. But no mutilations. So is she ...Lisa, did you say? ... part of the pattern? Or... Are these two killings tonight nothing to do with our serial killer? Find out when these pair of dykes were last seen together."

"Guv, I think all the killings are being done by one man," said Walters. "The murder in the hotel was done to draw us away from here. The wastepaper bin was deliberately set on fire to set off the smoke alarm."

"Well, if he is the same killer, then he is a shooter as well as a slasher," premised Edmunds, "So, did he also kill Reece? They were both shot in the back of the head. Was it another execution? Get forensics to see if the bullets match."

By now Warren was getting very agitated, she couldn't contain herself any longer. "Sir, don't you think we should send a patrol car to Mitre Square?" she suggested. "If Sharon's murder was intended to draw us away from here so Lisa could be killed, then if Max is right, it was also intended to draw us away from where Kate was going to be killed.

"Ellie, I cannot see how the killer could possibly have known you and Jim were staking out Max's hypothetical locations. How could he have known that Max even told us anything like this? No. You are crediting him with super-human powers. And you, Jim, you're beginning to worry me. You're buying too much into Max's story. However, what I want to know right now is where is the little bleeder? What was he doing here and why did he run away?"

"Sir, Max was here because," returned Warren, "-even though you may not believe his theory but he certainly does... therefore I think he is heading for Mitre Square. That's why we should get a patrol car over there immediately.... Sir."

Edmunds looked severely at his female subordinate and wondered if he should castigate her for trying to tell him his job, but thought she deserved better. "Send one over and bring him in for questioning," Edmunds ordered.

CHAPTER 33
Butchery in Mitre Square
21st August. Tuesday

CK allowed himself a little smile as he saw that here in Mitre Square, yet another primary school had been built on top of a Jack the Ripper murder site. Again CK had no difficulties gaining access to the very spot where Catherine Eddowes on September 30th in 1888 had been butchered. He gently lowered the naked Kate to the ground, at the corner of the building now housing the pupils' art room. He then roused her from unconsciousness by injecting a swift acting antidote. Her eyes slowly opened and then widened with terror on seeing her tormentor. The soul-less psychopath swivelled her round, facing her away from him and briskly slashed her throat from left to right. As the light died in Kate's eyes, the killer stretched her out on her back, and with the bayonet, ripped her abdomen wide open from the breast bone to the pubes, laying it out, which allowed him to then detach her intestines. He draped the intestines over her right shoulder. He then sliced away two and a half feet of colon and draped it over her left shoulder. Taking Kate's jacket, he soaked it in the blood pouring from her stomach, he then placed in a plastic bag. This was followed, by a deft surgically experienced incision through the peritoneal lining and the careful removal of Kate's left kidney. The womb was then cut through horizontally, leaving a stump of three-quarters of an inch. He took the rest of the womb out and wrapped it, together with the left kidney, in a piece of material severed from Kate's blouse, which he put in another plastic bag.

Not content with having done all this, CK proceeded to mutilate Kate's face, cutting both eyelids, then cutting over the bridge of her nose, extending from the left border of the nasal bone down near to the angle of the jaw of the right side. He sliced the tip of the nose and detached it. In everything he did, there was no display of anger or demented rage. He worked like a craftsman, as if he were carving out a Holy relic from a piece of wood. His actions continued to be cold and ruthlessly efficient as he sliced Kate's eyebrows off and her lips. Finally, the possibly reincarnated demon surgeon completely severed her right ear lobe.

Having done all this, CK straightened up and held aloft the plastic bag containing the womb and kidney, offering them up to the Heavens.

"Beloved Unholy Provider," beseeched the Occultist Ripper. "With this Life - the Fifth and Penultimate Blood of the Great Hexatron, I with Thee WED. Upon the Sixth and Final Blood shall our Consummation be complete...and Henceforth, with the Passage of Nine Dark Moons, will be born, the Third and Final Lord of Hate and War. So Mote It Be."

Not since she was a child, when she would imagine she was being pursued by a monster, has Sophie had to run so fast, madly pushing Max along Aldgate High Street, heading towards Mitre Street on their right. As they got close to their goal, Mitre Square., a police patrol car suddenly raced up the road from behind them. It looked like it was going to pass them by, when it screamed to a halt and reversed back towards them, its blue light flashing. The cop car stopped in front of them, and two police officers got out of the vehicle.

"Are you Maxwell Abberline?" demanded one of the policemen, approaching Max and Sophie.

"Yes I am," replied Max. "Thank God, you've arrived. There's going to be a murder further up the road in Mitre Square. If you go there now, you may be able to stop it. Quick."

"We have orders to take you in for questioning."

"Fuck those orders," shouted Max. "Just get up to Mitre Square now before it's too late... if its not fucking already."

"Oye, you!" shouted back the police officer. "I won't tolerate any of this bad language. Now just come quietly to the car." The cop was just about to grab Max by his wheelchair, who in response immediately jammed on his brakes, when they were interrupted by the radio sounds of police coming from the patrol car. The second police officer quickly went over to their vehicle to listen to the message.

"Jesus, " spat out Max. "Why are our police so pathologically stupid? I suppose if I told you it was a Brazilian or an Arab in Mitre Square, you'd be up there like a shot... with guns blazing."

"Come along now, Mr. Abberline. I told you, we don't want any bother. You too, Miss Riley"

The second police officer ran back from the car, frantically beckoning and shouting urgently at his colleague, "Officer Watkins! Just got word that some people in Mitre Square have reported finding a dead body."

"Oh no! Sophie, we're too late. Again!" cried out Max in dismay. "FUCK. FUCK. FUCK. Why won't the fucking bastards believe me?"

"What are we going to do about these two?" asked the first cop.

"I don't know" his colleague replied. "Leave 'em to later, we have to go immediately to Mitre Square." And with that, the two officers quickly got into their vehicle and with lights flashing and sirens blaring, they raced up Mitre Street.

Stunned into silence, both Max and Sophie just stared up Mitre Street. After what seemed like an eternity, Sophie finally, but reluctantly, dared to break the spell, and asked Max, what were they now going to do?

"I don't know," replied Max with a heavy heart, "but there's no point in us going to Mitre Square now. And I don't want to see the horror that will be there."

"Oh, Kate. Poor Kate," sobbed Sophie, collapsing to her knees.

"Jesus, why?" cried Max, also unable to hold back the tears." WHY? What a waste. Women are for loving... not for killing." Silence again reigned as they held each other in mutual commiseration, until another police car raced up the street.

"Come on," said Max, snapping back into action, "we've got to go to Goulston Street."

"Where's that?" asked Sophie.

"About north-east from here. Less than five hundred yards away."

"Why have we got to go there? Not another murder, please!"

"No, reassured Max. "No. Nothing like that. But we may find something of Kate's there. If this killer is strictly following Jack the Ripper's footsteps, then the next thing he will do is write some graffiti on a wall in Goulston Street."

Sophie pushing Max along St. Botolph Street, passing Aldgate tube station on their right, listened with fascinated horror and dread as the diminuitive Ripperologist, in an attempt to take their minds off their current nightmare, explained more of his theories to her.

"Goulston Street. Aptly named. Ghoul-ston Street," he repeated in a tone reminiscent of Vincent Price, the well-known Hollywood chiller star. Sophie tried to reward his weak impersonation with an appreciative laugh but it came out very half-hearted. She really wasn't in the mood for it. Neither was he but he felt compelled to lift the atmosphere somehow.

"It was this graffiti," continued Max, "left in Goulston Street immediately after Catherine Eddowes' murder, that provided me with the Ripper Code, which finally enabled me to discover the true identity of Jack the Ripper - " Max paused to point out an alley, "Here, go right. Goulston Walk. Nearly there."

"Carry on," urged Sophie as she hastily swerved the wheelchair into the alley, nearly tipping Max sideways. As soon as his stomach returned to its rightful place, Max felt able to carry on, "This Ripper graffiti contains a code that is numerologically based. There are five lines to this graffiti and they create a mathematical sum, which creates a sixth invisible line of numbers. Catherine Eddowes, as with our Kate, was the fifth victim when this graffiti was written. The invisible sixth line of numbers point to a number which identifies the sixth victim to be. Jack the Ripper was such a self-publicist, but very obtuse in the way he wanted the world to know how clever he was. He creates this Magic Square of numbers to tell us, first, that he is a Black Magician Mason... and second, to give us all kinds of clues about the five murders... when, where and who and... about the sixth one he has yet to commit... Mary Jane Kelly."

"Kelly," blurted out Sophie, suddenly stopping in her tracks, causing Max to be nearly thrown forward out of his wheelchair.

"Yeah, Mary Jane Kelly," replied Max, wondering if he should push himself the rest of the way.

"What did this graffiti actually say?" asked Sophie, continuing to push the chair, at an even greater pace.

"You'll probably see any minute. We're just coming into Goulston Street."

On reaching the entrance into Goulston Street, they paused, not knowing whether they should go left or right.

"It will be somewhere along this street," insisted Max. "Near a doorway. Written in chalk. If my hunch is correct. Keep going."

"Which way?" asked Sophie.

"Er. Lets hang a right," replied Max. Sophie turned the chair to the right, and walked sharply down the street, while half-wondering if Max was making some kind of political double-entendre. However, she quickly returned to her original question.

"But what was it that Jack the Ripper wrote on the wall?"

Max took from his pocket a piece of paper which had the original words of the Ripper graffiti.

"Jesus, you brought it with you," she exclaimed in astonishment. "You expect to see it on the wall, don't you. You really believed your predictions would come true."

"And they have. So far. Unfortunately." he replied, studying the slip of paper in his hand.

"This is what the Ripper wrote 'The Juwes are The men that Will not be Blamed for nothing." Max held the paper above his head, so Sophie could see that the graffiti words were arranged in a square....

The Juwes are
The men That
Will not
be Blamed
for nothing.

"*J, U, W, E, S* ?" queried Sophie. "That's an odd way to spell Jews."

"It's a Masonic way. It's also numerologically convenient. He changed the spelling so that the word would give a 6 because he wanted the top line to give 6 6 6. '*The*' equals 6. '*Juwes*' equals 6 and '*are*' equals 6. It was discovering the 666 on the top line of the graffiti that suggested to me that the Ripper was a numerologist and that he was giving a code whereby someone in the future could discover the truth about him."

Suddenly Max shouted, "Stop. What's that across the road?"

They crossed the road to a doorway, where Max had spotted a bundle lying on the ground. Sophie knelt to have a closer look.

"Looks like a jacket," she said and touched it. "It's very wet. Oh Jesus, it's blood." she yelped, backing away from what was once a smart black satin jacket, now drenched in thick, sticky red gore.

"It's Kate's jacket," moaned Sophie, very distraught. "She loved that jacket."

Max, meanwhile, was looking up, straining to see in the dark, if anything was inscribed on the wall.

"Yes! He affirmed. "There it is. Graffiti. In chalk. Oh God, he is so predictable. Why?"

Max squinted his eyes, "I can't quite read it from down here. Is it the same?"

Sophie looked up and shook her head, "No, he's written Muslims instead of Jews...and there are some other word changes.

"Good God, he's updated the graffiti," exclaimed Max astounded. "Back in Victorian London, there was a huge influx of Jewish immigrants, refugees and asylum seekers, escaping from Polish and Russian pogroms. Then as today, your typical xenophobic Brit wanted to blame immigrants for everything. Then, it was the Jew who was suspected of all things evil, even the Whitechapel murders. Jack the Ripper played on this anti-Semitism by including it in his graffiti. Today, it's the Muslim who is being blamed for everything."

The Ripper Code

Meanwhile, further down across the street, standing in the shadows, lurking behind a doorway, CK, with wry amusement, silently watched the two amateur sleuths.

Max feverishly searched in his purse, and found what he was looking for, a pen and paper.

"Can you write out exactly the words, and how they are arranged?" Max asked, handing her the piece of paper and pen. "I want an exact replica."

Sophie began to scribble down what she read on the wall -

> *The Moslems   are*
> *The males   that*
> *   Will   not*
> *be Answerable*
> *   for   nothing*

As she did so, Max suddenly looked around, feeling they were being watched, "He's here," he announced in a low voice.

"What?" cried Sophie, startled.

"He's watching us. I can feel him," he whispered, looking up and down Goulston Street but he couldn't see anyone.

"Oh stop it, Max," begged Sophie as she quickened her scribbling. "You're scaring me. He could easily kill us both."

"Have you finished copying it down?" demanded Max impatiently.

"Yes," she whispered, thrusting the paper into his hand.

"We'd better go. But go slowly. Don't run. And stay in the light."

"Where shall we go?" asked Sophie, nervously gripping the handle bars on Max's wheelchair.

"Back to the car. I left my moby. I'll ring a friend, see if she'll pick us up. She won't be pleased at this time of night but I'm sure she'll do it. Then I'll get the garage to pick the car up in the morning."

Sophie pushed Max warily down the street, trying not to panic, trying not to look around, trying hard to maintain a normal walking pace. She looked down at Max, and sensed that he was also not as calm as he was trying to appear.

Waiting until they had disappeared from view, CK stealthily left his hiding place and nimbly nipped round the corner to his car, got in and drove several blocks north to Bishopsgate, where he parked the vehicle near a pub called '*The Jack in the Box*'.

Quickly surveying the seemingly empty street and satisfied that there were no potential witnesses about, he got out of the car, removed the number plates - MIB 666R, and hid them in his doctor's bag. He then went to the boot of his car, took out a can of petrol and poured most of the contents all over the car, and a small remainder on a piece of fabric from the late Kate's knickers. Using a cigarette lighter, he set the rag ablaze, which he tossed into the car, and quickly dodged around the street wall, to shield himself behind a rubbish skip. Within six seconds the car was engulfed in flames, and another six seconds later, it exploded, creating shockwaves that shattered windows on both sides of the street.

CK stood up and slowly walked away, talking into a mobile phone.

"Am I talking to the Camden Police Station?" he asked imperiously. "Good... A message for dear old Bobby... you don't know a "Bobby"... Yes, you do. Detective Inspector Robert Edmunds...That's my man...Tell dear old Bobby, I was not joking, when I gave him the tip. Double event this night. Number one problematic. Pity. Couldn't finish the job. Had not time to get ears for Bobby. Never mind. Tell him to go to 42 Goulston Street. He will find something to his advantage... Who shall I say is speaking? Tell him... Saucy Jack. Toodle-pip, old bean." And with that, CK switched the mobile phone off and threw it into a litter bin, and continued his nonchalant stroll until he reached Liverpool Street underground, where he got on the first available tube train.

Back at Berner Street, Max and Sophie had been waiting at his abandoned car, for nearly half-an-hour, when at last, another car arrived, flashing its lights and pulled up alongside. It was Claire.

"You're an angel, Claire," greeted Max.

"Only when asleep, which certainly isn't now," grumbled Claire. "Come on. Lets get you both to your beds."

"Claire, this is Sophie," said Max, as he got onto the front passenger seat.

"Maeve," reminded Sophie, putting his folded wheelchair on the backseat and squeezed next to it.

"Oh, yeah. Maeve," he corrected. "Maeve, this is Sophie. Ooops. Wrong again," and in a feeble attempt at a Neddy Sea Goon voice, he went on, "I'm sorry, I'll read that again....Maeve – Claire. Claire – Maeve."

The two girls tried to smile but they were just too tired. Claire had just enough energy to hit the gas pedal, and drive them back to Max's apartment.

CHAPTER 34
Code Ripping
21st August. Tuesday

Max, with the two women at either side of him, was at his computer, hammering at the keyboard, typing in the text of Goulston Street new graffiti, displaying it on the screen in accordance with Sophie's copy.

> *The Moslems are*
> *The males that*
> *Will not*
> *be Answerable*
> *for nothing*

"Are you sure this is how he wrote 'Muslims?' *M, O, S, L, E, M, S* ?" he asked Sophie who was standing at his left shoulder

"Yes," asserted Sophie. "I copied it exactly as I saw it."

"Interesting," mused Max. "He could have written it two ways. M-U-S-L-I-M-S or this way. He chose this. Interesting." He double-clicked on "NUMERIZE", and on the screen the Graffiti was instantly transformed into a column of numbers.

6	6	6		=	9
6	5	4		=	6
		2	4	=	6
7	1			=	8
	3	6		=	9
------------------------					----
1	6	9	4	=	2

"Ah-ha. That's why," he grasped. "He's changed some of the words from the Ripper original. But they've all kept exactly the same numbers. See." Max tapped some keys and brought up the "Juwes" version on the screen -

>   The Juwes   are
>   The men   That
>   Will   not
>   be Blamed
>   for   nothing.

Again he double-clicked "NUMERIZE" icon and the very same columns of numbers appeared, beginning with 6 6 6.

"Look," said MAX, pointing at the screen, "He's changed '*Juwes*' to '*Moslems*', '*men*' to '*males*' and '*Blamed*' to '*Answerable*'. He contrived three new words that would keep the same numbers."

He turned round to face Sophie and Claire, and went on, "This means our Mad Killer knows about the Ripper Code... because he has endeavoured to keep the sequence, the layout and the arithmetic of all the numbers... totally intact.

"But why?" asked Sophie.

"Because numbers and gematria..." began Max

"What?" interrupted Sophie, unsure whether she could take in any new information so late in the night.

"Gematria...sacred geometry," explained Max. "Numbers and Gematria mean everything to him. He has adopted Ripper as a role model for his killing spree because he too, is, at heart, an occultist, probably a necromancer."

Max then clicked on the icon labelled "WMC", and the computer immediately displayed a chart of the original Whitechapel murders.

"What does 'WMC' mean?" asked Claire.

"Do you know, I've forgotten," said Max, making a sheepish face. "It's such a long time since I wrote this program."

The Ripper Code

"Perhaps 'Whitechapel Murder Chart'," she suggested helpfully, which made Max groan, "Durrrr...silly me. Me brain's gone AWOL."

"And mine. Please Sir, can we crash soon?" pleaded Sophie.

"I thought you wanted to know why the Killer was playing with numbers in his bit of graffiti?"

"Yeah, okay, but get on with it," conceded Sophie.

"Take a look at the chart," Max turned back to the monitor.

```
1. martha tabram,    7th August – george yard, whitechapel high street
   7       3         7           3     3         2     5     6      = 9

2. "polly" nichols,  31st August – bucks row
   8       8         4            2     2                           = 6

3. annie chapman,    8th September – 29 hanbury street
   7       2         8              2     8     6                   = 6

4. elizabeth stride  30th September – 40 berner street, dutfield's yard
   7         3       3                4    8     6      1       3   = 8

5. "kate" eddowes    30th September - mitre square
   1      3          3                2     9                       = 9

6. mary jane kelly   9th November - 13 miller's court, 26 dorset street.
   3    3    2       9              4    7     5     8    9     6   = 2
```

He then clicked on the "*Ripper Code*" icon, and the "Juwes" numbers appeared alongside, allowing for a comparison to be made.

```
    6   6   6           =   9
    6   5   4           =   6
            2   4       =   6
    7   1               =   8
        3   6           =   9
    -----------------       ----
    1   6   9   4       =   2
```

"See how these final numbers – 9, 6, 6, 8, 9, 2 – are identical to these final numbers – 9, 6, 6, 8, 9, 2. This is what I call 'The Ripper Code',"

"I still don't get what the Ripper Code is telling us," sighed Sophie, wearily.

Max reached out and gave her hand a comforting squeeze, which Claire couldn't avoid seeing, and feeling a twinge of jealousy.

Max went on, "This Code is telling us that every decision the Ripper made concerning the six murders, the dates, the places, the victims were all arranged to fit in with a specific collection of numbers he believed to be important. He probably imagined he was some eccentric mathematics professor, scribbling esoteric equations on a blackboard, but instead of chalk he was using blood."

"He didn't write it in blood," countered Sophie. "He wrote it in chalk."

"I know," replied Max tetchily. "I was being allegorical."

"Well, don't be. These are my friends we're still talking about," Sophie snapped.

"This Ripper was some kind of perverted Einstein," interceded Claire, trying to ease the tension.

"That's probably it – apart from all his black magician mumbo jumbo rituals-" agreed Max. "Jack the Ripper, i.e. Roslyn D'Onston, was trying to tell the world he was a genius."

"All he's telling me," spat out Sophie, proceeding to pace back and forth. "...is he was a fucking nut case, 'toys in the attic' maniac, a total fanatic. Fancy him going to all this effort, all these numbers and geometry, maps, compass, rulers, word play... for what? Eh? To kill six innocent women. I mean, he thinks he's got such a great fucking brain but all his pathetic imagination can do is dream up a sick scheme for killing women. And, I worry, Max, that you secretly admire him." Max felt quite hurt at this totally unjustified insinuation, but he wasn't inclined to defend himself as he understood how exhausted and fraught she must be.

"Have you noticed," piped up Claire, who was studiously staring at the computer screen, "that with this Ripper Code, all the numbers lead to one particular number?"

"Yeah, number 2," replied Max.

"Well, look at the name of the woman he plans to kill next." Claire pointed to the chart. "He is actually giving us the number of her name. Two."

"Mary equals 3. Jane, 3. Kelly, 2," read off Max. "Kelly."

"Maybe we should be looking for a woman called Kelly," Claire proposed.

"God, I'm knackered," yawned Sophie. "Got to crash."

"Just my luck, Max thought, here I am sharing my bed with two gorgeous women, and we are all too shattered to take glorious advantage of this ménage a' trois." Indeed, there he was on his back, wide awake, staring up at the ceiling, with both Claire and Sophie fast asleep, on either side of him. Their arms were heavily draped across him and he seemed uncomfortably pinned down. He had been lying like this for nearly four hours, desperate for the toilet and wishing morning would hurry up.

Finally, as he was about to doze off, he was jolted awake by the sound of a package coming through his letter box in the hall, and dropping to the floor with a dull thud. Max stirred himself and struggled to get out from beneath the heavy blanket, weighing him down, between the two women. He carefully moved their arms without waking either and pulled himself out. He, as with his two friends, was still fully dressed, so without causing any disturbance, he quickly got into his wheelchair and slipped out to the hallway, where he immediately espied the brown rectangular package, narrow enough to pass through the letter box.

Max picked it up and weighed it in his hand. He noticed the package had no postage stamps. Perhaps, it had been hand-delivered. Yes, it must have been, because it did not have a proper address. All it said, in thick, black marker ink -

"The Real (Wheel) Chairman, the Whitechapel Vigilante Committee."

"What is it?", came Claire's voice behind him. Max turned and saw that both Claire and Sophie, were up and anxiously staring at him.

"A package. Just arrived. No stamps or anything. Must have been delivered by hand," replied Max, showing them the package. "And look how it's addressed."

Claire took the package and read aloud, '*The Real*... brackets – *Wheel* – close brackets...*Chairman, The Whitechapel Vigilante Committee.*' Eh?"

"What does it mean?" asked Sophie, baffled.

"I fear, something very nasty," answered Max, taking back the package.

"Is it from him?" Sophie nervously inquired.

"Of course. Who else would send a package to me, addressed to the Whitechapel Vigilante Committee. He's taking the piss."

"I don't get it?" complained Claire, though unable to take her eyes off the package, which to her was screaming to be opened.

"I told you," said Max, "this mad man is copying Jack the Ripper. After the double event of Catherine Eddowes and Elizabeth Stride murders, the Ripper sent a package to the Whitechapel Vigilance Committee, which had been set up, to try to catch the Ripper, by a George Lusk, self-appointed chairman."

"You're not going to open it, are you?" cautioned Sophie.

"Uh-uh. No way," Max reassured her. "I'm taking it straight to the police."

"I'd better give you a lift then, hadn't I, since I'm the only one with wheels," said Claire, then laughed when Max tapped his wheelchair, "Well, you know what I mean!" she added.

"I'm coming with you, if you don't mind," said Sophie, grabbing her things as Max and Claire prepared to leave.

CHAPTER 35
WheelChairman of the Whitechapel Vigilante Committee
21st August. Tuesday

The desk sergeant had mixed feelings of both relief and dismay, when he saw Max, and his two women companions, enter the police station. On the one hand, he had been ordered to bring in the bloody little nuisance, and in wheels the little tyke, bold as brass, saving the sergeant the bother; and yet, on the other hand, nothing was ever simple with Max, he always brought trouble and strife with him to the cop shop.

"Is Detective Inspector Edmunds in?" inquired Max, going up to the desk, while Sophie and Claire kept in the background.

"Afraid not, Mr. Abberline. But if you would like to wait here until he returns. I know he is very keen to talk to you," informed the Sergeant.

"Can you get him on the blower? It's urgent we see him now."

"I'm sure it can wait." the Sergeant replied dismissively.

"Look. This package," warned Max. "It suspiciously arrived on my doorstep this morning. I don't know what's in it. It could be a bomb," Max placed the said dodgy item on top of the desk.

"Good god!" shouted the Sergeant, nervously stepping backwards." And you brought it here... to a police station!"

"What better place," retorted Max mischievously, turning to wink at the two girls behind him.

"Are you a suicide bomber?" accused the Sergeant, reaching for the emergency alarm beneath the desk

"I doubt it's a bomb," said Max hastily, "but I think it's something from this lunatic killer you got."

"Why do you think he would send you anything?"

"The Inspector will know. Get him here. Then you can ask him."

"Ask the Inspector what?" demanded Edmunds, who, at that very moment, had just come through the front entrance.

"What are your thoughts?" inquired Edmunds after he, Walters, Warren and Max had convened in his office, to consider the unopened package which was now carefully placed on his desk. Claire and Sophie had been ordered to wait out in the Reception.

"Well, I think we can safely say it's not an explosive device," replied Max with smug-like confidence.

"Oh? Really? What makes you so cock-sure?" came back Edmunds.

"Because this creep only does what Jack the Ripper does, and the Ripper did not send bombs in the post," returned Max.

"Well, for your information, this killer has been doing a lot more than your Ripper. He shot a prostitute in a hotel before he killed the two in Whitechapel. And with the same gun, we believe he killed one of our police officers. So, he is not exactly following your Ripper pattern, is he?"

"My God. Who did he shoot in the hotel?" cried Max, appalled.

"Sharon. Lezzie Lisa's partner," answered Warren.

"Oh no!" he groaned. "Jesus! I was dancing with them both, earlier. Sort of dancing."

"So, it goes to show, doesn't it Max, that it's not safe to make too many assumptions," countered Edmunds. "Question is – do we bring in the Bomb Squad?

"Well, I'll tell you what I think, is in the package," offered Max. "Half a left kidney belonging to Kate. And a letter that will be similar to the one sent to a man called Lusk."

Edmunds stared intently at the brown package, wishing he could strip away the wrapping with his eyes. After a deep sigh, he turned to Walters and said, "Jim, get this package over to forensics for x-ray examination and, if non-bomb, opened up. Then have them send over the contents immediately and a preliminary report."

The Ripper Code

"We'll need a sample of your prints, Max," said Walters as he put on a pair of rubber gloves and slid the package in to a plastic bag. "Anyone else finger the parcel?"

"Er, Claire I think...and possibly Sophie -"

"Maeve," interjected Warren.

"I mean, Maeve," Max assented.

"Ellie, take fingerprints from all three before they leave," ordered Walters as he went out, carrying, with great trepidation, the package. After he had gone, the gruff old Inspector turned to face Max and patted him on the shoulder. "Young man, I have to be honest with you," said Edmunds, "my opinion of your abilities are changing. You've been pretty accurate anticipating the killer's next moves...and we've been plodding along in your wake, with our thumbs firmly up our own rectums. What can you tell us about Goulston Street...and the killer's next move?"

Suddenly Max sat up straight. "Hold on a minute," he exclaimed. "I just remembered. I know the killer's car registration number. Twice I saw it last night in the vicinity. A big black car. The second time, the bastard rammed me as I approached Dutfield's Yard when he was leaving."

"How do you know it was the killer, and not some drunk driver?" suggested Edmunds.

"First," began Max. "Because I've seen this car three times altogether. It seems like it's stalking me. Or..." Max went quiet, as a troubling thought took hold of him.

"Or what?" Edmunds demanded impatiently.

"Sophie knows him," Max continued. "She got in his car one time. Is Sophie, I mean Maeve, still out in the reception?"

Warren quickly went out the office but soon returned with, "Apparently she went home. Claire is still waiting for you."

"Ah, good old Claire," smiled Max.

"And the second reason?" reminded Edmunds

"His number plate. It's like he's got this perverse need to advertise himself."

"That characteristic is not unknown amongst many serial killers. So? Tell us the car's reg. And we'll check it with the NPC and the DVLA."

The Ripper Code

"You won't believe it," warned Max. "MIB 666R."

Warren immediately wrote down the number, and then spoke softly on the phone.

"MIB?" Edmunds raised his eyebrow. "Men In Black? 666? You have to be taking the piss?"

"No," Max emphatically denied, "but I think he is."

"Chief," Warren broke in. "The National Police computer has no record of it, either missing or stolen... The vehicle licensing agency say there's no such number on record. It doesn't exist."

"Max, you story is getting a teeny bit silly, again," said Edmunds in exasperation.

"You asked me about Goulston Street just now," reminded Max. "You found graffiti chalked up on the wall, didn't you? It was above a blood-soaked jacket belonging to Kate." Edmunds couldn't help nodding in the affirmative, and dumbfounded that Max had got there before him. Max then handed him a piece of paper, "This was what was written, wasn't it?"

Edmunds read it, whistled softly in amazement, and gave it to Warren to read.

"Keep talking," he commanded Max.

"Me and Sophie nearly got to Mitre Square but when we saw the police already there, we knew Kate must have...you know. So I said, lets go on to Goulston Street."

"Why go to Goulston Street?" demanded Edmunds.

"Because I am a Ripperologist. That's why. How many times have I got to tell you," Max snapped back. "I expected him to write the graffiti. Admittedly, I didn't anticipate the changes he made to the text. But what he didn't change was the number structure... which I won't go into now... but suffice to say, the killer, our local maniac, knew that the original graffiti was a code... what I call the Ripper Code, which tells us many things about Jack the Ripper and the games he played... but the most important thing it tells us... is who he is going to kill next, when and where. Our killer, advertising the same code, is also telling us who his final victim is going to be."

Edmunds put his hand out and waved at Max to stop, "Alright, enough of this. I don't want to know how you worked all this out.

Bloody mumbo-jumbo." This so incensed Max, he was ready to start a shouting match but just then, Walters returned from forensics, carrying a cardboard box. The contents were placed carefully on Edmunds' desk. A human kidney, presumably the one previously missing from the body of Kate, and a note addressed, "*From Hell*". Horrified, Edmunds and Warren examined the items. Edmunds then turned to Max and said, "He wrote this for you," And handed him the note. Max studied it, noting the idiosyncratic English.

"Maxy. Sir I send you half the Kidne I took from one woman prasarved it for you. tother piece I fried and ate. It was very nice. I may send you the bloody knif that took it out if you only wate a whil longer. Signed Catche me when you can Maxy."

"Well, he's mimicked all the Ripper's contrived spelling mistakes," said Max, handing back the note. "He's also called me "Maxy" - not Max. Adding a "Y" on the end. He is equating me with Lusk by giving my name the same number as Lusk - 9. Yep, our killer is a numerologist. And one hell of a sick bastard."

"So, we better catch him before he kills victim number 6. You say you can name her?" questioned Edmunds.

Max nodded, "The Ripper Code tells us her name is... Kelly. I thought it would be Mary or Jane, but it's Kelly." All three officers look startled, and yelled the names out at once.

"Riley?" bellowed Edmunds

"Maeve?" cried Warren

"Kelly?" stammered Walters

"Pardon?" shouted Max in frustration.

Warren grabbed Max's wheelchair and swung him round to face her, "Maeve Kelly Riley," she said with painstaking emphasis. "You're talking about your Sophie".

"Sophie is Kelly? stuttered Max, his face suddenly drained of colour. "Oh no. Shit! Where is she?" Max snatched his mobile phone, and dialled her number. He listened impatiently to the three rings, and then, the voice mail announcement.

"Fuck!" yelled Max, angrily stuffing the phone back in his pocket. "No wonder he was picking her up in his car. Posing as a regular client. He's been playing with her like a cat with a mouse." Max rushed to the door, yelling, "We got to get her back. Put her in protective custody or something."

"Put out an APB on Maeve Kelly Riley," Edmunds ordered Walters, who immediately dialed through to the desk sergeant and repeated the command down the telephone

Warren, taking a chair, sat down close to Max, and looking up at Edmunds, asked "Shall I, boss?". He nodded "Yes".

"Max," she began gently, "it looks like it's even more complicated than we thought. Maeve or Kelly or Sophie, however you want to call her, is our number one witness against gangland boss, Sinclare."

"Then why didn't you put her in protective custody from the start?" yelled Max. "Then, none of this would have happened. None of the girls would have been killed."

"What do you mean?" spluttered Warren, her eyes widening.

"This killer is on a contract. He was hired by your Sinclare to kill Sophie, to stop her from testifying but they didn't want to make it obvious... so, the hired assassin cooks up this Jack the Ripper killing spree as a diversionary tactic with Sophie as the end target. So that when she finally dies... before her court appearance, of course... you Birks in Blue won't connect her death - and all the nasty attendant Ripper mutilations and disembowelling - with a Sinclare hidden agenda. And you'll just write her off as another victim in a long line of prostitutes murdered by some crazee who wants to be Jack the Ripper."

"Jesus, Max, how do you know all this?" exclaimed Edmunds."

"Sophie was suggesting this scenario about five days ago, when Anne was murdered. It was an idea that was haunting her but of course, I didn't realise she was talking about herself." Max groaned, as he opened the door to the reception, where Claire was still waiting patiently for him.

"I have to go," he added with grim determination. "I need to get my car sorted out and I need to find her."

"We all need to find her, Max. Leave it to us," ordered Edmunds.

"Oh yeah, you were brilliant at protecting Lisa and Kate weren't you?" replied Max with embittered sarcasm. "Remind me not to call the police next time I'm in trouble."

And with that, Max took his leave, closely followed by Claire, who was, of course, all agog as to what had transpired behind closed doors. Max told her everything as she drove him back home.

CHAPTER 36
Another Victim for The Great Hexatron
21st August. Tuesday

Sophie, or should we now say Kelly? Aye, Kelly it is. She hadn't yet come home to her flat. The sitting room was in darkness, the curtains still drawn. And CK sat, waiting for Kelly to return, in her old grandmother's moth-eaten armchair, shipped all the way from Ireland when she left it to her favourite grandchild in her will, eleven years ago. The Master Assassin, sat in quiet repose, his hands in a seeming attitude of prayer, fingertips touching, as he listened to what he took to be her footsteps, climbing the stairs.

The sound of a key turning in the front door lock brought a thin smile to his face as he swiftly got up and went into the bedroom. He dived under the bed and listened to the front door opening and footsteps entering.

The unsuspecting Kelly dropped her coat, and immediately went to the bathroom. There, she switched on the shower. Next, she entered the bedroom, and began to undress, clothes dropping to the floor. CK peeping at her from under the bed was not, in the remotest, sexually aroused by the sight of her now naked body as she walked out of the bedroom.

In the sitting room, she pressed the "PLAY" button on her answer machine

"You have one message," came the male AnsaVoice, followed by a beep, and then the voice of Max, *"Sophie, I mean Kelly. Yes, I know you're Kelly. I now know you are in terrible fucking danger. Oh god, Kelly, why didn't you tell me? It was you he was after all along. And you knew that, you silly cow. We could have run away and hid somewhere. I know somewhere he would never have found us. We could have stayed hid until the court case. His assignment might then have gone past it's sell-by-date. Kelly, I'm going home. When you get this message, drop everything, come straight here. The police will protect you. God, I hope you pick up this message soon. Ring me. Love you."* The message concluded with a click, and "You have no more messages," from the AnsaVoice

Kelly stood looking at the telephone, wondering if she should immediately return Max's call, but hearing the shower in the bathroom, beckoning her, she decided it could wait a few more minutes. She went into the bathroom and began her shower.

CK quickly and silently got from under the bed and headed for the bathroom. Kelly didn't stand a chance. She had her back to him, when he noiselessly entered. At the last moment, some primeval instinct told her to turn round, she caught a glimpse of her intruder and tried to scream, but it was all too late. The chloroform-soaked cloth was pressed to her mouth and nose, and within seconds, she was out like a light.

"When's it going to be ready?" asked Max down the telephone, back at his apartment. Claire was sitting on the sofa, sipping tea. "Three days!" he protested, aghast. "No. It has be sooner. I need my wheels. I'm a prisoner at home without them. Surely the damage wasn't that bad? Well, can you supply me with a replacement loan? You've got none available? Great. Well, can you do it as quick as you can. Thanks." He sighed, slamming the phone down.

"I'll be your Wheels," Claire offered eagerly.

"No. Thanks but... you've got to go to work... and you got your own life to lead."

"I'll call in sick. They'll manage."

"No. It'll be too much hassle for you. I have to go round the red light districts to find Sophie. I wish I could remember where she lived. Only went there the once."

"You did it with her in her place?" Claire asked, trying not to sound disapproving, though she knew she was secretly uncomfortable with this business of Max and his prostitutes thing.

"Yeah. Actually it was a bloody laugh. Mad. She's crazy," replied Max, already feeling nostalgic.

"You really like her," said Claire, in a tone that failed to disguise her sense of loneliness. It was times like this that made her really feel inferior. She was sure if she wasn't disabled, Max would prefer her to other women.

"Hmmm," Max mused thoughtfully. "Yeah, well, Sophie's not like all the others. She's different. Sure she took my money. Would never forget to take the fee. But she never made me feel that it was just about money. If ever a woman came close to making me feel like a real man, it was Sophie. I mean Kelly."

Claire sighed wistfully, and then, "We'd better find her, then," she announced business-like, getting into her wheelchair from the sofa. "How long have we got?"

"What do you mean?"

"Before he tries to kill her. If he is still working to a strict timetable."

"You're right," he exclaimed, wagging his finger at her. He quickly went to the computer and opened the "Ripper Files" and then, "WMC file". On the screen appeared the table of the Victorian Whitechapel Murders.

Date	Victim	Location
Tuesday 7 August 1888	Martha Tabram	George Yard.
Friday 31 August 1888	Mary Ann Nichols	Buck's Row
Saturday 8 September 1888	Annie Chapman	Rear Yard at 29 Hanbury Street
Sunday 30 September 1888	Elizabeth Stride	Yard at side of 40 Berner Street
Sunday 30 September 1888	Catherine Eddowes	Mitre Square.
Friday 9 November 1888	Mary Jane Kelly	13 Miller's Court, 26 Dorset Street

"Mary Jane Kelly was killed on the 9th of November," Max points out. "Well, that's too late for our killer. But it'll be a date that will add up to '9'. He's working to a tight schedule, so I reckon it will be the next."

"Today is the 21st, so the next '9' has to be the 27th. 2 and 7 equals 9. Therefore, he will surely aim to kill Sophie on the 27th. Next Monday," Claire concluded.

"Six days time. SIX!" observed Max significantly. "What a convenient coincidence. His final sacrifice after a six day interlude."

"Don't you think you should tell the police?"

"What's the point? They're crap," declared Max. "Still, I owe it to Sophie. Yeah, I'd better." He picked up the phone and dialled.

"Can I speak to Detective Inspector Edmunds?" he asked he got through. "He's not in. What about Walters? ...He's not there either. Is Emma there, I mean Ellie... no... um... Eloise. Warren! Is WDC Warren there? She is! Great. Can I speak to her please. Tell her it's Max."

He waited a few seconds, nervously biting his lower lip, only relaxing slightly when he heard Warren's voice on the other end.

"Ellie?" he asked, wanting to be absolutely certain. "Hi. It's Max. Listen..."

CK stood, poised in the shadows, soaking up the delicious fear-laden atmosphere as he surveyed the huge, dark, cavernous near-empty space contained within the aircraft hanger turned-warehouse. After taking six long deep breaths, he began walk slowly towards the four-poster double-bed strategically positioned in the middle of the place, surrounded by a circle of black candles on ivory candle sticks that were three foot high. The candles were lit and flickering vigorously. Behind the head of the bed stood a 12 foot black crucifix standing upside down. At the foot of the bed, there stood a 12 foot high white pentacle, which was also upside down. The bed was not empty.
There lay Sophie, naked, on her back, strapped down. Each of her limbs were tied to the four corners of the bed. The helpless woman was wide awake but she could barely make a sound as her

mouth was taped. On seeing CK approach the bed, she shook with fear and loathing, and renewed her struggle to be free of the bondage, but it was no use.

"Hello Kelly, my Darling, my last but not least," purred CK. "I know it is going to be quite a discomfort for you to be bound in this position, especially as you will have to stay like this for six days but it will be convenient for me. I will, of course, come every now and then to feed and water you... and tend to your hygiene. You will have noticed there is quite a large hole cut in the mattress beneath your pelvis. Below is a bucket for your convenience. I will empty the bucket on my visits."

He turned his back on her and began to light the black candles, all eighteen of them, forming a hexagonal around the bed. As he put each candle to flame, he continued to talk to her with his hypnotically soothing voice, "Kelly, you will be pleased to know that you are to be the Vessel of my Seed, nurtured by your blood and the blood of your five sisters who have already made the supreme sacrifice. We have six days before the Final Conclusion of the Blessed Alchemical Wedding between my humble self and The Great Hexatròn. And in those six days I shall inseminate you three times a day. I shall visit you every eight hours. Ah, the Blessed Eight. Three Eights. It was in 1888 when the Second Lord of Hate and War was conceived. They called him the Antichrist. Did you know he was born in the Year of the Ox? They also called Napolean the Antichrist. He too was born in the Year of the Ox. As Antichrist he was the First Lord of Hate and War. Interesting, don't you think, how neither Hitler nor Napolean were originally native to the nations they were destined to lead to war. But I digress. I shall plant my seed in you three times a day for six days. Three Sixes! A potent schedule, don't you think?"

Sophie wriggled and struggled more frantically, as he bent over her and lightly touched her nipples with his fingertips.

"Ah but no doubt you are wondering," he went on, as he lovingly stroked and caressed every inch of her body, "surely the point of the exercise was to take out a nuisance police informer, stop her from testifying, save Sinclare's bacon. Admittedly, that was so but when I took on the contract and saw the incredible coincidence of Sinclare's list of whores actually including the six Ripper names, well I could hardly pass on this Cosmically Synchronous opportunity, especially when I have been nurturing such an ambition for so many years. And NOW everything is in place. Sun and Saturn are conjoining, Moon and Venus are opposing, Mars opposes Jupiter. Moon and Neptune will conjoin. And ... of course, you are here." His ice blue eyes momentarily closed as he listened to the cosmic music of the spheres..

"And now, I shall mount you," he grandly announced as his classically beautiful body climbed on top of the struggling, writhing Sophie, who was now wishing she had never been christened Kelly.

"Try not to fret yourself unnecessarily," crooned CK soothingly. "As we often say, just lie back and think of England." Suddenly her body went numb and she could no longer keep up the resistance. Satisfied that the preparatory charm had taken effect, CK proceeded with the ritual rape.

That night, Max was feeling desperate as he sat, a passenger, in Claire's car, riding around the streets of Kings Cross. Why should Sophie disappear now? Has she gone into hiding? Or has the fiend snatched her already, even though there are six days to go before the anticipated murder? Max tried again to push such gloomy thoughts from his mind as he leaned out of the car window to ask yet another street-walker, the ninth one in over an hour, if she had seen Sophie or Kelly or Maeve. And as with all the others, the answer was still "No."

"Do you know where she lives?" asked Max.

"No, she never tells us anything," replied the prostitute, quickly losing interest and walking away.

"I don't think they'd tell you, anyway, even if they knew," observed Claire.

"Not surprising really," answered back Max. "They have to protect each other's anonymity."

A police car pulled up alongside but when Max held up a street map of London, indicating to the enquiring officer that they were lost, the patrol car callously drove on.

"We might really have been lost," complained Claire, quite shocked. "And I genuinely believed the British police were wonderful."

"Not any more, they're not. And I wonder if they ever were. Probably just a fairy tale put out by 'Dixon of Dock Green'."

"Who?"

"Oh, just a TV Cop series, back in the 1960s, long before you were born."

"Hark at the Old Man!" gently teased Claire.

Max smiled wanly and said, "I think we should call the search off for the night, and head home." Claire agreed, but was disappointed when outside his flat he merely kissed her cheek goodnight and didn't look like he was going to invite her in.

"Shall I pick you up tomorrow evening?" she asked.

"If you want. If it's not too much trouble," he replied.

"You can never be too much trouble." To which Max merely grunted.

"See you tomorrow then? Six thirty?" suggested Claire.

"Yeah," said Max without much apparent enthusiasm, going inside.

"Well, at least I can be his Doctor Watson," she thought, comforting herself, as she drove back to her apartment.

The next night, Wednesday, the 22nd, was no different. Max, being chauffeur-driven in Claire's car, around the Kings Cross 'red light district'. Still, nobody had seen nor heard anything of Sophie. After several hours of fruitless enquiring and searching, Max asked Claire to take him home.

Again, at the front door, a very depressed Max routinely went to kiss Claire goodnight on the cheek, but she suddenly moved her mouth to his and kissed him full on the lips. Although Max was taken by surprise, he nonetheless didn't immediately pull away. For a blissful sixty seconds they passionately snogged, until a neighbour's cat yeowed. Max stopped and slowly drew Claire's attention to a rubbish bin, half concealed in the shadows.

"Keep still," he whispered. "See the fox."

Claire looked to where he pointed, and then gave a soft gasp of delight.

"Oh yes," she whispered excitedly, staring with disbelief at the urban fox, which was carelessly scavenging around the abandoned city detritus. "I've never seen one this close before." She felt so thrilled to share this beautiful moment with Max.

"They're lovely," murmured Max. "I prefer wolves but I'd have a fox for a pet if I could. Anyway, goodnight, Claire. Thanks for everything."

"That's okay, Max. Good-" But before Claire could finish her sentence, Max was inside, with the front door resolutely shut.

CHAPTER 37
Pass the Parcel
23rd August. Thursday

Edmunds sat in his office, staring with a vacant look in his eyes, at the files on London's gangland bosses and the recent prostitute murders. The tired detective inspector was wondering, yet again, if it was not time for him to take early retirement. He felt he was becoming useless in his old age, as he seemed to be getting absolutely nowhere with this nightmare of a case. He jerked out of his reverie at the knock on the door, and shouted, "Come." Walters entered, carrying a long rectangular package.

"Guv, this just arrived in the post," he said, putting the elongated parcel down on Edmunds' desk. "It's addressed to Maxwell Abberline."

"Max?", questioned Edmunds, most perplexed.

"Yes. Care of Detective Inspector Edmunds, Camden CID."

"What's the postmark?"

Walters looked down at the package, "Looks like it was posted in Shrewsbury."

"Very shrewd," replied Edmunds drily.

"You think it's from 'Jackabee'."

"*Jackabee?*" queried Edmunds, raising a quizzical eyebrow.

"Well, he's a Jack wannabe, so I call him 'Jackabee'," replied Walters with a half-smirk.

Edmunds gave a little appreciative grunt, then said, "You better get Max over here. Have him open his parcel."

"You don't want forensics to give it the once over, first?"

"No point in wasting time. We know from the last package, there won't be any prints."

Thirty-six minutes later, Max was at the police station, looking with dread at the parcel addressed to him.. Edmunds, Walters and Warren watched him as he held it before him very tentatively.

"Well, aren't you going to open it?" Edmunds impatiently demanded.

"Aren't you afraid it's a bomb?" asked Max.

"It was x-rayed when it arrived," replied Edmunds tersely. "Standard procedure."

"Then you should know what's in it," responded Max, throwing the package back onto the desk.

Walters picked up the offending parcel and handed it back to Max, saying, "Some of the finer detail is missing, but we know there are no explosives or detonating devices.

With a sigh of reluctance, Max slowly unwrapped the parcel, until it was eventually revealed to contain a pair of number plates - *MIB 666R*, and wrapped around them were a pair of ruby red silk knickers, laced in black. In horror, Max dropped the items on to the desk. His eyes began to leak tears as he simply stared ahead, mute. Edmunds was about to speak but Warren stopped him with, "You don't have to ask him, Chief. I helped Kelly choose them."

"But does this prove that the bastard has actually taken Kelly?" argued Edmunds. "He could have just stolen these. Could be just playing with us. Playing with Max."

"Oh, he's got Kelly, alright," pronounced Max, his voice thickened with emotion. "And he's keeping her until he's finished with her. Until he has killed her, somewhere in Dorset Street, on the 27th. Monday morning, between one and two."

"Yes. You said that to WDC Warren."

"Are you going to believe me this time?" challenged Max, glaring at Edmunds.

"I promise, we will make sure the area around Dorset Street is well covered," replied Edmunds in a sympathetic, though determined tone. "Meanwhile, we'll pull out every stop to find her before Monday. I swear."

"Yeah, well...that's it. I guess," shrugged Max. "Can someone give me a lift back home?"

"Chief, shall I?" volunteered Warren

"Sorry, I can't spare you. Arrange for one of the squad cars," ordered Edmunds, and turned to Max, who was already on his way out, "We'll do everything we can, Max, I promise you."

"Whatever," replied Max, unconvinced, and was quickly gone.

An hour later Max was back at his flat, working feverishly at his computer. From the Internet, he had downloaded satellite maps of the south and north-west of England, and was drawing circles around Shrewsbury, extending the radius to include London, east and south-east. At the same time, he had the computer perform numerological calculations of place names, and then draw straight lines, in an attempt to make geometric connections.

Suddenly, his frantic activity was interrupted by the telephone ringing. He paused momentarily, staring hard at the phone. Finally, he chose to ignore it. "Let the bloody answer machine deal with it," he thought, and continued working. Anyway, he had been in the habit of screening his calls for several years now. When he heard Claire's voice, his heart skipped a beat, and was nearly tempted to grab the handset. But he just sat there, and listened, trying to enjoy the sound of her voice, all the while wishing it was Sophie's.

"Hi, Max, it's me Claire. Pick up the phone," she begged. "Are you there? Max? Did you get your car returned? Do you want me to come round? Shall we go looking for Kelly this evening? Give me a ring if you need me. Bye."

Give me a ring if you need me, thought Max. "Oh Claire, if only I wasn't afraid to need you..." He was almost tempted to return her call, but instead turned his thoughts to Roslyn D'Onston, and Rosslyn Chapel. Picking up a book entitled "Exploring Occult Britain", he looked in the index to see if there were any references to Rosslyn Chapel. There was, one on page 66. He quickly flicked to the said page, and read -

"One of the most tenacious pagan customs to survive Christian domination in Britain, is the paying of tribute to the Green Man or Jack-in-the-Green, who for centuries has been a fertility

symbol for the arrival of spring and the rebirth of greenery or vegetation. In the Wicca or Witchcraft traditions the Green Man is identified with the Horned or Phallic God. This custom of worshipping such a Nature deity seems to be a relic of ancient tree worship,that predates Druidism and Christianity by thousands of years. And yet, one ought to consider it very strange and anachronistic, even blasphemous, that it is in churches, and almost entirely rural churches, where such remnants of this pagan homage can be located. In fact, one such medieval church, famously known as Rosslyn Chapel, has over one hundred stone carvings depicting the Green Man. Rosslyn Chapel was also decorated, by the fifteenth century architects, with many examples of Masonic symbols. It wasn't just witchcraft that kept alive the homage to the Green Man. That other Craft, otherwise known as Freemasonry, has also been responsible. In fact, many masonic lodges are allied to local witch covens. And where this is the case, there will be a village pub called The Green Man, that serves as a regular meeting place for witches and masons alike."

Exactly, thought Max, the Craft of Wicca and the Craft of Masons, two sides of the same coin, they both chant "So Mote It Be" as a refrain during their ceremonies, and they both claim ancient pagan roots which originally involved paying homage to a fertility god that often demanded human sacrifices. Rosslyn Chapel for centuries has been the Masons' code book in stone, enshrining this occult knowledge. This, Max concluded, was why the man who was Jack the Ripper, an occult magician, also named himself Roslyn. Rosslyn Chapel, Roslyn D'Onston, Jack the Ripper, Jack o'Lantern, Spring-heeled Jack, Jack in the Green, the Green Man. I always suspected there was something dodgy about pubs called *The Green Man*, Max thought, and went back to creating circles and straight lines with the computer.

CHAPTER 38
Jack in the Green
24th August. Friday

If only Max could have been aware of the extraordinary synchronicity of him reading the passage on the Green Man, and a certain top civil servant, the very next day, waiting to meet with the contract killer, in a village pub called *The Green Man*, near Ongar in Essex. But if he had known, what use would it have been to him? Sceptics would say 'None'. They would argue synchronicities, coincidences, chance were merely nomadic tricks of Fate that rarely have a practical value beyond symbolic significance.

CK stepped into the lounge of The Green Man and instantly spotted Sir Oscar Edward Molyneux, the permanent under secretary at the Ministry of Defence, sitting at the bar, and casually sauntered over to him.

"So good of you to come," gushed Sir Oscar, giving CK a hearty handshake that spoke volumes. "What will it be?"

"Dry Martini," came CK's laconic reply.

"Ah. Indeed."

As if on cue, the barmaid was there to hand CK his Martini. Sir Oscar stood up, "It's a pleasant evening. Mind if we stroll outside?" he asked. "The garden is quite a delight." CK nodded and the two gentlemen leisurely walked out, carrying their drinks,

"We need another 7/7," Sir Oscar said quietly as they strolled together around the 'chocolate box' beer garden outside the pub.

"You having problems getting the new anti-terrorist laws passed?" guessed CK.

"The New Broom is demanding tougher bristles. Plus, the Americans insist we help them take India. We have to build an argument."

"Bloody Yanks. When will they ever learn?" growled CK. "India? Too big. It's not a nation of little Gandhis any more."

"Yes, it will be another bloody nightmare of a quagmire. But we did remove Pakistan's nuclear weapons. Now it's India's turn," sighed Sir Oscar.

"Quite. So now you want another 7/7?"

"Will you organise it?"

"Pity you didn't ask me three weeks ago," replied CK. "I could have given you an 8/8. You know how the Yanks like their 'Buzz-numbers'. Dates that are simple and easy to remember – 9/11. Emergency Call and all that."

"Enough said," interrupted Sir Oscar.

"If you don't mind waiting until next month I could give you a 9/9."

"No," Sir Oscar shook his head. "We need the fireworks to soften the public a.s.a.p."

"Very well. You'll get your whizz-bangs in a few days. What are you paying me?"

"Afraid not a lot this time," answered Sir Oscar. "Treasury a bit strapped for cash. A million suit you? Half now, the rest upon delivery?"

"That'll do nicely," agreed CK. "I suspect this show will run and run. There'll be plenty more opportunities coming my way."

"Naturally, old chap," beamed Sir Oscar Edward Molyneux. "You're the best we've got." They shook hands and parted company.

CHAPTER 39
Devilishly Handsome
24th August. Friday

"You said I would get my car back today," insisted Max on the phone, becoming increasingly agitated. "You said it would take three days, well, it's three days. Why isn't my car here?" Max looked at his watch. Time was escaping him. "You haven't got a driver to bring it here. But the car is repaired? Right, well if I get someone to give me a lift to you, I can drive it away? Great. I'll be right there." He quickly dialled another number. "Claire, can you do me a favour? Yes, to the garage. Yes, it's repaired, so I can take it away. Thanks, you're an angel."

Forty minutes later, Max was, at last, sitting in his own car, parked in the garage forecourt of Camden Motors. A despondent-looking Claire, parked alongside him in the opposite direction, was about to drive off.

"Thanks for the lift, Claire," smiled Max, blowing her a kiss.

"Max, why didn't you pick up the phone when I rang you," demanded Claire. "I must have rung about ten times. I know you were there. Am I annoying you?

"No, of course not. I rang you didn't I?"

"What, you mean half an hour ago?" she snorted sarcastically. "Yeah, when you wanted something. When you wanted me to give you a lift to your bloody car."

"You're the one who volunteered to be my wheels," Max countered.

"But you could have picked up the phone when I rang you. You ignored me. Ten times. Do I deserve that? If you don't want me around, at least, have the decency to tell me to fuck off." She felt like crying, but she was determined she wasn't going to let Max see any of her tears.

"I'm sorry... if it seemed I shut you out," responded Max in all sincerity. "It wasn't deliberate. Honest. I didn't mean to hurt you. I...Forgive me. I know I'm a prick sometimes." Max looked down, unable to say another word. He wanted to drive off but he didn't want it to look like he was trying to get away from Claire.

"Max, I know you're worried about Kelly," Claire quietly spoke. "We can still drive around Kings Cross tonight. You never know, we might see her."

Max looked up at her, tears seeping from his eyes. "She's been kidnapped," he said hoarsely. "He's got her hidden away somewhere."

"Oh my God," came her shocked response. "How do you know?"

"He sent a message, with an item of her clothing."

"Oh, no. Oh Max, I'm so sorry. Is there anything I can do? No, of course, there isn't. But Max, if you do need me, please, please ring me. Just don't sit there, suffering in silence. Even if I could be just a little shoulder."

"Yeah, well, maybe I could do with some extra brains," Max said, giving her a weak smile.

"You trying to locate her by using numerology and sacred geometry?" she asked.

"Yeah but I think I'm wasting my time. He's not going to select a hiding place based on any principle he's used before. I might just as well randomly stick a pin in a map."

"Well, I'll come round this evening if you want," offered Claire.

"Okay. I'll give you a ring. I promise." With that, Max started his car, give her a little wave and drove away.

That night Max was back on the streets of Kings Cross, trying to find prostitutes he could question. After an hour of fruitless driving, he came across one in Camley Street, and another in York Way, but all he got from either of them was a bored "No idea".

Then as he was heading east towards Islington, down Copenhagen Street, he encountered Fran, who on recognising him, ran away from him. Max drove after her, shouting, "Fran, I need to talk to you about Kelly." She stopped and looked back at him warily. He beckoned her over to him, and when she reached his side window, he asked, "You knew her? Well, she knew you."

"Kelly knew everyone," shrugged Fran. "She made it her business to. She was a copper's nark."

"Did all the girls know she was working with the police?"

"Don't be stupid," Fran laughed.

"But you knew."

Fran made no reply, but instead fidgeted on the spot, feeling the urge to fly.

"Did you grass on her to Sinclare?" demanded Max.

"What do you take me for?" snapped Fran. "Anyway, you know what they do to messengers who bring bad news. It was the cop, Reecy. He told Sinclare... just as he told me."

"Greasy Reecy?" exclaimed Max. "Was he working for Sinclare?"

"What do you think?"

"Why did Reecy tell you that Kelly was going to testify in court?"

"He wanted to cover his back," replied Fran. "He hoped that if I told the Boss then the police couldn't point the finger at him if anything happened to Kelly."

"But you didn't tell the Boss?" Max asked sceptically.

"I'm not stupid," sneered Fran.

"You know Kelly has been abducted," Max informed her slowly, watching her reaction closely. Fran's eyes widened, her jaw dropped. She almost collapsed. He reckoned she was genuinely shaken.

"Sinclare?" she asked in a whisper.

Max shook his head, "The serial killer."

Fran was terrified. "How do you know?" she stammered.

"He sent the police something of hers."

"An ear or something?" she asked, dreading the answer.

"Not yet but he will, when he finally kills her," replied Max harshly.

"How do you know he hasn't killed her already?"

"We know. He's playing a sick game with us. But I can assure you, in a few days time Kelly will be dead if we don't find her before then. Have you ideas?"

"No, of course not," squealed Fran defensively. "How can I? Nicking ten quid off you doesn't mean I'm a kidnapper or murderer. Here, take the fucking ten quid." Fran threw a ten pound note at Max. "Leave me alone," she yelled, and started to walk away

"It's alright, Fran," Max tried to reassure her. "I don't want the tenner. I'm not angry with you." He drove to overtake her and stopped in front of her, "I'll give you more than ten quid if you'll talk with me some more," He held out to her two twenty-pound notes, which she snatched out of his hand.

"Did you ever share any of Kelly's regular clients?" interrogated Max.

"I never knew who her clients were. So, I wouldn't know if had them, would I?" Fran moodily replied.

"When a girl gets picked up by a punter driving a car, do they normally make a note of the car's number plate? You know, for their own safety sake?"

"I don't know about other girls but I do sometimes. Especially if the bloke feels really dodgy."

"Did you ever take a note of this number?" asked Max, showing her a piece of paper with 'MIB 666R' written on. Fran quickly glanced at it, nodded and asked, "Mind if I get in the car?" Not waiting for an answer, she got in, and sitting beside Max, instructed him to drive down the street. At the Mecca bingo hall, she told him to drive right, into the car park at the rear of the dilapidated building.

"Stop here," she ordered, and quickly looked about her.

"Yeah," she said after being satisfied the yard was safe, "I've been with a guy who had a car with that reg. number. These last couple of weeks, in fact."

"Why did you write down his number? Did he feel particularly dodgy?" asked Max.

"Nah. Far from it. He was a real gent. I really liked him. I remembered the number because it intrigued me. You seen the movie, '*Men in Black*'?"

"Yes, it was total crap," replied Max, making a face that looked like he wanted to vomit.

"Yeah, well, there's no pleasing everyone. I liked it," asserted Fran defiantly. "Anyway, the number plate made me laugh," she continued. "I thought it was a bit of an overkill. MIB, Men in Black? 666? Antichrist? *The Omen*? You seen that movie?"

"Yes," Max replied.

"S'pose you thought that was crap, too?" sneered Fran.

"No, I really enjoyed it. But that was made in the Seventies, a golden age for brilliant movies."

"Maybe," said Fran thoughtfully. "Godfather, Cuckoo's Nest, Exorcist, Clockwork Orange, French Connection, Deer Hunter, Jaws, Taxi Driver, Apocalypse Now." She paused, silently thinking of a few more, and then pronounced, "Yeah, you're probably right."

"You were saying about the registration number?" prompted Max.

"Yeah, it just made me laugh. I asked him if he was a film buff or something."

"What did he say?"

"He said yes."

"What did he look like?" enquired Max.

"Really gorgeous," Fran sighed wistfully. "Tall, dark, handsome, charming. Very Pukka English. A sort of Pierce Brosnan, Timothy Dalton and Roger Moore all rolled in one...Really tasty."

"You don't include Sean Connery?"

"Nah, he's too Scottish," snorted Fran dismissively. "This bloke had something of the military about him. An officer type. I called him 'The Colonel'."

"Was he a colonel?" Max asked, taking out a notepad and pen.

"I don't know... but he certainly acted like he was. He was a gentleman but he knew he was in command."

"What colour eyes?"

"Blue...a chilling blue...like Henry Fonda. You know like in *Once Upon A Time in The West*."

"What colour hair?" asked Max as he wrote down "*Henry Fonda psycho-blue eyes*".

"Blond, I think. No, possibly a light brown. Dark maybe. Oh I can't remember. But he was really gorgeous," she said, smiling nostalgically.

Max grunted disapprovingly and came back with, "Huh, if he was so physically attractive and charming, why was he having to pay for sex?"

"It's not just ugly and charmless men who go to whores, you know," Fran sharply retorted. "You do yourself a great dis-service, thinking like that. There are loads of reasons why men pay for sex."

"What about the Colonel's reasons?"

"I asked him once... I did actually think like you in this one instance," admitted Fran. "I said 'What's a good looking bloke like you doing, paying for an ugly old whore like me?'"

"Now, you're doing yourself a gross dis-service," came back Max's swift rejoinder.

"I was joking, really," Fran giggled. "You know us women, always fishing for compliments. He said he was some kind of philanthropist. He was filthy rich and going to prostitutes was a way of redistributing his wealth. It was his idea of doing charity."

"What a load of patronising bollocks!" spat out Max

"Of course, but I made a few quid. Didn't do me any harm."

"You were one of the lucky ones," Max tartly reminded her. "You had the wrong name. If you saw what he did to Kate or Lezzie, Lisa or –"

"Stop it," she cried, grasping her head with her hands. "You're right," she said, looking up at Max, a little tearful. "He is a monster. That's the kind of charity we can do without. Sorry. I forgot who we were really talking about."

"I don't suppose he gave any idea as to where he lived?"

"Nope. He never talked about himself. From his accent and behaviour, he's obviously a Posho. Probably Home Counties or South East England."

"What sort of age would you say he was?" asked Max.

"Mid to late forties. Probably. That's all I can say. Sorry I can't be more help."

"No, that's been great," Max assured her. "Really. You've been great. Thanks."

"Sorry I cheated you last time," replied Fran genuinely penitent. "Trying to make a fool of you."

"Never mind," Max said, giving her arm a gentle squeeze. "Anyway, I was a prick, imagining I could get a proper fuck for just ten quid. You were simply taking advantage of my gullible greed. You can't be blamed for that."

"So, since we here... could you be looking for business?" suggested Fran, looking hopeful.

"Not tonight, Fran," Max attempted a little smile. "Another time, maybe."

"Promise?"

"Promise."

"Alright. See you later," said Fran, and gave him a quick kiss on the cheek before leaping out of the car. She looked around her, searching the shadows in the car park and once she was reassured it was safe, she sprinted away, only pausing briefly when she reached the main thoroughfare, to give Max a shy little wave, then she was gone.

CHAPTER 40
Holmes... and Sweet Holmes
25th August. Saturday

"What are you doing?" asked Claire, who was looking over Max's shoulder, as he worked on the computer, which had on display a map of the Home Counties, over which he moved the curser, dragging and manoeuvring a floating representation of his number matrix of the Ripper Code...

```
6   6   6               =   9
6   5   4               =   6
    2       4           =   6
7   1                   =   8
    3   6               =   9
-----------------------------
1   6   9       4       =   2
```

"I'm trying to see if the numbers or the shape of the Ripper Code matrix, when superimposed on the map, with the number "1" centred on the middle of London, could point to the location of where Kelly might be hidden," explained Max, feeling a little sheepish, as this may confirm any theory she may harbour that he was a complete crank..

"Do you really think he would allow the Ripper Code to betray him like that?" Claire asked doubtfully.

"Well, he's been following the Ripper rules up to now." Just then, the phone rang, and the answer-machine kicked in. Max and Claire looked at each other, and then at the telephone, in suspense, waiting for the caller's voice to identify itself.

"Max, it's Jim Walters here," announced the detective sergeant's disembodied voice. "When you pick up this message, can you pop over to the station? We'd like to pick your brains." When the answer-machine beeped, signifying the conclusion of the call, Max turned back to Claire, and saw, with some pride, that she was most impressed.

"Do you mind hanging on here," he asked, "while I check out what the Peelers want with their Sherlock in a Wheelchair?

"Sure thing, Chief," saluted Claire, which made him smile. As he wheeled away to the door, he stopped at her side, and gave her a little kiss on the lips. Not wanting to linger, he nonetheless allowed her hand cling to his hair, as if she were refusing to let him go. In response, his own hand reached out and cupped her left breast, enjoying its comforting round, soft, warmth. Realising that if this continued much longer he may not want to get away, Max pulled out, shaking his head. "I have to go," he said, laughing happily. "Don't go away." As he wheeled towards the front door, grabbing his jacket on the way, he glanced back at Claire and saw that her eyes were brimming with tears of joy, which filled him with gladness. But, once he was outside, he cursed himself. How dare he feel this way, knowing that another woman close to his heart was, at this moment, being horribly abused, and terrorised with the certain knowledge that, very soon, she will be murdered.

As soon as Max entered the Camden police station, he could feel overall that there was a more positive change in attitude towards him. The officers around him seemed to be accepting him as a valuable member of their team. He was directed into the Incident Room where he was greeted with friendly smiles from both Walters and Warren. The Detective Inspector also looked pleased to see him.

"We are scouring all over the country, but we haven't a clue as to what we are looking for," confessed Edmunds, as he hastily removed an obstructing chair from the conference table, so that Max could sit alongside him. "Is there anything in your studies of the real Jack the Ripper that could throw some light on this particular nasty character? And since he is also a numerologist, and this does stick in my throat having to ask you - Can numerology give us any more clues?"

"As it happens, I am currently doing just that, trying to see if I can use the Ripper Code to locate his hiding place," replied Max.

"How are you getting on?"

"Nowhere," said Max with regret, and then in a more positive tone, he continued, "With regards this nasty character. Well, it seems there are several similarities between today's and yesterday's Ripper. We know they are both numerologists. Roslyn D'Onston had a military background. It appears our Jack is or was in the army..."

"How do you know this?" demanded Edmunds.

"I was questioning one of the prostitutes last night," replied Max. "She recognised the car registration number belonging to one of her more regular clients. She could him 'the Colonel'. I get the feeling she thinks he was trained at Sandhurst." On hearing this, both Walters and Warren leaned forward. This could be their first break.

"But she's got no evidence of this?" queried Edmunds.

"No. But... presumably you are questioning all of Sinclare's skin traders."

"We haven't started on that yet."

"Might I suggest you do," counselled Max. "Pull in all his sex workers, make sure you include a woman called Fran. She may give you more info than she gave me."

"Guv, I like the idea of taking all his girls off the streets," put in Walters.

"And his rent boys. Disrupt his business for a while," added Warren.

"Maybe we could put pressure on Sinclare to put pressure on his hired killer to release Kelly... unharmed?" Walters suggested.

Edmunds stood up, fired with enthusiasm, "Right, well, in that case, let's go the whole hog and pull in all his organisation - drug pushers, porn merchants, racketeers, the lot. Let's really screw him up tight." And turning to Walters, "Get it organised, Jim," he ordered.

"With pleasure, Guv," said Walters, grinning wickedly.

"Max, anything else you can tell us?" asked Edmunds, sitting back down.

"According to Fran, he's in his mid to late forties, which roughly coincides with D'Onston's age - 47 - when he was on his killing rampage. In terms of physical appearance, Fran considered him a bit of a dish, a right pin up boy... tall, dark, handsome, debonair - all the cliches... a real gentleman, she says," Max said, mimicking her cockney sparrow voice.

"How could she be turned on by such monster?" tutted Edmunds.

"History is full of monsters in angelic disguise," rebuked Max.

"And some of the ugliest people have been the greatest heroes," came in Warren.

"Why are you looking at me when you say that?" complained Max, as if his feelings were hurt.

"I don't think you're ugly," protested Warren. "You're quite cute, actually."

Edmunds slammed his fist on the table. "Oye, less of this," he reprimanded. "I refuse to play gooseberry in my own office." He stood up and strode over to the rostrum, and pulled down a retractable screen that was bolted to the wall.

"Detective Constable, get everybody in here," he ordered Warren, who immediately went out and returned with about twenty officers, with more trying to squeeze in. Suddenly, the Incident Room was heaving and cramped.

Once he was sure everyone had gathered, Edmunds switched on the slide projector. A map of Whitechapel and Spitalfields instantly appeared on the screen, and he began to describe the plan, indicating with a laser pointer, as he spoke, "On the east of the target area, we will have people on Commercial Road - here at Whites Row, covering the south - west, we'll have officers at Crispin Street. And north of the target, we'll be covering Brushfield Street. He'll be totally surrounded, he won't even be able to fart without us knowing about it. We will have Dorset Street covered from every angle, armed officers, SWAT teams behind every window and door."

"Excuse me, sir," interrupted one of the officers, "but if he knows we know he is going to this location to kill his hostage, why would he come? Is he an moron or is he crying out to be caught? I mean, pardon my French, but what's his bloody game?"

The Chief surprised everyone when, instead of answering the question, he signalled to Max that he should come forward. "This is Maxwell Abberline. He has kindly agreed to assist us with our enquiries," cracked Edmunds, which made everyone laugh, including Max, as they all knew this was often a euphemism for being "under arrest".

"Well, Max?" coaxed Edmunds.

"You are dealing with a very arrogant man," began Max. "He is ultra confident at being able to outwit us at every turn. He so admires Jack the Ripper, that he even employs his catch phrase – 'Catch me if you can'. I think he believes he has supernatural agencies protecting him...of course, I'm not saying he has, but that is what he believes. Which isn't surprising because the original Jack the Ripper also believed this about himself, and that he had powers of invisibility. So, our man is quite happy to inform us that he will be at a certain place on a certain date at a certain time with a certain victim and he will kill her and get away with it. He enjoys believing it and he wants to make fools of you all...Just as Jack the Ripper did over a hundred years ago. He thinks he has immunity. Maybe he has. The Ripper certainly had, he was a Freemason, and the Police Commissioner heading the Whitechapel murders investigation, was also a Freemason -"

"Thank you, Max," Edmunds quickly interjected, while at the same time, giving Warren a nod to escort Max out.

"Right," laughed Max, taking the hint, "I guess I'll be off then."

As Warren helped Max put the wheelchair in his car, she tried to reassure him, "Max, we will have over a hundred officers around that square. Don't worry. We'll rescue Maeve Kelly alive, I promise you. And I won't abandon the post, no matter what."

"Yep," replied Max, not particularly convinced.

Claire was still at the computer when Max returned to his apartment.

"Max, I think I solved the puzzle," she declared excitedly. "The Ripper Code may point to Kelly's location after all."

"You're joking?" he exclaimed, giving her a big hug.

"Ever heard of Roxzi Road, Southend-on-Sea?" she asked.

"Of course not. Haven't even been to Southend, let alone Rock Sea Road."

"No, ROXZI," corrected Claire. "R. O. X. Z. I. Roxzi Road. It's a new road. Only completed last year but it leads to Peter Pan's Adventure Island."

"Peter Pan's Adventure Island? Jesus, that sounds pretty bizarre. You think he's keeping Kelly captive there?"

"Well, there or somewhere along Roxzi Road. But I go for the Peter Pan Island. It's the sort of sick, surreal thing he'd do," shivered Claire.

"How did you come to Southend-on-Sea... and this odd sounding road name?" Max asked, intrigued.

"I found it through your Ripper Code. He really is a creature of habit. Perhaps someone addicted to Sudeko. He just has to organise his moves according to the parameters set by the Ripper Code."

"Okay, so what have you got?"

Claire quickly showed Max on the computer, a map of Southend-on-Sea, homing in on Roxzi Road, and Peter Pan's Adventure Island, and then returned to the map of London, and the Ripper Code number matrix.

"I carried on doing what you started off, superimposing the Ripper Code number matrix over Jack's murder sites, placing number 1 on top of *Murder 1*, and saw that number 2 of the code could also be placed over *Murder 2*."

Claire illustrated her point by having the computer graphically zoom in on the Whitechapel murder locations and moving the Ripper Code number matrix over them.

"As you can see," she continued, "we also get this 6 superimposing over *Murder 6*."

"But the other three numbers don't fit," objected Max.

"They do, if you subtract, Kelly's number, 2 from each of them. The five, subtract 2 gives you 3, which gives us "murder 3". The

The Ripper Code

7 minus 2 gives us the fifth murder and 6 minus 2 gives us the fourth murder site."

"Wow, Claire that's brilliant," whooped Max. "*Fucking brilliant*, as my old professor would say."

Glowing with pride, Claire enthusiastically continued, "Notice how you need the '2' three times to make these three sites fit into the plan. And, in keeping with the theme of Six, what are three twos but Six."

"Okay, I'll go along with what you've said thus far, but we've still got the top line of 666 and this '3', and this '4' unaccounted for," he said, tapping the display.

```
     6    6    6              =    9
     6    5    4              =    6
          2         4         =    6
     7    1                   =    8
          3    6              =    9
     -----------------------------
     1    6    9    4         =    2
```

"I'm coming to those," replied Claire. "The '4', I think, is telling us the direction '2' went, i.e. Kelly."

"It's pointing east of '2'," observed Max.

"Exactly," exclaimed Claire in triumph. "East. That's Essex. Which fits perfectly for the top line, 666. Essex is 666."

"Well, that could explain Essex Girls," surmised Max with a cheeky twinkle in his eye.

"Excuse me, I'm an Essex girl," protested Claire, punching him on the shoulder.

"Oops," said Max, wincing, and then more seriously, "Okay, so how did you conclude Essex was 666?"

"Simple. Look. E is Five. S is One, giving us Six. S is One. E is Five, giving us another Six. And finally, you have X, giving us the third Six. Essex as a word gives us the whole number of 18 - which is what '6, plus 6, plus 6', gives us."

"So, the top line of the Code, 666 is telling us to look in Essex for Kelly," summarised Max. "But where in Essex? How did you

The Ripper Code

come up with Southend? And more precisely, Roxzi Road in Southend?"

Claire gave a little grin. She knew what was next was going to really impress Max.

"You were asking about the '3' and '4'" that's still unaccounted. I decided to assume these numbers gave us the number of miles from *Murder site 1*. So, I asked the computer to draw a straight line on the map 34 miles due east of George Yard, Whitechapel." As Claire spoke, she typed on the computer, double-clicked on a few icons and the computer drew a straight line from Whitechapel ending in Southend.

"As you can see, the line stops at Southend-on-Sea," she pointed out. "Next, I had to see if these numbers...", indicating the row and column of summations – 1,6,9,4 and 9,6,6,8,9 - of the Ripper Code number matrix, "could tell us the address in Southend."

"The first thing I noticed was that the numbers of this row would make up the letters for the word "road" – '1' is A, '6' is O, '9' is R and '4' is D."

"An anagram for ROAD," said Max softly. "Very nice. So we possibly have a street name ending with *road*, and we can discount *avenue*, *lane*, *street*, *close* etc."

Claire nodded and continued with her exposition, "So, I looked on the map around this part of Southend, for streets ending with 'road', having a word in front of five letters beginning either with an I or an R."

"Why?"

"Because this column of numbers in your Ripper Code told me to," she explained, tapping the computer screen.

"Ah. Right. 9,6,6,8,9," agreed Max.

"And lo and behold, I found Roxzi Road," beamed Claire proudly. "A perfect match. I couldn't believe it."

"My god, that's incredible. Claire. You're a genius," congratulated Max. "I love you. Marry me."

"Don't be silly," she laughed. "You don't mean it."

Max starred at Claire's graphic presentation on the computer screen, and shook his head in wonderment. "The thing is, I can't

The Ripper Code

believe he's really that dumb," he said. "That he would give clues as to where he has hidden Kelly before he can sacrifice her on the appointed day, at the appointed place... Unless..."

"Maybe he isn't trying to give clues," interrupted Claire. Perhaps he doesn't realise someone else has cracked the Ripper Code. Maybe he thinks it's his own special little secret."

"In which case, he is simply using the Code to guide his actions and make his decisions for him. So when he was wondering where to hide Kelly, he went to the Ripper Code as a kind of oracle and he interpreted along the same lines as you. So, I think you're right. The killer does think he is the only one who knows of the Ripper Code."

"Well, Max, that was his fatal mistake...he hadn't reckoned on a Sherlock Holmes in a Wheelchair also discovering it and is now using it to read his mind." Claire gripped Max's shoulder, her eyes shining.

"That wasn't me," disputed Max. "That was you. He hadn't reckoned on two Sherlocks in Wheelchairs." Max moved to the telephone and began to dial.

"The big question now is," he went on, turning to Claire, "can this be convincing enough to persuade the police to go to Southend and search Roxzi Road."

CHAPTER 41
Peter Pan and Wendy
26th August. Sunday

Claire was both excited and very frightened. Never in her wild imaginings, did she think that she would, one day, be doing something like this. Sitting in her own car, playing private detective, surveying an empty street in Southend-on-Sea, on the look-out for a dangerous serial killer.

"Do you think they'll come?" Claire asked Max, who was keeping his head down, out of sight, leaving her to do all the watching. He knew the killer would recognise him if he spotted him. That was why they were staking out the only building on Roxzi Road, a large disused hanger-cum-warehouse, in Claire's car, which hopefully, the murderous "Colonel X" won't have been acquainted with yet. They were parked at the end of the road, just two hundred yards from the target. Behind them, across the water, was the now abandoned Peter Pan Adventure Island, which had had to close down, when the new MacDonalds Amusement Park, half a mile away, hijacked all their custom.

"Max, will the police come?" Claire asked again.

"I don't know," he shrugged. "Edmunds is impossible. I think he secretly wants to believe me but his detective orthodoxy gets in the way."

"What did he say?" she whispered.

"He'll examine both the material and your conclusions, and then discuss it with his chief. He doesn't hold out much hope. It's all too wacky-backy."

"Do you really think Kelly could be prisoner in there?" asked Claire, mesmerised by the sight of the bleak looking steel and concrete building.

"Well, it all adds up, according to your analysis," replied Max.

"I wish we could get in there and rescue her ourselves."

"So do I. If I was Mulder and you was Scully, we could. But we're not. We're just a pair of useless crips."

"Shut up. Don't say that, wanker!" snapped Claire angrily. "I'll show you we're not a pair of useless crips...." And with that, Claire started the car and began to charge towards the forbidding-looking warehouse...

"Hey, hold on a minute, Claire!" whelped Max, taken completely by surprise.

The words were barely out of his mouth, when suddenly, police cars, vans, and ambulance with sirens blaring arrived. Claire instantly pulled the car to a halt, as the warehouse became surrounded, with SWAT teams, led by Edmunds with his assistants, Walters and Warren, taking up positions. For a moment, Max and Claire watched in stunned amazement, then Max sprang into action, threw his wheelchair out of the car, quickly got in, and raced across the road to Warren to get a better look, but she frantically tried to wave him back. Max turned as if to retreat, but instead headed for some police vehicles, using them as cover so as to get as close to the action as possible. He dodged and scooted around the perimeter of the warehouse building, searching for an entrance not covered by the police.

Meanwhile, other doors to the old disused aircraft hanger were smashed open, shattering the darkness with blinding shafts of light. Armed police charged in, acting like they were in some kind of American FBI movie, all noise, tear gas smoke and belligerent yells, and, of course, gun barrels pointing in all directions. Once the "Action-Cop" commotion had died down, there was a moment of stillness as they took in the fact that the cupboard was bare, except for an empty bed bang in the middle of the spacious warehouse.

Edmunds and Walters entered, on the heels of the SWAT team. A brief glance around made the detective inspector think they had been sent on a wild goose chase.

"Bloody Max," Edmunds cursed bitterly, furiously disappointed. "He's making a laughing stock of me. Nothing.

Why did I listen to him?" He swung on Walters angrily, "I hold you to blame."

"Me?" bellowed back Walters.

"Yes. You keep telling me, him might have something. Well, I'll tell you what he's got. He's got a fucking screw loose."

"What about this bed?" pointed Walters, and going over to it, "and these chains? What are these black spots on the floor?"

Edmunds joined him, in examining the bed, and the chains.

"What do you think, Guv?" asked Walters, scraping up a sample of the dark stains from the floor, into a forensics plastic bag.

"Clearly, someone has been lying on the bed very recently," Edmunds then looked under the bed and said, "Seems to be some kind of commode-type 'set up' under here."

"Someone being kept prisoner?" suggested Walters.

"More likely an S and M scene," Edmunds grunted dismissively. "Essex is famous for it. Especially Southend. All the kinky East End gangsters end up here."

Suddenly at the far end of the warehouse, another door banged open. All the police swung their guns round, pointing them straight at Max, who looked down and saw a hundred red pin-pricks of light swarming all over his chest. "Oops", he went.

"Max, you idiot!" yelled Edmunds, storming over to him.

"Where is Kelly?" demanded Max, frantically looking around him.

"As you can see. Nothing. Zero. Zilch. Why the hell did I listen to you, Max?" complained Edmunds, and then, turning to Walters, said, "Jim, You sort him. I'm off." the detective inspector marched off in a foul temper. He paused, on his way out to give instructions for forensics to be carried out and photographs to be taken. The rest of the SWAT teams were starting to gather their equipment, and leave the hanger cum warehouse.

"How long have you been here?" demanded Walters.

"A couple of hours, casing the joint," Max nonchalantly replied.

"What?" cried Walters in disbelief. "Hadn't it occurred to you that your presence here drove him away? Arriving on the scene,

The Ripper Code

he spotted you and he took off with Kelly? What was the point of you telling us he was here and then you scare him off before we could get here? How stupidly irresponsible is that?"

"No one was scared off," argued back Max. "There weren't any vehicles moving the whole time we were watching. And anyway, we were well hidden."

"We?" questioned Walters.

"Me and my partner."

"Where were you parked?"

"See. You didn't spot us," said Max triumphantly.

"But he knows your car."

"Exactly. That's why we came in my partner's," explained Max. "Anyway, I wasn't sure you lot were going to show up. You wouldn't give me a yes or no, so what was I suppose to do?"

"Do nothing. It's not your job," reminded Walters, trying to pull rank.

"I gave you the tip off," Max threw back at him.

"Yes. And you keep blowing it for us," retaliated Walters.

"Bollocks!" Max vehemently denied

"Just keep away when we're trying to do our job," insisted Walters.

"It's my responsibility too, you know. You people aren't exactly perfect."

"You want us to save Kelly, you just keep away from Dorset Street tonight," warned Walters, losing patience with Max's constant answering back, and walked away.

A disgruntled Max returned to the waiting Claire, and climbed in the car, beside her, de-assembled his wheelchair and lifted it in onto the back seat behind him.

"What's happening?" asked Claire anxiously.

"Nothing. Kelly wasn't there," he replied bitterly.

"Were we wrong?"

"I don't think so. We were just too late. He's moved her. Probably closer for tonight's... horror."

"What shall we do now?" asked Claire, feeling very despondent.

The Ripper Code

"I guess we have to wait near Dorset Street...avoiding the police, of course. They'll be swarming all over the place," sighed Max bleakly.

"That's what you want, isn't it?"

"Yeah, of course, if it means catching him before he kills Kelly."

"Is there any real point in us being there as well as the police?" Claire questioned. "We're not going to be much help," she added. "As you say, a pair of useless crips."

"You don't have to be there," grumbled Max, "but I...have to. All my life I wanted to be a knight in shining armour."

"Yeah but you don't want to be a Don Quixote, do you?" Claire gently cautioned.

"And you don't want to be my Sancho Panza," countered Max. "Ow!" he yelped, as Claire affectionately punched him on the arm.

"Anyway, Kelly is no windmill," asserted Max, his face becoming serious again. "She is a genuine damsel in distress, about to be ripped apart by a real monster. And no, this isn't just a fantasy game. I hope Edmunds and his crew will be successful but it can't hurt to be back up. I want to be there, just in case."

"Okay," consented Claire, "but there's loads of hours to kill. Let's go home, have something to eat, get ourselves ready for a long night."

"Yes, Sancho Panza," teased Max.

"Well, at least you didn't call me Rosinante, his decrepit old horse," she laughed, turning the ignition, and began their drive back to London.

Warren looked at the luminous glow of her watch; 11.55 pm. Not too late, she hoped. She and Walters had just arrived at the empty darkened room on the fourth floor of the Countrywide Building Society building in Whites Row, overlooking Dorset Street. Equipped with infra-red cameras and night-vision binoculars, the pair of them looked down out of the window, hiding behind lace curtains. Ready for anything, they and their police colleagues were armed with service hand-guns.

"We're all in position, Chief," Walters, spoke softly on his police radio. "The area is well-covered. No tell-tale indications of surveillance. We have successful obscurity of all units."

Down in the street, Edmunds was inside a parked unmarked van. With him were three other police personnel monitoring surveillance equipment.

"Keep your officers in position, especially the marksman, but I want you and Warren down here with me," replied Edmunds. He then punched in the Open Police Channel, and announced, "Here is a general order to all *Jackabee* units. All radios switched to Receive Only until further notice. Any sighting of target will be conveyed by one click of the Transmit button followed by two clicks in quick succession."

CHAPTER 42
A Fox loose in the Warren
27th August. Monday

Kings Cross Railway was the first station to be hit. The time was just one minute past midnight. By a cruel twist of fate, Fran, the only street-walker who had been able to give Max what little information there was on his adversary, just happened to be loitering around the platforms, hoping to attract a potential customer, when the planted time-bomb exploded. She was caught at the centre of the blast, and killed instantly. Many others were also annihilated in that first second. After that, it was general mayhem with countless injuries, screams, secondary explosions and outbreaks of fire, and more death and wounded.

It was at two seconds past midnight, that there was a second bomb explosion. This time, Oxford Circus Underground was the target. Late night revellers were thrown in the air by the blast. The scenes of death, screaming injured, terror, chaos were repeated...as they were also at Camden Town Underground station, when a third bomb exploded at three minutes past midnight, and a fourth at four minutes past zero hour at Holburn's underground. At the fifth minute and at the sixth minute past, bombs five and six exploded, ripping apart underground railway stations at Euston Square and Baker Street respectively. Six bombs erupted, spewing death and destruction, within the space of six minutes, at six railway stations. Not since the Blitz of World War Two had Londoners ever experienced anything quite like it. The devastation was heart-breaking. And yet, it would have been more than a thousand times worse, had the bombing outrages occurred at peak commuter times. For most of the general public, it has remained a mystery, as to why the perpetrators chose an hour when the human carnage would be less.

The streets around Dorset Street, were in uproar as police officers frantically emerged from buildings, rushing to their vehicles, speeding away with sirens blaring and lights flashing.

Warren ran up to Edmunds who was shouting multiple orders into his radio, as he leapt into his squad car.

"Sir," Warren tried to speak.

"I know," Edmunds interjected. "We have to get back to Camden." He returned to bellowing down his radio, "Listen, when I say, 'order all units back to their respective bases', I mean ALL UNITS!"

"What's going on, sir?" begged Warren, looking very confused and a little frightened.

"Explosions at five underground stations," Edmunds brusquely informed her, "Camden Town, Euston Square, Baker Street, Holborn, Oxford Circus and Kings Cross rail station. It's a bloody massacre. Anti-terrorist predict more south of the river." Edmunds went back on the police radio, talking rapidly to Walters, "Jim, meet me at Camden Town underground. We're clearing out of here. We need all available manpower for rescue teams. Get to it."

Edmunds slammed the radio down, and groaned, "Jesus, I dread to think what we're going to find. Over a hundred casualties and still counting. That's at Camden alone."

"Bombs?" asked Warren, staring at Edmunds with disbelief.

"Not clear. But they think so. Fucking bastards."

"Al Qaida?"

"Too early to know. Could be the new bunch, I. M. R. A. N."

"Oh?" queried Warren, "The International Muslim Revolutionary Arms Network?"

"You never know," replied Edmunds, throwing his hands in the air, as if grasping at straws. "Could be any of them. These fucking Mussy nutters are popping up all over the place."

"What about Kelly, sir?" Warren asked quietly.

"Kelly?" Edmunds starting his car's motor.

"Maeve Kelly Riley, sir." Warren said slowly.

"I'm sorry... but I can't think about her now," responded Edmunds, dismissively.

"Sir, her life is at stake," Warren reminded him, with almost insolent insistence.

"Right now, Sergeant Warren, there are hundreds, possibly thousands of lives at stake," snapped Edmunds.

"But sir..." she tried to protest.

"Sergeant, we have a different kind of crisis on our hands which takes precedence and I can't afford the manpower."

"We promised, sir."

"She's probably dead by now, Ellie. He's had her for six days. I'm sorry. We have to have priorities. Come on, we must go. Get in the car," he commanded.

"I already have a car, sir," replied Warren pointing to it, across the street.

"Fine. Rendezvous at Camden Town," barked the Detective Inspector, slamming his car door shut, and just had time to hear Warren's "Yes chief," before putting his foot down hard on the accelerator, and speeding away.

Detective Constable Warren, highly-trained undercover cop, stood, watching the area around Dorset Street quickly empty of all police and their vehicles. Soon she was quite alone, seemingly frozen to the spot, wracked with conflicting thoughts and emotions. With a deep heavy sigh, she finally moved from her static position, and hurried to her waiting car.

With the police gone, and everyone, not asleep, glued to their television sets, watching in horror the latest reports of the multiple train station explosions, it seemed that there was nobody around to notice the ominous-looking black van slowly cruising down the empty road of Whites Row towards the corner of Crispin Street. It drove round the corner and continued slowly north to Brushfield Street, turning right at the T-junction. No one intercepted the vehicle as it moved towards Commercial Street, where again, it took a right hand turn and continued until it was back at the entry into Whites Row. There, the van halted, pausing for a few seconds. Having ascertained that the coast was clear, the vehicle moved slowly back into Whites Row until it reached Dorset Street, which it then entered and, turning left into Miller's Court, finally stopped outside Number 13.

After a few seconds pause, the van's motor was switched off, and the driver's door quickly opened. Stepping noiselessly to the ground, CK, wearing a long coat and hood over his head, moved rapidly to the front door of 13 and unlocked it. With a hand-held remote control, he switched on the lights inside the house, and then, twisting the door handle, he kicked the door open. Sensing no threat lurking inside, CK returned to the van and opened the back doors, and pulled the seemingly lifeless body towards him from inside the van.

"Soon, my lovely, all your trials and tribulations will be over," CK softly murmured. "Soon the final Act of the Cosmic Consummation will set alight the Dawning of the New and Terrible Age. They thought our times were bad enough... they ain't seen nothing yet." He gave a quiet chuckle as he stood the inert body of Kelly, who, with her hands taped behind her back, was slowly reviving from a semi-conscious state. Her eyes opened as CK, propping her on his shoulder, carefully tried to help her walk with him to the door of number 13 Miller's Court. Kelly tried to pull away from him, but he had her firmly in his powerful grip. She wanted to scream but her mouth was taped. As he forcefully frog-marched her, SUDDENLY ...out of the shadows...emerged Warren, holding at arms length a police handgun, lethally aimed at the hooded CK.

"Stop!" she ordered. "Don't move or I'll blow your fucking head off."

CK, taken completely by surprise, swivelled round to face the woman detective, nearly dropping Kelly. He quickly recovered and using her as a shield, walked slowly towards Warren.

"Ooo-eee, Detective Sergeant Eloise Warren," CK mocked. "Well, well, well, what a pleasant surprise."

"Stop fucking moving, arsehole," demanded Warren. "If I have to shoot through Kelly, to get you, I fucking will." Of course, this was a bluff. Warren knew she didn't have the psychopathic ruthlessness for sacrificing Kelly's life, as a means to ending the Kings Cross Terror.

"You know, Ellie, one of the sexiest things on earth is a tough woman. I admire you for that," crooned CK as he kept advancing towards Warren, pushing Kelly in front of him.

"I mean it, stop now," screamed Warren, desperately trying to aim her gun so that the bullet would just scrape past Kelly's head, and catch the fiend in his left eye. "Any closer and I will take you out," she warned.

CK was now close enough to Warren to be able to shove Kelly onto her. and as he was about to do so, a car driven by Max, screamed around the corner and smashed into the back of CK's van, sending it forward. At the same time, another car coming from the opposite direction, charged towards CK, who had no choice but drop Kelly, in order to get out of the way, which enabled the second car, driven by Claire, to come between the predator and its prey. Warren, stunned at first at what had just happened, regained command and screamed at Kelly, who was still very dazed and confused, to get into Claire's car. Kelly stared without recognition at Claire, who had now opened the passenger door, and was yelling at her to get aboard. But Kelly just stood there, frozen to the spot like a rabbit caught in headlights.

In that moment of hiatus, CK saw an opportunity and began to move towards Claire's car, with the intention of trying to hijack it, but Max, quick as a flash, reversed his car from the rear of the van, swung his vehicle round and charged straight at CK, forcing him to dodge further away from Kelly, and Claire's car...Warren ran around the cars and succeeded in getting behind CK. He froze, as he felt the barrel of her gun pushed hard into his back.

Meanwhile, Claire tried again to persuade Kelly to quickly get into her car. Max also shouted, "Go on, Kelly, get into Claire's car. You're safe now."

On hearing Max's voice, Kelly ran towards his car instead. Max quickly opened the passenger door and she threw herself in. Max immediately accelerated away, the car door slamming shut. Claire not wanting to be left behind, executed a mad U-turn and chased after him.

The Ripper Code

"Claire, stop! Don't go!" Warren shouted after her...but it was too late. She was left alone in Miller's Court with CK, who had started to hum very quietly a theme from Rimsky-Korsakov's *Scheherazade*. Warren, still keeping her gun trained on his back, pushed him forward to create some space between them. With her other hand, she took out her walkie-talkie.

"So, what are we going to do now, Ellie?" CK asked.

"Stop calling me Ellie," snapped Warren. "I don't know you and I don't want to know you. So, just stand still and shut the fuck up."

"I'm sorry, Eloise, but I can't shut the fuck up," objected CK. "I don't want you to jeopardize such a promising career. Believe me, you're about to make a big mistake. Radio your boss, Chief Superintendent Robert Edmunds. That is his name, isn't it. Call Bob Edmunds, tell him he must ring a number. I will give you the number. I have it on a business card in my left pocket. Allow me to slowly turn towards you and I will give it you..." He began to turn towards her.

"Don't move, I said," screamed Warren, waving her gun at him.

"But WDC Warren, you have to allow me to give you this phone number. It's a Special Branch number. Edmunds must ring it before you do anything else. Both yours and his careers depend on it." Warren didn't like the sound of this. Also the creep was much too calm and self-assured.

"Keep your back to me...with your left hand, take the card from the pocket, nice and slow and drop it on the floor and move ten paces forward. Do it, now," commanded Warren. With a careless shrug of his shoulders, CK did exactly as he was ordered.

"Keep your back to me and drop your hood," demanded the policewoman,

CK lowered his hood. Warren was aghast. The man was still hidden by a mask.

"What the fuck is that?" she exclaimed, feeling slightly rattled. In answer, he slowly turned towards her, revealing that he was wearing a smiling *George Bush Jr.* Halloween mask.

"Jesus, you really are sick," Warren muttered, fighting hard not to laugh. "Take that stupid mask off. Do it. Now."

"I'll do it when you pick up the card."

"Do it now!" she said, menacingly, taking a step towards him.

"Sergeant Warren! Pick up the card and call Edmunds," urged CK. "You are wasting time."

"I said, take off the fucking mask." Warren raised the gun, aiming it at his forehead.

CK reluctantly did as he was told and removed the President Bush joke mask. Warren took some time examining his face, wondering where she had seen him before. Finally, still none the wiser, she knelt down and quickly picked up the business card from the ground while still keeping her gun pointed at CK. As she quickly read the card, she failed to notice he had moved slightly closer to her.

"This your name?" she demanded.

"Yes."

"Commander Fox?"

"Yes."

"Is that all? Just *Commander Fox*?" queried Warren doubtfully

"You don't need anything else," replied Commander Fox in his suavest matter-of-fact voice. "Now call up your Boss. Tell him to phone the number on the card."

"Why the hell should my Chief do what you tell him to do?"

"He will when you tell him the number. Believe me. It's a magic number. It opens many doors and calls forth all kinds of spirits...some good, some bad, some carefree and indifferent. What will it be? Will it be your lucky day?" teased Commander Fox.

"You're off your fucking head, you are," accused Warren sarcastically.

"Of course, you ordered me to remove it," the Fox laughed, standing, hands on his hips. "Why do I get the feeling I'm not the one in control here?" thought Warren, suddenly feeling very frightened and uncertain.

"What sort of number is this?" asked Warren, desperate to get it over and done with. She couldn't stand being locked in this man's creepy atmosphere any longer.

"Special Branch. Home Office. Intelligence Liaison Section. Take your choice," offered Commander Fox. "Where the number goes... is unimportant. How it affects your life hereafter... is." He moved an inch closer, which the detective constable again failed to notice, so intent was she on trying to operate the radio with one hand, while still pointing her gun with the other.

"Chief," cried Warren, relieved to have finally got through to Edmunds. "D. C. Warren here.... I'm still in Dorset Street...well, Miller's Court, actually... Yes, chief, I know what you ordered......but......Chief......please.....Chief...I've got him.....I've got him......the killer......yes, my gun is pointing straight at him......Sir, Listen. Don't do that. He insists you ring this Special Branch number..... He gave me a phone number which he says you must ring. Yes, before you do anything else... I don't know what nonsense this is, sir.......Over 600 casualties in Camden alone! Oh god...... I know, but... please ring the number, Chief... I'm alone and I..."

Commander Fox interjected, "Constable Warren, when Edmunds phones the number...he must mention my name, Commander Fox. Tell him that."

"Sir, this lunatic says when you ring the name... Sorry, I mean, the number.... say Commander Fox... yes, Commander Fox.... he says that's his name-"

"Good Girl, Ellie, there could be promotion for you," Commander Fox spoke condescendingly. "When your Guv'nor gets back, put him onto loudspeaker. I want to hear what he has to say."

"I don't take orders from you," snarled Warren.

"You already have."

From Dorset Street 'the Rescue Party' drove straight to Claire's apartment. Max had heard on the radio about the bomb explosions, so while Claire took Kelly to the bedroom, he switch on the television, tuning into *24-Global-News*.

"It has been confirmed that just after midnight," the Newscaster sombrely announced, "bombs had exploded in six transport locations around central and north west London, killing at least 700 and injuring four times as many. The Prime Minister speaking at Number Ten has promised that the evil perpetrators will be found and punished. He believes that after tonight's horrible outrage all Parliament will vote for the new law introducing the death penalty for terrorists..." On seeing Claire come in from her bedroom, Max muted the volume of the television with the remote.

"How is she?" enquired Max

"Asleep at last, replied Claire. "What she has been through doesn't bear thinking about. I don't think she will ever recover."

"Who could?" said Max, and then pointing at the television images of destruction at the six rail and tube stations, "And this? It's madness. Six targets. One Kings Cross and one here Camden. Of all the nights for the Al Qaida to strike, it's weird."

"And it's been quiet for so long," said Claire, bewildered. "Do they know it's Al Qaida?"

"No. Still pure speculation. No one has claimed responsibility yet. A spokesman for the anti-terrorist intelligence unit thought it had all the hallmarks of IMRAN but I think he's just saying something to fill the void."

"You think they will grab the first Muslims they can and pin it on them, just to placate the public fury."

"Or fan the flames," Max predicted. "I don't think, as with all the others, we'll ever know the truth."

Claire moved her wheelchair alongside Max, and dropped her head on his shoulder.

"Why is the world so evil, Max?" she asked, tears welling up, as she stared at the silent images flickering chaotically on the television. Max put his arm around her shoulder.

"I don't know," he replied, at a loss for anything comforting to say..

Commander Fox knew it wouldn't be long now. That bitch detective, Warren, was getting weary, standing, waiting for Edmunds to radio her. The gun was still trained on him, but he could see the barrel was beginning to drop down a little. He chanced moving forward slowly, but she instantly sensed the movement and snapped to attention.

"Stay back," she warned. "You move one more time and I'll throw caution to the wind. You'll die and I'll happily take the consequences. As was once said in a great movie 'Go on, make my day'," she added, pointing the gun at his crotch. Just then, the police radio speaker crackled with Edmund's voice, "D.C. Warren. You still have the prisoner?"

"Yes, Chief," affirmed Warren. "Where's the back up, Chief?"

"You are to let Commander Fox go. Put your gun away," came back the Inspector's voice, sounding distinctly unhappy.

"You must be joking, chief," protested Warren.

"That's an order, Detective Constable," bellowed the loudspeaker. "Tell him he's free to go. And, Ellie, forget you ever saw him."

"Sir, I can't. That is madness. Why? What are you doing? How can you do this?"

"I'm not doing it. It has nothing to do with me... or you? It is way above both our heads. The orders come from on high."

"We can't let this homicidal maniac go, sir," implored Warren, tears of anger and fear streaming down her face. "I'd rather shoot him now, where he stands and claim it was an accident."

"Warren, please for all our sakes, obey an order for once in your life," urged Edmunds' cracked voice.

"Yes sir," came her reluctant reply. Warren switched off the radio, and, with pure hate in her eyes, looked up at the gloating Fox.

"Well, Lady Policewoman? Am I free to go?" he laughed.

"I give you five seconds to piss off out of my sight," growled Warren, raising the gun level with his head.

"Hmmm. I'm not turning my back while you still have a gun in your hand," Commander Fox shook his head. "As you said, accidents can happen. Put the firearm in your holster and turn your back."

Warren stared at the Commander, momentarily indecisive, then with great reluctance, she flicked the safety catch on, put the gun in her holster on the inside of her jacket, and as she turned her

291

back... the Fox rushed at her, with one hand he grabbed her by the hair, yanking her head back, exposing her throat, and with the other wielding a large bayonet-like knife, he made two quick slashes. Warren's throat was deeply severed. The look of uncomprehending surprise in her eyes was pitiful, as her blood spurted out, relentlessly robbing her of her life.

The killer quickly picked up her shaking body, and as he carried it towards the still open front door of number 13 Miller's Court, he whispered in her ear, "Well, well, well, my beauty. As one door closes, so another door opens. And you have all the qualifications. You worked undercover as a prostitute. A whore is a whore...even if it is in the line of duty. And your name, Eloise, has the right number, too. Two. Yes, as a last minute substitute prostitute, you'll do nicely."

CHAPTER 43
The End of Community
27th August. Monday

Tom McCarthy was a rarity. He was one of the last remaining milkmen who actually delivered milk from a milk float. There were still parts of London where the local people, steeped in nostalgia, actually preferred to wake up in the morning to find pint bottles, genuine traditional glass bottles, of milk on their doorstep. Not for these people, the inconvenient bleary-eyed drive to the impersonal Tesco or Sainsbury or any other hyper-store, that is killing local trade and destroying the sense of community all over Britain.

However, the days when good old reliable friendly Tom McCarthy delivered milk in the Dorset Street area, came to a gut-wrenching end during the early hours of that Monday morning of August the 27th.

Whistling Tom arrived at Miller's Court, and was annoyed to find an abandoned black van blocking his access. It seemed the bloody thing had crashed against a wall belonging to an old bakery. He got out of his milk float to investigate, when he noticed that the door to Number 13 was wide open. He called out, as he knocked on the door. "Hello? Hello? Anybody there? Is that your van out here? Hello? It's causing an obstruction. I'll have to report it to the police. Hello?" Finding that his knocking and calls were going unanswered, and slightly uneasy about going in uninvited, he walked to a window at the side, where the glass had been broken. He reached inside and pulled back the curtain to look into the interior. He immediately wished he hadn't. What he saw so horrified and nauseated him, he vomited there and then. A young woman's naked body, unbelievably mutilated, lay sprawled on the bed. It took Tom the milkman several minutes to compose himself sufficiently to dial 999 on his mobile phone. Even then, as he was reporting what he had found to the police, he still had difficulties breathing, his heart was in such distress.

The first police officer to arrive on the scene, warily entered the small, sparsely furnished, yet cluttered room. Even though he had been briefed as to what he may expect to find, he nonetheless had great difficulties looking at the unrecognisable corpse of WDC Eloise Warren, and had to rush outside to vomit.

When Edmunds and Walters finally entered the den of carnage, they turned a deathly pale at what they saw. Poor Ellie's corpse had suffered the exact identical set of mutilations as her predecessor, Mary Jane Kelly, Jack the Ripper's sixth victim.

The whole of the surface of her abdomen and thighs was removed, and the abdominal cavity emptied of its viscera. Her breasts were cut off, her arms mutilated by several jagged wounds and her sweet face, her assassin had hacked beyond all recognition. The tissues of Warren's neck were severed all the way round, and down to the bone. The uterus and kidney with one breast had been placed under the head, the other breast had been placed by her right foot. The liver between the feet, with the intestines by the right side and the spleen by the left side. Tissue flaps removed from the abdomen and thighs were on a table.

What was once a hard cynical detective inspector who thought he had seen every evil under the sun, was so shaken that he had to be helped out by his sergeant, Walters, whose own angry tears were streaming relentlessly down his face. On their way out, the police surgeon, Dr. Llewellyn Hawkey arrived in great haste and immediately began a preliminary post-mortem in situ.

Outside, Millers' Court, and the main Dorset Street, was crowded with police vehicles and officers, grey drained faces and hushed tones, where occasional talk did not rise above that of whispers. Mostly, however, the air was filled with mortified silence. Edmunds sat in his car with the door open, stared blankly into space. Walters was standing at his chief's side, at a loss as to what to say or do. His heart dropped even further as he saw Dr. Hawkey approach them, his face grim and ashen.

"You probably don't want to hear this," began Dr. Llewellyn Hawkey.

"Tell it, anyway. My brain is already half numb," came back Edmunds, tonelessly.

"Frankly, I have to say I am utterly astounded by the ferocity of this murder. The victim's..."

"Detective Constable Eloise Warren," interrupted Edmunds.

"...Detective Constable Eloise Warren," the doctor quickly correcting himself, "the cause of her death was the severance of the carotid artery in the throat, slashed with such force that the tissues have been cut all the way down to the spinal column. The face has been gashed in all directions with the nose, cheeks, eyebrows and ears being partly removed. The lips were blanched and cut by several incisions running obliquely down to the chin. There are also numerous cuts extending irregularly across all of the features. The victim's skin and tissues of the..."

Edmunds again interjected, "Detective Constable Eloise Warren."

The police doctor took in a deep breath, and continued "Yes, of course. Detective Constable Eloise Warren's... skin and tissues of the abdomen from the costal arch to the pubic area have been removed in three large flaps. The right thigh has been denuded in front to the bone, the flap of skin, including the external genitalia and part of the right buttock. The left thigh has been stripped of skin, fascia and muscles as far as the knee. I would say that all this was done with a very sharp, strong knife about an inch in width and at least six inches long, which leads me to conclude that it was probably the same murder weapon as employed on the other women. With the implication that it's the same killer."

There followed silence as all three took time to digest the verbal autopsy report, then Edmunds let out a long heart felt sigh.

"Terrible," he muttered, burying his face in his hands. "Terrible. To have to live and witness such horror." Edmunds looked up at Hawkey, almost hating him for giving so much grisly information, "Is that it?" he vehemently asked. "Can I go back into unconscious mode?"

"There is one other thing," Dr. Llewellyn Hawkey tried to break in gently, "Detective Warren's heart has been cut out. It's nowhere to be found. Looks like it has been taken away." Another bout of screaming silence underscored the utter incomprehension produced by this new startling revelation. As if in response, Edmunds slowly pulled out his handgun and stared at it, and began rubbing the barrel. Wanting to protect his boss, Walters gave a signifying look at Hawkey, who with an acknowledging nod, said, "Well, I better go and put all this down in a formal report. Bob, I'm really sorry about Ellie."

Edmunds lost in thought, suddenly remembered he was a professional with a job to do, and looked up at the doctor, "Aye. Thanks Lew." After the doctor had gone, "Jesus Christ, what do I say to her Mum and Dad?" he groaned. With a quiet chuckle to himself, he took a wallet from his jacket's inside pocket, and pulled out his detective's identity card, and then tried to balance it on the gun barrel. Walters looked on, very concerned, wondering if his chief was about to crack up.

"Jim, I'm getting too old for this," sighed Edmunds. "God, how this job has changed. I use to like being a policeman. Even as a kid, I dreamed of being the Blue Knight, protector of the weak and vulnerable. Righter of Wrongs. When I first started - Jesus, nearly forty years ago - we never had any of this rubbish where so-called Health and Safety Regulations prohibited you from rescuing some boy from drowning. In those days, you didn't care if you had the training, you just leapt in and tried to save someone's life. Being a copper really counted for something. You could go out on the street, and *know* you had the respect and cooperation of the neighbourhood. Today, you're regarded with suspicion, and considered scum, no better than trigger-happy bully-boys in uniform. And you know why? Because now, policing has become too political. It's not about catching criminals any more."

"Well, Guv, don't quote me on this but maybe it's because the biggest criminals are in Government," suggested Walters with bitterness.

"Poor Ellie," grieved Edmunds. "Jim, I didn't think I could still be shocked. Eloise. Oh Eloise. How could anyone do this? Oh Jesus. I abandoned her. Left all alone to deal with this monster."

"No, you didn't, Guv," contradicted Walters. "First, she took it upon herself to single-handedly challenge the killer, which was really terribly misconceived. Secondly, your superiors got it horribly wrong. There was nothing you could have done to prevent this from happening. We had no choice but to leave the scene, to deal with the bomb explosions in Camden Town."

"No, I had a choice. For one moment, we had in our hands a suspect serial killer and we could have brought him in. I could have disobeyed GPI.9... but... in accordance with today's rules, I have to worry about keeping up my mortgage payments, securing the pension, feeding my family, and not catching a stray bullet."

Edmunds quickly put his I.D. card and gun away, and stood up, giving Walters the hard business-like look that was his trademark.

"Alright. Someone has to pay," Edmunds growled. "If we can't have the assassin, then, at least, we can grab one of his paymasters."

"Sinclare?" queried Walters. "What evidence do we have to tie him in with the Jackabee murders?"

"Fuck the evidence. I've decided to retire, anyway. Are you with me?"

"All the way, Guv," replied Walters.

"Let's go to it, then." ordered the Detective Inspector.

CHAPTER 44
Farewell, My Lovely
27th August. Monday

Max had volunteered to drive Kelly to London's third airport at Stansted. It was the least he could do. Kelly had wondered if his badly beaten up car would make it, but for old times sake, she'll risk it, she said, attempting to make a joke of it, though the mood on the road was far from jovial.

"I won't tell you the details of how I suffered those six days, but -" said Kelly, resting her head on Max's shoulder. "You were right about him. Like Roslyn D'Onston, he was using us girls to bring about a new Antichrist."

"So, he was trying to follow in Jack the Ripper's footsteps," said Max, feeling vindicated. "Did he believe D'Onston had successfully created Hitler's dark soul?"

"Oh yes, I think he envied D'Onston's occult midwifery."

"Anyway, enough of him," ordered Max, knowing that there wasn't much time left for them to be together, the signs for the airport had loomed into view.

"You can drop me off here," requested Kelly, as they drove past a bus stop.

Max stopped the car as directed. They both sat awhile, looking straight ahead. With a deep sigh, Kelly took his hand and gave it a little squeeze.

"Max," she said. "You and Claire. It could be good. Give your heart a chance."

"I was hoping to give you my heart," choked Max.

"I know but I have nothing to give in return. Give it to someone more deserving, who knows how to give. Goodbye Max. I'll never forget you saved my life." She gave his hand another squeeze.

"Well, it wasn't just me," argued Max.

"But it was your lovely crazy-mindedness that set the wheels in motion."

"Where will you go?"

"Back to Ireland," replied Kelly.

"Dublin?"

"No. I hate cities now. To my real home in the west of Ireland, where the light of the native soil may heal my aching soul and repair this ripped body."

"I wish you'd stay this side of the Pond."

Kelly shook her head emphatically, "I have to get away from England and all who sail in her."

"You're leaving the sinking ship, then," quipped Max enviously. "Well, good luck Kelly...or Sophie. Dammit! What shall I call you?"

"Sophie, if you like. In memory of our playfulness," Kelly took Max in her arms, squeezed him tight and gave him a long passionate snog on the lips. Just as Max was beginning to weep, she stopped and leapt out of the car, "Max, come and visit... in a few months... when I'm ready. And bring Claire with you," she shouted as she walked away very quickly, not looking back.

Max, his eyes awash with tears, could barely see as he executed a U-turn with his car, and drove away, as fast as he could, in the opposite direction.

CHAPTER 45
Triptych
27th August. Monday

Sinclare was feeding raw meat to his new pet, a black panther, when the Heavy, Mister Pink, entered. The tanks of piranhas were gone.

"Who's a lovely girl, then?" clucked the Boss, bursting with pride, tickling the big cat under the chin, which, to the intense relief of the gang, was restrained by a long silver chain, securely attached to a wall in the Reception Room. The satin-black feline, with its diamond encrusted collar, was comfortably reclining on a red velvet covered sofa.

"Isn't she gorgeous?" Sinclare asked rhetorically, as the overlarge 'pussycat' snatched the meat from his fingers.

"If you say so, Boss," replied Mister Pink, looking nervously at the panther, which immediately growled at him as the Heavy attempted to approach Sinclare.

"Boss, we've got company," Mister Pink cautiously announced, knowing his Boss hated receiving bad news when he was feeding his pride and joy. "The Filth are outside. Armed to the bloody teeth. They want you to come out quietly."

"Edmunds is it?" groused Sinclare.

"Yes, Boss," apologised Mister Pink, as if he were personally to blame, still eyeing the black panther with trepidation.

"How do I get rid of this annoying itch? The bastard's not content with his constant harassment of my people, his cunt-stant undermining of my business operations and his fucking cunt-stant disruption of my Kingdom but he has the fucking gall to come here and fucking arrest me. For what? What have I done?"

"Shall I let him in, Boss?"

"No, you fucking won't," yelled Sinclare. "Not yet. Get the rest of the crew in here, pronto."

As the Heavy goes to a side door at the back, Sinclare unhooked the panther's chain and held it out to him, saying, "Take Petula back to her cage."

"Do I have to, Boss?" moaned Mister Pink, to which Sinclare gave him his most chilling '*Don't fuck with me*' look..

"Alright, Boss," came the speedy acquiescent reply.

"What's the size of Edmunds' army?" asked Sinclare.

"He brought six of the fuckers with him."

"Only six," exclaimed Sinclare. "He's got balls." He turned and glared at Mister Pink who was still loitering at the door, trying to get a grip of Petula's chain and coax her to come with him

"Oye, what are you hanging around for?" shouted Sinclare impatiently. "Get the boys. We can't keep the Filth waiting."

Yet another case of synchronicity, for at that very moment, back at Max's apartment, the ex-Sherlock-in-a-Wheelchair was sitting with Claire on the sofa, watching, on the television, the final shoot out scene in the movie, *True Romance*. Claire, who wasn't that interested in the film, though she did think Gary Oldman in his Rasta dreadlocks pretty sexy, was looking out of the corner of her eye at Max, as he tried to keep his focus on the Cops and Gangsters action at the screen. Claire decided to make the first move, and reached out to take his hand. She was gratified that, instead of pulling away, Max gave her hand a soft squeeze. Then, when she let her head rest on his shoulder, he responded by putting his arm around her and pulling her close to him, holding her tight. Claire turned her head towards him, and looked wide-eyed at him. He looked back at her and they gazed into each others eyes, slowly drawing together as if tiny threads attached to their lips were being pulled by microscopic web-weaving spiders. Their lips touched and there was an eruption of passionate kisses. Hands reached hungrily for erotic zones. Breasts and groins feverishly caressed and groped. Max finally indicated with a gesture of his head, the bedroom, to which Claire nodded her assent. They got into their wheelchairs and headed for the bedroom.

***

Somewhere in the rural hinterland of Essex county, north of Southend, not far from the village of Canewdon, lay a de-sanctified church of St. Ann's, where terrible rumours abound of satanic rituals taking place on certain festive days in the Pagan calendar. This particular church had been built on the sacred site where aeons ago, Tan, the Celtic god of fire, was worshipped and sacrifices performed. The hill (in Roman times it was called Saturn's Hill) upon which the defunct church bestrode, had a mysterious power that seemed never to allow too much deviation from the sound of its archaic name - Tan, Saint Ann, Saturn, Satan.

Although this day of August the 27th was not one of the traditional eight sabats of the year, nonetheless, ponderous organ music could be heard coming from inside the old mediaeval church. Within the dark, cavernous, dusty space with shafts of light, streaming from shattered stain-glass windows, seemingly invisible voices intoned the Lord's Prayer spoken in Latin, but backwards. Curling wisps of incense smoke danced like wraiths on a moonlit night. At the alter stood a nine foot black inverted Crucifix. At its base was marked upon the floor in red wax, a six pointed star with a diameter of eighteen feet, known to the initiates as the Hexatron. Around the circumference were twelve tall black candles a-flame. Opposite the inverted Crucifix, stood a six foot white inverted Pentacle.

At the conclusion of the chanting, the hooded High Priest, holding aloft a Black Chalice, stepped into the centre of the six pointed star. From the shadows emerged twelve other hoods, each stepping alternately onto the points and inner angles of the Hexatron, creating a total gathering of thirteen i.e. a coven. When all were assembled and in their designated place, the High Priest spoke aloud, his voice reverberating eerily in the desolate shell of what was once a home for benign worship, "I had hoped to bring the Womb filled Thrice Times Six with my Seed but subsequent events denied this Perfection. No matter. In the great scheme of things, it is of no consequence. It is the Will which Excites and Summons the Power. In the Beginning was the Will and the Will was made Flesh. I Dared...as my predecessors So Dared... and from their Daring... from their Will, was born the First and the Second Beasts of the Apocalypse."

"So Mote It Be," came the response from the Twelve Hooded Ones, also known as the Cunning Men.

"In this Black Chalice, the UnHoly Graal, is the Miracle of Miracles... a Heart that still beats because the Will of my Seed is its Living Blood. The Heart lives because I anointed it with my Seed."

"So Mote It Be," came the refrain.

The High Priest then took out from the Black Chalice, a gleaming pulsating steaming human heart, and held it high for all to see and gasp, in awe and wonder.

Back at Sinclare's Lair, Detective Inspector Edmunds, Detective Sergeant Walters and five other heavily armed police officers were waiting in the hallway, warily watched over by three of Sinclare's heavies, their jackets also bulging with hidden firearms.

Suddenly, a door was flung open with a bang and in walked Sinclare, flanked by four more heavies. Another door opened behind the police detectives and five more heavies entered. All of twelve Sinclare's heavies fanned out around the room, encircling the cops in the middle of the tastlessly furnished hallway. Edmunds, Walters and their colleagues also slowly spread out, each moving to an item of furniture which may serve as some cover in the event of fireworks. There was a sense on all sides, that at any moment there could erupt a scene from the '*Gunfight at the O. K. Corral*'..or better still, from one of Sergio Leone's Spaghetti Westerns.

"Well?" growled Sinclare. "What do you want, Edmunds?"

Carefully taking from his trouser pocket, a piece of paper vaguely resembling a summons, Edmunds in his most official sounding voice, began to read out aloud from it, "Auguste Sinclare, we've come to arrest you for the murder of police officers Sergeant Reece and Detective Constable Warren...and for the murders of six of your very own call girls..."

Sinclare laughed out loud, trying hard to hide his growing sense of disquiet. His henchmen nervously joined in. Then, after snapping his fingers at them to cease their gorilla-like guffaws, he launched into a sarcastic tirade.

"Am I to suppose that I personally killed these people?" shouted Sinclare, in his most exaggerated Cockney accent, as if he were trying to sound like Bob Hoskins in *The Long Good Friday*, "Or were they stupid fuckers who got hit by a bus, or slipped on a banana skin, or bitten by a rabid squirrel, or some such irrelevant shit... and you are trying to pin their unfortunate deaths on me?"

"We have irrefutable evidence, enough to put you away for a thousand years... or more."

"Oh yeah and I believe in the Tooth Fairy as well. Pull the other one, it's got bells on."

The heavies laughed even louder, whilst at the same time, were getting ready with the various weaponry concealed about their persons. Some of them had chosen to hide their weapons inside rolled up newspapers, mostly editions of *The Sun*, and *The Daily Mail*.

"Maeve Kelly Riley. Mean anything to you?" asked Edmunds.

"Ain't she one of them six tarts that got snuffed by that crazy sex killer?"

"No. No, the idiot...YOUR idiot...YOUR Incompetent... killed the wrong one. He took out Sharon Kane by mistake. Funny, you just can't get the staff nowadays, can you? And how much did you pay? A million? Two million? Phew. You were ripped off, mate. I'd demand my money back, if I was you."

"Yer fuck off. Yer talking bollocks," jeered Sinclare, who was also getting ready with his machine gun, wrapped in a rolled up copy of the *Financial Times*.

"You better believe it, sunshine," replied Edmunds, noting with grim satisfaction all the sly surreptitious little movements. "Maeve Kelly Riley. I think she was a former mistress of yours. Secrets of the Boudoir and all that. Lovely bedtime reading. She's

The Ripper Code

agreed to give evidence against you. We have her in protective custody. So, are you going to accompany us, nice and quiet like... or are we going to have to do the dance of a thousand mosquitoes?"

As if this was the cue, Sinclaire dropped the newspaper wrapping and began blasting away with his machine gun, yelling "Let them have it, Boys!" His men took his signal and opened fire at Edmunds, Walters and fellow officers, who had already anticipated the suddenness of the attack, and were quick to drop to their knees and take cover behind tables, chairs, settees and other assorted best forgotten furniture. Bullets whizzed, screaming, shattering bits of furniture, ornaments. The grandfather clock exploded. Mirrors smashed. Flying shards of glass ripping clothes and flesh, cops and gangsters alike. The noise was deafening. Screams as heavies begin to take bullets. More screams, and curses as the cops also fell, bones shattered, ribs smashed, blood spurting.

"Fuck!" shouted Walters, as a bullet broke his left arm, but he was able to carry on with his right hand, which holding the gun. Edmunds managed to get a shot at Sinclare, who was having to fire on his belly, both his legs shot away. As the gun battle continued to roar and rage, more cops and gangsters collapsed, creating ever-expanding pools of blood.

"Jesus!" gasped Edmunds as he felt the bullet pass through his chest, tearing one of his lungs and exit near his spinal column. He collapsed to the ground, as the gun battle boiled over. Silence fell like a heavy curtain. When the smoke finally cleared, Edmunds, lying on the carpet saturated in blood, with eyes struggling to remain open, saw that nearly everyone was on the floor... either dead or wounded.

Walters, hearing Edmunds groan, crawled painfully on his knees over to him.

"Bloody hell, Jim," wheezed Edmunds, struggling to take breath, and coughing up blood. "I caught that stray bullet. Life's a bitch, eh?"

"Guv, take it easy," said Walters, gently propping up his Chief. "The paramedics are on their way."

"Sinclare?" enquired Edmunds, his throat gurgling in blood.

"Dead," reassured Walters.

"Good," muttered Edmunds, and promptly died in Walters arms.

***

The High Priest, hidden in his cowl, held up the glistening, beating, human heart to the ongoing cries of adulation from the twelve hooded disciples.

"This Heart," he intoned triumphantly, "...ripped from the sixth Whore of Babylon shall be the Vessel, the Womb, the Grail that Transports and Transfigures the Seed of Pure Will so that He, the Third and Final Beast of the Apocalypse, may be born in eight months hence."

"So Mote It Be," responded The Twelve as their priestly necromantic Grand Master, taking the Heart and the Black Chalice, walked to the alter and picked up the Black Dagger, and plunged it into the Heart which, nonetheless, uncannily continued to beat vigorously. The Coven took up a chant as the Heart's Blood poured into the Black Chalice, which it was rumoured had been purloined from the secret underground vaults beneath Rosslyn Chapel. The High Necromancer Priest then put the chalice, now full of the heart's blood, down on the alter, and placing the Heart on a silver dish, proceeded to carve it into thirteen pieces. He returned with the chalice and dish to the centre of the Hexatron and beckoned each of his disciples, in an anti-clockwise order, to be fed the pieces of Heart and drink from the Black Chalice.

"Drink of the Blood of The Great Hexatron and your Will shall become One with His... and the Day of His Dark Son shall come."

"So Mote It Be," came the supplicant's refrain, after drinking the blood.

"Eat of the Flesh of The Great Hexatron and your Will shall become One with His... and the Day of His Dark Son shall come."

"So Mote It Be." came the supplicant's refrain, after eating the flesh.

As each partook in this Black Mass, their Leader dubbed both shoulders of the supplicant with his black Masonic Sword, after which the supplicant dutifully returned to their position on the six-pointed star.

When the last member of the Coven had received the UnHoly Sacrament, the hooded High Priest turned six times, and addressed the congregation circled around him.

"In the name of the Father - Jahweh the Dragon, in the name of the Son - Baal the Antichrist, and in the name of the Holy Ghost - Isis the Whore, I consummate this day." And then drinking the final drop of blood and eating the final piece of heart, he lowered his hood, to reveal the Green Mask of the Horned God.

"So Mote It Be," concluded the Necromantic High Priest Hereditary Grand Magister of the Cunning Men.

"So Mote It Be," rapturously responded his followers, The Unjust Twelve.

***

The bedroom glowed from the flickering flames dancing on white candles. On the old fashioned gramophone player, a vinyl disc revolved, playing the Moody Blues hit, "Nights in White Satin", while on the double bed, lay Max and Claire who were slowly undressing each other, kissing and caressing as they became gloriously naked. Max kissed Claire's breasts and nipples, then moved down her belly, kissing all the way, licking and sucking her navel, until he reached between her legs and buried his face in her soft mound, licking and kissing, making Claire gasp and shudder. In ecstasy, she pulled his hair, clamping her knees tight against his skull, making him yell. He buried his face deeper between her legs, flicking his tongue mercilessly. Claire moaned as her orgasm gripped and shook her. Max gently entered her, and they slowly, lovingly made love. Pure joy radiated on their faces as the love-making became more passionate and wild.

Their rhythms quickened to a crescendo that exploded into the ecstatic tingling climax they always hoped for. After which, they collapsed on top of each other, kissed and then, thoroughly contented, fell asleep, snuggling in each other's arms.

EPILOGUE
Return of the Grand Inquisitor
24th September.

One month later at a U.S. Air Force Base near Chirchik in northern Uzbekistan. The atmosphere vibrated with the sound of the helicopter rotor blades as they sliced the air, causing dust to swirl and catch in the onlookers' throats. Commander Fox, immaculately dressed in his Naval Intelligence uniform, stepped lightly to the ground from the military helicopter that had just landed. He shielded his eyes from the glare of the midday sun, and saw the two officers walking towards him, across the airfield. One was an American Marine Major. The other was an Uzbeki officer in one of Uzbekistan's many national security services.

"Commander Fox, welcome to Uzbekistan," greeted the American Marine Major, most heartily with a smiling mouth full of gleaming white perfect teeth. "Good trip?"

"Excellent," replied Commander Fox. "You're Major Alvin Scott, I take it."

"You bet," grinned Major Alvin Scott. "This is Colonel Bahodir Mirzaev, local chief of the National Security Bureau," he continued, introducing the earnest looking Uzbeki officer, with an avuncular slap on the back.

"It is such a pleasure to meet you, Commander Fox," smiled Bahodir Mirzaev. "The Minister of the Interior speaks highly of you."

"I like to do my bit for the War on Terror," replied Commander Fox.

"Don't we all," agreed the American major, as they walked across the tarmac to a waiting U.S. embassy limousine. "I understand you were here five years ago."

"Yes, at Chirchik Prison. Coalition Interrogation Liaison Officer."

"But you're a hands-on man. You're not just theory. You walk the talk, which we like. A man with your experience in these terrible times is always invaluable," said Scott.

The Uzbeki colonel sighed heavily, "The Muslim fundamentalists are winning the propaganda war. Rebellion is everywhere. The prisons are bursting with these fanatic extremists. The IMRAN especially."

"And there's the usual problem with interfering human rights watchdogs," complained Major Alvin Scott, as the three of them climbed into the back of the car. "The U. N. are particularly irritating. Continually bleating that most of the suspects are innocent. Don't they realise the Free World is fighting for it's very existence? Extreme times demands extreme measures."

When they had settled in their seats, the American major opened the cocktail cabinet and poured a dry Martini for the English commander, and a bourbon for himself. The Uzbeki was left to serve himself.

"My dear chap, forget the United Nations," replied Fox. "They are an irrelevance. A toothless pussy cat, well past its sell-by-date. Now it is our time. To prevail, you defeat terror with terror. You want confessions, I will get those for you. And if you want an atmosphere of fear and terror, I can give you that too. Just hand me the detainees."

"It is good to have you aboard, Commander Fox," laughed Colonel Bahodir Mirzaev, raising his glass of gin and tonic.

"I'm glad to be of service," responded the Englishman, with a supercilious air

The American Marine looked with satisfaction at the English officer's uniform, "I guess, you're Naval Intelligence?"

"Was," corrected Commander Fox. "Did a stint with the SBS, and then the SAS. Helped the SPG with some of their interrogation problems. You might say, a Jack of all trades."

"But not, I trust, master of none?" drawled the American.

"That will be for you to judge," came the softly voiced reply.

The Ripper Code

Nabil Shaban
Dreams My Father Sold Me
Poems and Graphic Art

With a *Foreword by Lord Richard Attenborough Introduction by Colin Baker*.

Dreams My Father Sold Me is Nabil Shaban's first published anthology of his poetry spanning 20 years (1983-2003) and graphic art spanning 30 years (1975- 2005)

"This magical book is fascinating...."
- Lord Richard Attenborough

"...direct and stark anthology..." - Colin Baker

"...loved the book. particularly like the art work...really gets under the skin...truly the stuff of nightmares...the poems really very moving...singular perspective...unique and utterly familiar at the same time..." – Douglas Hodge

"...an excellent production, very high quality... a book to be proud of... poems...images -- word play -- riddling speech -- which can be felt intuitively in the instant...The paintings...the emotion comes through -- strongly!   I can look at them for ages...." – Cathy Lester

"...I rather rashly bought your book and instantly regretted doing so... It reminded me of all those scary stories and pictures you told me when I was a kid which gave me nightmares and got you banned from coming to see me (in the children's home)" - Jazz Shaban, the author's sister

"...I can honestly say I have never owned such a book! It's beautiful!"
- Meaghan

ISBN 0954829409 £14.99

SIRIUS BOOK WORKS publishing

Nabil Shaban
The First To Go
an original theatre play
about disabled people in Nazi Germany

Everyone knows about the millions of Jews who died in the Nazi extermination camps. Countless books, plays and films have been produced to ensure that we never forget and so remain vigilant against any likely recurrence. Yet until Nabil Shaban decided to do something about it, there has never been a play or film which seeks to tell the story of Hitler's Euthanasia program for disabled people. In fact, THE FIRST TO GO, the First Victims, in Hitler's systematic drive to purify the Aryan race were people with physical, sensory, mental and psychiatric disabilities. Gas chambers were originally created to speed up the culling of such unwanted "Useless Eaters", the term used by Hitler to describe disabled people.

Nabil Shaban's play doesn't just tell the story of Disabled Victims, it also tells of Disabled Heroes and Disabled Villains.

The Disabled Victims, **Siegfried**, **Heide** and **Helmut**....it is their destiny to be given lethal injections.

The Disabled Villain, **Dr. Josef Goebbels**, a man who so hated being crippled with a clubbed foot, he chose to hate all disabled people, he masterminded the propaganda campaign advocating Euthanasia.

The Disabled Heroes, **Claus von Stauffenberg**, the one armed, one eyed "terrorist", who attempted to blow up Hitler
And **Brunhilde**, the German Army nurse who becomes disabled and consequently joins the ranks of the persecuted but in doing so, helps thwart Hitler's plan to rid the world of so-called "imperfect" people.

"...brilliant... moving and funny and very scary." Linda Rogers

"...this play flies very justly in the face of all the stereotypes holding every one of us hostage to this day." Jessica Sharp

"...engaging and poignant..." Robyn Hunt

ISBN 978-0-9548294-1-4 £7.99

SIRIUS BOOK WORKS publishing

Other books by Nabil Shaban soon to be published
by Sirius Book Works

Diary of the Absurd

Ivarr the Boneless

I am the Walrus

King of the Incurables

No One Knows Eddie

SIRIUS BOOK WORKS publishing